PRAISE FOR

THE EFFORT

"Page-turner of the year! In the grand tradition of Stephen King's *The Stand*, Pat Frank's *Alas, Babylon*, and J.T. McIntosh's *One in Three Hundred*, this book is the story of a massive comet that threatens to end human existence and those who fight to prevent that catastrophe. Call it a techno-thriller, call it apocalyptic fiction—I call it great writing. This is an important and provocative novel, one that should be read by all who care about the future of the planet and humanity's role in its preservation. Claire Holroyde is an exciting new voice in modern fiction, and we're lucky to have this stirring and fully imagined book."

—David Heska Wanbli Weiden, Author of *Winter Counts*

"Claire Holroyde's *The Effort* artfully mirrors an allegorical warning on the state of our planet's climate with a more imminent threat of complete and total annihilation of the human species. It speeds up the doomsday clock—that's ticking relentlessly on every page—but with a lingering and aching glimpse at everything that's about to be lost. Heart-pounding and heart-wrenching all at once, it's ultimately, somehow, a story of immense hope. Just a stunning debut."

—Jane Gilmartin, Author of *The Mirror Man*

"*The Effort*, by Claire Holroyde, is a supreme demonstration of how to write a compelling and engrossing literary thriller. It is masterfully plotted, and a worthy addition to the pantheon of great doomsday stories: an astute, unflinching look at what 'civilization' means at the twilight of human perseverance."

—David W. Brown, Author of *The Mission*

"[Claire Holroyde's] prose is measured and clear, and the plot arcs nicely from the scientific issues to more personal stakes. An adept contribution to the realm of apocalypse fiction."

—*Kirkus Reviews*

"Twisty...Holroyde displays a keen vision of societal and diplomatic breakdown amid imminent disaster. The deeper themes about human nature make this apocalyptic thriller more than escapist reading."

—*Publishers Weekly*

"*The Effort*, in the tradition of science fiction novels past, manages to sweep aside national, sectarian, and governmental boundaries to...offer a glimmer of hope. It serves as a small, miraculous contrast to a world which, for the most part, simply folds its wings like [an] eagle and sinks when threatened with space debris, or with its own consumption patterns...Do we die with a bang, with a whimper, or both? Or do we find some way to live? *The Effort* suggests maybe all three at once."

—*Observer*

"*The Effort* offers a vision for how humanity could avoid an existential crisis with international collaboration, while also highlighting the environmental threats created by humans."

—*Electric Literature*

"*The Effort* is ultimately a novel about the desire to live. Struggle is everywhere, on the individual level and in the broader sense as a species. Working together is proven essential. In the end, Holroyde has faith in an intangible human condition: survival depends on our willingness to help each other, and that quality allows humanity to thrive through adversity."

—Ian MacAllen, *Chicago Review of Books*

THE EFFORT

THE
EFFORT

CLAIRE
HOLROYDE

GRAND CENTRAL
PUBLISHING

NEW YORK   BOSTON

Grand Central Publishing
Hachette Book Group
1290 Avenue of the Americas, New York, NY 10104
grandcentralpublishing.com
twitter.com/grandcentralpub

Originally published in hardcover and ebook by Grand Central Publishing in January 2021

First trade paperback edition: January 2022

Grand Central Publishing is a division of Hachette Book Group, Inc. The Grand Central Publishing name and logo is a trademark of Hachette Book Group, Inc.

The publisher is not responsible for websites (or their content) that are not owned by the publisher.

The Hachette Speakers Bureau provides a wide range of authors for speaking events. To find out more, go to www.hachettespeakersbureau.com or call (866) 376-6591.

Library of Congress Cataloging-in-Publication Data

Names: Holroyde, Claire, author.
Title: The effort / Claire Holroyde.
Description: First edition. | New York : Grand Central Publishing, 2021.
Identifiers: LCCN 2020030171 | ISBN 9781538717615 (hardcover) | ISBN 9781538717608 (ebook)
Classification: LCC PS3608.O49435656 E48 2021 | DDC 813/.6--dc23
LC record available at https://lccn.loc.gov/2020030171

ISBNs: 9781538717592 (trade paperback), 9781538717608 (ebook)

Printed in the United States of America

LSC-C

Printing 1, 2021

To my early readers Chris, Bernadette, and Matt...

and to the beautiful, blue planet we all share

"Sooner or later there will be one with our name on it. It's just a matter of when, not if."

—Alan Duffy, lead scientist at the Royal Institution of Australia

Allyson Chiu, "'It Snuck Up on Us': Scientists Stunned by 'City-Killer' Asteroid That Just Missed Earth," *Washington Post*, July 26, 2019.

THE EFFORT

PROLOGUE

NONE OF THE SPACEWATCH personnel could later remember if it was Jeff or Jim who discovered it; they were such similar individuals, and neither wanted the credit. Both men were postdoctoral students in their late twenties at the University of Arizona's Lunar and Planetary Laboratory. They each arrived early at the lab on the morning of July 30 dressed in cargo shorts and Birkenstock sandals. After rubbing sleep from their eyes, they settled at their computers to review results from the previous night.

Jim and Jeff were asteroid hunters, and like most hunters faced with a crowded field of vision, they used movement as a means to track. Automated software controlled the university's two telescopes at the summit of Kitt Peak for twenty-four nights each lunation. Images of the same slice of night sky were captured minutes apart in order to detect changes in position. These digital images looked like photographic negatives with the dark, light-flecked universe converted into something that looked like white static.

Reviewing fainter solar system objects from the larger 1.8-meter telescope took priority, as these were less likely to be observed by other asteroid hunters at stations around the globe. Jeff and Jim worked side by side, but one of them must have seen it first: a new object that wasn't visible the night before—a very large object recently emerged from the blinding edge of the sun's glare. *Am I seeing this, or am I crazy?* the one man probably called out to the other. *Because I'd rather be crazy...*

It must have been worse for the owner of the second set of eyes. Once he rolled over in his ergonomic chair and leaned in until his bearded face was several inches from the computer screen, he would have to confirm the faint black dot located out by Jupiter's orbit. Realizing what he was seeing, and what that meant, he must have jumped back and knocked over his chair.

ONE

OUT FROM THE SHADOW
OF THE SUN

PASADENA, CALIFORNIA
JULY 31

■NE WEEK BEFORE the discovery of dark comet UD3 went public, Dr. Ben Schwartz's phone rang in the middle of the night. No caller ID. Ben sent it to voicemail, but his phone rang again minutes later. *Who's dead?* he wondered. *Aunt Rachel? Mom or Dad?* Ben scrambled to put on his glasses and answer the call. A creaky, accented voice asked for him by name.

"From NASA's Jet Propulsion Laboratory," the man added.

No one from the lab bothered with a full pronunciation. They used "JPL" along with all the other acronyms for the verbally efficient. *Was there an emergency at the lab? A security breach? An explosion?*

Ben's girlfriend, Amy, groaned when he flipped on the punishing overhead lights. She shielded her face, flashing the peacock feather tattoo tickling the soft underside of her forearm. Amy's hair was now platinum blond, but it had been flame red and tucked behind elfin ear-tip prosthetics when they met at a CosCon sci-fi/fantasy convention. *Eat your heart out, Tolkien!* It had also been black during a steampunk phase but never brown. Brown was too normal, and Amy had no interest in normal.

"This is Ben," he confirmed. "And *you* are?"

The names of famous old masters are dropped all the time in

scientific circles, so it took Ben a few groggy seconds to realize that he was actually speaking to one.

"Holy shit! Really?" he asked.

Amy cursed and hurled a pillow. If anything heavy or sharp was within reach—an alarm clock, a lamp, a mace on a chain—she would surely have knocked out his teeth. Ben shut off the bedroom lights and moved to the hallway, stepping barefoot across wall-to-wall carpet the color and texture of oatmeal. His 655-square-foot condo was suitable for the bachelor years of his twenties and early thirties but was now cramped with two people. Amy required space. Ben wished for a larger condo, but South Pasadena real estate was crazy, and he worked for the government, not Google.

"Sorry," Ben said, "but do you mean Tobias Ochsenfeld the astrophysicist? Like, *the* astrophysicist?"

"Yes," the man said. "I dabble in writing books as well, but no one seems to give a damn."

Actually, the old bugger had won a MacArthur with his collections of essays on symmetry. Born in Austria and tenured at Oxford, he was as brilliant in mathematics as one can be without losing too much ground on the autism spectrum. Rumor had him as both a lover of Proust and Fermat's Last Theorem.

"I can't believe this," Ben said with a flat laugh. "I studied your theories in school. I mean, when I picked up this phone, I'd never have guessed you were on the other end."

The famous octogenarian turned gravely serious. "That's unfortunate. I heard you're rather good at guessing."

Dread returned. It sat heavily in Ben's belly and restoked his imagination. He started asking questions but didn't get very far.

"I'm going to interrupt you, Ben—May I call you Ben?"

"Sir—"

"And you may call me Professor, if you like. I've worked in academia most of my life, and I'm older than dirt. Now, Ben, you need to get to the airport in Los Angeles. Immediately."

Ben halted and spoke the only word that could pull sense from the situation.

"Why?"

"Because the UN is arranging your flight to French Guiana," the Professor replied. "You'll need a yellow fever vaccination before you clear security."

Ben took a tentative step into his combined kitchen and living room.

"Why—"

"I'm calling from Brussels," the Professor interjected, "but I'll be boarding my own flight before the day is over. I promise to brief you in person. Now, there is a car waiting outside your residence. It will drive you straight to the airport. All you need is your passport."

After a moment of shock, Ben lowered his phone and crept over to the sliding glass door leading to his second-level balcony. The property's front lawn looked just as it did when he bedded down for the night; Astroturf blanketed everything but a concrete walkway lit with spotlights.

When Ben first moved in, there were perennial gardens and grass lawns with automated sprinklers, but California's historic drought and water conservation measures made such decorations unpopular. Replacement pebble gardens and flowering cacti washed away afterward in flooding from El Niño. Astroturf was the best surrender to such erratic climate conditions, according to the homeowners' association. They couldn't help complaints that the property could double as a miniature golf course with the addition of a few holes and putters lying about.

Ben spotted a sedan parked at the curb. Under the streetlights, he saw shadow movements behind the driver's-side window. Goosebumps puckered his skin. Then everyone started shouting: Ben shouted questions; the Professor shouted that there wasn't time for questions; Amy shouted from the bedroom for Ben to shut the hell up so she could sleep.

"I'm not going anywhere," Ben insisted, "until I know what this is about."

"I can't have you losing your head," the Professor warned. "Because I need that head."

"Just try me."

Ben crossed to the center of his living room for a better thinking position. He stood in boxer shorts and a white undershirt, looking at his wall-mounted flat screen. Central air kicked in with a whirring sound as he regarded the narrow chest and bony appendages of his own five-foot-nine silhouetted reflection. Ben's extraordinary brain was housed in a less substantial vehicle.

"A dark comet was discovered yesterday," the Professor said. "It just rounded the sun on an eccentric orbit—"

"I *knew* it!" Ben shouted.

In autumn of 2014, the subject of comets earned Ben his fifteen minutes of fame. Comet Siding Spring had just whizzed past Mars at less than half the distance between Earth and its moon. Astronomers in Australia discovered the comet only twenty-two months beforehand. As manager of NASA's Center for Near-Earth Object Studies (CNEOS) at JPL, Ben gave a press conference and used the opportunity to discuss the dangers of "dark," or unseeable, comets. For the first time in his life, Ben's warnings got picked up by mainstream media.

"Congratulations," the Professor said with a note of hostility.

Ben sobered and tried to keep his mouth shut so the old man could continue.

"The comet has no name, only its label, UD3. No one at Spacewatch wanted to put their mark on it."

"Hang on," Ben cut in. "You mean those guys in Arizona called *you* first?"

"No. They called the NASA administrator first. He called your executive office."

Ben waited only a couple beats.

"And?"

"And your country's leadership wanted certainty," the Professor said. "They wanted proven trajectory, definite odds of impact...all things we don't have with an initial sighting. What they *didn't want* was any early estimations that might be wrong and only cause a nationwide panic."

He made a sound, a mix of a sigh and a harrumph.

"I suppose extinction is...inconceivable," the Professor added. "Not just to the creationists in the administration but to the others as well. I guess we're each the center of our own universe—"

"Extinction? How big is the comet?"

"Eight kilometers."

There was silence on the line.

"So," the Professor continued, "that's why the NASA administrator called *me*. I was able to connect with the United Nations and the European Union. We have their cooperation."

Ben gasped for breath, just realizing that he had been holding it.

"Did you say eight kilometers?" he asked.

"Yes. Most unfortunately."

Ben could hear his own panting. With less than twenty-four hours of tracking, not much could be determined outside of the comet's size and speed, which were terrifying enough.

"What's the plan?"

"That's why I called *you*," the Professor said, losing patience. "You manage NASA's Center for Near-Earth Object Studies. You are the expert, are you not?"

"Well, yes," Ben stuttered, and stood up straighter. "Asteroids and comets have been my life's work."

Ben often ran out of breath talking about cosmic impacts. Even Amy, a Star Wars follower, fantasy gamer, manga reader, and arguably the hottest ticket on the sci-fi convention circuit, had to ask, *Do you* ever *shut up about asteroids and comets?* In a word, no. And Ben would argue, how could anyone?

His first love had been dinosaurs. At six years old, he collected their miniature plastic likenesses and orchestrated epic battles on his parents' shag rug. As Ben grew older, he learned of a much greater force of nature. The terrifying teeth of a *Tyrannosaurus rex* were no match for a ten-kilometer asteroid. The 150-million-year reign of dinosaurs ended after an impact generating more than a billion times the energy of an atomic bomb. Nothing posed a greater threat to complex life on Earth than cosmic impacts...aside from humans, anyway.

"And I'm chair of the IAA Planetary Defense Conference," Ben added. "We've played out one hundred twenty-two hypothetical cosmic impact scenarios—"

"Good. Because we need to plan for the worst-case scenario. Now, unless you'd like to waste more time, I suggest you get on that plane and draft up names for your core team."

The Professor cleared the moths and cobwebs from his throat and concluded, "I'll be seeing you at the equator."

The line went dead. Ben returned to his bedroom in a daze and flipped on the lights.

"Jesus," Amy hissed. "I'm trying to sleep. I have work in the morning."

Ben flipped off the lights and stood in the darkness. He wasn't sure how much time passed before he flipped the lights back on.

"What?" Amy yelled. "What's so damn important about space? It's not like it won't be there in the morning!"

Ben's lips and eyelids fluttered with mental-processing overload. Seeing him struggle, Amy threw off the down comforter and jumped to his side.

"Sorry, babe," she said. "Tell me what's wrong."

There was no way Amy could force her way into his head. She had to gently draw him out of it.

"Ben?"

Amy took his small hand in her smaller hands. Ben had long, delicate fingers, which he hated and she loved.

"Ben!"

"Do you remember some years back when comet Siding Spring did a flyby? You got pissed because I was sleeping at the office while we corralled all the Mars orbiters on the other side of the planet—"

"The duck-and-cover maneuver," Amy finished for him.

Ben's small smile disappeared, soon as it reached his lips.

"There's another dark comet," Ben said slowly.

Amy tried to interrupt and demand the estimated trajectory, probability, and date of impact, but Ben cut her off.

"They got a first glance yesterday—and it's fucking huge."

There was never a question of talking straight with Amy. Ben never assumed superiority with age, he being forty-two to her thirty-four, or with intelligence. Ben told Amy everything for the plain reason that he always wanted to. At his core, he was a lonely, nervous person. Amy added brass and steel to his intricate mettle.

"I have to go," he said. "There's . . . a car waiting outside."

They stared at one another in silence before Amy asked where he was going.

"Airport. South American equator. We have to plan for the worst. That's where they'll launch an intercept vehicle, if it comes to that. Or, should I say *I*? That's where *I'll* launch. I'm the one who has to make a plan."

He paused and let his imagination step into a room with seemingly endless rows of options, only to have it freeze with indecision. Bile crept up Ben's esophagus and soured his mouth. Blind spots grew in the corners of his peripheral vision. He neared that part of a dream when he fell and lost equilibrium, only to jolt awake.

"He warned me. I can't lose my head."

Ben sat down on the bed and closed his eyes, but it wasn't enough. Stumbling, he made it to their adjoining bathroom and vomited into the toilet bowl. Amy tiptoed in as he finished a round of dry heaving. She pulled a toiletry bag out from under the sink and dropped in her toothbrush, floss, deodorant, and tampons.

"Wait," Ben said. "What're you doing?"

He sank to the cool tile floor and wiped his mouth and jutting chin.

"Packing," Amy said, ducking into their shower. "I'm coming."

Ben shook his head and wobbled. When he tried to argue, Amy whipped around and glared with her gray eyes.

"You're not leaving without me."

Amy was a military brat raised on several bases until she got her GED and became a legal adult at eighteen. She worked several different jobs and lived with several boyfriends while taking night courses at several community colleges. Every time Ben mentioned that he wanted to move to a larger living space, Amy leveled her eyes at him and said, *I'm done with moving.* She wanted her idea of a settled home where Ben was a permanent fixture.

"Cap it."

"What?"

"Cap your razor," Ben said, pointing to the pink disposable in her hand. "Or you could cut yourself."

Amy towered above his crumpled form, wearing a ratty *Mystery Science Theater 3000* T-shirt and a stolen pair of his boxers, which he hated for the sole reason that they fit better on her flat navel.

"C'mon," Amy said, not urgently. "You need to get over your shock and get dressed."

She left the bag of toiletries on the sink and grabbed Ben under the arms. Leveraging her weight, Amy leaned back and stood Ben up.

"Now, go find our passports," she prodded.

Ben usually knew where things were because he was the one who put them away in the first place. Using walls for support, he followed Amy back into their bedroom. Two empty suitcases were already on the bed with unzipped mouths gaping open. Amy grabbed armfuls of clothes from their closet and dumped them into the suitcases with their plastic hangers. Ben pulled on a pair of jeans and tucked his wallet and their passports in his back pockets. A car horn sounded briefly from the street.

"Cool your fuckin' jets!" Amy hollered.

Ben flinched at the loud noises. His hands were shaking, but hers were steady and determined. All those hours she spent alone in her tiny bedroom reading science fiction novels and comics had prepared her.

"Amy, you know this is for real, right?"

She nodded. Amy had been waiting to save Earth since the fifth grade.

"Everything we know and understand is at stake."

"Yeah, I got it," she said, and grabbed their suitcases by the handles.

Ben watched her struggle. A braver, simpler man would have rushed to help, but Ben was neither brave nor simple. His mind was still reeling.

"My God," Ben whispered. "What's gonna happen when the world knows what's coming?"

TWO

DARK COMET

PACIFIC NORTHWEST
AUGUST 7
T-MINUS 178 DAYS TO LAUNCH

Jack Campbell was on layover in Seattle on his way to Alaska when his eyes caught "dark comet" on an overhead monitor. The news ticker looped as Jack blew steam off the surface of his franchise coffee. His pursed mouth froze when the full headline came into view: SPACEWATCH DISCOVERS DARK COMET UD3. He didn't know why it sounded ominous, so he googled it.

Online articles described dark comets as those that are out of sight from Earth's perspective. UD3, according to a NASA report, was a long-period comet that approached from the other side of the sun and slingshotted around the massive star, hurtling into the view of telescopes. NASA stated that there wasn't enough information to estimate the comet's trajectory or provide comment on probability of impact. Jack looked up from his phone and studied the other travelers waiting at gate 36. Danger felt more real when shared with others, but everything appeared normal. Men, women, and children were either bent down toward phones, laptops, books, or magazines or cat-napping until a flight attendant flipped on her microphone and welcomed all passengers—especially American Airlines AAdvantage program members.

Jack boarded the plane and secured his camera bag in the overhead compartment. He was a photojournalist headed to an assignment aboard an Arctic expedition. It was an opportunity of a lifetime, and he should have been over the moon with excitement.

"What do you think about this comet?" Jack asked the silver-haired passenger in the window seat. "The one that was just on the news?"

He tried to show her the screen of his phone, but she waved it away.

"Oh, I don't follow news, honey. Too depressing. Are they giving us food on this thing, or do we have to pay for snacks?"

~~~

THE PLANE LANDED in Anchorage just after three p.m. Alaska daylight time. The faces of other passengers were set with a sense of urgency as they hurried on to jobs, family, or more travel. One boy studying his phone and likely hunting for Pokémon bumped into a wall, rebounded, and continued on his way. He was another reminder that life was mostly keeping your head down, only catching fleeting glimpses of the great wide open and all its implications.

Jack's editors at *National Geographic* had arranged for a driver to take him the remaining leg of the journey to Seward. Travel schedules for his profession were grueling, but at thirty-two and with no strings attached, it was a price Jack was willing to pay for a job he loved. He kicked off his sneakers and stretched his lanky six-foot-two body across the back seat of the town car, and he was on his way.

During the flight from Seattle, Jack had web surfed and discovered that cosmic impacts were nothing new. It was the larger bodies that were rarer. For the last 70 million years, Earth had had a lucky streak . . . but luck could run out. Probability said it would.

Jack pulled out his phone and ignored all the new emails and texts from friends, colleagues, and ex-lovers from all over the world. He didn't answer his mother's latest emails, so it was no surprise when she called at the end of his three-hour drive. She asked about the flight and other niceties, but Jack was only interested in discussing the comet.

"You shouldn't believe everything you read," his mother advised.

"Mom, it was on CNN."

"Exactly!"

He knew where this was headed.

"Why would this be fake news?" Jack asked. "There's no political gain in scaring people..." But he knew there was, so he switched tack. "There was an asteroid the size of a school bus that came closer than the moon back in March," he countered. "It was discovered *five days* before it zipped past. And back in 2014, there was another of these dark comets called Siding Spring. It came out of our blind spot from behind the sun and almost hit Mars."

"I never heard that."

"Me neither, until I read about it today. Just because we're not paying attention, it doesn't mean these things don't happen, Mom."

"I can hear you sighing. How would you like it if I sighed every time *you* gave an opinion?"

"These are *facts*. Facts are not *opinions*."

"I didn't call to argue."

Jack heard his own sigh too late to stop it.

"Are you still leaving?" she asked.

It was the question his mother always asked.

"Because if you change your mind, your father and I could come visit..."

Jack tapped the speakerphone button so he could listen while checking what was trending online:

1. Red Sox vs. Yankees
2. Taylor Swift concert
3. Autism and antidepressants in utero
4. FIFA World Cup

5. Hair loss from shampoo
6. ...

Comet UD3 came in at number 16, bumping Manchester City Football Club. It appeared that Jack's mother wasn't the only one who missed its headlines.

"We wouldn't take up all your time," she assured him. "We can do a matinee and then meet up for dinner. It's been so long since we took a trip up to the city..."

"I gotta go, Mom. With all the flights, I'm beat."

It was true. On some things, his mother didn't argue. Jack said he loved her, which was also true, and ended the call.

As his town car reached Seward, Jack made one more Google search. Some of the articles he read on the flight referenced an official document released several years ago by the outgoing executive administration. Jack typed a few of the words he could remember and clicked on the first auto-fill option: *National Near-Earth Objects Preparedness Strategy*. The top link sent him to an unavailable webpage on the current whitehouse.gov site, one of several removed indefinitely.

Thank you for your interest in this subject, Jack read. *Stay tuned as we continue to update whitehouse.gov.* In sharp focus, contrasting with a blurry American flag in the background, were twin microphones atop a lectern with the presidential seal, as if any minute someone important would step up with something to say.

Jack's driver parked at the Seward waterfront and unpacked his bags onto the concrete. Jack didn't move when he came around and opened his passenger door. Never had he felt such hesitation before a long assignment. Not when his father needed heart surgery, not when an on-again-off-again girlfriend called him sobbing, not when an old sports injury acted up and left him limping in pain with heavy camera bags. Jack wasn't one to believe in premonitions, and yet he had one even as all the people he encountered continued to function with an expectation of normalcy.

The driver ducked down, confused, but then saw Jack's face.

"I could drive you back to Anchorage. I'm sure they'll understand," he added, nodding over his shoulder to the massive ship in port.

Jack quickly thanked the driver for his patience and shook his hand. He stepped into moist air that smelled of salty rot. The mist billowing down the snow-veined mountains surrounding Resurrection Bay was thick as smoke. Jack hoisted the weight of his bags onto both shoulders, ever mindful of his camera, and walked across the long and narrow dock with his head bowed.

He felt that all his assignments were of great significance, and documenting the last Arctic expedition by the US Coast Guard cutter *Healy* was no exception. There were only two guest slots available, and Jack had practically begged his editors to pull strings to secure one. They had all met at Washington, DC, headquarters back in June to discuss the magnitude of such a mission. *It's like you're capturing the Yangtze River dolphin,* one editor told Jack. *Aboriginal Tasmanians. The Javan tiger. The Bo of the Great Andamanese peoples. Passenger pigeons whose flocks could blot out the sky . . .* The editor winced and shook his head. *All beautiful and extinct. All that's left are fossils and pictures.* Jack was assigned to capture the beauty of the Arctic with his camera before it was gone.

It wasn't until he neared the water's edge that Jack could see more than fifty large, feathered carcasses floating in the bay. He walked up to the edge of the dock, stood beside a piling wrapped with ropes thicker than a man's wrist, and gaped at the dead dark birds of prey. A large young man walking several yards behind suddenly dumped his duffel bag and joined Jack to stare at the awful sight. He wore a navy brimmed cap and hooded sweatshirt with HEALY CREW in yellow block letters stretched across his wide shoulders.

"These are eagles," the young man said, frowning in surprise. "It's only been murres before."

He scanned the water and pointed to the carcass of a penguin-like bird.

"There's a murre. With the global weirding and all, things got out of whack and they starved. Thousands of 'em."

Jack asked about the eagles, but the younger man shrugged and said he didn't know.

"Maybe they saw the headlines about the comet," Jack said, squinting up at the sky, now empty of eagles. "Or know something we don't."

"Aw, I heard that comet was a conspiracy. But enough of politics—I'm Ned Brandt."

The beefy Coastie had the jaw, neck, and torso of a quarterback. His cheeks were flushed in the damp wind, and his face held an honest, open expression. He was handsome in a Chris Pratt kind of way. Ned was a Coast Guard lieutenant and helicopter pilot returning from mid-patrol break.

Jack gave his own name and a handshake.

"I'm one of the guests," he explained.

"The poet?"

"No, I'm the other one. Photojournalist."

"Yeah? Well, if you're looking for aerial shots, I can take you out in the helicopter," Ned offered. He suddenly smirked. "Unless that comet of yours leaves us SOLJWF."

"What?"

"Shit outta luck and jolly well fucked," Ned explained. "We've got lots of acronyms in the military."

He jogged back to his duffel bag and lugged it over his shoulder like a sack of potatoes. The two men continued on together to the end of the dock. Looming ahead was USCGC *Healy*, the country's most technologically advanced polar icebreaker. The ship was longer than a football field and nine stories high, and for all the eye could see, there was another thirty feet of ship below the water. Despite this, Jack felt sure it would become claustrophobic on their late-summer deployment. Everything familiar became claustrophobic.

The two men approached *Healy*'s 420-foot hull, painted bright red for visibility on ice. Ned elbowed Jack in the ribs and nodded for him to follow as he cut ahead of the long, single-file line of civilian scientists waiting to check in with their luggage. A Coastie stood by the bottom of a steep gangway greeting the new arrivals. She gave a bright smile to Ned and checked Jack's name off her passenger list. When she handed him a pager, Jack snorted a chuckle at the outdated equipment.

"Last time I saw one of these, it was hanging off the shorts of my freshman year pot dealer."

The woman also handed Jack a welcome aboard packet and a new passenger card held together with a paper clip. The card listed his emergency life raft, pager number, and stateroom assignment. Jack was to share quarters with the other guest passenger, a poet and Nobel laureate in literature. A poet was an unusual pick for the expedition, as guest slots had previously gone to wildlife surveyors, filmmakers, photographers, and Indigenous community observers. Jack wondered if the selection committee was more sentimental in this final round and wanted the Arctic preserved inside the immortality of the written word.

Ned led the way as the two men lugged their bags up *Healy*'s metal gangway and into the red belly of the ship. Immediately on the right was a ladder well labeled MAIN DECK. Ned bounded up like a mountain goat, but Jack had to be cautious on the steep and shallow stairs while balancing the weight of his bags and camera. He turned down the passageway of 02 deck and found the door to his stateroom closed. Jack knocked and entered the dark, windowless room. After flipping on the lights, he jumped back, cursing. There was a small man sitting at a desk.

"Sorry," Jack said quickly, "but you scared me."

The other man stood, only as tall as Jack's collarbone. Deep crescent lines arced from the inner corners of his black eyes down around gaunt eye sockets and into broad cheekbones. His hair—

chopped bangs in the front and long and straight in the back—was still black and thick, though the skin of his face was weathered. Jack guessed the man was somewhere in his late forties to early fifties, but it was difficult to tell.

"Jack. Nice to meet you."

"Gustavo," the man said without a smile.

His sagging denim jeans were cinched up high on his frightfully thin waist with a leather belt. It was no surprise when Gustavo quickly excused himself for being unwell. Jack stood aside to let him pass; it was difficult to get out of the way in such a small room. Gustavo kicked off worn leather shoes and unbuttoned his linen shirt. Stripping down to jutting bones and dingy white underwear, the poet climbed nimbly up to his top bunk and drew its curtains for privacy.

Jack glanced around their stateroom, but there wasn't much to see. The boxy cabinets, bunk beds, and closets were made of cheap sheet metal. On the wall to the left of the door hung a phone with a pager directory. Farther along, there was a small sink with a cabinet and vanity mirror and then a couple of desks and chairs. Jack saw nothing on Gustavo's desk—not a phone, laptop, book, magazine, or journal. The poet must have been sitting in the dark at the mercy of his own thoughts.

Jack dumped his bags in the closet that stood open and empty. He was still jet-lagged from all the travel and followed infantry wisdom: *Never miss an opportunity to sleep, eat, or shit.* Jack took off his sneakers and jeans, climbed into the bottom bunk, and drew its curtains closed.

∿∿∿

JACK WOKE AFTER three in the morning. He turned back and forth in his narrow bunk, but the same premonition of danger kept him alert. Outside his stateroom, *Healy*'s corridors were lit with red light like the darkrooms from Jack's earlier days developing film. A network of exposed cables and pipes ran along the ceilings. In the red light of after hours, they looked like arteries or intestines inside a great beast, like Jack was Jonah in the whale.

In his restless wanderings, Jack found the science lounge on 02 deck. It had long tables with computers and chairs, cheap couches, and widescreen TVs. There was only one other person: a youngish woman hunched over the keyboard of a Mac Mini workstation against the wall. Her straight black hair was gathered into a thick ponytail that stopped just short of the floppy hood of her dark sweatshirt. After the woman didn't turn to acknowledge him, Jack walked to one of the inferior HP laptops on a long table in the middle of the room.

He signed in to a guest account and pulled up a browser. His fingers strummed with impatience as each webpage loaded slowly until the woman cleared her throat in annoyance. Jack searched "conspiracy UD3" and skimmed the reader comments sections beneath online articles. One user posted:

Fake news! Photo made with CGI!

Jack scrolled up to the image accompanying the article and saw a caption beneath it that read, *Artist rendering of a comet in space.*

The only plausible conspiracy theory was that the comet was invented by NASA after its Asteroid Redirect Mission was defunded back in March. Jack finally logged off and looked to the woman sitting by the wall. If he could have a real conversation about the comet and exorcise that topic from his head, then he might be able to sleep.

The woman didn't hear him approach but remained mesmerized by the white-blue glow of her screen, which washed out her skin and reflected in the lenses of her glasses. Jack apologized for startling her but couldn't help glancing at her screen at the negative image of stars. The largest black splotch was circled in red and labeled UD3.

"Doesn't look too intimidating," he admitted. "But isn't it weird that NASA hasn't released any details?"

She sighed and turned her body toward him. Block letters on the front of her sweatshirt spelled out BERKELEY.

"I don't know," she admitted with the shrug of one shoulder.

"But you're worried?"

"I wouldn't be sitting here instead of sleeping if I wasn't worried."

She wasn't trying to be rude, just stating a plain fact. The woman added that there had been quite a few scientists reading into the night but they left one by one to try to sleep before sunrise. Jack wished her goodnight and let her be.

He left the science lounge and wandered farther down *Healy*'s corridors. The crew lounge was delightfully noisy. Jack ducked in for a peek and blinked at the harsh fluorescents. A few computer workstations lined the walls, and several laptops rested on long tables, but none of the Coasties were using them. The mood was lighter and friendlier as a dozen graveyard-shifters enjoyed downtime.

Two men stood in front of a large flat screen, swinging their arms as they watched their Mario Tennis Aces avatars on Nintendo Switch. More lounged on couches in their socks or played cards at a table. Three women gathered in a corner knitting and chatting about work in a good-natured stitch 'n' bitch. The crew already had the company of friends and familiars. Jack wished he could just walk in, sit at the table, and ask the dealer for a hand of cards.

Back in his stateroom, Jack tried to be as quiet as possible as he returned to his bunk. In the silence before sleep, he heard muffled sobbing from the man lying parallel less than five feet above him.

THREE

ARRIVAL

AMY MADE THE BEST of a jet-lagged, early morning. She had just finished ironing her best silk blouse when there was a knock on the door of her hotel room. Amy peeked through the door's fisheye lens and saw Ben's colleague Chuck Maes. He had accompanied them on the flight from Los Angeles to French Guiana and now stood yawning in the hallway, wearing rumpled khaki shorts, thong flip-flops, and a T-shirt. Ben emerged from their foggy bathroom moments after she opened the door. Like Chuck, he dressed in the same anti-style of someone who didn't need to give a shit about appearances. In less than five minutes, Amy changed into a denim skirt, sandals, and one of Ben's science conference T-shirts knotted at her slender waist. When in Rome, do as Caesar does.

The three of them piled into a courtesy shuttle before dawn, armed with their laptop bags and paper cups of coffee. Their hotel was on the edge of the town of Kourou, less than five minutes' drive from the Guiana Space Centre. Chuck asked Ben if he had received any updates.

"Nothing," Ben said, reflexively checking his phone again. "I assume the Professor wants to debrief me in person."

There was a nervous silence before Ben launched into their continued discussion of the plan. Amy opened her laptop and put on her tortoiseshell cat-eye reading glasses. She listened to Ben and googled terminology, organizations, and especially people until motion sickness forced her to look out the shuttle's windows at the moving landscape.

On the flight, Ben told Amy that an equatorial launch at the European Space Agency's spaceport would leverage the rotational velocity of the Earth and provide extra speed. There wasn't much knowledge of world geography between the three Americans, however. Amy stared at her laptop keyboard a bit before giving up and typing "Where the hell is French Guiana?" into a search engine.

The French region was on the northern coast of South America, bordered by Suriname to the west and Brazil to the south and southeast. The elevation was low, and most of the thick vegetation had been cleared, leaving only scraggly palm trees, grass, and clumps of bushes along the road. Everything was remarkably green compared to California's rain-starved terrain. The tropical temperature was already 88°F, but the interior of the shuttle felt like an icebox. Amy considered asking their driver to turn down the air-conditioning, but Chuck was heavyset and Ben was a nervous ball of energy; both were sweating at the temples.

Amy rubbed the goose bumps of her pale blush skin and massaged a biceps still sore from vaccination. She caught Chuck staring and gave a friendly smile. He was a sarcastic sweetie who tried to be discreet and never openly leered, like a handful of other NASA trolls. Chuck smiled sheepishly and turned to Ben, who was using him as a sounding board for a roster of engineers and physicists. Amy tried to keep tabs on the names dropped in between technical speak.

"Who is Ariane?" Amy interjected.

"Not *who*," Ben clarified, "but *what*. Ariane is a brand of rocket, like Dr Pepper is a brand of a soda."

Ben explained that a carrier rocket was needed to launch a spacecraft past Earth's gravitational field.

"The Ariane rocket at this spaceport is the first part of our plan," Ben said, already arranging props for his full explanation.

Amy was the one student Ben lived to teach, and he took great care not to talk down to her smarts or over her head. It was a bit of a tightrope, but it was one he was willing to walk. Ben pulled two green bills out of his wallet and crumpled them in his left fist, which he called the "spacecraft" for the purposes of demonstration. Next, he waved his empty right hand and called it the "Ariane rocket carrier." In one motion, Ben grabbed hold of his left fist with his right hand and made like he was throwing it up like a fly ball.

"At a sufficient altitude, the Ariane rocket carrier jettisons our spacecraft," he said.

Chuck watched the demonstration in stupefied silence, no doubt shocked by Ben's sudden show of patience as he held up his left fist and pulled out one of the paper bills.

"This is the leader impactor," Ben said, giving the single dollar bill to Amy. "Our spacecraft is gonna shoot this at the comet and blow a crater into its surface. Then the spacecraft will ram into that crater and detonate a nuclear explosive for optimal disruption."

Ben held out his left fist and opened his palm, revealing a twenty-dollar bill. Amy pocketed the bill before asking how Ben knew that this was the right plan when they knew so little about the comet. Ben started to shake his head and winced. Over the last forty-eight hours of vigorous planning and no sleep, Ben mentioned headaches. His habit of shaking his head was made all the worse by these heightened stakes. *I feel my brain bruising*, he joked. In the final hours before landing in South America, he gripped a fistful of his thick, dark waves and held his head still with one hand while the other gave Chuck's ideas a gladiatorial thumb up or down.

"The worst-case scenario is that we have a high probability of impact with less than ten years to deflect it," Ben said in rapid staccato. "A nuclear impactor would be the only viable option for a comet this large and fast. Modeling has shown that an existing nuclear weapon could deflect a one-kilometer near-Earth object. I mean, with all the impact scenarios..."

Amy knew about the 122 impact scenarios, some played out in person at the biannual Planetary Defense Conference and some played out virtually within an online forum. The scenarios helped prove what would fail—in theory—with computer simulations, probability, and human role-playing. Ben had already experienced the majority of all imaginable actions, reactions, and outcomes. Of course, the scenarios weren't real, nor were they current enough to account for the world's newer leaders and administrations.

"It's the right plan," Ben insisted.

But he looked suddenly ill and full of doubt. And who could blame him? If there was a high probability of impact, not even Amy would want to voice the question, *What if you're wrong?* The answer was obvious anyway: Ben might fail to prevent an extinction event, that's what.

"We're here," Chuck nearly whispered.

The three-mile drive was over before they even finished their coffees. The shuttle driver turned onto a European roundabout with colorful flags and a large WELCOME TO THE GUIANA SPACE CENTRE sign in French and English. He drove past the tourism entrance on the right and continued parallel to a long security fence topped with barbed wire. Amy had read online that the spaceport facilities stretched across an area nearly the size of New York City.

Through the windshield, she saw a checkpoint ahead with five armed guards in dark uniforms. Ben had had to throw a fit over the phone with UN headquarters to get Amy on the flight out of Los Angeles. Gaining security clearance on premises would likely be more difficult. They had strategized together on the plane until Amy grew frustrated: *You can tell that Professor Och-Ochsss—.* The name didn't exactly roll off the tongue. Ben quickly interjected with the right pronunciation. *Him!* Amy picked back up: *You tell him that one of our presidents got his daughter and son-in-law security clearance to the frickin' White House. Take a lesson: the big man calls the shots—and right now, that's you, Ben.*

The checkpoint's metal gate slid open as guards waved them forward several yards and then held their palms out flat, motioning them to stop. A guard spoke to their driver in French and had him exit the vehicle so that he could step up and take the wheel. The shuttle's side door opened, exposing them to bright sunlight and hot air. Amy saw a woman in professional dress approaching, her high heels rapping the asphalt.

"Welcome," the woman said, leaning into the interior. "I'm Marielena Acosta with the United Nations. I understand there is an extra passenger?"

Her dark eyes focused on Amy.

"Perhaps she would like to wait inside with me at Security?"

Amy opened her mouth, but Ben was quicker to respond.

"This is Amy Kowalski," he said calmly. "I asked your headquarters to distribute her resume ahead of our arrival. Ms. Kowalski has her own corner office in Modis Burbank because she's one of the best tech recruiters on the West Coast—and the only one I trust. The Professor said I could pick my team. Well, here's my HR director, and she takes her coffee black."

The woman nodded, considering.

"You selected Ms. Kowalski," she clarified.

"Every day," Ben replied with utmost confidence.

She nodded again and then waved to the guards. Amy clasped Ben's hand as their shuttle accelerated past a one-story building labeled SÉCURITÉ and entered an administration complex of tall buildings labeled with names of celestial bodies. A lone woman was waiting by the entrance of a building named Janus. She was very tall with a broad forehead and short, ash-colored hair. The woman barely paused for an introduction before ushering Amy, Ben, and Chuck indoors.

"Director Durand and Professor Ochsenfeld are expecting you

in the Janus meeting room," she said, overtaking them with wide strides on square-heeled pumps.

It had been three days since the Spacewatch discovery of UD3. Several sober-faced staffers stared at the three newcomers like rubberneckers passing a traffic accident in the hallway. These men and women certainly knew something.

"Dr. Schwartz!" one of the staffers whispered, and rushed out to intercept the group. "We've met," he told Ben in a thick German accent. "I worked for NASA on a visa. I was there when you led the Mars orbiters duck-and-cover maneuver for comet Siding Spring!"

Their tall guide gave sharp looks of disapproval as she reminded everyone that they were expected to report directly, but Ben stopped her.

"I'm sorry, I don't remember all of my colleagues," he said, shaking the man's hand. "That flyby was nuts, and I didn't get a lot of sleep."

It was the truth, but it was also true that Ben was unobservant when it came to meeting new people. That was Amy's strength.

"You were incredible," the man said in awe.

Ben beamed with pride and then thanked the man for reaching out, but really it was for recalling a moment in time when Ben was exceptional. Nothing could take away or change that triumphant piece of the past. It was Ben's forever. He seemed to breathe easier as they continued down the hallway to an elevator. Their guide used her security badge to gain clearance to the top floor. Amy was able to read "Assistant Director" before it retracted on its lanyard. The elevator doors shut behind the group, forcing them to stare at one another in awkward silence.

"I can't place your accent," Amy said to fill the silence.

The woman's eyebrows lifted and rippled her broad forehead. Amy had a voice like rusty knives that gave strangers pause. She had suffered from croup as an infant and screamed until she scarred her vocal cords. Then she smoked like a fiend from the age of thirteen until she moved to California and dropped the habit cold turkey.

"Dutch," said the assistant director.

"Ah, I'm sure it's a pretty language."

"Not at all."

The elevator slowed to a stop, but Amy wasn't giving up.

"Speaking of language," Amy added, "what does *Janus* mean?"

Ben was quick to blurt out that Janus was a moon of Saturn, but the assistant director added, "This is the first building in our headquarters facility. We bring heads of state to the meeting room."

The elevator doors parted with her synchronized exit.

"Janus was the Roman god of gateways... Also of beginnings and endings, and duality. He was depicted with two faces, one young and one old."

There were closed, double doors at the end of a short corridor. The assistant director opened the doors and nodded to the newcomers. Ben was the first to step into a large conference room with long tables forming a square studded with chairs around the sides, all facing center. Two of these chairs were occupied by men sitting side by side. Both rose, but only the man on the left was quick about it. The man on the right battled gravity as he fought to stand. Photos of him on the internet were all dated by several decades. Amy wasn't prepared for Professor Ochsenfeld's current state of steep decline.

"Sir," Ben said. "I mean Professor. It's such an honor..."

Ben blathered on. Amy had never seen him offer such respect to the living. The Professor had to be a true legend—not that he looked the part. The dapper cane with mother-of-pearl handle that supported his stooped weight was the only outward sign that he was an eminent Oxford don. Otherwise, his clothes were drab and dated.

"Professor, let me introduce you to Chuck Maes," Ben said, motioning back to his friend. "Chuck is from my JPL crew."

Chuck nodded with a nervous smile and fidgeted. Ben looked to Amy next. He had to fight for her inclusion.

"Amy Kowalski," she said, walking over to the men.

Introductions were important; she always handled her own with a smile, direct eye contact, and a firm handshake—but not too tight. As Amy got close, the smell of sickness hit her nostrils. Some organ or internal process had gone foul, but Amy still took the Professor's gnarled hand into her own. Old age and sickness were absent from the army bases where she spent the first eighteen years of her life. While these mortal reminders were still strange and frightening, Amy would never let them get the better of her.

"It's such an honor," she repeated, following Ben's lead just as he followed hers in the right situation.

Thick spectacles magnified red-veined eyes draped with lids like unfolded origami. The Professor's face held no expression but moved with an occasional tremor. It was only his pause that spoke to his momentary surprise; no one would pick her out of a lineup to be Ben's girlfriend.

The assistant director stood beside Director Durand after securely shutting the doors. Amy found him handsome for his age; sixties with a strong body, thick white hair, and startling blue eyes. It was only as she studied his expression very closely that she sensed danger.

"What's wrong?" she asked immediately.

The director took a halting breath and introduced both himself and the assistant director as Marcel Durand and Anneke Janssen.

"But what's *wrong?*" Amy demanded.

The Professor cleared his dry throat and announced, "The comet is accelerating even faster than expected."

Ben was no longer smiling, no longer giving deference. He was back in crisis mode. He stood protectively by Amy and stared into the Professor's unblinking eyes.

"How many years do we have, Professor?"

Ben could well have said decades, that was his hopeful estimation, but the Professor shook his head.

"What do you mean, 'No'?" Ben asked, raising his voice.

They didn't have years, the Professor explained. JPL's Sentry impact monitoring system and the European Space Agency's CLOMON system had calculated three very approximate, possible trajectories between them. The shortest of these estimated a potential impact as early as June.

"June," Ben repeated. "As in *this* June?"

The Professor rapped his cane on the thin carpeting and yelled back.

"Yes, *this* June! You must initiate your plan. Now!"

Ben took a breath and made several mental calculations with the speed and accuracy of a pocket calculator. He told the room they needed a February 1 launch for a spacecraft with solar power. Both of the spaceport directors protested at the same time.

"Is it even physically possible?"

"We'll find that out, won't we?" Ben said. "Now set the clocks."

FOUR

THE ARCTIC WEST EXPEDITION

SEWARD, ALASKA
AUGUST 8
T-MINUS 177 DAYS TO LAUNCH

SLEEP GRANTED JACK a reset. Worrying was tiresome, after all, and he needed a break from it. The curtain to Gustavo's top bunk was still fully closed, so Jack quietly grabbed his towel, toiletry bag, and a pair of flip-flops. The shower in the passageway bathroom was the size of a small closet and had a printout taped up on the wall with instructions. All passengers had to make do with a "sea shower" no more than once a day using only two bursts from the showerhead: one to get wet and one to rinse. Jack understood that heated, drinkable water on demand was still a luxury to the majority of the world's population. On top of that, he didn't mind getting dirty and smelling like the mammal he was; it was another form of freedom and truth.

At 0730 hours, freshly shaved with his short, light hair gelled up in stylish tufts, Jack found the cafeteria-style galley. Crewmembers and scientists sat in the mess deck at long tables chatting and chewing. It was easy to spot which group was which: the Coasties wore navy sweatshirts or work shirts, and the scientists sported plaid button-downs, jeans, facial hair, thumb rings, and fleece vests.

As a guest passenger, Jack was the odd man out. He helped himself to a stack of chocolate-chip pancakes and sat alone. Flipping open the welcome aboard packet, Jack read an introduction by the ship's own Captain Weber:

> Welcome aboard *Healy*. Please review the enclosed materials.
> The inherent hazards of life at sea require that we all understand
> and follow the basic safety practices which are described...

Jack skimmed the rest. Mostly, he looked for instructions on getting access to his *Healy* email account. Once the ship reached 75°N latitude, bandwidth would be so limited that only the bridge would be authorized to access the internet. The computer labs in the lounges would only provide email through *Healy*'s server onboard.

The Coasties and scientists surrounding Jack made more haste with their breakfasts. Their mornings were booked with scheduled activities listed on the plan of the day posted throughout the ship. Safety drills occupied the crew and one unlucky man-overboard dummy named Ralph. The scientists were to split their numbers in half to inventory equipment lockers and lab spaces while also testing the cranes on deck. Jack was left to his own devices.

The weather was warmer than he expected; high sixties, set to creep up to 73°F, according to plan of the day posts. Jack stuffed his hat and gloves into the pockets of his parka and thought it unusually warm for Alaska. Or maybe not so unusual, considering that the previous year brought the hottest global temperatures on record by the largest margin to date. The current year was already set to break more records. Jack often remembered the allegory of the frog plopped in water that was slowly brought to a boil—no cause for alarm until you're already served up on a plate with garlic and lemon.

The mist had burned off, and Jack could see Seward's mountains clearly. He walked aft and back again to the bow, checking different vantage points with the viewfinder of his camera. There were more dead eagles in the water, many more, and yet the air was full of healthy, obnoxious gulls that swooped and drafted large ships in the bay.

Jack craned his head up to the three boxlike structures rising from *Healy*'s hull.

The structure closest to the bow housed living quarters: staterooms, lounges, mess deck, gym, laundry, and so on. It was the widest and tallest of the three structures with small, evenly spaced portholes dotting its sides all the way up to a crown of windows and satellite antennae at the bridge, *Healy*'s central command. Sprouting from the bridge, like a mast and crow's nest, was a small lookout. No doubt those windows afforded the best panoramic view.

Jack ducked into the closest ladder well and encountered two Coasties loping down single file.

"Wrong way, sir," one of them called out.

"What?"

"Yah have to go to the starboard side if yah want to go up."

The reasoning was immediately apparent as they squeezed past each other. Jack climbed to the bridge four levels up at the height of a six-story building. He stood and gaped at the view over the tip of *Healy*'s bow and onto the slate-colored horizon. A crewmember approached and introduced herself as Ensign Sokolov. Stocky, formal but helpful, she offered a tour of the bridge that Jack gladly accepted.

The other crewmembers were all patient, and each took a moment to give their names, ranks, titles, and assigned tasks. They tried to explain various functions of a long control console with clunky buttons, lights, and radar screens. Captain Weber even walked over to give a handshake. He was tall and lean, like Jack, but with a chiseled profile that belonged on Mount Rushmore. His eyes were blue as worn denim, but unfocused with distraction. After excusing himself, the captain walked up to the windows of the bridge and lifted a pair of binoculars. He didn't look out to the horizon but down at the dead eagles floating in the water.

Jack's pager sounded. He pulled it from his waistband and squinted at the display.

"What's this code mean?" he asked Ensign Sokolov.

"Abandon ship."

"We're still in the harbor!"

Her eyebrows lifted as she stated that safety drills were explained in the welcome aboard packet and his assigned emergency location was listed on his new passenger card.

"Yes, it is," Jack agreed, pulling the card from his back pocket and using it to salute her.

The abandon ship locker was halfway up *Healy*'s starboard side. A group of scientists were gathered by the doorway. Jack recognized the woman he had spoken with in the science lounge. She had light brown skin in the true light of day and barely came up to his shoulder in height.

"Might as well introduce ourselves," Jack said, and approached with a smile.

He studied her oval face with rounded cheeks, nose, and chin. Her mouth had soft, mauve-colored lips, as if lightly stained by red wine. Sunglasses and gloves concealed her eyes and ring finger.

"Maya," she said, after a pause. "Dr. Maya Gutiérrez. And this is one of my bunkmates, Dr. Nancy Stevens."

She motioned to a tall woman standing beside her with paint-spatter freckles and red hair that curled and fluffed around her jawline.

"I'm Jack," he said, shaking their hands. "Mr. Jack. Definitely not doctor."

A Coastie holding a clipboard walked to the center of the group and called out above the wind.

"Good morning, life raft number five!"

They mumbled good morning and each raised their hands when he took attendance.

"Gustavo Wayãpi?"

Jack swiveled his head around but didn't see his bunkmate.

"Gustavo Wayãpi going once? Going twice?"

The Coastie made a mark by Gustavo's name. After roll call, he explained *Healy*'s abandon ship procedure: what supplies each individual had to bring along, what to wear, and how food would be rationed. Jack scrolled through his email, trying not to count all the new messages from his mother. He was subtle, but the Coastie was watching his audience carefully.

"You gonna remember all this?" he asked Jack.

"It's okay," Jack assured him. "I can't die. I'm an only child."

The man wasn't amused.

"Doubt your mother can save you out here."

"You haven't met my mother!" Jack said, but he tucked away his phone and made a better show of listening.

"Any questions before we get you all fitted for immersion suits?"

The Coastie was quick to add that no one knew why the eagles were dying, but the EPA had been alerted days ago. Dr. Nancy Stevens raised her gloved hand.

"What if the ship needs to turn around?" she asked. "Because of the comet?"

The Coastie asked Nancy to repeat her question before looking at the rest of them for assistance. He hadn't heard of any dark comet, but the scientists wouldn't let him off the hook so easily. The Coastie finally radioed his supervisor, who joined the group ten minutes later with a reply that wasn't an answer.

"We hear not much is known 'cause they just spotted the thing," the supervisor explained.

The thing still didn't have a name, only the label UD3.

"And this is *Healy*'s last scientific mission," he added, visibly affected, "so we're gonna see it to the end."

Healy's Arctic West expeditions had been recently defunded. Climate change wasn't considered a factual threat by many in the administration. Those who did accept the science still understood that the Coast Guard's budget had to be slashed where it could in order to fund a multibillion-dollar wall along the country's southern border.

As life raft number fivers peeled off to head toward the next station of the abandon ship drill, Jack sidled up to Maya. Here was a new person in a totally new environment, and Jack lived for assignments that dropped him like a paratrooper into unfamiliar territory that required his full focus. Nancy looked back to her bunkmate with an arched red eyebrow, but Maya gave a subtle nod for her to go on ahead. Jack was not unaware of this exchange. Men were trouble, no doubt about it. Jack was nothing if not self-aware and avoided sex with women near his apartment in Brooklyn because there could be no exit plan. (Of course, he still had occasional, messy slip-ups when alcohol or a nostalgic birthday was involved; drunken, nostalgic birthdays were *always* calamitous.)

Jack meant to play it safe on this assignment. *My stash of emergency condoms is exactly that: for emergencies,* Jack promised Nancy in his head, *because there can be no exit plan on a ship in the middle of the Arctic.* While Jack loved the intensity of new friendships and infatuations, the maintenance of long-term relationships hadn't proven worth the effort—not yet, anyway.

"Can I take your picture?" he asked.

Maya immediately shook her head, sweeping her black ponytail across her shoulder blades.

"I hate cameras."

Jack mimed a punch to the gut. He would have made a great class clown if he had ever felt the need for attention. Maya's upper lip curled under her teeth as they caught up with the rest of the group: a barely suppressed smile.

Immersion suits were stored in the helicopter hangar at the top of *Healy*'s second boxlike structure. The hangar complex was the largest room on the ship and housed two helicopters parked by a folding metal wall leading to the flight deck. Ned Brandt, *Healy*'s pilot, looked like a solid bench-presser in a short-sleeved navy shirt. An even bulkier Coastie named Malcolm flanked him with large, brown biceps and raised veins like cables.

Once the stragglers had all gathered, Malcolm held up an immersion suit that Ned called a Gumby. Malcolm demonstrated how to step into the floppy booties, pull on the big-fingered gloves, pull over the hood, and zip up the front. There was even a face flap leaving all but the eyes, nose, and brows safely sealed. Ned pointed to shelves where the immersion suits were stored and told the group to "have at it."

Some of the scientists donned the suits, laughed, and waddled around. Others took a more sober stance to the idea of floating in the Arctic Ocean and waiting for rescue. Jack had both feet secured in his Gumby booties when Ned ambled over and playfully poked Jack's average biceps. He passed an open invitation to the CrossFit classes he taught with Malcolm on Saturday afternoons.

"There are more dead eagles today," Jack said suddenly.

Ned nodded but said nothing.

-᷈ᴧᴧᴧ᷈-

JACK KNOCKED QUIETLY and entered his stateroom. Gustavo was seated at his metal desk but with the noticeable improvement of overhead lights.

"You missed the abandon ship drill," Jack said, with a smile he hoped was disarming. "The Coasties took attendance. You're gonna get busted."

Gustavo continued to stare straight ahead.

"Look, I know these close quarters aren't easy," Jack offered. "I'm sure you're not used to having another man stuck to you like glue."

Gustavo blinked rapidly, like he was coming out of a dream or the daze of a head injury.

"I am used to it," he said. "Or, I was." Gustavo struggled to say the simple words: "I had a twin."

As he leaned forward to stand, a chain spilled free of his shirt collar and dangled from his neck. Attached to the end was a crushed piece of metal: a spent bullet. Gustavo crossed the small room, climbed into his bunk, and drew the curtains closed.

Jack couldn't imagine the loss of a twin sibling, but he could understand the need to retreat into grief.

In the silence that followed, tugboat engines revved as they pulled *Healy* away from the dock. The last Arctic West expedition was underway.

～＾＾＾＾＾＾～

HEALY SAILED OUT of Resurrection Bay and into the Gulf of Alaska. Keeping land in sight, Captain Weber navigated coastal waters until *Healy* reached the base of Alaska's long-tail archipelago at Katmai National Park. Jack was on deck for a few hours before sunset. Coasties bustled about but were friendly about interruptions. One pointed to the view from *Healy*'s starboard side and said that the park drew lots of tourists with its brown bear population. Jack stood by the deck railing and trained his lens at dark volcanic rock, emerald forests, and blue-toned mountains crowned with snowcaps. He was all business with landscapes, like a jeweler inspecting a diamond. People were another matter entirely. He fell in love with everyone behind the camera: women and men, old and young. The day he didn't love and empathize with his subjects was the day he had to quit photojournalism.

Jack heard the eagle's splash before he saw it. He zoomed his lens to the highest magnification and saw a bald eagle with a white tail and crown floating on the surface of the water. With its hollow bones and feathers, submergence was slow and difficult to watch. Jack thought he saw the bird blink before slipping just below the surface. Air bubbles unsettled the water. The eagle was alive but drowning, motionless instead of struggling to live.

~~~~~

JACK FOUND DR. MAYA GUTIÉRREZ in the science conference room, where more than twenty scientists were gathered. One of them stood at the front of the room. He was a stout white-haired man with a full beard that looked like a cross between a college professor and Santa Claus.

"May we help you?" he asked Jack.

Jack looked to Maya, who wordlessly stood and joined him in the hallway.

"We're kinda busy right now," she said quietly.

Jack regarded Maya's black eyes, unplucked eyebrows, and full lashes. Her unwavering gaze felt open and intense at the same time.

"You're staring."

"Sorry," Jack stuttered. "First time I've seen your eyes without glasses. What...What's wrong with the eagles?" he asked. "Why are they dying like this?"

After Jack explained what he saw, Maya's tone changed. She looked sheepish when she shook her head.

"But you must have some ideas?" he pressed.

"There was a fishing town on an island in Japan..." she whispered, and continued to describe the once healthy ecosystem of Minamata Bay. In the 1950s, mullet, shad, and lobsters started to disappear. Dead fish rose to the surface one by one; birds dropped from the sky. The cats of the village began to spastically dance and bash themselves against walls. They jumped into the sea and drowned. Then the fishermen and their families—and their newborn babies— exhibited damaged nervous systems. Their bodies were racked by convulsions that left them speechless and immobile. And then they died.

"They called it Minamata disease," Maya said. "It was caused by severe mercury poisoning that destroyed the brain's cerebellum, for starters."

The people of Minamata all knew that wastewater from the local Chisso chemical plant was the cause. But they were poor, and—in the eyes of Chisso, the chemical industry, and the Japanese government—expendable. Evidence was suppressed while Chisso steadily increased production and the resulting poisonous wastewater. The strange Minamata disease continued to spread to an estimated ten thousand people.

"I don't know if they're related," Maya was quick to interject, "but there have been documented cases like what we're seeing right now."

"Could it be the comet?" Jack whispered.

Maya tilted her head and squinted her eyes at him. She asked *how* a near-Earth object farther out than Mars could be killing eagles. Jack shrugged and pouted with his lower lip. He thought of his own premonitions.

"Maybe some things can't be explained by science," he said defensively.

"All phenomena have cause and effect," Maya stated, but had to add, "we just don't always understand what those causes and effects are."

Jack sighed and shook his head once.

"I'll let you get back to your meeting," he said, just as Maya was about to take a step closer.

FIVE

MORE GATEWAYS

MAYA WAS SURPRISED to see Jack waiting patiently at the front of the breakfast line at 0645. His casual-cool clothes and easy manner didn't identify him as an early riser, but the camera hanging from his neck did. As a photographer, his agenda was dictated by the sun, and being late had consequences.

Jack smiled when their eyes met as they filled up plates with food. Maya's stomach and heart fluttered on reflex. She nodded hello but retreated to the small side of the mess deck, where the scientists gathered at three long tables. Jack tried to catch her eye again, but she studied her scrambled eggs and Tabasco sauce until he sat alone across the room.

The man's forwardness could be explained by his profession; photographers made their subjects more comfortable in order to get what they wanted. And it wasn't like Jack had lots of options when it came to flirting among ninety-three crewmembers and fifty-one scientists, excluding all the men and married women (she hoped Jack excluded married women). Either way, Maya told herself not to be flattered.

As soon as his attention was diverted, Maya stole a greedy glance. Jack had well-proportioned, angular features and a square jaw. His sandy hair wasn't exactly blond, ginger, or light brown but was all three at once. There were crow's-feet at the edges of his eyes that were paler than the surrounding, unlined skin. He must have a bad habit of squinting under the strong sun to get a good look at his surroundings.

From a distance, Jack was good-looking in a nondescript way until his features lit up with a smile; then he was gorgeous. *Muy guapo!* Maya's mother would say out loud, in her Latina whisper. Maya didn't respond to her mother's prompts because good-looking men were mostly self-aware. The wealthier ones from good families, with polite manners and business suits, needed even less encouragement. Maya had bedded exactly three of these unattainable types, the sum total of her sexual activity in thirty-six years of age.

It wasn't hard to interest men in a one-night stand. Maya was attractive in a well-formed way; most said "cute" and some said "pretty." She was so petite and reserved, sipping her drink with watchful eyes, that those three men were each shocked to feel her body suddenly brush against a hip as she stood on tiptoe to whisper in their ear. Maya always left them with one less curiosity to satisfy.

As for the decent men who were interested in more than sex, the ones who could have made good life partners and fathers, Maya kept a kind distance. She was a first-generation American and the eldest of four daughters. Showing the most promise in school resulted in the most attention from her father, a man who believed that education was the surest and most honest way out of poverty. He pushed Maya hard until she pushed herself even harder and made all the necessary sacrifices. Her younger sisters all had children who were the spoiled loves of their grandmother's life, but Maya was forever studying and uprooting her life for a bachelor's degree, doctorate, post-doctorate, and finally professorship.

Jack abruptly stood up and walked by her table. Maya tried to get a better look at the scars she had noticed when they first met. They weren't the usual clean and faded scars of men who were once boys who crashed their bikes or fell against a radiator. One jagged scar on Jack's neck looked dangerously close to his jugular vein. Maya was hungry for more. As with all her appetites, the key was moderation. Maya allowed herself a few breaks from good behavior as reward for a very disciplined life, such as the empty potato chip bags that came with all-night study sessions. Maya had to run five miles a day in order to stay petite and not just short, but some things were worth a steep price. Luckily, *Healy* had a gym with a treadmill.

Maya stopped into the science lounge on her way back from breakfast. Instead of scouring for updates on the comet, she searched the roster on *Healy*'s intranet and found Jack, aka John S. Campbell. Maya googled his name and poked around until she found his portfolio website: a patchwork of documentary-style photography. Most of the photos contained people who looked through the camera to the man behind it. It was only one side of the lens, but it was the one that mattered. Jack must have seen the unique vitality in these people and captured it to share. Maya felt her barrier walls cracking.

She quickly logged off and prepared for a day of work on deck. *Healy* had several safety requirements: steel-toe boots, insulated socks and gloves, neon anti-exposure suit, and hardhat. Add a dose of Dramamine for motion sickness, and Maya was ready for her first water sample cast—more than ready.

Conditions on deck were low sixties with dazzling sunlight and strong winds. Maya allowed herself a moment to breathe the moving air through her nose and mouth to both smell and taste the salt and algae. Despite growing up in California, Maya had seen the ocean for the first time at seventeen. She never looked back at a life without it, which was fortunate. Her parents' approval and her own ambition wouldn't have been enough to keep her on such a long and difficult path. In the end, it was her love of the ocean that made her trudge on to a tenure track at UC Santa Barbara's Marine Science Institute. It was the same love that got her out of bed every morning and eventually on a ship bound for the Arctic.

Healy had just passed through a gap in the eastern Aleutian Islands, a gateway from the Gulf of Alaska to the Bering Sea. The islands' steep volcanic shores, colorful harbors, and fishing towns diminished in their wake. Ahead lay open water and the first opportunity to collect samples. Maya walked to the back of the ship and waved to another team of scientists as she passed. They hovered around a coring device, collecting soft sediment, or "delicious muck," as Charlie referred to it.

Dr. Charles Brodie—"Just call me Charlie"—was *Healy*'s chief scientist. He was also an important figure in Maya's life with a history that dated back to her graduate school years at Berkeley. Aside from Charlie, who had handpicked and interviewed all expedition candidates, the other fifty scientists were mostly strangers or acquaintances who read each other's publications and chatted at conferences. While the Coasties were predominantly young males, the science party had an even gender split and wider age range, from twentysomething graduate students to sixtysomething senior scientists, but all had the fraternity of a shared purpose: to study the ocean and gather hard data.

Facts were what scientists needed to identify change and sound the alarm. Forty years of NASA satellite imagery proved that ice extent in the Arctic had decreased significantly in that time by an average of 11 percent per decade. However, the chemistry of the Arctic waters had only been mapped for the first time in 2015 aboard this very ship. It was important groundwork that Maya and fifteen other scientists aboard *Healy* would continue over the course of the expedition—starting today.

A group of seven scientists stood beside a large crane at the stern of the ship, comprising half of the chemistry mapping team assigned to the first twelve-hour shift. Maya would have admonished herself for being on time and not early, but seeing Jack's photos was well worth that price.

Most of the faces in the team were already somewhat familiar after two days on the ship. Maya quickly introduced herself to the others: a middle-aged professor and a young postdoc, both from Oregon State University. Both had trimmed beards surrounding their smiles and gentle handshakes. Maya spotted her smiling bunkmate, Dr. Nancy Stevens. Nancy was from Woods Hole Oceanographic Institution in Massachusetts. The two women were getting to know each other quickly, trading family history, jokes, and worries over the comet.

Nancy and the OSU professor were the most senior scientists with multiple research excursions in their CVs. They took charge and split the team in half. Three scientists followed Nancy in removing their boots and entering the two twenty-foot-long ISO van workstations in their socks. The OSU professor remained outside and pulled a tarp off the cylindrical frame of *Healy*'s rosette water sampler. Maya and two other scientists followed him in a revolving line as they opened the doors to one of the workstations, received a thirty-liter GO-Flo bottle from one of the scientists inside, and then walked over and attached it to the rosette frame. Maya moved quickly and felt the rush of endorphins that comes with reaching the summit of a steep climb to lifelong achievement. At that moment, Maya wouldn't have traded places with anyone alive.

Once the rosette frame was full of the empty containers, the team hooked it up to the crane by a wire cable. A scientist on the team would handle the controls for opening and closing the bottles at specified depths to capture samples, but a Coastie had to operate the crane itself. Three of them arrived just in time. Maya stood barely five-foot-two next to their towering height, but she had stopped being intimidated by such things—or anything, really.

"Good morning, scientists!" the one named Malcolm called out. "I'll be your crane operator today. So who's ready for some action?"

Maya immediately lifted both hands above her head with her palms out. Malcolm laughed and jogged over to slap a high-ten.

"True soldier," he whispered.

〜〜〜

GUSTAVO MOSTLY LEFT his stateroom to use the toilet. After a couple of days, he even ventured to the galley to eat a few bites of food, but he was still dropping weight. In the middle of poking another hole in his leather belt with a pocketknife, Gustavo heard a knock at the door. He expected Jack to walk in, but the cabin door remained shut. Gustavo waited until another knock sounded, louder this time. A muffled voice called out.

"Gustavo Wayãpi?"

The woman standing in the corridor took a quick step back when he opened his door. She repeated his Brazilian name until he acknowledged it with a nod.

"I'm Ensign Camila Ortiz," she said. "We saw each other when you boarded."

The ensign waited for Gustavo to nod again, her eyes scanning his face carefully. She asked if she could enter the room after he didn't offer.

"*¿Prefieres español, Gustavo?*"

"No," he said. "I don't speak much Spanish. I'm better at Portuguese and French, and best at English."

She scanned his physical form again, clearly confused as to why this was the case. Gustavo understood that he was confusing—even to himself.

"I know *Healy* has tons of regulations," the ensign continued in English, "but they all exist for a reason..."

Gustavo's focus wavered. He wished she would just state her purpose so he could say whatever words would get her to leave. All he wanted was to be left alone.

"The accountability form lets the crew know that all hands on deck are alive and well," said the ensign.

Gustavo nodded immediately, but she repeated herself anyway.

"So you *must* log in to our intranet and sign the form. Twice a day, by eleven a.m. and again at five p.m.—"

He kept nodding.

"*Or*, we will have to keep repeating this conversation," she insisted.

Gustavo saw Jack cautiously walk through the room's open door.

"Should I come back?" he asked.

"No," the ensign said. "We're done here, right?"

Gustavo nodded one last time. Soon as the woman left the room, he closed the door with relief.

"I read some of your poems online," Jack said to his back. "From a collection called *The Majesty*."

When Gustavo turned around, Jack was eagerly waiting.

"I didn't read all of them," Jack admitted, "but most. They were beautiful, but they also hurt."

He paused.

"I'm not a violent person," he said, and smiled to help prove the statement, "but your poems left me with...a taste for blood."

Gustavo nodded. Jack had understood his words and meaning.

"You know, I had an assignment in Brazil last year," Jack said.

He reached for the laptop on his desk.

"These are the Guarani-Kaiowá people."

The image on Jack's screen featured three men and one woman standing or squatting beside a plastic tarp fashioned into a shelter. They carried bamboo spears and wore body paint but also jeans and plastic flip-flop sandals. The woman was fully clothed with a sleeved shirt.

"They were evicted from their lands and had their water resources poisoned by fertilizers and pesticides from factory farms," Jack explained. "These families were living by the side of a busy road. They have one of the highest suicide rates in the world."

Gustavo was already aware of the Guarani-Kaiowá peoples' plight. He had even traveled to Europe with one of their leaders, Marcos Verón, before the old man was beaten to death by a rancher's henchmen. Gustavo asked Jack why he took pictures of the Guarani-Kaiowá.

"To make the international community aware," Jack said without hesitation. "That's the work of good journalism."

"And did this awareness help the Guarani-Kaiowá?"

Gustavo smiled at Jack's troubled expression. Now they understood each other even more. It was good to be understood by a young man who was trying to be kind in such a forbidding place. Gustavo turned away and picked up his belt. Jack watched him loop it through his loose jeans and cinch it at the newest notch.

"I was on my way to lunch," Jack said. "Why don't you come with me?"

"I already ate."

"Looks like you could eat some more..."

Gustavo told him to go on ahead, firmly but kindly. Hunger was for the living. Grieving in a metal box floating on a freezing ocean wasn't living; it was hell and purgatory combined, where all one could do was wait. *Is this a dream?* Gustavo often wondered. *Or is this death?* Had Gustavo died instead of his twin brother? Or, had sorrow left him numb and frozen like the frigid sea surrounding them?

SIX

THE DEFENSE EFFORT

KOUROU, FRENCH GUIANA
AUGUST 9
T-MINUS 176 DAYS TO LAUNCH

LOVE MWANGI HAD never seen rain like this. The airstrip of Kourou, French Guiana, was flooded in water that puckered and warped with constant downpour. Less than a mile in the distance, ground traffic controllers sloshed around in fluorescent rain suits. Love stood by her plane's open hatch and smelled the soupy climate, ignoring the flight crew as they tried to maneuver around her six-foot frame. None said a word as Love continued to stretch her cramped muscles. As a lean and leggy East African woman wearing tight jeans, studded motorcycle boots, bead and metalwork necklaces, and a striped feather earring, she made for an imposing beauty.

An entourage of Humvees pulled onto the airstrip and parked several yards from the plane. The men who stepped out of them carried assault rifles and wore green camouflage and sky-blue helmets with two bold letters stenciled in white. In Love's early youth, the sight of UN peacekeepers signified both grave danger and the only safety she could count on. When Love began employment at UN African headquarters in Nairobi in her late teens, those two letters took on a whole new meaning: a path away from poverty, loneliness, violence, and stigma.

Love went and stood with the other passengers on the plane; thirty-some UN civilian personnel who all had remained tight-lipped on the fifteen-hour flight from New York City. The first peacekeeper to enter the plane's fuselage addressed them as a group.

"Welcome to the Defense Effort for Comet UD3," he said. "You are now part of an international collaboration toward collective action to defend the planet."

Several more peacekeepers entered the plane and shook off raindrops. One called out for an interpreter, and Love stepped forward. He handed her a plastic packet containing the same camouflage poncho that the peacekeepers wore.

"Come with me," he said.

Love donned the poncho and gathered her luggage. Passing by the armed men, she kept her hooded head bowed to avoid the eyes of those who could end her life with the pull of a trigger finger. The peacekeeper led her to a Humvee at the front of the line. Love hefted her duffel bag and carry-on suitcase onto the back seat and climbed in. She pulled off her poncho, left it in a dripping heap, and then stretched out on a diagonal. The knees of her jeans were already drenched and clinging like a wet skin.

The peacekeeper got into the front passenger seat and rested his assault rifle in his lap while the driver shifted gears and eased off the brake.

"Am I in danger?" Love asked.

"We all are," the peacekeeper said simply. "That's why you're here."

His accent wasn't derived from French but probably some other Romance language. His skin was a light gold while the driver's was as richly dark as Love's, and yet they seemed to be fellow countrymen. Love waited quietly until the driver whispered in Portuguese while nodding back at her. His words roughly translated to "Not what I expected."

Love peered through her passenger window as they exited the small airfield. Behind a blur of rainfall, Love saw thousands of light blue helmets. In less than a mile, the Humvee turned and drove down the length of a Kourou golf course converted into military barracks with rows of tents and parked trucks that stretched on into gray mist.

Love leaned forward and asked the soldiers more questions to distract them as she smoothly pulled out her phone. Pointing the screen down to hide its light, she typed a message to her girlfriend, Rivka:

Landed safe. Remember what I told you.

Love slipped the phone back in her pocket as the Humvee reached a roundabout with flagpoles dotting its circumference. Against gray rainclouds, the colorful flags of the European Union looked brighter. To Love, they called out, *Welcome! Welcome, France. Welcome, Portugal. Welcome, Germany. Welcome, Norway. Welcome, Croatia. Welcome, Netherlands...* Love smiled. Here was her final destination: the equatorial spaceport in French Guiana, now entirely dedicated to the international Defense Effort for Comet UD3.

Trees and dense foliage cleared at the corner of a security fence where more than a hundred armed peacekeepers stood yards apart along its perimeter. Through the windshield, Love saw a large group of soldiers clustered around a security checkpoint. They wore dark uniforms with GENDARMERIE stitched onto bulletproof vests.

The Humvee's driver pulled to a stop and rolled down his ballistic glass window.

"Interpreter!" he shouted.

One of the gendarme soldiers stepped forward with a clipboard in a clear plastic bag. With a thick French accent, he asked for her full name and country of origin.

"Love Mwangi," she said, leaning into the front of the cab. "I was born in Kenya but I live in New York."

"Bienvenue," he said, finding her name on his list.

Welcome.

The Humvee crept past the checkpoint's sliding metal gate and barbed wire after the soldier waved them through. It was a short drive to the nearest building, which had a sign that read SÉCURITÉ. The peacekeeper riding in the passenger seat turned around.

"Sorry," he said, pointing to the crumpled-up poncho. "You'll need that today."

But Love had already taken a step outside. Getting soaked was no trouble if it allowed her to escape cramped quarters. Rubbing warm rain over her shaved scalp, Love hoped for a shower and a clean toilet at the end of this long journey. She shouldered her duffel bag and pulled her rolling suitcase along the flooded asphalt. Six gendarme soldiers stood by the front exterior of the security building with their helmets dripping. Two peeled away to escort Love into the building. A woman wearing a suit was waiting just inside.

"Welcome. I'm Marielena Acosta with the United Nations," she said, with the same accented English as the peacekeepers. "We've been expecting you."

Love introduced herself with a perfectly casual, flat, and nasal American accent.

"From New York City," she added, standing very tall and very wet.

Acosta removed her tailored blazer and offered it as a towel. Love told her the clothing was too nice to wrinkle, but Acosta reached up to gently pat Love's wet cheeks. The gesture was tender, but there was no forgoing procedure.

"Please empty your pockets," Acosta said, pointing to a nearby plastic bin.

Love did as she was told. When the soldiers unzipped her luggage and carefully inspected all her things, she gave them the stink eye.

"Is this all necessary?"

Acosta plucked Love's cellphone out of the bin, dropped it into a Ziploc bag, and handed it to one of eight workers seated with laptops.

"Hey, I need that!"

"Sorry," Acosta said. "But the Effort will require your full focus."

"Then how am I supposed to let someone know I'm safe?"

Acosta shook her head, no answer for her question, and beckoned Love to follow her toward a long desk against the back wall. Love insisted on dragging her luggage along.

"Look up, please."

Love heard a click and saw a printer spit out her photo. Acosta slid it into a plastic holder at the end of a lanyard she placed over Love's bowed head. Acosta instructed her to wear the security badge at all times. As an interpreter, Love had general access to the premises but was only allowed into cleanrooms, labs, and hangars when accompanying an engineer.

"I thought it was a terrorist attack," Love muttered, inspecting her new security badge.

"Pardon?"

"You know, when I got an urgent call from the UN's New York headquarters, I thought Al-Shabaab had gone and beheaded an American journalist or aid worker, or something."

It was the explanation that made the most sense: Love spoke all the Kenyan regional dialects, she had no living relatives in the country to endanger, and there was leverage with Love's request for American citizenship hanging in the balance.

"I thought I had it all figured out until they told me there was a natural disaster coming, something unexpected," Love said. She laughed with her white teeth and their front gap bared.

It was only on the flight to French Guiana that Love was finally briefed in full.

"They got the 'unexpected' part right. I mean, a comet, of all things..."

Love rubbed her dry and heavy eyes. It had been thirty-two hours since she was awakened in the middle of the night with a summons.

"Were you able to sleep on the plane?" Acosta asked.

Love shook her head. She couldn't understand how anyone could sleep in a crowd of people, so exposed and defenseless.

"My colleague can take you to camp if you must sleep," Acosta said with visible disappointment. "You'll have four hours of rest before he takes you to Janus."

Love didn't bother to ask what or who Janus was. No one explained anything. Acosta pulled a large plastic bag out from behind her desk and handed it to Love.

"Your Effort kit," she said, already hustling Love out the back door. "Please review the materials as soon as possible."

The UN civilian personnel from Love's flight had arrived for processing. One by one, they filed into the security building and emptied their pockets.

"Should you need anything," Acosta added, "don't hesitate to ask. You'll find my business card in your kit."

She held open the door to the exit with the parting words, "Welcome to the Effort."

To Love's dismay, there was a Humvee parked in the back lot ready to take her on yet another leg of the journey. A small man in a trench coat emerged from the passenger side and introduced himself as Bradley without clarifying if it was his first or last name. Love quickly surmised that he was an American but not a New Yorker.

"You're not from headquarters."

"Washington, DC," he said, scrambling to open an umbrella. "Georgetown alum."

He grabbed the handle of Love's rolling suitcase. Love lunged and pulled against his grasp. It was instinct, but she didn't let go.

"Thank you, but I handle my own bags," Love said firmly.

Bradley was too taken aback to reply. On closer look, the man wasn't as young as he first appeared; just short and stout with a close-cropped haircut that made his big ears look bigger. As they walked to the Humvee, Bradley sheltered Love with his own umbrella. She didn't have the heart to refuse his help a second time.

In the passenger seat, Bradley paused to listen to his earpiece.

"We're taking you to the engineers' camp?" he asked.

Love nodded and said that she needed sleep. Bradley's mouth grew pinched, but he nodded to their driver. As the Humvee accelerated, Love inspected the contents of her Effort kit. Pawing through, she saw a glossy folder thick with documents, a digital watch, a box of antimalarial tablets, a protein bar, a bottle of spring water, and a hygiene kit.

Love pulled out the folder and started reading documents, but she nearly fell asleep. Instead, she opened her window and leaned her face into the wind and rain. Blinking rapidly, Love saw a huge museum styled to look futuristic only in the eyes of architects from the past. The effect was clunky and kitschy. Love's Humvee pulled up to the front entryway, and Bradley darted out to open her passenger door.

"The engineers are camped out in a *space museum?*" Love asked.

Bradley sounded defensive when he told her that it was a logical space with perfect proximity. Love followed him across a concrete walkway and under a large overhang that was spilling rain. The two doorways on either side of the ticket office had been repurposed into a security checkpoint.

"Can I borrow four euro for a ticket?" Love asked.

Bradley ignored both her joke and the soldiers manning the office. They ignored him in return but eyed Love carefully as she rolled her suitcase inside. The museum's air-conditioning puckered her wet, shiny skin. Bradley disappeared into the gift shop entrance and returned with a towel and rolled-up sleeping bag.

"The gift shop now stores dry goods," he explained, handing her the towel, "and medication. Are you taking any?"

Love shook her head but nodded gratefully at the towel. She was shivering.

"May I at least carry a sleeping bag for you?" Bradley asked.

There was no edge of sarcasm that she could detect, but it wouldn't have mattered. Love would not apologize for who or how she was. It drove Rivka mad with frustration.

Bradley led her across the lobby and through an entrance to a vast and cavernous exhibit hall. The smell of human bodies was unmistakable despite the industrial fans that could be heard, if not always seen, against black walls. Back-lit displays were turned off, but small lights running along the floors, stairways, and balcony railings illuminated a floor cluttered with suitcases, sleeping bags, and horizontal bodies. Love barely made out silhouettes of mockup satellites suspended from the forty-foot ceiling with their planar extensions and gold-foil bodies.

"I gotta be dreaming," she said softly. "This has to be a nightmare that will end by morning."

Bradley touched his index finger to his lips with respect for the sleepers. Then he whispered back, "You won't be the first to wonder. Or the last."

He pointed ahead. Love squinted and saw a man sleeping with a piece of fabric draped over his eyes, a black dress sock. To his right was a clear space on the floor where Love's body and bags might fit.

"No," Love insisted. "This won't work."

Bradley tried to shush her, but she only raised her voice.

"I need a room with a lock."

A nearby body pulled up and out of a sleeping bag, a shapely female body. The young woman stepped lightly around luggage and limbs while lifting her arms to yawn. Love watched her T-shirt lift to expose a taut stomach with a delicate, whorled dimple at its center.

"Who's that?" Love whispered.

"Amy," Bradley grunted. "The girlfriend."

Love appraised "the girlfriend" as she sauntered over: early thirties, Caucasian, attractive, and self-aware with movements that carried the grace and calculation of a gray-eyed lioness. Amy was less subtle in her own appraisal of Love, who kept her cool and stood her ground.

"You don't exactly blend in," Amy said with a wide smile.

Before anyone could be left to wonder, she nodded to bureaucratic Bradley and added, "That's a compliment."

Amy licked her fingers and used them to smooth the part in her ice blond hair.

"So, your whole look," she said. "What is it? Like, Afrofuturist?"

Love shrugged.

"So cool," Amy gushed.

Love couldn't help smiling. She was an adjunct professor at Columbia University, where she had a devoted fan club of undergraduates— or so Rivka always claimed. Love supposed it was true.

"There's a broom closet, or whatever, on the second floor," Amy continued. "It's locked now, so you just need Bradley here to go find a key."

Here she leveled her gaze at the short man while still speaking to Love.

"Because if you weren't important, you wouldn't be here."

Bradley tried to pointedly stare back, implying Amy was a glaring exception to that rule, but the young woman was already headed for a glowing exit sign. When Amy glanced back and caught Love staring, she winked.

SEVEN

FORTUNE-TELLER

BRADLEY HAD TO knock and then bang on the door of the locked utility closet to wake Love. She had no idea if it was still day or night without her phone. Love continued to burrow into her sleeping bag cocoon until Bradley could entice her with a hot shower.

The dress code for UN interpreters was business professional with no flags or crests from one's homeland. Love removed all her jewelry and pulled on a short-sleeved blouse, skirt, and ballet flats but also draped a cotton scarf around her neck and shoulders: a royal blue, black, tan, and canary yellow repeating pattern she bought from a Nairobi market on the few occasions she could afford the airline tickets back to Kenya.

Love left her luggage in the utility closet and relocked it. Bradley was on the verge of impatience, but as she moved closer, he must have noticed that Love's nose was slightly skewed from a past fracture. The sandpaper pattern of her shaved scalp was interrupted with keloid scars, and one of her dark pupils was permanently dilated. His mouth shut with a snap.

Bradley would never know what it was like to be a single woman, an orphan defending herself for thirty-seven years, sometimes keeping a large piece of herself secret—but he could see the body of evidence: her body. As for Love, it was easier to pretend she was an undamaged person with a spotless past, a rooted person living among family, someone who belonged. When Love concentrated, she could speak American English with all its slang like a true native. It made her pretending all the more believable.

Bradley led Love outside to the museum's water-logged parking lot. In drizzle and dusky twilight, Love saw queues of people waiting for heated showers inside parked Red Cross vans. Bradley complained that they were wasting precious time, but Love said that Dr. Benjamin Schwartz and Professor Ochsenfeld (whoever the hell they were) could wait. Bradley finally pulled rank and waved her to the front of a line.

Love emerged from a van fifteen minutes later, still bleary-eyed and exhausted but clean, at least. Amy stood waiting with breakfast from the museum's cafeteria.

"Don't worry," she said with a sideways smile. "I got rid of Bradley."

Love gladly accepted a paper cup of steaming hot coffee.

"I didn't know how you take it," Amy added, and handed her a brown paper bag. "Next to the muffin, there's sweeteners and creamers. They didn't have soymilk. Are you lactose intolerant?"

Love snorted a laugh. How charming to be mistaken for the picky bourgeoisie. It was a credit to her pretending.

"Your CV is very exciting," Amy said. "You've worked with the UN all over the world."

In Love's experience, excitement was an appetite for the rich, free world. Stability was the luxury she craved.

"I've stopped working as an interpreter," Love replied, "for the most part."

She taught at Columbia's Institute for Comparative Literature and Society and freelanced on the side, providing literary translation for the big publishing houses.

"I only continue to work with the UN on an emergency basis," Love explained. "This is an emergency—"

"This is *the* emergency," Amy corrected, suddenly sober.

The two women reached an idling jeep on the perimeter of the parking lot. Instead of joining the driver in the front, Amy sat with Love in the back. Love tried to eat her blueberry muffin while returning the other woman's flattering attention. It was unnerving to have a total stranger know so much about her.

"And you are...someone's girlfriend?" Love asked.

"Who said that? Bradley?" Amy asked, curling her thin lip. "Look, as a self-made woman, I've had my share of haters that hate. I've learned to ignore them and let my results speak for themselves."

After Love nodded in understanding, Amy took the opportunity to pitch.

"I've always understood the value of human capital, but it wasn't until I became a tech recruiter that I really found my professional calling."

Amy described her placements with top tech firms—Google, Lyft, Slack, Automattic—and the aerospace industry—Boeing and Raytheon. Love nodded here and there, sucking sweet muffin paste from her back molars. The jeep turned around the familiar round-about (*Welcome!*) and continued along the manned security gates. Love muttered that, for once, the UN response had been quick in sending thousands of peacekeepers.

"Oh, this was a Brazilian mission stationed in Haiti," Amy said, dismissing their numbers with a wave of fashionable blue nail polish. "They're nothing next to what's already mobilized. The Professor has a lot of clout."

"That's who I'm supposed to meet," Love interjected. "Who is he? The Professor?"

Amy was more than happy to prove her research and said the Professor was an academic who had published preeminent work in the field of astrophysics while mentoring younger generations of theorists, engineers, and astronauts for the past sixty years.

"And Ben, well, he warned everyone about all this," she said, gesturing up beyond the jeep's ceiling to hints of stars growing brighter as the sky grew darker.

Their driver spoke into his headset to clear them past the security checkpoint. He drove to a cluster of large administration buildings and parked in front of the one labeled Janus. Love hopped out as a military jet streaked low in the sky overhead. Amy reached for the front door of the Janus building and held it open. As soon as it shut behind both women—the first time Love could catch any of these Effort people alone—she rounded in front of Amy and got in her face.

"Where's it gonna hit?"

Amy stuttered. Her cheeks and ears flushed. When Amy stepped back, Love stepped forward and continued her interrogation.

"The comet. Where's it gonna hit us?"

"We don't know if or where," Amy said, jutting her pointy chin upward. "We don't have an accurate trajectory, just approximations."

Their faces were less than six inches apart; bodies almost touching.

"We just know it's big and *fast*," Amy said.

Love heard a noise, a sharp rap of a cane followed by the soft drag of orthopedic shoes. Someone was slowly approaching from the corridor. As Love turned, Amy ducked out of reach and sprinted down the corridor out of sight. She reemerged, grinning and arm-in-arm with a very old man. It was as if she and Love were playing a game of tag and Amy had narrowly escaped to safe base.

"Love Mwangi!" the ancient called out, after catching his raspy breath.

If his voice were a wine, it would carry notes of both Central and Western Europe aged in several decades of tobacco smoke. The man made no moves to introduce himself but could be none other than the Professor.

"Renowned translator, interpreter, and polyglot," he marveled, disentangling his arm from Amy's so he could wave Love closer. "We'll soon be in desperate need of your linguistic talents."

Not only did the Professor move like a tortoise, but he seemed to embody one as well. Small and stooped, his neck had to extend out and up toward her height, pulling on its pendulous flap of skin. Love, on the other hand, stood straight and proud with ropy muscle and taut skin. Her long neck, sharp jaw, sculpted lips, high cheekbones, broad forehead, and slightly flared nostrils gave her a regal bearing.

They inspected one another with the curiosity of opposites.

"Love," the Professor repeated. "I couldn't forget a name like that. Not even in my decrepitude."

The nuns at Love's orphanage fed her, clothed her, and gave her a formal education. They taught her their languages and lent her their books. Those strict but decent and devoted women instilled the idea of purpose very early, a purpose outside of marriage and childbirth. This purpose had a name: Love.

"The names of saints and virtues were all taken at my orphanage," Love said with a shrug, and this was also true. "Our nuns had to get creative by the time I arrived."

The Professor snorted. "In Austria, the nuns had mustaches and made me stand in the snow without my jacket."

In perfect German, Love asked if he deserved it. The Professor smiled at his native tongue and beckoned Love back the way he had come. Amy gave the pair a respectful distance, but not so respectful that she couldn't hear their conversation.

"You are known to speak and write in at least thirty-six languages and dialects," the Professor continued, "but you yourself won't confirm the total number."

Love said nothing. She was never interested in the fame that came with quantity and chose instead to make her mark in mastery. Growing up, she learned Bantu Swahili along with local dialects from the other children at her orphanage. She learned English, French, Spanish, and German from the nuns and did extra chores in order to borrow their books and magazines from abroad. By the time she had to leave the orphanage at seventeen, Love had labored through Achebe, Proust, Steinbeck, and García Márquez all written in their original languages.

"Whatever the number," the Professor said, "use it. Engineers from all over the world will converge here. You must translate all that you hear. Technical details, instructions, conversations, even insults... You must go room to room—and tear the walls down."

The Professor said they must fly one flag only, that of the Effort. Love looked into offices and cubicle workspaces as they walked past. The people packed inside didn't look up but remained focused, murmuring in French, English, and Dutch. By the time the three reached the end of the corridor, the Professor's breathing was labored. Amy stepped up and used her security badge before helping him into an elevator.

"The core team is in the Janus meeting room," she said to Love.

Love figured those words would make sense in due time. At the top floor of the building, Amy nodded for her to get a head start out of the elevator. Love walked up to the open doors of a large conference room and peeked around the frame. Long tables formed a square with nine people seated around a corner to the right and another thirty or so gathered at the opposite sides.

Amy helped the Professor as far as the doorway. It appeared that someone had dragged a padded armchair up from the lobby and placed it flush against the wall. The Professor dropped onto its cushions.

"Love," he said, between breaths. "Allow me to introduce you to... the knower of one hundred twenty-two impact scenarios, the seer of likely futures... Ben Schwartz, our fortune-teller."

He used the end of his cane to point to a slight, hairy man in thick glasses somewhere in his early forties who was presiding at the corner to the right with the smaller group of people.

"Grab a seat," Ben said, pausing only a moment to address Love with a hoarse voice.

As Love approached the table, she nearly tripped on a pair of high-heel pumps that someone had left on the floor. Nude pantyhose lay close by like molted snakeskin. Amy immediately claimed the empty chair to Ben's right, evening out the numbers so that five people were seated on each side of the corner.

Love sat in the sixth chair, next to an Asian man with silvered hair and smile lines around his eyes and lips. His face looked haggard, but all of their faces looked haggard. All except Amy's. In accented English, the man introduced himself as Dr. Jin-soo Lee, director of the Asteroid Deflection Research Center at Iowa State University. He projected his voice and looked expectantly at Ben. Only Amy caught his social cue and turned to kick Ben under the table.

"Ow, what?"

Ben rubbed his shin and looked to Amy. He followed her stare to Love and Jin-soo.

"Again?" he sighed. "Ahh, fine."

Ben stood on sandaled feet and motioned to the men and women in disheveled corporate dress gathered at the other end of the room.

"Those are UN minions," he said, as they continued to converse, talk on phones, and/or work on laptops. "And their two overlords are sitting on either side," Ben said, sweeping his finger to a woman on the far left and a man on the far right.

"The rest of us sitting at this corner form the Effort's scientific core. Here's Chuck to my left," Ben said, nodding to a heavy man with ginger-colored hair and beard, glasses, and faded freckles on his meaty arms. "He works with me at NASA JPL. Next to him is Ed from Sandia National Labs. Then there's...sorry, guy, I forgot your name already. Hey, who do I have to screw to get some name tags around here?"

One of the UN minions across the room lifted her phone off the table to go find the answer.

"Anyway, Ponytail Guy is from NASA Goddard and was once a student of the Professor's. Next to him is Jin-soo, who you've already met—"

Amy interrupted to claim human resources for herself. Ben nodded and picked up with the scientists sitting to her right.

"That's Julie from Livermore. Ziggy from Stanford and Los Alamos back in the day. On the end, we have Marcel, the director of the space center and his very tall assistant director, Anneke. Duck, duck, goose. Where were we?"

Discussion among the science core continued. Love spotted a photographic image on the screen of Jin-soo's laptop. The scientist followed her stare and whispered that the image was recently captured by the Hubble telescope and showed UD3 at 1.5 billion miles from the sun. The comet's frozen nucleus was pure white, and the hazy aura of dust surrounding it was glittering blue—a killer beauty.

Love tried to listen to the scientists, but their strange words were practically Greek. (Not literally. Love was fluent in modern Greek.) Jin-soo was too polite to ignore her frustration. Instead of asking if Love had a question, he asked for the first one.

"What is a high civ?" she asked. "You all keep using that word."

Ben did the answering. His attention was everywhere at once.

"Hypervelocity comet intercept vehicle. HYCIV. Check the folder in your Effort kit. There's an acronym sheet—we can't have our interpreter needing an interpreter!"

Love had left her paperwork back in the utility closet with her luggage.

"I just got here," she said. "I haven't had time to memorize your literature."

More than several people winced.

"No time?" Ben asked in mock concern. "Gee, I wonder what that's like."

His voice cracked on the last word. Ben grabbed a bottle of spring water off the table and chugged. Amy crossed her arms and stared daggers that Ben willfully ignored. Jin-soo tried to be more helpful.

"The HYCIV is the spacecraft we need to build in order to deflect the comet," he explained, and turned his laptop to face her.

Using the trackpad, Jin-soo opened a file into a new window that visualized what looked like a large potato floating in outer space.

"That's an asteroid rendering," Jin-soo admitted, "but the same rules apply to a comet."

He clicked the Play button and started a crude animation of a boxy spacecraft—a HYCIV—propelling toward the potato asteroid. Love watched as the front of the spacecraft separated and detonated against the asteroid's surface, leaving a crater. The rest of the space-craft maneuvered into the crater and detonated in a large, pixelated blast that nudged the asteroid into a new orbit.

"The HYCIV on Jin-soo's monitor takes five years to build and test," Ben called over. "And guess what?"

Love's stomach sank as their brown eyes locked.

"I thought guessing was your job, Ben?" Amy said with a casual edge. Her expressive eyebrows were drawn low as she added, "You're the fortune-teller. Love here is our star interpreter."

"We don't have five years," Ben said, to the point. "So we can't start from scratch."

He lifted a stapled pile of spreadsheets off the table and held it up for Love.

"This is a global inventory of all spacecraft and satellites in their final stages of production. We're going to reengineer the HYCIV on Jin-soo's screen by using repurposed subassemblies that've already been built and tested."

The scientist called Chuck smirked in a way that shifted his beard.

"We're gonna beg for good Cadillac parts," he said. "And *you're* gonna help."

"Also on this list," Ben added, "are all the nuclear arsenals worldwide, according to research for the nonproliferation treaty—"

"Ben?"

There were microphones sprouting up from the tables so that anyone could be heard throughout the large room. Love located a UN minion tapping his spongy microphone for attention.

"Ben? Iran's insisting on keeping their satellite."

"What?" Ben squeaked. "Why!"

"They said it cost them four hundred million."

Ben started to violently shake his head but winced and held both palms against his forehead. One of the UN overlords showed no hesitation or emotion of any sort as she stated, "The Islamic Republic approved thirteen billion in defense spending last year. Our HYCIV is an investment in defense."

"The only defense that might matter in the history of *Homo sapiens*," Ben shouted.

He pointed to Love.

"Do you speak . . . Iranian?"

Love coolly stated that she spoke most of the Persian and Turkic dialects, Kurdish and Arabic.

"I told you she was good," said the UN overlord, with a smooth smile.

Ben admitted, in a rare show of appreciation to a humanities scholar, that he had flubbed Hebrew school. The other UN overlord spoke into his microphone.

"Troy Andrews," he said, lifting a hand into the air.

He was a good-looking, tall man with gelled hair combed back to expose silver temples. His shirtsleeves were rolled up and his collar was unbuttoned, but he still looked somewhat crisp and alert. He reminded Love of Lower Manhattan's Financial District, where such elites went to move around money and make their fortunes.

"We're speaking to translators and scientists, in the more difficult cases," Troy explained to Love. "But we need to talk to decision makers in their own language. Can you help us?"

Love rose to her full height, ready to heed the call of the UN and repay an old debt.

EIGHT

BURNING, BERING SEA

AUGUST 13
T-MINUS 172 DAYS TO LAUNCH

Jack's phone lost all signal as *Healy* sailed farther into the Bering Sea. He busied himself taking pictures of offshore oil rigs emerging from cold fog. Their flare stacks extended sideways like the nozzle of an Arabic oil lamp, reminders of the burning fossil fuels contributing to climate change. Jack's editors wanted him to keep an eye out for heightened development now that an Obama-era executive order had been reversed to open more drilling in the Arctic.

Jack made his way around *Healy*'s perimeter until he spotted Maya's boots with telltale purple laces lying by the door of an ISO van. He lingered before finally removing his own boots and quietly stepping inside. Maya sat on an overturned bucket in front of a row of plastic tubes. She wore surgical gloves and held a small sample bottle that she was labeling with painstaking detail. Jack snapped a picture of her bent form and tangled ponytail. The click startled her.

"You didn't ask to take my photo."

"I didn't capture your face," Jack said smoothly. "Just your back and hands. Whatcha doin'?"

Maya considered his words before answering.

"Bottling and labeling seawater from our rosette casts. I test these samples for trace elements of mercury—"

"Like what's paralyzing the eagles?" Jack asked.

Maya shook her head. The current levels were dangerous. Mining and fossil fuels had tripled the amount of mercury in the surface of the ocean since the Industrial Revolution, but it did not explain the strange phenomenon of the eagles.

"Why does your hand keep dipping in and out of your pocket?" Maya asked suddenly.

"I remember there's no service just as I'm reaching for my phone," he said, and shrugged. "Habit, I guess. The feeds are good company, but not like the real thing."

Jack tried to look in Maya's eyes, but they were trained on his left hand. When he moved, Maya grabbed his hand on reflex.

"Sorry," she muttered quickly, and dropped it like a hot poker. "I was looking at your scar."

"Little bastard of a parasite," Jack said ruefully. "Picked 'em up in Afghanistan."

He held out his hand with its round, shiny, and raised scar like a plastic button. Maya no longer wanted to inspect it and looked annoyed with herself as she pulled off her gloves, now contaminated with his germs.

"I might as well ask about the one on your neck while we're at it," Maya muttered.

"Hmm? Oh, that was from a piece of shrapnel in Syria."

Maya looked up at Jack. The skin between her thick brows was pinched.

"I never expected to live this long," he admitted.

There was a commotion from the crew outside. Jack propped open the door of the van and stuck out his head to listen.

"Whale sighting!" he called back.

Maya moved fast. She reached the outer rail of the ship's deck with unlaced boots and only one arm through her parka. The gathered crowd had to wait until the impossibly giant mammal surfaced and exhaled in two misty towers.

"Gray whale, I think!" Maya called above the wind. "Two blow-holes."

When she smiled at him, Jack saw her teeth for the first time. They were small, crooked, and pointy. He wondered how it would feel to get a nibble or bite and almost shivered.

Their whale swam beside *Healy*, dipping and spouting. It jumped in a back flip with its barnacled snout and flippers rising out of the water. Most of the scientists clapped, but Maya let out something between a yelp and a scream.

～⋀⋀⋀～

THERE WERE MORE sightings of the comet. All major news outlets had picked up the story by now, managing the risk of overhyped sensationalism while reporting on the very real sense of growing alarm. Online news articles posted images of a bright gradient of light scattering dust beside the full heat of the sun. The comet's tail wasn't visible because UD3 was pointed directly at Earth like an arrow.

Scientists were still gathering and reporting a trickle of facts but gave no assurances—at least not in the *New York Times*, *USA Today*, *Los Angeles Times*, *Chicago Tribune*, or *Washington Post*—that the comet's trajectory would miss Earth. Jack's fingers banged on his keyboard as he typed out his frustrated questions into a search engine. Instead of facts, there were opinions sometimes presented as facts. Jack once worked with an editor at the *New York Times Magazine*, a grizzled old-school journalist who smoked cigars and didn't sleep. *Opinions are like assholes*, he always said. *Everyone's got one.*

Jack typed, "will comet ud3" and read the autofill options:

kill us all?

miss Earth?

prove there is no God?

be a tool for terrorists?

be a tool for infidels in the holy war?

. . .

So many of the same unanswered questions in cyberspace, and yet Jack felt alone. The science lounge was full of people, but none who wanted to talk. All were busy typing, either searching for more information on UD3 or writing home to their wives, husbands, children, lovers, and old friends.

As for Jack, he had no wife, girlfriend, or children. Everyone wanted to be Jack's friend, and Jack was friendly with everyone, but only his editors could rely on him at any given moment. Jack had fallen out of most social circles by his own lack of participation. This he only realized with a sinking ache in his gut when no one responded to his email messages and posts. In the advent of UD3, no one had time for a charming acquaintance, a colleague, a Brooklyn neighbor, or even an ex-boyfriend whose love had been intense but as brief as a lightning bolt.

Jack left the science lounge and passed *Healy*'s barber station on his way to lunch. Ned, the pilot, was seated stock-still in an apron for a fresh buzz cut.

"I hear you were poking around some off-limit zones," Ned called out.

Jack stopped and said he was only taking pictures of the ship and documenting *Healy*'s journey.

"What does off-limits mean to you?" Ned asked.

His smile had always been sunny and simple when they joked

around or passed each other in the corridors. The one he gave now was more complicated; it had the usual chumminess but with an edge that spoke to his feelings about a fuck-up guest passenger with no respect for rules and regulations.

"Camila says your bunkmate could also use some help with accountability," Ned added, and then bent his head with closed eyes so the barber could shave his nape.

Instead of heading on to the galley, Jack turned toward the living quarters. He usually avoided his stateroom when he could. Gustavo wanted to be left alone for the most part, but Jack needed to talk to someone, and he was quite sure Gustavo needed to talk as well. They had to help each other, because there was no one else. They weren't crew and they weren't scientists; they were troublemaking artists who needed solidarity.

Jack knocked on his stateroom door and entered. The curtain on the top bunk was fully drawn. Gustavo rarely ventured out of their room during normal hours, preferring instead the empty, red-lit hallways of the graveyard shift and the quiet meal served at midnight. Judging by the restless turning in his bunk, he didn't sleep much.

"You've got your own Wikipedia page, you know," Jack called out.

Gustavo pushed back his curtain, looked down at Jack, and waited.

"There was a link to a *New York Times* article on there," Jack continued. "It reported on the time you hijacked the floor of the Brazilian senate. I mean, I don't know you, but I want to. We're strangers now, sure. But given these circumstances, stuck in this tiny room while we try to wrap our heads around that comet..."

There was no language, figures of speech, quotes, comparisons, or poetry for the annihilation of all known life. It left one speechless but not blank-faced like Gustavo. Jack was a practiced outsider who chose when to admit or hide a lack of understanding. He could see the same about the man in front of him.

"D'you know about the comet, Gustavo?"

Gustavo inhaled a long breath through his nose before finally asking, "What is this word?"

"What, comet? It's like a huge ball of ice and rock, floating in space."

Gustavo frowned and squinted with disbelief, but any further explanation would assume a material understanding of celestial bodies in the solar system. It was quite a thing to assume, the more Jack thought about it.

"The important point," Jack continued, "is that this comet might fall from the sky, like a falling star, and strike Earth."

Gustavo finally blinked.

"Wormwood?"

It was Jack's turn to stare. Gustavo climbed down from his bunk to rifle through the meager belongings in his closet. He walked over to Jack with a worn, leather-bound Bible fat with dog-eared edges. After leafing through the dog-ears, Gustavo handed the open Bible to Jack and pointed to a passage in the Book of Revelation:

...and a great star fell from heaven, blazing like a torch, and it fell on a third of the rivers and on the springs of water. The name of the star is called Wormwood. A third of the waters became wormwood, and many people died from the water, because it had been made bitter.

Jack skipped to the end.

...Then I looked, and I heard an eagle crying with a loud voice as it flew directly overhead, "Woe, woe, woe to those who dwell on the earth..."

NINE

IMPACT SCENARIO 122

BEN TESTED HIS headset before stepping up to the lectern and addressing nearly one hundred audience members of the sixth biannual International Academy of Astronautics Planetary Defense Conference in Maryland. As the chair of the conference, Ben wished a good morning to the gathering of representatives from NASA, the European Space Agency, the Federal Emergency Management Agency, the UN, and a host of academics from the international circuit. Bespectacled eyes blinked back at Ben above the glow of laptops in the dark conference room. Ben spotted his NASA colleague Chuck Maes in the front row of the audience with his clip-on tie already lying on the table next to a notepad. Chuck gave him a thumbs-up.

"I just want to remind everyone to be really careful on social media," Ben said slowly. "*Be clear* that this is all an imaginary exercise. Some of your live posts have already scared some folks, and I don't want to scare any more."

He turned to the screen backdrop spanning half the stage and clicked a remote to advance his presentation. The bottom corner of each slide had the word *EXERCISE* in red capital letters.

"Welcome to day two of our hypothetical asteroid impact scenario. You all saw the date on today's press release..."

Day 1 had kicked off their conference in the present, but day 2 advanced the scenario storyline three months into the future, to the end of July 2019.

"After several months of tracking the asteroid post-discovery, we have a better grasp of its orbital path and have updated the probability of impact to ten percent in the year 2027."

Ben absently pulled at the noose of his tie. He always hated the damn things. As if in protest, several strands of dark chest hair poked up from his starched white collar.

"With such a narrow time frame, space-capable nations need to move quickly to develop deflection missions. Hopefully"—Ben slowed to accentuate his words—"they will do this in coordination."

He locked eyes with an old man in the third row and recognized Siegfried "Ziggy" Divjak, a nuclear physicist of Los Alamos fame. The man had partnered with Russian scientists during the Gorbachev years to secure the nuclear arsenal of the dissolved Soviet Union. Ziggy had worked hard to keep weapons of mass destruction from falling into the wrong hands. And here he was, sitting rod straight and alert, probably wondering if Ben was going to use the spotlight for his own political soundbite.

Hell yes, he was.

"In a time of nationalist politics, we have forgotten our allies," Ben said. "But now, with a cosmic threat of this magnitude— the greatest threat humanity has ever faced—now is the time to remember and join our allies and friends and stand *together*."

Ben forced himself to pause a moment before transitioning slides. His next visual charted the long, elliptical orbit of their fake asteroid intersecting with the tight, circular orbit of Earth.

"And I hope you've all downloaded JPL's NEO Deflection app," Ben interjected eagerly, resuming his usual warp-drive speed. "We've uploaded all one hundred twenty-one of our previously simulated asteroids and comets with their trajectories and deflection calculations. Seriously, guys, it'll help when we break off into groups."

Ben scanned the audience for enthusiasm and saw several people take long pulls of coffee. Caffeine was key to asteroid busting on an early Tuesday morning.

~~~

COLLEGE PARK, MARYLAND
MAY 3, 2019
DAY 5 OF THE IAA PLANETARY DEFENSE CONFERENCE

BEN AND AMY joined the other tourists walking along the National Mall, killing time before dinner reservations in downtown Washington, DC. Perfectly content with each other's company on any occasion, they glowed with excitement over a new impact scenario and the impressive scenery of the United States capital.

"So here we are on day five of the conference," Ben recounted. "It's 2029, and the biggest chip of the asteroid we shattered on day four is going to hit New York City in ten days."

He had ditched his tie by now. Ben's shirt was unbuttoned at the top, and his sleeves were rolled up to his elbows.

"Can you imagine evacuating all of Manhattan *and* the boroughs in that time frame?"

Amy whistled and shook her head. Her platinum hair swooped down on a side part and glanced her eyelashes until she smoothed the locks behind an ear.

"Me neither," Ben agreed. "So I had reps from FEMA do it for me."

"Weren't those the guys that handled Hurricane Katrina? Because *that* went real well."

"Well *my* FEMA reps were successful," Ben boasted, but had to add, "theoretically."

It was so easy to get wrapped up in the role-playing and forget that it was one of many impact scenarios meant to prepare for the real thing.

Ben pulled his phone out of his pocket to check the time. Whenever he came to DC on business, he tried to meet up with his sister, Becca, who lived inside the Beltway with her husband and two children. Within the satchel that Ben carried were gifts for his nephew and niece: difficult Lego sets that he knew they could conquer. The kids couldn't open their boxes at the restaurant, so Ben already made his sister promise to video the moments when they each dumped all the plastic pieces onto the floor at home, skimmed the instructions, and formed a battle plan.

Ben wasn't up to the job of being a father, but he loved being an uncle. And his niece and nephew were turning into such great little humans. Ben couldn't wait to show them the world; it wasn't kind, but it sure was fascinating. And kids absorbed everything so quickly. The last time Ben called from California, his niece and nephew prattled on, interrupting one another on speakerphone in order to detail the latest adventures in their Minecraft video game and their neighbor's new calico kitten named Periwinkle. Ben made so many plans for the future: shipping his favorite books one by one to their DC address; watching *2001: A Space Odyssey* together with Amy; flying them out to California to teach them how to drive on the calmly winding Route 1 with the Pacific Ocean stretching farther than the eye could follow...

"Your sister doesn't like me," Amy said suddenly.

Ben immediately shook his head but had to pause and think before answering.

"She's just *surprised* by the two of us."

Amy countered that they had been living together for five years already.

"She's still surprised," Ben said. "Hell, *I'm* still surprised!"

Amy didn't bring up parents, luckily. It was too nice a night to ruin. And there wasn't much to talk about, besides. Ben's parents didn't approve, and Amy hadn't introduced Ben to her family. That was that. It hadn't stopped Ben from getting down on one knee at their favorite restaurant a year after Amy moved in, and Ben couldn't imagine life without her. Amy kept grinning as he proposed and had to press a glass of ice water against her flushed cheeks.

After they got engaged, Ben expected to see wedding magazines appear on all the tables and countertops. He expected a deluge of ridiculous questions (Seating chart or place cards? Do we risk the smell of a salmon entrée?), but Amy continued on as usual. She didn't even wear her engagement ring, a large fire opal for her October birthday. *I would lose it*, Amy explained. Knowing Amy's habits, Ben had to agree that it was a likely possibility. Amy kept the ring squirreled away in a shoebox instead, part of a collection of precious objects that she wanted to keep safe and only bring out to touch and enjoy every blue moon.

Ben wondered if Amy was concerned about her family, but he knew so little about them, it was hard to guess what might be the problem. Amy's father was retired Army and her mother was a housewife, living modestly in Kansas, so it could be financial. Amy's parents and brother were all devout Christians, so it could also be religious.

The ceremony will be nondenominal, Ben told Amy one night while they were reading in bed. *We'll pay for the reception ourselves, and it can be small. I've got some savings that will cover it. My family can supply the ring bearer and flower girl, obviously.* Amy looked up from her novel and stared, blinking behind artsy, cat-eye reading glasses. *My family can supply the drag queens and strippers*, she finally said. *And the Elvis impersonators, obviously.*

She smirked but added that she hadn't told her family about the engagement and didn't plan to tell them about a wedding. Amy seemed more interested in getting back to her novel. When Ben asked about timeline, Amy shrugged. *What would we have gained while married that we don't have now?* she asked. Ben had to think on that. *When I die,* he said, *you'd get my entire anime collection.* Amy nodded with lifted eyebrows and said she would take it under consideration. That was four years ago.

"I'm so glad you're here," Ben told her. "With me."

He reached out to hold Amy's hand.

"Wouldn't miss it," she assured him.

Amy wore an orange top and a long pink silk skirt that billowed in the breeze and wrapped around her legs. Gold bangles decorated one wrist and jingled with her steps. Amy had many different distinct styles and rocked them all, looking just as good in combat boots as spiked heels. This early evening, she wasn't going for any particular style. *I thought it looked pretty*, she said absently, in front of the hotel's bathroom mirror. The colors were more than pretty and made Amy look radiant, like the setting sun.

They continued walking under a long row of cherry trees. Amy opened her notebook and read a fact aloud: the three thousand cherry trees were a gift from the mayor of Tokyo in 1912. A large, man-made body of water stretched out like a lake on their left. It doubled the beauty of the tree branches with a clear reflection on still water. Farther out, two-seater paddle boats puttered around or drifted, carrying couples wearing bright orange life vests.

Ben inhaled the fragrant, quiet riot of spring on the East Coast and passively wondered if existence could get any better. Here he was on a Friday with the fruitful challenges of the workweek behind him and a beautiful evening unfolding. His light-speed imagination was happily slow and lazy in offering obvious suggestions for improvement: Winning lottery ticket? Peace in the Middle East? A new Star Wars movie? *Hold on to this,* Ben told himself. *Keep this moment as a memory of what happy feels like...*

"This is a beautiful walk—"

"Of course it is," Amy said. "Would you doubt my reconnaissance?"

Never.

While Ben was at the Planetary Defense Conference all day, Amy explored. She was technically on vacation. So, after checking her work email and voicemails, Amy laced up her sneakers and hit Washington, DC's sidewalks and national parks. When Ben was free in the late afternoon, they met up for a happy-hour drink and debriefing. Amy showed him her notebook with detailed entries logged in atrocious handwriting. All the locations that she wanted to share had five-pointed stars scribbled beside them. This had also been their routine two years ago at the conference in Tokyo and four years ago in Frascati, Italy.

Ben and Amy stepped out from under the tree canopy and gazed up at the obelisk of Washington Monument. One of the world's tallest stone structures cast a long, fading shadow. Ben remembered a poem, something about the ruins of a giant monument with the inscription:

My name is Ozymandias, King of Kings;
Look on my Works, ye Mighty, and despair!

Ben couldn't recall all of the poem but he remembered the next phrase:

Nothing beside remains.

Ben had spent his adult years staring down the possibility of a cosmic impact that could end modern civilization and bring the downfall of his species, but he hadn't spent much time imagining the aftermath of such an event. Ben wasn't a biologist, but he knew that ecosystems could be zero-sum games of survival. After all, the decline of the dinosaur reign spurred the rise of mammals like him.

Would every other creature under the sun rejoice at humanity's demise? What would prosper and rise around their ruins?

TEN

BEN'S LIST

THE MAJORITY OF BEN'S attention remained on Jin-soo as the man proposed a detailed plan of the HYCIV assembly, and the majority of Ben Schwartz's attention was weighty enough. Jin-soo spoke carefully into his microphone. He was only four chairs to Ben's left but was soft-spoken and too polite to halt interruptions from the other scientists.

Ben's eyes continued to drift back to the list of complex components that they needed to acquire and repurpose for their intercept vehicle. He could spot lots of little check marks but just as many empty boxes as well. Without enough subassemblies or nuclear missiles, they were screwed—screwed to the nth degree.

"How's China coming?" Ben interrupted, lifting up the list and tapping a section of empty check boxes with his index finger.

Jin-soo stuttered, blinked, and looked to Chuck.

"I told you," Chuck sighed. "They pledged support."

"That was Taiwan. I'm talking about mainland. *Dios mío*, our geography blows."

Chuck flipped up his middle fingers as Ben leaned into his microphone to address the opposite side of the Janus meeting room, where forty UN workers were trying to be quiet as church mice.

"UN overlord of the male gender?" Ben called out.

The man perked up and pointed to two HELLO MY NAME IS stickers on the chest of his dress shirt. TROY was scrawled in oversized capital letters on the top sticker, ANDREWS on the bottom.

"Yeah, fine." Ben began again. "Troy, how're we coming with mainland China?"

"Promising," Troy said, and gave a thumbs-up.

Much of the developed West had already pledged their resources and support: the European Union, Britain, Canada, Mexico, India, Japan, South Korea, Australia, Brazil, and Argentina. However, the Effort still wanted the support of Pakistan, Turkey, and South Africa. They still *needed* the support of the United States, China, and Russia. Negotiations with these superpowers all seemed to go well until a lack of action proved how cheap talk really was. Disbelief was met with disbelief. *How?* Ben yelled at the walls. How could the Effort not have the support and resources of the United States? *Leave it to the diplomats*, Chuck told Ben. *That's what they do. We are the science.* But Ben let his shock turn to anger as he screamed foul expletives and murderous oaths and invoked plagues of biblical proportion upon the houses of the US president, vice president, and majority speaker, all the way down to the staffers and interns behind the scenes.

A UN minion approached Troy Andrews and whispered nervously in his ear. Troy's charming smile sank. He looked to his peer, the female UN overlord, and shook his head.

"What?" Ben demanded, and tapped his microphone for attention. "What's wrong?"

Troy took a breath and leaned into his microphone.

"The Kremlin's canceled all departing flights. They're going to manage their own defense effort with their own resources."

Troy looked to Marcel and Anneke, director and assistant director of the Guiana Space Centre, before adding, "Including the change-out Soyuz spacecraft."

Marcel's crisp blue eyes teared up as he sniffed back a runny nose and swallowed hard. The awful silence that followed ended with him standing up, covering his face, and leaving the room. Anneke stayed seated but could only look down at her hands folded in her lap.

Ben decided not to think about those astronauts on the Space Station. *No*, he told that line of thought, already sprinting ahead on its own. *No, no, no.* There were so many bigger problems to solve.

"No Russian support means no Russian engineers, satellites, orbiter, uranium, supplies, or troops," Ben listed out. "They're leaving us with nothing but the men and women stuck on that Space Station without a working Soyuz for escape, all shit outta luck."

Ziggy shook his head, his wispy white hair looking like an unraveled cotton ball. The nuclear physicist croaked, "We had an agreement…"

But he didn't finish, for the US-Russian agreement on planetary defense was never formalized. It gained serious momentum after the 2013 Chelyabinsk meteor explosion, and then quietly continued in spite of Russia's annexation of Crimea. Ziggy was the lead negotiator of these talks. Ben took off his glasses and closed his eyes, but he could still see Ziggy's expression: failure, despite decades of effort toward noble ends. Still failure.

Ben screamed. His hands made fists that he used to cover his eyes. Tendons in his forearms strained like he wanted to squeeze something hard until it popped. No one spoke. Slowly, Ben lowered his fists and opened his eyes. Love, the interpreter, had jumped from her chair, but everyone else hunkered down to take what was coming. Ben turned to look at the Professor, but the old man had no interest in sympathy. Politicians did what they did. Others had to work within the fallout.

"Please, please," Ben begged the air, "*please* tell me Oleg and Yuri got out of Russia in time. Our nuclear team needs their expertise. Ziggy? Julie? Back me up here."

Ziggy piped up.

"They were our counterparts in the Cold War," Ziggy explained to the room. "After the fall of the Soviet Union, we became collaborators and worked on nuclear strategies for planetary defense for over two decades."

He looked to Julie Schmidt, who nodded agreement. Ben leaned in to shout into his microphone, "Throw us a fucking bone, people!"

Several minions picked up their phones and scrambled to dial.

"I'll call the Kremlin," the other overlord said, and rose with her security badge dangling from her matronly bosom. Ben shook his head and winced. Rogue Russia was a feature of impact scenario 51, and there was no helping it then or now.

"That gold-chain-wearing thug won't change his mind," Ben told her.

Jin-soo's pleasant face turned sober.

"Well," he said into the quiet, "that saves us from having to make a difficult choice with the Space Station."

"There was no *choice*," Ben hissed. "We needed those Soyuz parts. Anyone who knows *anything* knows that. I already added them to the list."

His whole body was shaking with fury and fear. The science core team looked to him, the UN staff looked to him, Love and the Professor looked to him—and Ben hated them all in that small moment. Chuck finally spoke up. Chuck was Ben's rock through all these dealings, albeit a soft and pudgy one.

"Ben's right, there was no choice. Without the Soyuz subassemblies from the Russians, it'll take at least two years to build our HYCIV. And that's only if the US and China come around with full resources."

Love was still standing. She looked around her, trying to read expressions so she wouldn't have to ask what the rest of them knew but avoided in all discussion.

"Do we have two years? Before the comet gets close?"

No one said anything, which was answer enough.

"C-could you be wrong?" Love asked Ben.

He wouldn't look up or respond. Chuck finally cleared his throat.

"Ben predicted the trajectory of asteroid Toutatis to within thirty kilometers when it was 8.5 billion kilometers away. That's a fractional precision of point zero zero zero zero zero zero zero four."

Ben picked up a pen with a shaky hand and slashed X's on page after page of his list.

~~~~

BEN FLUCTUATED TOO quickly between the extremes of tireless frenetic energy, caustic impatience, and defeated emotional exhaustion.

"You *need* to eat and sleep—" Chuck yelled at Ben.

He was the only one who would dare, so surely Ben deserved it.

"Either you're gonna collapse, or I'll have to knock you on your scrawny ass next time you flip out."

"I'll order food delivery—" Ben muttered.

"Go to camp!"

Ben cringed at Chuck's volume and then wobbled as he stood.

"Someone call me a jeep," he said. "Please."

Several minions reached for their phones at once. Ben didn't look like a man who called the shots in any situation outside of the present, but the present was all that mattered.

"I'll go, too," Love said, and stood.

The Professor didn't look up as the two walked out of the Janus meeting room. He was bent over in his armchair with his forehead nearly touching his knees. It might have looked like he was napping if it weren't for his arthritic, white-knuckled fists squeezing his cane. Whatever caused him pain, the Professor tried to keep it to himself.

"It's no secret the Professor's got one foot in the grave," Ben told Love, once they were alone in the elevator.

"Is that a fortune from the fortune-teller?" Love asked.

Ben looked up at her and tried not to take her height as a personal affront.

"It's a fact."

There was nothing further to say, so they continued to the lobby.

"Oh, it stopped raining," Ben said absently, as he walked out into the clear night.

"It stopped raining three days ago," Love told him.

I'm so tired, Ben thought. *And we've only just begun.*

Ben had always been terrified of failure. His family and teachers were shocked when he quit competitive chess in his junior year of high school. As national champion, all Ben had to do was defend his title. No one could understand the move, but no one saw Ben sleepless during the tournaments, sick to his stomach at the thought of facing off against an opponent in front of a live audience with media attention. Winning was not a victory, only a relief.

Ben and Love waited for a jeep in the dead of night. Harsh spotlights cast either blue-white light or black shadow on all the moving staffers, converting a spaceport to a defense effort piece by piece.

"How...how did this come together so quickly?" Love asked, over the loud vibrations of a passing helicopter overhead.

Ben could see there was so much Love didn't understand, but she paced her questions with his failing stamina and her own patience.

"There've *always been* comets and asteroids," Ben replied, "and there will *always be* comets and asteroids. It's humans that have no precedent. We're the variable—"

"So you always knew it was a possibility," Love interrupted. "But how did you get all these different people and governments to work together?"

"Science has no borders," Ben said simply.

It sounded like a bumper sticker, but it was true. For as long as Ben could remember, there had been an international network of scientists dedicated to collaboration in the name of planetary defense. Despite wars, espionage, broken promises, cyberattacks, and sanctions between their countries, scientists kept communications open with a flow of ideas. When UD3 was discovered weeks ago, these scientists didn't wait for public opinion or permission from demagogues.

"We acted with the allies we had—"

"The UN and the European Union," Love finished for him.

"This space center already had an Ariane rocket close to complete," Ben explained. "And thank God. It was slated for a mission to resupply the ISS. Sorry, that's the International Space Station. You'll get used to all the acronyms."

"What about the Space Station? How will they get supplies now?"

"They won't."

Love continued to stare. She was going to make him state the obvious, awful truth.

"Evacuation could have been a possibility," Ben continued, "if the Russians had rotated out the defunct Soyuz capsule with a new one. But they're keeping their new Soyuz to repurpose its subassemblies. Just like I would have."

When Love opened her mouth, he held up a hand.

"We need to worry about the seven point five billion humans and, like, nine million different species of creatures living on Earth. As in, the only known life *in the universe*," he said, staring into her eyes to drill in the point.

After a silence, he added in a whisper, "Those astronauts are strangers to you, but they are no strangers to this spaceport. Marcel and Anneke can barely—"

He changed the subject.

"By the way, if I pass out, or scream at you, or start crying uncontrollably...just gimme some space and try not to hate me. Deal?"

Love had to consider. She nodded; it was a deal.

"I should probably hit up the meds station in the gift shop," Ben said.

There was no more astronaut ice cream, but anyone could get plenty of Zoloft, Adderall, and Malarone to ward off depression, anxiety, sleep, and malaria.

"And if you need anything else," Ben said, "Amy's usually floating around helping out."

"The girlfriend?"

"*My* girlfriend," Ben clarified. "And she's got her own skill set, so everyone needs to cut her some slack."

"How'd they let you bring her here?"

Ben shrugged.

"They needed me, and I needed her. Not that Amy gave me much choice," he added. "But she was right. Love makes saving the world less lonely. I guess it makes everything less lonely."

"I do things on my own," Love whispered, like it was a curse.

"It's a weird name, Love," Ben mused. "Must be annoying. You know, popping your head up every time someone says that word in conversation."

"People say it less than you think," she said. "And mean it even less."

Ben closed his dry eyes and considered this. He wobbled and nearly stumbled. Love asked if humans could survive the impact of an eight-kilometer comet.

"Maybe," Ben hedged. "In some parts of the world."

"So, where's it gonna hit?"

Ben shook his head and winced. He told Love that an accurate trajectory required a thirty-day observation arc, at the very least. Any premature estimation would be grossly negligent, unethical on an unprecedented scale.

Love cut in, but Ben interrupted her interruption as the faster talker. "You need to understand impact scenarios fifty-three, fifty-four, fifty-five, and fifty-six..."

He tried to describe the simulations where a nuclear power, upon learning that the site of an impending impact was safely on the other side of the planet, decides to jeopardize all defense efforts and shoot down interceptors that could knock the asteroid or comet into a new, less favorable trajectory or even split the thing into several dangerous pieces. The glazed look on Love's face was the same look everyone gave when he spoke too fast in an uninterrupted gush of words with no pauses between them. Only the Professor could understand Ben when he spoke this way, and only when the old man wasn't doubled over in pain.

"The site of impact will be classified," Ben said, much more slowly. "It's too dangerous to release. That's why we need to keep it secret until we can knock UD3 safely off course," he said.

"So knock it off course, then."

Ben rolled his eyes. "Yeah, thanks. That's why they pay *you* the big bucks, right?"

Love put a hand on her slim hip and waited for the inevitable lecture.

"First of all," Ben said, lifting his index finger, "we've never built anything with that kind of capability. Jin-soo's Iowa team has a model for a HYCIV, but it's only been tested with simulation software.

"Second, we don't have time to build the subassemblies, let alone assemble the whole damn thing and prep for launch. That's why we'll have to scavenge for parts, but lots of politicians can't accept the likelihood of world calamity or even human extinction. And others...Others will never release their grip on power. Never."

Ben took a few breaths while his words hung in the air. He asked if Love was fluent in Russian. She nodded with her eyebrows raised.

"We've got two nuclear physicists hopefully on their way here. Ex–Cold Warriors like Ziggy and Julie. They were trying to slip past the Russian border, but...easier said than done."

"Can they find a way? To make the Effort work?"

Ben attempted a weak smile. If only they had met under usual circumstances: some SoCal hipster bar, where Love could dismiss him for being a plain old nerd with no stock options instead of a failure to his entire race.

"Please don't put this on just their shoulders, Love. Or mine. It's gonna take all of us. There's hundreds of engineers and physicists headed our way. The cavalry is coming..."

But can we do it? Ben wondered. That triggered the million-dollar line of questions: Could they launch an interceptor and destroy an eight-kilometer comet? Could they launch before mass hysteria hit, before the talking heads declared World War III, before they all starved or went insane...before the doomsday clock hit zero?

"How much time do we have?" Love finally asked.

Ben held his digital wristwatch right up to her face. It was the same black plastic watch that came in every Effort kit that security doled out. Ben pressed a button on the side of the face to switch from military time to a countdown with T-minus 172 slipping away from their February 1 launch window.

ELEVEN

IMPACT IMMINENT!

JACK'S MORNING BEGAN with the activity of a hornet's nest. The science lounge was packed with people waiting for twenty-minute slots of internet time.

"What's wrong?" Jack asked one of the scientists, as he penned his name at the bottom of the waiting list.

"Comet might hit Russia," the bearded man whispered.

When Jack took his turn at a computer, he gaped at the biggest, boldest news headlines he had ever seen:

IMPACT IMMINENT!

That's a lot of i's *and* m's, Jack would remember thinking, or something just as stupid.

Scrolling down the article, he read that a high-ranking Pakistani scientist had leaked calculations for an estimated comet trajectory to a British tabloid for an undisclosed sum. The estimate placed UD3's impact site in eastern Siberia with a thirteen-month timeline. The international press was trying to locate more expert sources, but many had refused to comment or had disappeared altogether. A Dr. Benjamin Schwartz from NASA's Jet Propulsion Laboratories had called into the *New York Times* headquarters to announce an international body gathered for preemptive action: the Defense Effort for Comet UD3. Schwartz dismissed the estimated comet trajectory with the following comment:

> An accurate trajectory requires a 30-day observation arc, at the very least. Any premature estimation is not only inaccurate, it is unethical.

When asked whether the rumors were true that this Pakistani scientist had used Schwartz's own NEO Deflection app to help calculate his trajectory, or when NASA's own trajectory calculations would be released, Schwartz had the same response:

> No comment.

Jack's Gmail inbox had five new messages from his parents, who were four hours ahead, on East Coast time. His father wrote to assure him that humans had harnessed nuclear power, eradicated smallpox, and sequenced a genome. If nothing else, they were resourceful, he argued. Something would be done about the comet. (And if not, there wasn't a damn thing the Campbell family—a tax lawyer, housewife, and photojournalist—could do about it.)

The first of his mother's four emails contained only one sentence:

> I want you to come home.

Jack switched over to social media and witnessed the world awakening through the bright pixels of his monitor. People were suddenly yanked out of the microcosms of their professions; families and failing bodies now faced a widened scope of the solar system and questions they couldn't answer. The 280-character language of Twitter proved either inadequate or perfect:

Fuck! Is anyone else following this?

Whaaaaat?

A tweet from the US president tried to quickly reassure the public:

My own scientists are working on it. Ignore the dishonest media. Stay calm!

The tweet came paired with an ad banner in the margin. Some entrepreneurial soul was already hawking UD3 merchandise with KEEP CALM AND FIND A BUNKER slogans ripped from World War II posters by the British Ministry of Information.

Jack searched posts on Weibo, but Chinese censors had already updated their algorithms. His searches on UD3 returned:

Sorry this content violates 《微博社区管理规定(试行)》 or related regulations and policies.

A wave of fear unsettled him. Jack heard a sob and turned to see Maya's bunkmate with the fluffy red hair start crying at her computer. Maya stood up from a nearby computer and quickly moved to comfort her friend. Shock and horror were evident on all the faces of the scientists. The more news Jack read, the more he realized that shock and horror were the least of people's reactions.

England's tabloids had posted more than ten hours ago, giving Eurasia, Africa, and Australia time to let the news sink in. Religious leaders on those continents put forth the question: Are the people of this godless age praying enough? They called for Latin masses, live televangelism programming, pilgrimages to Mecca, dances, smoke ceremonies, prayers, readings of religious texts, and singing. The more severe religions called for desperate measures to match these desperate times. Followers sacrificed goats, chickens, and infidels. Embassies of the Western world were targeted with explosives.

Jack felt powerless as he sat stock-still. It was like he was a little boy again, waiting by the curb of his kindergarten for his mother's white BMW. One day, he watched with mounting fear as every other child got picked up and taken home. The school called his house, but no one picked up the phone. Terror overtook that six-year-old Jack, but his feet stayed planted. He would have waited forever for his reality to normalize, waiting and watching that empty road.

The next thing Jack knew, Maya was squeezing his shoulder.

"You've been staring off at nothing for more than ten minutes," she whispered.

Jack closed his jaw and realized that his mouth was completely dry. He looked around and saw that the scientist on his left had changed from a young woman to a man with a white mustache and beard. He didn't know how he lost time—not then.

~~~~~

THE AFTERNOON COFFEE date was Maya's idea. All the scientists were deeply troubled by yesterday's news, but Nancy was a mess. Maya heard her bunkmate tossing into the late hours before finally lacing up her boots and leaving before dawn. Nancy met up with the chemistry mapping team for morning duties on deck but kept breaking to pace back and forth, wringing her hands. When their rosette casts were complete, she didn't follow everyone to lunch. She said she couldn't eat but, at Maya's insistence, promised to join up for coffee afterward.

By the time Maya reached *Healy*'s dry goods store at 1300 hours, Nancy had already finished her weak cappuccino. She stood beside the wall, drawing on her empty Styrofoam cup with a permanent marker.

"You got a head start," Maya called out, temporarily relieved of worry.

"This is my fourth cup," Nancy replied without looking up. "Couldn't sleep."

Maya nodded to the Coastie behind the counter. He stepped up to the coffee machine along the back wall, oversold as the Java Hut, and made a cappuccino that would add another buck fifty to Maya's tab.

Nancy had drawn the name Derek on her cup and surrounded it with boxy robots.

"Your son likes robots?"

"He likes dinosaurs," Nancy replied, "but I'm trying not to think about them right now. So robots it is."

She couldn't speak of her seven-year-old son without frowning and tugging down on her freckled lips and brow. Before the latest news of the comet, she had resigned herself to the longing of temporary separation in order to grab the opportunity of *Healy*'s last Arctic expedition. "Impact Imminent" changed everything for everyone.

"Shall we shrink it at the North Pole?" Maya asked, nodding to the cup.

It was an oceanographer's tradition to decorate Styrofoam cups and attach them to water-sampling devices. The cups shrunk to a fifth of their original size under immense water pressure, making miniature mementos of the journey.

"No," Nancy said. "I'll shrink it now. Before *Healy* turns back."

They walked along together, but Nancy turned left at the corridor's junction as Maya turned right.

"Charlie called a meeting," Maya said.

"I can't take his speeches," Nancy said abruptly. "What good is studying the sixth mass extinction event when the seventh might be headed right for us?"

Maya said nothing.

"I'm going to talk to Captain Weber," Nancy sighed. "I should be with my son. I just never thought..."

She walked away, shaking her head. Maya watched her friend go and thought, *Are we turning back? Is the comet really going to hit Earth? Is there anything I can do—or anything anyone can do? Will we have to just wait it out together like death row inmates with no bars to keep us safe from one another...*

Maya knew she couldn't stop and think. The overload of questions paralyzed her with fear and dread. She had to keep moving and doing.

Most of the scientists had already gathered in the science conference room, although Nancy wasn't the only one absent. Maya took a seat as she counted thirty-four heads out of the fifty-one who had boarded. She sipped her cappuccino and tried to listen to their nervous whispers.

"Charlie needs to let us leave," one postdoc said, projecting her voice for all to hear.

All but Charlie. None of these detractors would make a peep if he were in the same room. The man was larger than life in all ways; he dined with Leonardo DiCaprio one weekend and sat at the Intergovernmental Panel on Climate Change the next. That was not to say that Charlie was unapproachable. Despite his star power, Charlie always insisted that Maya treat him as an equal, even in the years that he served as Maya's thesis advisor at Berkeley. Charlie continued to arrange opportunities and offer career advice whenever she asked (and even when she didn't). Maya's place on *Healy*'s last Arctic expedition was due in part to his characteristic kindness. She intended to crack open an incredible Bordeaux-style blend from Napa Valley once they entered the Arctic Circle—but only to share with him.

All whispers died when Charlie entered the science conference room. Coasties called him Chief Santa, and he looked the part with his stocky frame, white beard, wire-frame glasses, and full cheeks with red blooms of broken blood vessels. For the last three Arctic expeditions, Charlie had donned a fuzzy red Santa costume when the ship anchored at the North Pole. He read aloud Christmas wish lists from the children of crewmembers and posed for photo ops. Charlie could even be called jolly, but there was an underlying intensity at his core. It was a trait that he and Maya shared.

"Good afternoon," Charlie said with a smile, and immediately addressed the issue. "The news reports gave us a preliminary trajectory—one that is unofficial and already judged to be inaccurate. It was leaked for one reason. Money."

Charlie stared down his audience. He always had the fire of the self-righteous. "I know there's going to be disagreement about this, but I told Captain Weber I want to see this last mission through. You all know its importance. The musician Joan Baez is quoted as saying, 'Action is the antidote to despair.'"

Maya nodded when their eyes locked. She didn't have children who needed her back on the mainland, and she didn't know how to save Earth from a potential cosmic impact. What she did know, and what she could prove, was the grave damage being done to its oceans. In sounding the alarm, she hoped to save humanity from itself, if it still had a future. That was the original plan anyway, and she had yet to make another.

"So let's do what we can," Charlie urged the scientists, "while we still can."

~~~~

JACK THOUGHT *HEALY*'S Arctic expedition would be canceled, but the majority of the world was still in a state of disbelief: this Pakistani scientist had to be wrong; an impact event couldn't happen; humans were not dinosaurs, they were masters of the solar system (for sheer lack of competition, but still). And there was the habit of duty, after all. US Coast Guard Cutter *Healy*'s military crewmembers and its latest batch of scientists had a duty to further understanding of the disappearing Arctic. Jack had a duty to document the ice-breaker's last scientific expedition through an ecosystem already slipping from existence.

True to its motto *Promise and Deliver*, *Healy* heeded the call of duty and stayed the course. In the meantime, a voice projected from loudspeakers, or what the Coasties called the pipes, announcing a partial evacuation by helicopter to Wales, Alaska. Scientists, guest passengers, and nonessential crewmembers with small children would be given first consideration.

Jack half-listened to the announcements. Of course he was shocked and frightened by the rumor of an imminent impact; his mind spun off on tangents that threatened to pin him immobilized under their weight. Still, Jack wouldn't evacuate. Those were the very words he used during the interview process with a new employer: *I won't evacuate*. Jack felt obliged to warn editors and address the issue up front, as he already had a reputation.

Jack had been called an "adrenaline junkie" by one editor who refused to work with him again. Another claimed he was exhibiting signs of PTSD after refusing to leave a Syrian battlefield. Jack didn't care what they called him. All he knew was that every evacuation he had made early in his career filled him with some type of regret: survivor's guilt when other journalists died doing their jobs, or jealousy toward the ones who managed to survive and document harrowing events in order to bring them into the eyes of the public. Journalists who stayed to get the job done had made their lives meaningful and relevant, while Jack chose to be sidelined with fear. Never again.

He passed Ned and Malcolm as they headed toward the helicopter hangar, wearing flight suits. Jack backed against the corridor wall to let them pass and overheard Ned whisper in conversation with his friend.

"I wonder if the government is keeping secrets about the comet."

"They don't know shit about shit," Malcolm grumbled. "Haven't you been paying attention?"

Jack continued down the corridor and saw Maya standing by the Java Hut.

"Hey!" he called out. "You waiting for your bunkmate?"

"Nancy. You've met her—"

"Right, Nancy."

"I was," Maya said, "but I think she's leaving *Healy* to go be with her son and husband."

Jack nodded and continued, but Maya blocked his path. He knew walking away made Maya want to chase him.

"I'm staying," she said.

With those dark and intense eyes, it was half invitation and half challenge. Jack was never one to back away from a challenge.

"Then I'll see ya around," he promised.

TWELVE

SPACE AND TIME

Bob Nowak would be forever grateful for receiving the worst news of his life. No one had to tell him, least of all NASA's administrator on an unscheduled Skype call in the lavatory of the International Space Station.

"You will receive full honors and respect," the administrator promised.

Bob had to assume he meant posthumously.

"Since our president is thoroughly engaged with the planetary threat..."

The administrator was careful with words because he was not alone. Bob could only see the man's upper body between a desk and white wall, but his microphone picked up more whispering and breathing.

"I've asked our vice president to do the honors of the last word."

Bob swallowed hard. Of course their president wasn't one for awkward situations, like talking to the walking dead. He would pass off the job, like all others.

"God bless you, Bob."

The administrator's lips contorted as he got up from his desk and stepped out of range. *Don't leave us*, a voice in Bob's head called out. It sounded like a small child too young to understand a hopeless situation. The vice president stepped into the webcam's range and sat down with a bookmarked Bible. His expression was an exaggeration of resolve, like an actor playing a general ready to address his platoon before sending them on to their glorious deaths.

"Let us pray," he said, by way of greeting, and opened the good book. "'Fear thou not; for I am with thee—'"

"Sir?"

"'Be not dismayed; for I am thy God: I will strengthen—'"

"Sir? I'm an atheist."

The vice president blinked.

"Then...my prayer won't be *with* you, but *for* you."

He continued to recite the passage as Bob sighed and waited. The vice president was a politician who had yet to be convinced of human evolution and climate change, whereas Bob was an astronaut who had given his life to science. A disconnect was to be expected.

After concluding his prayer, the vice president looked back up at the image of Bob. His expression finally softened.

"Thank you for your service, Robert Nowak," he said.

"Thank you, Mr. Vice President."

Did it make sense to thank someone for thanking you? All Bob knew was that he needed to end this formality before the shock wore off. He pulled out his headphones and closed his laptop, clutching it tight to keep from slamming it against the toilet seat. *Be grateful*, he insisted. *They could have said nothing.* That would've been easier for everyone with feet firmly planted on living soil through gravitation. The International Space Station could be so forgettable in the face of annihilation, just another satellite moving swiftly through the crowded night sky.

In a stricken daze, Bob opened the waste and hygiene compartment's curtain and pushed off a handrail. He would have to contact his wife, but what would he say? Everything? Nothing but *I love you*? Bob tried to focus, but his mind wandered back to the *Kursk*, lost at sea around the turn of the millennium. An initial explosion sank the Russian submarine to the bottom of the Barents Sea and a second collapsed the hull, killing nearly all the crew. Twenty-three men managed to survive by holing up in the turbine room. Russia refused international aid, so the world had to watch and wonder what was going through the minds of the crew as they died while waiting for rescue.

Now, I'll know, Bob thought, *firsthand.*

With the heaviest of hearts, he floated across *Tranquility* module. On the left, he passed ant farms bolted to the wall. They were an experiment on behavior in microgravity by students at the University of Colorado Boulder.

Little buggers have no idea they're doomed, Bob thought. *Keep those eyes on the tunnels ahead, boys!*

The Cupola observatory module was attached at a berthing location in the floor. Astronauts often visited the Cupola during off-hours to gaze back at planet Earth while they orbited at 17,500 miles per hour. Bob peered over the edge of the Earth-facing port, expecting a view like a glass-bottom boat. Instead, he saw white-socked feet belonging to Rémy, a French astronaut from the European Space Agency. Bob didn't want company, but he didn't want to be alone, either.

Still holding his laptop and trailing headphones, Bob pulled on the Cupola's handrails with his right hand and descended headlong. In a pressurized, zero-gravity environment, orientation didn't matter; upside down didn't feel any different from right side up. The Cupola was nearly nine feet in diameter but had tubes and consoles poking out of the sides. Two adult males could fit comfortably shoulder to shoulder, but any more had to be nuts to butts, as the saying went.

Rémy turned to see Bob by his side, hugging his laptop like a teddy bear.

"So now you know why the Russians didn't rotate out our

Soyuz capsule," Rémy said, making it a flat statement rather than a question.

Bob said nothing, but he couldn't hide his surprise.

"Unless you always take your laptop to the toilet," Rémy added. "And if you do, I don't want to know why."

"Funny."

Rémy agreed with a bitter smile that seemed to say, *To the last.* The Frenchman looked back to the dome of windows and said, "I already spoke to the director of the Guiana Space Centre. Marcel told me the situation."

And it was grave. A Soyuz capsule, the only method of transport for ISS astronauts, remained docked to the station in case of emergency evacuation, but the capsule currently attached had an onboard system failure that had been discovered in late July. The Russians were scheduled to change out the inoperable capsule with a new one, but then canceled the flight and cut all communications with no explanation. The astronauts had no escape. They also had no way to keep living. The European spaceport wasn't going to launch a transfer vehicle with new supplies. All rockets, spacecraft, and satellites were being repurposed for countermeasures against the comet threat. The ISS crew would be out of luck and, more important, oxygen.

"How many medals did they promise your widow?" Rémy asked.

Bob ignored the question. "Should we tell Sergey?" he asked. "You know the Russians won't."

Rémy shrugged. He had one of those dimpled donut chins that was all the more noticeable in harsh, artificial lighting.

"Only if he wants to know," Rémy said. "Peggy did."

"You told Peggy?"

By which Bob meant, *You told Peggy before you told me?* But of course Rémy did. Peggy Whitson was his favorite. She was everyone's favorite with her wide smile and Iowan decency. Peggy had broken the record for the most time spent in orbit by an American.

When she and Bob had once watched a sunset together, the sixteenth and final sunset in their waking hours, Peggy whispered that she wanted to keep exploring right up to the day she died. Poor Peggy would get her wish.

Rémy placed his index finger on the innermost layer of aluminum ceramic composite glass. Bob supposed he was pointing to the spaceport in French Guiana, but when Bob looked 248 miles below, past the minimal cloud cover, French Guiana was too far northeast. Rémy was really pointing to dark plumes of smoke drifting above Brazil's Amazonia.

"It's still burning," Rémy muttered.

"What?"

"Clearing fires along the Xingu River."

Rémy dragged his finger in a squiggly line, tracing the river that glowed like a filament in a light bulb. He told Bob that he first saw the fires at the beginning of his six-month mission on the ISS and watched them spread wider and farther along the headwaters into what was left of virgin forest.

"You know, I almost ventured into the Amazon last time I was stationed at the space center," Rémy mused. "When I couldn't fit it into my schedule, I told myself I had time. I was ... forty-three."

He shook his head at his own ignorance. For here he was, using depleting oxygen, and there *it* was, burning until there was nothing left.

Bob tried his best to comfort the man beside him.

"You are not alone," he said quietly. "We always think we have more time."

THIRTEEN

USCGC *HEALY* KEEPS ITS PROMISE

ALL TOLD, THIRTY-TWO scientists and twenty-seven crewmembers were evacuated by the time *Healy* sailed past the Bering Strait and into the Chukchi Sea. It wasn't long before the ship crossed the Arctic Circle perimeter. The summer sun didn't fully set at these latitudes; it only dipped low to an eerie twilight.

Healy's corridors, mess deck, and lounges grew quieter with a third less people. Maya tried to keep herself busy working, walking, and talking. Ruminating was dangerous in the face of a comet and its apocalyptic potential. She tried to focus on crossing into the Arctic, a region she knew only from every possible method of secondhand experience. It was cause for a small celebration.

Maya reached the chief scientist's stateroom carrying her bottle of Bordeaux by the neck. For the last couple of days, none of the scientists had seen Charlie working on deck or eating in the galley. A few of the Coasties floated a rumor that he wasn't signing his accountability forms. Charlie's door was slightly ajar, and there was a three-inch hole where there should have been a knob. Maya knocked on the wall by the open door.

"Charlie? It's me, Maya."

Silence. Fluorescent light shone through the hole in the door.

Charlie was very energy conscious and wouldn't have left his room with the lights on.

"Charlie, we crossed into the Arctic Circle."

Maya crouched down quietly and peeked through the hole with one eye. Charlie was seated at his desk along the far wall. Maya couldn't see much beyond the slope of his round shoulders. Was he asleep, or was he lost in some kind of mental fog like she had witnessed in the other scientists?

Maya slowly walked into the room calling his name, but Charlie didn't stir. The stare from his watery-blue eyes was as level and empty as the ocean's horizon. It raised the hair on Maya's skin. What if he was dead?

Maya reached out an unsteady hand and touched his thick neck, fearing cold flesh. Consciousness rose from some deep depth as his eyes came to life.

"Mongolia this time," Charlie said, like he was answering a question.

Maya jumped back and nearly screamed. Charlie blinked up at her and further explained.

"A new trajectory calculation puts the impact in Mongolia, not Siberia."

Maya sank to the floor and sat shaking. Charlie continued to draw her into the middle of his own conversation. An Argentinian scientist, he said, had calculated an alternate trajectory and posted his findings to his personal website. The Associated Press had gotten word of it before the site's server crashed with an overload of traffic. The scientist said no one paid him for his research. He was acting alone and for the sole reason of serving truth.

"Did anyone confirm it?" Maya asked, once she could speak again. "No one confirmed the last one."

Charlie shook his head and said he didn't know. Maya hesitated. There were some questions you weren't supposed to ask.

"If there's nothing we can do, Charlie, do you really want to know?"

Again, he shook his head.

"I was just asking myself those sorts of questions," he admitted. "But I only came up with more questions instead of answers. Like, have you ever wondered about a single word and how it came to have meaning? You say it slowly to yourself and it sounds like babble. When you go to write out the letters, they look wrong even though you've spelled it the same way all your literate life. So what if...what if all the meaning that we've assigned to things comes undone all at once? I'm talking beyond language. All societal structures and the fictions we tell ourselves every day just come apart at the seams? What's left of us when there are no rules and no future?"

Maya saw his facial muscles twitch.

"What happened to your door, Charlie? Charlie!"

He looked at her, confused. She had to point backward until he muttered something about being distracted and not hearing the Coasties when they knocked on his door.

"No one's seen you at meals," Maya said.

She pulled a stolen turkey sandwich out of the front pouch of her sweatshirt. Hoarding food was against *Healy*'s rules and regulations, but Maya was worried about her avuncular old thesis advisor. He barely looked at the sandwich wrapped in a paper napkin as she placed it on his desk.

"Not hungry?" she asked. "What about thirsty?"

Maya presented the bottle of Bordeaux with the proud panache of a waiter at a Michelin-starred restaurant. Charlie finally remembered his manners and placed a hand on her arm.

"Rain check?" he asked, with the kindest, saddest smile.

─〜〜〜─

JACK RETURNED TO his stateroom after breakfast. Gustavo was seated at his desk with his hands in his lap.

"Looks like we're both in for the long haul," Jack said, stating the obvious to fill the silence.

Gustavo nodded and said, "I can't go home to Brazil."

"What, are you dodging extradition out here?"

Jack meant it as a joke. He kept trying and failing to get his bunkmate to smile. When Jack caught Gustavo's meaningful stare, he thought, *Oh shit. Me and my big mouth.* He quickly changed the subject and asked if the Nobel laureate had written any poetry on their strange journey.

"I haven't the heart to speak," Gustavo said. "Only listen."

Jack understood. He listened with his camera and took pictures of his surroundings: the choreography of dust motes in the light of a porthole; a photo of a Coastie's baby daughter that was taped up by the wall next to the Java Hut; Maya's expression as she looked to the sky.

"I spoke to Camila at breakfast," Jack said. "She asked if I wanted a reassignment."

The partial evacuation had left many staterooms empty. Camila offered to pull strings for Jack. It was widely known that Gustavo was deeply troubled and that Jack avoided his room because of it. Camila could give him an out, if he wanted it.

But he didn't. Jack didn't want to be alone with his spinning mind. He also didn't want to abandon Gustavo to misery.

"I could stay," Jack offered. "I think we could both use the company."

Gustavo eventually nodded. Jack fixed him with a patient stare until some instinct of self-preservation finally forced his bunkmate to verbalize: "Yes. Please stay."

So it was settled. Jack said he was on his way to the science lounge and offered to take Gustavo with him.

"You need to know what's happening with the comet," Jack said gently.

He didn't want to broach the topic of human extinction, but even the lesser outcomes included devastation beyond recorded history. It wouldn't matter if UD3 struck Mongolia or Siberia or whatever site was named next; all of Asia would be SOLJWF—shit outta luck and jolly well fucked, as Ned the pilot would say.

"If it hits, half a continent could be annihilated—"

"Annihilation is nothing new to Indians," Gustavo said sharply. "We've suffered genocide. Millions are dead and many tribes extinct. The few survivors are . . . shadows that stay silent or get shot."

Gustavo struggled to stop.

"I know a priest who had an expression," he said, more controlled. "He was Canadian. Maybe you have a similar expression in America . . . 'Welcome to the club.'"

-∿∿∿-

WITH LESS THAN half of *Healy*'s scientists choosing to remain aboard, Jack didn't have to wait for a computer in the science lounge. New emails from his father no longer dismissed the comet threat or the dangers that it caused. Stating the situation matter-of-factly, he wrote that locals were hoarding food, bottled water, batteries, and gasoline, leading to panic in their northern Virginia suburbs.

Jack's mother had also written several new emails that were all strangely fragmented. In some paragraphs, she talked only of the comet and its effects on her surroundings. There was a neighbor who used to make pecan pralines for Jack's birthdays. Now an elderly widow, she was discovered in a catatonic state.

Although, Jack's mother conceded in her less than charitable way, *Mrs. Allen was always a bit untethered.*

Other paragraphs veered back in time to memories that she described with a mix of love and sharp barbs:

As a little child, you were in awe of the most ordinary things. You reached out to touch dogs, dandelion puffs, even dirty puddles

with rainbow oil slicks. You made me see my world with your
new eyes. I'd never have guessed how quickly you would grow
bored of it...

What could Jack say to that? A better son would have written
something other than:

Mom,

I will be losing internet as we head north. I'll still have access to
email on the ship's server. You can reach me at this address:

Jack.Campbell@healy.polarscience.net

PS. Hang in there.

Jack wasn't that better son, but two stillbirths kept his mother
from trying for more. She had to cling to the memory of her smiling,
towheaded toddler like a religion.

⌁⌁⌁

THE POSTED PLAN of the day listed satellite information in its
margins. *Healy* was heading through fifty miles of ice drifts at 40 to
60 percent coverage. Jack would have to work quickly in such harsh
conditions. A spare lithium battery was taped to the warm skin of
his chest, ready to go. The air was clear and frigid on deck with a
staggering wind chill. Despite a bulky anti-exposure suit and the
awkward face mask that looked like a fabric beard, Jack snapped
photos with effortless coordination.

Work wasn't a means to life for him; it *was* life. In entering
the full concentration and flow of a master practicing his craft,
Jack found something close to joy. He traveled the perimeter of

the ship, looking for different vantage points, and spotted Maya's boots outside one of the ISO lab vans. Maybe she was lost in her own concentration and flow, measuring trace elements with utmost precision.

The Arctic sky was pale blue with thin smears of cirrus clouds. When Jack focused his lens straight ahead, the white irregular shapes of ice floes alternated with dark water like white-and-black cowhide. Yet, when he looked down at the submerged ice, Jack saw gradations of some of the most beautiful blue-green colors nature had to offer.

Jack spotted a group of walruses all trying to clamor onto a wide, anemic floe. They used their tusks like pickaxes, but the ice was too weak and broke under their weight. A lone bull, farther in the distance, managed to find a small floe strong enough to support him. He sat atop it and watched *Healy* pass. Jack focused in on his blunt, whiskered snout and rolls of blubber. Never had such a cuddly animal looked so solemn.

Are we all goners? Jack wanted to ask him.

Of course humanity had to come to an end one day—everything did. Didn't it?

Two crewmen walked behind Jack as he snapped pictures.

"Shoulda been more ice at this latitude," one said to the other. "Least, that's how I remember it."

FOURTEEN

CRAZY

WHEN IT CAME to loving Love, there was no choice. From the moment Rivka first saw her, all she could think was—*Good God!* Love carried herself like a queen with soaring cheekbones and full, pouty lips that could smile wide when you least expected it. One day, she caught Rivka's adoring stare on Columbia University's urban campus.

"Which languages can you speak?" Love asked, as a way of introduction.

"English, French, and Spanish," Rivka replied.

Love laughed with a wide and flirtatious smile, revealing a charming gap in between her front two teeth.

"Three? That's it?"

Rivka was a goner. Love taught a few classes in comparative literature and society but earned her reputation as a literary translator. The two women stayed awake into the early hours at Rivka's apartment in Harlem. Love pulled papers from her satchel and read sections of novels from all over the world. She would pause and touch Rivka's haze of hair, which spilled over her pillow in brown ringlets. When she continued, Love's Russian was a thick staccato; her Italian, smooth and honeyed.

Despite the intensity of their relationship, there was still an unsaid understanding that Love was exactly where she needed to be, doing exactly what she needed to do in order to survive in the long term. Or, as Love put it, "until a computer program can properly translate the beauty of a novel." At twenty-nine, Rivka was younger than Love and in an earlier stage of her career. In order to launch, she would have to leave. Rivka stopped applying to postdocs. After defending her thesis, she took an underpaid adjunct position.

Rivka's parents couldn't forgive a lapsed-Catholic lesbian lover from Kenya. *Are you trying to put me in an early grave?* her father shouted into the phone. Rivka was disowned and cut off emotionally and financially from her family. She sublet her Harlem apartment and moved into the South Bronx with Love. Colorful drapes, blankets, throw rugs, and pillows couldn't warm the drafty rooms or muffle the traffic and shouting.

Rivka could tell that Love didn't put much faith in the longevity of their relationship. Through her Kenyan eyes, Rivka and her fellow Americans were spoiled, fickle, and untested. While there might be truth to that, it didn't mean they were weak. Rivka vowed to prove herself as resourceful and strong. When their apartment was vandalized and all her grandmother's jewelry stolen, Rivka said nothing. A decent chunk of her savings disappeared in exchange for a new deadbolt and floor guard.

And she stayed. The sex was amazing; it was the intimacy that sucked. Rivka wanted a sense of ownership between them, but Love, an orphan and nomadic scholar, was never allowed to own anything. She was only allowed to learn the language of a given land before she had to pack up and move on. When a call came in the middle of the night—Love put it on mute and whispered that a rep from the United Nations was on the line—there was no hesitation in answering the call of duty, all despite Love's claim to be finished with UN contract work. When the call ended, Love stood dumbstruck.

"I thought it was Al-Shabaab," she said, "or just more of the usual danger."

She recovered enough to wrestle her old, battered suitcase out from the back of their bedroom closet.

"I have to go now," Love said. "There's a car outside waiting."

Rivka asked what the hell was going on, but Love said little as she packed up some clothes and essential toiletries. The UN needed expert interpreters, she said, and they needed them fast. Love stripped off her oversized T-shirt and pulled on underwear, a pair of straight-legged jeans, a cotton blouse with bright patterns, and her leather motorcycle boots, despite the August heat.

Rivka grabbed Love by the shoulders.

"This is crazy—"

"I *have* to go," Love insisted, wresting herself from Rivka's frightened grip. "I don't have a choice."

"Everyone has a choice," Rivka shot back.

She was a hypocrite and didn't care. Love finally looked her in the eyes.

"Stock up on food and water," she said.

"What?"

A car horn blared from the street outside.

"Food, water, supplies—and cash," Love said. "Empty your bank accounts. There's some kind of natural disaster on the way. Something big."

She strode over to their bed and leaned across the mattress to reach Rivka's pillow.

"You need to prepare," she called over her shoulder.

That was it. That was goodbye. Rivka listened to Love's unlaced boots travel down the stairwell.

"You know your name?" Rivka asked the walls. "Love? In America, we call that false advertising."

She had saved that great line only to waste it on a closed door. When Rivka returned to bed, she saw Love's switchblade resting on her pillow. Love never left the apartment without it concealed on her person. Here she had left it for Rivka. If the switchblade could talk, it would say, *Stay alive.*

∿∿∿

RIVKA SCOURED THE news the next day. No one seemed particularly concerned about the discovery of comet UD3, so Rivka thought the "something big" was still unannounced and looming. Then she got a text from Love:

Landed safe. Remember what I told you.

Rivka did remember. She immediately liquidated her meager bank account into fifty-dollar bills and rode the subway back, clutching Love's switchblade. At the local market, Rivka stocked up on cases of bottled water and foods like canned soup, rice, beans, granola, nuts, and dried fruits. She even hit up the fancy camping stores in Manhattan and wandered the aisles, tossing freeze-dried food packets into her cart along with a hand-crank flashlight. She tried to look inconspicuous but, as a born and bred New Yorker, Rivka's idea of nature was the man-made slopes and lakes of Central Park; her idea of "roughing it" was Yonkers.

Rivka returned to the Bronx lugging three large shopping bags. She saw her neighbor Lamar from 1B dash in front of her and hold open the door to their apartment building.

"Wait," he said, frowning. "You still a Mets fan?"

With that, he shut the door on her. Rivka waited outside until Lamar opened the door and stepped out with a shit-eating grin. She laughed and grinned back, always a fan of the goofy, friendly giant from the first floor.

"Hey, Lamar, have you seen anything big on the news lately? I feel like I'm missing something."

He cocked his head, thinking.

"You mean, like the robbery four blocks down?"

"No, like the national news? International even?"

Lamar shook his head and shrugged, already losing interest but gaining curiosity about her shopping bags and such conspicuous consumption. He stuck a finger into the lip of one and tried to peek inside, but Rivka told him not to bother.

"I just spent more than two hundred dollars on shit for *camping*," she admitted with self-disgust.

Lamar shook his head sadly.

"White people be crazy," he observed.

"Yes," she agreed. "Yes, we are."

And life continued. Everything seemed normal except that Rivka was heartbroken without Love. And then the media released the initial trajectory of UD3 in late August, and the world flipped upside down. Rivka saw change manifest on the bustling sidewalks of New York City. People slowed to a standstill because they couldn't walk and think about a cosmic impact of this magnitude at the same time. It left the sidewalks crowded with slack-jawed, motionless people.

Students stopped attending classes. Rivka's vice provost sent an email that the campus would be closing so that students, faculty, and administration could all process the news with their loved ones. Rivka stopped by the university's administrative offices to try to change the man's mind and keep the doors open. She needed the routine and socialization that her job provided, because she didn't have loved ones, not anymore.

The vice provost wasn't in, so his secretary took down a message. Half of the desks around her were empty.

"Where is everybody?" Rivka whispered. "We haven't closed yet."

The secretary looked up and lost her professional polish as her lower lip trembled. Some employees called out for personal time, she said. Some quit outright, and others hadn't contacted the office at all. The secretary motioned to a nearby desk.

"That's where my friend Shonda sat. I tried to call her landline after she didn't show up at work, but it was off the hook."

After the breaking news on the comet's initial trajectory, cellular service failed due to network overload. The vice provost's secretary, whose name was Adelle, had to walk over to her friend's apartment building and ring the buzzer for a good twenty minutes before she heard Shonda's voice over the intercom.

"She said she needed to be home to pray with her family," Adelle said. "She wouldn't even buzz me up."

Rivka was a secular Jew, a lazy agnostic who was suddenly envious of having something to believe in and somewhere to go. She went for a long walk that evening and lingered outside several houses of worship. The buildings were all packed with long lines of worshippers trailing out the open doors and into the crisp night air. Some held hands as they prayed, like a chanting paper-doll chain that wound around the block.

When Rivka returned to her apartment, there were several automated emails from her commercial bank. One took the form of a letter from the chairman and CEO, asking customers to remain calm because their money was as safe as it always had been. The news reported on riots at dozens of division branches. It appeared that those who weren't busy praying were panicking and making a bank run. The Federal Reserve issued a warning to the Associated Press that the stability of financial institutions was at stake.

Rivka couldn't help rolling her eyes, but it wasn't just about money. Panic caused rampant hoarding as well. Rivka tried three different grocery stores in the course of a weekend, but the shelves were mostly bare. A vicious fight broke out when a man reached into the overflowing cart of another and took several boxes of cereal.

"You don't need all this," the man yelled, with an armload of Cheerios. "You're selfish. The rest of us got nothing."

The other man landed a punch with a sickening thud and sent the cereal boxes cartwheeling on their corners.

The city's supply chain couldn't keep up with so much stockpiling. Rivka had to tap into her fancy camping food after she finished everything in her fridge. She opened a salty mix labeled "gorp" and stood by her window listening to the rumble of private helicopters. The *New York Times* reported that the president and his family had fled for Mount Weather in Bluemont, Virginia, with the rest of the civilian leadership of US government. They would all be safe in an underground city that could house thousands. The bunker had sewage treatment plants, reservoirs for drinking water, and an extensive computer system to keep communications open. Rivka imagined all the upcoming renovations from the president and First Lady: crystal chandeliers, gold lacquer walls, and enough ostentatious wealth to give the Vatican a run for its money. She fumed and picked out the tastier chocolate M&Ms and dried fruit, leaving the nuts and granola in the bag because Love wasn't around to yell at her.

Rivka felt abandoned as New York's rich and powerful made their way to summer cottages in the Berkshires and Catskills or beachfront property in the Hamptons, Nantucket, and Martha's Vineyard, seemingly safer places with better access to local farms. The modern world had always fled to the cities, but now there was a reverse course back to rural fields. The Midwestern states sealed off access to their borders through major highways. News coverage had aerial images of gridlocked traffic and abandoned automobiles. The governor of Indiana was rumored to have said, "Flyover country needs to take care of her own."

The streets in Rivka's neighborhood remained functional, but delivery trucks had no entry access through the city's outer limits, if they were even trying to operate business as usual—and that was a big *if*. Grocery stores in a fifteen-block radius were empty and locked. There was no one to ask when there might be food again, which was an answer in itself.

On her way home from walking all day in search of groceries,

Rivka passed two young men carrying desktop computers with the wires trailing behind them on the street. In a block, she reached a small office with a shattered glass front. As Rivka stood to gawk, three women approached. New York City wasn't a place where you talked to strangers, but they were all suddenly in it together. Anyone could pick up the continuing conversation around the question, *What the hell is happening?*

"Where are the police?" Rivka asked them, with her arms lifted and palms up.

Two women were instantly furious on the subject, with lots of expletives and head-shaking. The third was more measured.

"My friend's husband is a cop," she called back as she kept walking. "The ones that showed up for work got sent over to the Hell Gate and Harlem River Yards power plants."

The women were right to keep moving. A small mob was gathered on the same block as Rivka's apartment building. They faced a lone gunman standing guard over a locked-up convenience store across the street. Several people in the mob tried to talk him into laying down his weapon. The loudest was a woman who shouted that she had hungry children at home with nothing to put on their plates. Maybe the gunman didn't speak English, or maybe he had his own children to feed. When the loud woman broke from the others and stalked off toward the storefront, he fired a shot over her head. Rivka sprinted into her building and didn't look back. *We can all get away with murder from now on*, she thought.

Once Rivka's apartment door was safely locked, she shed hysterical tears and screamed at the police through her walls like a crazy lady. But the more she paced around her small apartment and calmed down, the more she got to thinking that her overwhelmed local government had made a smart move. The modern world ran on power, right down to the basics that no one bothered to think about. What would happen to all these people in New York City if there was no drinking water? What about no sewage system? That's when the oatmeal was really going to hit the fan.

And what about nuclear power plants? By design, they needed power for cooling systems—this she learned from the radioactive spill in Fukushima, Japan, after an earthquake. How many nuclear power plants were there in North America, and did they have a way of shutting down without emitting radiation?

Rivka intended to look it all up on the internet, but next thing she realized was that her mouth and eyes were very dry. The sky outside her window was dark when it had been light only moments earlier. The clock on her microwave read 3:06 a.m. Rivka decided not to think about the subject again.

The last time she left her apartment alone, Rivka set off at the break of dawn. She hoped to find food or even someone to talk to, someone who wouldn't hurt her. Loneliness wasn't a cause of death, that she knew. But Rivka was starting to lose her shit, and that could lead to death in times like these. White pillowcases hung from some of the windows in her neighborhood, signaling hope of rescue. Others had cardboard signs with letters scrawled in black marker:

Looters will be shot.

One sign was made from plywood and painted with brushstrokes:

I have a big dog a big rifle and a staple gun.

It was a nice touch at the end. Rivka turned a corner and found two sleepy men smoking cigarettes and sipping from steaming travel mugs. Aside from the handguns tucked into their belts, they could have been taking a break from a morning shift at a regular job on a regular weekday.

"Fuck off," one of them yelled.

Rivka forced her feet to quickly step one in front of the other.

They took her south. She hoped to catch a glimpse of home, but as Rivka neared the Harlem River, clouds of smoke blotted out the brightening sky. She checked the *New York Times* website when she got home. It still posted fresh content, although it was more like shocking announcements than in-depth coverage.

The first article under the nameplate reported fire barricades on all the bridges connecting to the New York City boroughs. There wasn't much detail. Rivka could only imagine what earthly possessions the Manhattan residents had to sacrifice to feed the flames day and night: designer clothes, top-of-the-line sound systems, leather interiors and floor mats from luxury cars, *New Yorker* magazines, novels and plays in progress, Ivy League diplomas, original Picassos...and in with them, the sweat and blood shed for the best of everything. Manhattan was spared the looting of the outer boroughs, but at a high price.

By mid-September, there was no food left to steal, and the real violence began. The president declared a national state of emergency from his bunker and sent troops to occupy thirty major cities to restore order. Paratroopers dropped into Manhattan with food and medical supplies, but the outer boroughs were left to themselves.

Rivka was alone in the dangerous chaos of the Bronx. Her door stayed bolted, but her windows couldn't bar the sounds of gunfire, shattering glass, car alarms, and screaming. She cowered in the corner of her bedroom and blamed Love for her banishment from Manhattan. She blamed gentrification—not the gentrification that attracted her to a Harlem apartment in the first place, but the gentrification that kept her from being able to afford it with an adjunct professor salary. Most of all, Rivka blamed herself. Perhaps she really did have a choice about Love and had made the wrong one.

What if Rivka had chosen from the string of nice Jewish boys her parents pushed on her at every family function? Her mother grew so frustrated. Here was a woman who married a successful lawyer before she could legally drink alcohol. *I was married with two babies at your age*, she kept harping. Rivka's mother didn't understand the value of a lover who made your body temperature rise. She didn't understand wanting to get wrapped up in someone and something too wonderful and crazy to last.

FIFTEEN

ICE AT THE END OF THE END

ICE DRIFTS WIDENED to 82 percent coverage at one week's distance to the North Pole. *Healy* slowed and fired up a second engine. Her 420-foot flanks were brightly colored but tough as a battering ram against the floes. Deep vibrations could be felt in the ship's walls and floors. Rooms in the bow of the ship, like the cafeteria and galley, were especially shaky and loud. In an email to her parents, Maya tried to describe it as a constant crunching and sandpapery static. During the quiet concentration just before sleep, she could feel it in her inner ears, lungs, and teeth.

Maya gave this latest email the same closure as all the others written in the three weeks since IMPACT IMMINENT! had stretched across her monitor: she loved them both and hoped to hear from all of her family and friends in California once things settled. There was always the panicked urge to write more. Three weeks was a long time to endure silence from the people you loved, followed by the lack of internet at such high latitudes. Maya worked long hours, ate food she couldn't taste, overslept because she didn't want to be awake, and stared at her inbox until she could see its glare of pixels when she closed her eyes.

Healy's tight-knit crew was better off; they had each other to stave off the aching loneliness. Malcolm tried to console Maya by offering to coach her at the gym and spot her bench pressing. Members of the Morale Committee stopped her in the corridor to ask how she was feeling, just like those TV news reporters back in California: *How do you feel after losing everything in that wildfire?* Maya wanted to answer them: *How the hell do you think I'm feeling?* But what she actually said was, "It's hard. I haven't heard from anyone back home. And without internet, I don't know what's going on with the comet."

The Coasties on the committee offered their sympathy and tried to relate. They had all heard from their families in rural Washington and Oregon. Most of their towns had imposed a mandatory curfew to combat looting and gas siphoning. Store shelves were bare, and vehicles were stranded. "My infant niece hasn't had formula or milk," one of them told Maya. "They're pushing solid foods at her, but she's still dropping weight. See, we're in this together." Maya nodded and rubbed at her teary eyes.

~~~~

THE CREW STATIONED on the bridge began their search for a wide and thick enough floe for ice liberty. Everyone was itching to get out and stretch their sea legs, but the floes were still so thin and new, not the solid multiyear ice they needed. According to satellite imagery, it was another record-breaking year of the lowest ice extent in history. When Charlie recruited Maya for the expedition, he told her that computer climate models projected that the North Pole would fully melt to open water in less than a few decades.

Healy finally came to rest beside an ice floe strong enough to hold their collective weight. The crew lowered the steep metal gangway onto the frozen surface below, placed orange cones at the edge of a safe work area, and conducted rescue drills. The remaining science party attended a safety on ice briefing before they were allowed to don insulated dry suits and head out. Maya looked at the snow-covered expanse as she descended the gangway. It looked like a windswept desert of white sugar with aqua melt pools in the recesses.

Almost everyone disembarked for ice liberty. It was the first time any of them had been off the ship in more than a month. Several Coasties stood guard on the perimeter with harnesses over their shoulders, ready to assist with any necessary rescues. Maya looked for Charlie but didn't see him. Instead, she spotted Ned with a rifle slung over his back. She heard he was a Coast Guard sharpshooter on polar bear patrol, although there had been no sightings to date.

The scientists took photos of the experience, posing in clusters and with the Coasties. Ned and Malcolm, the meathead bro duo, each posed with two snowballs in front of their real testicles. Maya wondered how many times they had made that joke, but she still laughed. The day's venture wasn't for standard operations or for science but for fun and, more important, morale.

She walked lightly across the snow. *Not land*, Maya had to remind her feet. Beneath the drifts was a sheet of ice more than two meters thick, forming continuously in layers, like a crustacean shell. Below the ice lay two miles of ocean. *I am walking on an ocean*, she thought, feeling so big and so small at the same instant.

Charlie had tried to describe the northern edge of the world, or "the end," as some called it. There wouldn't be another human soul to the north until you passed over the pole and headed back south to a military base on the tip of Greenland. But Maya didn't look north. She looked up to the sky, because up was now "the end." Maya usually avoided thoughts of mortality, but they couldn't be avoided here on the Arctic Ocean at the end of the end.

Her boot slid on refrozen ice. Maya fell and heard a crack beneath her. Jack broke from the crowd and ran toward her.

"Stay back!" Maya yelled, as she scrambled away on all fours.

Jack kept running but skirted the crack and lay down as he stretched out a hand.

"You run straight into danger," Maya said, angry. "How are you still alive?"

But Jack gave her that brilliant, beautiful smile and shrugged. "Luck?"

It felt like Maya's heart traveled painfully up and then had to be swallowed down; a gulp of something too large for her throat. She cursed herself silently in Spanish, then grasped Jack's hand.

~~~

CAPTAIN MARTIN WEBER stood by the windows of the bridge, watching ice liberty with binoculars. He searched for smiles and found a few here and there. One of the red-suited scientists loped around the ice in circles, probably to remember the feel of running. *We needed this*, Weber thought.

The Morale Committee was already getting a jump-start on the North Pole celebration. They hung ropes of tinsel and candy canes in the mess deck while Christmas carols played on the pipes. The committee didn't know that *Healy* would never reach the North Pole. In a matter of hours, the ship would make an about-face only three days short of 90°N latitude and cut its way home at a steady three knots.

That morning, the ship's commanding officers received an email brief stating that Congress had initiated an immediate transfer of the entire branch of the US Coast Guard to the Department of the Navy. Weber had to read the email several times to believe his eyes. This transfer had only happened twice in history, during the First and Second World Wars. All Coast Guard missions were canceled, and all ships were ordered to return to port for reassignment.

At least one of the captain's prayers had been answered. According to the brief, the majority of nations had agreed to make a defense effort imperative. The world's best engineers had already been summoned to South America along with astrophysicists and nuclear physicists. (Weber supposed hostile countries would now come together to use the very weapons they created for one another.) The US government backed the Effort with full support and now called upon its own specialized resources: interpreters, helicopter pilots, drone technicians, loadmasters, canine squads, and so on.

Weber immediately emailed his wife, Karen, with news about the brief. She was grateful but also wanted to know about any plan to address the country's immediate food and fuel shortages and the violence that came with them. Karen was patient (she was always patient with his long voyages) but said it would be easier to bear if she knew what steps were being taken if the crisis progressed. Their neighborhood watch had organized an armed patrol. Karen and the kids could be all right for a while, but the canned food in their basement larder wouldn't last forever.

Weber confided that he was just as much in the dark. Eventually Karen's patience wore thin:

> But you're a captain in the military! How can you not know what the government's going to do?

Karen taught fifth grade English. In her controlled sentence structure, Weber had never seen an exclamation point. He typed out:

> I don't think the government knows what the government's going to do.

He deleted the sentence. After three more attempts, he finally ended with:

> I loved to watch you comfort our children when they were sick. I've always meant to tell you that. You are my hero for always

trying to take away their pain. I know you will make the right decisions.

He heard footfalls behind him as *Healy*'s second-in-command approached the windows of the bridge and cleared his throat.

"We're ready with the new coordinates, sir," he said. "Want me to call everyone back on the ship?"

Weber saw one of the Coasties throw a wet snowball smack into the chest of another.

"In a bit," he said, trying to hide a smile in spite of it all.

SIXTEEN

THINGS ARE BEING DONE

KOUROU, FRENCH GUIANA
SEPTEMBER 10
T-MINUS 144 DAYS TO LAUNCH

BEN AND AMY sat in the back of a Humvee, fighting sleep. Four hours was not enough rest for a sleep-deprived body, but it would have to do. Amy took Ben's hand and squeezed. Back in California, in what seemed like an alternate reality, she used to say, *It's us against the world, babe.* But here they were, doing their very best to save that world. In terms of chess, they were the queen and king, sitting with a core team of bishops, knights, and rooks in a swarm of pawns. The queen was the power player, the mover and shaker; the king was admittedly the less glamorous piece, but he kept his army alive.

And what an army it was! Their defense effort was in full force at more than fifty thousand bodies encircled by two layers of protection: the original security gates of the space center and the outer Effort perimeter. The center's gates wrapped around security headquarters and its kennel, the administration complex, the Ariane rocket launcher integration facilities, payload prep and fueling stations, the railway tracks connecting them, and a new infirmary set up in the gutted Vega rocket facilities.

The Effort's security perimeter cast a much wider net that included the center's public facilities, the Effort's vast military barracks, the Pariacabo wharf by the Kourou River and the desalination plant they were installing beside it, the Kourou Station with its fifteen-meter dish antennae and no-break power supply, and the Kourou air-field. Ben was told about additional security that extended beyond the perimeter's southeast border for forty miles along the highway leading to Cayenne, the capital of French Guiana. Access to the international airport, main seaport, and French naval base had to be protected.

The Effort's security team had instituted a no-fly zone over the entire perimeter, but luckily for Ben, there was still a persistent swell of human activity. Noise helped ease his crippling anxiety with an assurance that things were being done. *Things are being done things are being done things are being done things are being done* looped in the background din of Ben's thoughts.

"You had to tell them the truth," Amy said, watching him carefully.

He did. Ben needed the brain trust of the world to solve the impossible. For one of a few times in his life, his own brain was not enough. On September 1, Ben had used the UN's back channels to world leaders in order to confirm a high probability of impact and call upon their resources.

"We needed the US to pledge support," Amy insisted.

Again, she was right. The president had sole authority over the country's nuclear arsenal, which they needed for the HYCIV's nuclear charge. In order to get cooperation, Ben had to divulge the full truth: that NASA's own trajectory calculations predicted 89 percent probability of impact. With that, the president finally committed the country's nuclear arsenal and military might.

"NASA's trajectory will leak to the public. Maybe it already has," Ben said, miserable. "The world's gonna go to shit, Amy."

"You don't know that."

But he did. At the annual Planetary Defense Conference, Ben had played out many impact scenarios where mass hysteria set off a chain reaction of events. First came the hoarding, looting, and runs on banks. Then came the breakdown of supply distribution networks and municipal services. With no access to clean water, food, medicine, waste disposal, electric power, currency, and all things that made habitation for dense populations possible, people grew desperate and violent. All impact scenarios drew upon the outcomes of real-life, localized disasters that were then multiplied up to a human population of 7.5 billion.

But even knowing the consequences, what else could Ben have done? The Effort needed a miracle, but short of that, it needed a nuclear arsenal and the best engineers alive.

Things are being done things are being done things are being done things are being done...

Amy sighed and rested her cheek on Ben's bony shoulder. He smelled her freshly bleached hair, a familiar aroma that wasn't unlike Chinese food. Amy had long stopped caring about her appearance, but she hadn't stopped caring about Ben's manic fear of time running out. She promised to keep her roots bleached a matching pale yellow to keep him from calculating how many days had passed since he last measured them (human hair grows 1.25 centimeters a month, he said). Ben already stared at the digital seconds of his watch for too long as they blurred with the speed of change.

Once their jeep cleared the center's security gates, Amy called out to the driver by his first name and asked to stop. (She always seemed to know the things he never bothered with: names, birthdays, who had kids, who had pets that were treated like kids, etc. She had read that Dale Carnegie book *How to Win Friends and Influence People*, like, a million times.)

"I'll help process the new arrivals at security," Amy said. "Then I'll review the rest of the engineer CVs."

She looked so exhausted and serious, so unlike his Amy.

"You could stay with me. I feel taller with you," he half-joked.

She kissed him goodbye and said, "Let's get to work."

Ben continued toward the administrative building complex. The Effort's scientific core team had split into factions, and the Janus building was now the residence of the nuclear team. In the next twenty-four hours—or however long he could stay awake—Ben would make two additional stops farther north within the space center grounds: to Jin-soo and the HYCIV team in the largest cleanroom at the payload prep facilities, and then to Marcel and the staff working to complete the Ariane rocket in the launcher integration building.

As Ben exited the elevator on the top floor of the Janus building, he immediately heard a loud swell of voices and languages spilling from the meeting room. The quiet UN minions and overlords were gone, transferred to another building in the administrative complex with the rest of UN leadership as they battled incoming government officials to remain a neutral arbiter of the defense effort. Comparatively, members of the nuclear team were loud as schoolchildren.

More than seventy physicists stood or sat in large clusters facing walls lined with electronic whiteboards. Lopsided diagrams and long equations were scrawled across one to the other as onlookers discussed and called out in their own native tongues. The nuclear team was responsible for a nuclear payload capable of a one-gigaton explosion. This was an unprecedented amount of power; twenty times larger than the biggest man-made nuclear bomb: the Russian Tsar Bomba, or King of Bombs, that detonated a yield of fifty megatons of TNT in 1961.

At the back corner table, where the science core once gathered, Chuck sat watching with his meaty arms crossed. The Professor sat a few feet from the entrance in his lobby armchair against the wall. The octogenarian was much more functional these days, admittedly with the help of strong pain medication. His expression was relaxed and loopy with opiates—or maybe he was just giddy to be surrounded by so much math. For inside this tropical Tower of Babel, math was the universal language. All the other languages were a barrier that required either several interpreters or one of the best.

"Love!" Ben shouted.

She was the only interpreter Ben used. Whenever he called her name—*Love! Love!*—all the English speakers in any given room would look at him like he was crazy. Ben took a seat next to Chuck as Love emerged from the babble dressed in rumpled culottes and a sleeveless shirt that showed off her shiny arms and collarbones. She had started growing out her hair, but Ben began to hallucinate that he could see it growing and humbly asked that she cut such an obvious indicator of passing time. As for the men, they had to be freshly shaven or bearded. Ben couldn't stand the in-between grizzle sprouting right before his own eyes.

"You look...better," Love said carefully to Ben. "You needed the rest."

But Ben ignored her, just as he ignored the needs of his body.

"What'd I miss?"

"Just lots of math."

"Just?"

She took a seat on Ben's right side. Both Ben and Chuck were left-handers who liked to write their own notes. In fact, there was a surprising number of lefties among the nuclear physicists. Ben spotted two members of his core team: Julie Schmidt from Lawrence Livermore and Ziggy Divjak from Stanford and Los Alamos. Julie used her left hand to point out a piece of an equation that Ziggy was writing, also with his left. Only the Professor used his right hand to hold up his cane like a pointer stick in a lecture.

Ziggy handed his marker to Julie when he saw Ben. He flashed an unmistakable grin that made his old, elfin face look a few decades younger as he excused himself from the fray.

"I have a surprise," Ziggy told Ben.

"I hate surprises."

Ziggy quickly got to the point.

"Oleg and Yuri have finally arrived in Kourou."

"When?"

But Ben knew before he finished asking the question; it had

to have been while he was sleeping. Only four hours of rest after days of no sleep, and he was already out of the loop. The arrival of the two Russian physicists was a long-awaited event. Luckily for the Effort, Oleg and Yuri were retired from the Russian Ministry of Defense, which meant they could travel freely outside of the country. Both men took the same flight from Moscow just before the Kremlin closed the borders and banned international travel. Russian diplomats had tried to block their connecting departure from Heathrow Airport, but the British government didn't want to force two individuals back on a plane against their will. Oleg and Yuri had to remain in London until the UN could successfully intervene on their behalf.

"They're on their way from security," Ziggy said, more than thrilled at the chance to reunite with more ex–Cold Warriors like himself.

In the winter of 1992, one month after the fall of the Soviet Union, Ziggy had contacted two directors of its secret nuclear weapons labs to invite them to the United States. The security of Russia's nuclear arsenal—which had kept the United States in its crosshairs for the last forty years—was now especially threatened in the political vacuum.

The ex-Soviet directors, Oleg and Yuri, agreed to a tour of Los Alamos and Lawrence Livermore National Laboratories. What's more, they returned the invitation. That February, Ziggy, Julie, and four other senior US scientists arrived in Sarov, a city that had long been removed from all government maps. Ziggy once described to Ben the surreal experience of stepping out of a Russian plane and into the strong hug of Oleg and the gentle embrace of Yuri. "Unknown enemies," Ziggy explained to Ben, "but here they were waiting for me in the bitter cold like old friends."

Both the Russian and US scientists were eager to collaborate. Most were active in the field in September 1983 when a nuclear world war was avoided by the split-second reaction of one Soviet official named Stanislav Petrov. Petrov saw an early warning system alert of a missile attack from the United States but reported it to his superiors as a false alarm. Not only was this gut decision correct, it also saved the United States and its NATO allies from a mistaken counterattack by the Soviets and the large-scale nuclear war that would have followed. Millions of lives were saved by one man holding a phone and acting on a hunch. This was the Cold War legacy. How could its retired warriors not jump at the chance of redemption?

Doors to the Janus meeting room opened with Acosta from the Brazilian United Nations in the lead. She stood to the side as Oleg and Yuri walked in. Oleg was large and thick with dark hair sprouting up from the collar of his shirt. Added to a full beard, and wide upturned nose, he resembled a silver-backed gorilla. Yuri, on the other hand, was reed thin and soft-spoken with sparse white hair. Ziggy rushed to them with open arms. Julie was close behind with her own crinkled, beaming smile. Even the burly and gruff Oleg kissed her age-spotted hand most sweetly.

Ben let the Cold Warriors have their moment. He had met the two Russians only virtually through email. Oleg and Yuri used to be more involved in their earlier days, especially after 1994, when comet Shoemaker-Levy 9 impacted Jupiter. Physicist Edward Teller, known as "the father of the hydrogen bomb," even made a public proposal for nuclear weapons designers of the Cold War to collaborate on future planetary defense. Who better, he argued, to leverage old arsenals of nuclear fusion warheads than the very men and women who built and tested them?

But Ben was only seventeen at the time of the comet's collision. Since then, national politics and acts of aggression interfered, as they often do. Teller's dream of collaboration was never realized. At least, not until now.

Ben wasn't a hugger, but he grabbed Oleg as soon as the man was within reach.

"You two are a sight for sore eyes," he sighed.

"Had to make sure you didn't fuck this up by yourself."

Oleg meant it as a joke—he was a ball-buster for sure—but it still made all of Ben's muscles quake. Oleg clapped him loudly on the back with a friendly smile, but whispered, "Breathe, man!" through his dentures. Ben had to be helped back to his chair.

I am not alone in this, Ben told himself. *Together, we are getting things done. Together...*

Oleg and Yuri took the two chairs on Chuck's left. Discussion among the physicists continued briefly until Ben caught his breath and yelled for everyone to shut up for a minute so he could summarize their main challenge to Love: nuclear weapons weren't built to vaporize a comet or asteroid flying through space at tens of thousands of miles per hour; they were built to hit static, terrestrial targets.

"Them, in other words," Ben said, pointing to the two former Soviets on his left.

Oleg chuckled and looked to Ziggy and Julie, his old counterparts in the Cold War.

"Or them," he said, pointing.

"Or them!" chirped a Pakistani physicist, pointing to an Indian physicist, who laughed and ruefully pointed back, happily surprised as anyone to be in a room full of enemies turned allies using weapons of mass destruction to save all of creation.

"It's a strange universe for sure," Ziggy remarked, speaking for all of them.

SEVENTEEN

MAYA AND JACK

REGAINING ACCESS TO the internet at lower latitudes came as a shock to *Healy*'s passengers. In the weeks where bandwidth was too limited, media outlets had reported multiple leaks of classified information from NASA claiming an 89 percent probability of impact with comet UD3. With that, all hell had broken loose, and the president had to call a national state of emergency to combat food scarcity and rampant crime.

When Maya visited the UC Santa Barbara website, she saw one of those yellow emergency announcement bars pinned to the top. The university had canceled classes and shut down administration indefinitely. Only one of Maya's colleagues at the Marine Science Institute had replied to her emails. Jennifer was a second-year postdoc who had gone to stay with her parents at their vineyard after the university shut down. She wrote:

> Needless to say I've been pretty drunk during the worst of this. And pooping. Grapes are the only fresh produce we have left, so we're eating them by the pound. So much pooping.

(Maya was envious. She missed fresh produce—and wine—and a good poop in her own private bathroom.)

Jennifer's parents were also hosting two migrant workers and their three children, who had nowhere else to go. The migrants' employer from the recent harvest was a wine hobbyist who owned the neighboring property and ran operations remotely. Jennifer said his land was taken over by "very unfriendly" squatters who turned the family away. Jennifer wrote:

Of course we wanted to save this hungry family. And we did. But we can't save the next one that shows up at our doorstep. Would you let your own family starve to feed five strangers? I mean, those are the choices we'll have to make in the short term. In the long term, I think we're all fucked anyway. That could be my hangover talking. Or not.

There wasn't much pause before she added:

I'm sorry about your family. And no, I haven't heard anything about your hometown except that it's one of the cities that've gone dark.

Jennifer wrote that the army was keeping order in major cities like Los Angeles, San Francisco, and San Diego. The rest had to make due with local law enforcement. Cities such as Oakland, Stockton, San Bernardino, Compton, Merced, and Modesto had "gone dark" with power blackouts and rampant violence. There was no reportage or contact because no one could safely get out and no one wanted to go in.

Maya hadn't received an email from her mother, father, three sisters, or neighbors on all sides of the small house where she grew up since news headlines announced the first leaked trajectory. She told herself to stop hitting Refresh only to stare at an empty inbox. The memory of her father's last visit to campus replayed in her head.

He came alone. Maya's sisters all had young children and husbands to care for. Maya's mother came less often because she was usually saddled with grandchildren and neighborhood children who needed watching by a good abuela who didn't say no. Mr. Gutiérrez made the four-and-a-half-hour drive to UC Santa Barbara every couple of months, not out of obligation but because his "heart sang with joy" to see his own daughter working as part of such an impressive institution of higher learning.

They always toured the university grounds and lingered at the library. Maya's favorite was the first edition of Charles Darwin's *On the Origin of Species*, and his was the collection of old Bibles and illuminated manuscripts. When there was enough daylight, they went to an early dinner. Maya chose a seafood restaurant by Goleta Beach so she could spoil her father with a view of the Pacific at sunset.

He didn't turn down the chilled beer she ordered, but he did nurse it with slow sips and long blinks against the wind at dusk. *Doctor Gutiérrez*, he said, and smiled before biting into a crunchy shrimp tail. He said it again to savor the wonderous pair of words with his meal and added, *You are our American Dream come true. Your mother and I never would've stayed for ourselves. It was too hard...* The hands that held his beer bottle looked twenty years older than the wrists they were attached to. Not that Mr. Gutiérrez wasn't careful. As a mason, his skilled hands put food on the table and a roof over his head.

When Maya asked after her sisters, her father pulled out a plastic sandwich bag that was tucked in his pocket. Maya's mother sent photos of her nieces and nephews from parties, communions, and weddings. Maya sorted through the photographs until she found her niece and godchild Angelina. The girl was still young enough for pigtails but old enough for missing milk teeth. The tip of her tongue poked out of the front gap in her smile.

Maya couldn't remember what shirt her father wore, or what dishes she ordered, but she clearly remembered that moment of loving her life and at the same time wondering if it had to come with such a high cost. She had been thirty-five at the time, an age that places you in the high-risk category for pregnancy—if you are still able to get pregnant at all. Maya wondered if wanting it all was asking too much too late. Even then, before the letters UD3 had meaning, she felt time escaping her grasp.

An hour slipped by before Maya could force herself to stand and walk out of *Healy*'s science lounge. A group of Morale Committee members were in the stateroom corridors. They no longer planned talent shows in the helicopter hangar or *Biggest Loser*-style weight loss competitions for the Coasties. They no longer asked about feelings and coping. They didn't say much at all as they knocked on each door, forcing entry if need be, to check on the occupants. Maya heard that more than a few of the scientists had to be checked into sick bay, but she wasn't curious about details.

The committee members finished removing a door handle with a power drill, but Maya's gaze didn't follow them into the stateroom's interior. She was determined to stay focused and functioning in the present. Looking to memories in the past—where Maya was in her parents' backyard surrounded by the noise of family and Latin pop music, grilled corn stuck uncomfortably between her teeth, the nightly breeze gentle on her bare skin, and the warm-toasted feeling of love, belonging, clear purpose, and an unquestioning understanding of reality—was just too painful. Looking to the future—anarchy, madness, starvation, and, unless UD3 could be stopped, the death of everyone and everything she knew with the planet scorched into one big fossil—was too terrifying.

Maya headed to the galley, where breakfast was just finishing up. The OSU professor had evacuated back in mid-August, but his postdoc was sitting idle in the mess deck, staring down into the small void of a black cup of coffee. It wasn't until Maya touched his shoulder that he jolted, blinked, and then nodded. He didn't ask why, as in *Why do we keep working? Why does it still matter?* Wordlessly, they sought out Malcolm and two other crane operators at the Coasties' table. All stood at the ready, needing to be needed.

∿∿∿

WHEN THEY FINISHED their water-sampling cast at the stern of the ship, Maya and the postdoc, Carl, packed up their equipment. Carl's eyes drifted south to open water. Maya wondered if Carl felt the same nail-biting impatience to return to civilization mixed with gut-twisting fear over what they would find.

"Hey you."

Maya turned to see Jack taking her picture.

"You should really ask for permission," Maya said, pulling down the brim of her hard hat.

Jack promised to stop taking her picture, but only if she promised to stop hiding her pretty face. When Maya looked up again, Carl was walking off toward the hatch, leaving them to the magnetic pull and push within their interactions.

"We're finished collecting samples," Maya said, "Just packing up. I'll test them later in the day—"

Maya stopped because Jack was trying not to laugh. His mouth twisted into a smile, then a grimace. Giggles slipped out like effervescent bubbles from below the surface.

"Sorry," he said. "It's just that it seemed so important. Didn't it?"

His inhale hitched like a sob.

"Our mission *was* important," Maya insisted. "It *is*."

Her hard stare suddenly softened.

"Remember our whales?" she asked. "Remember those giants doing backflips for us? Weren't they important?"

He winced at the shared memory but nodded. Maya stared up at him, soaking in every detail: his pretty eyes and gold-tipped lashes; his delicate nose; his violent scars and the way they left pale, warped tracks through the growth of his new beard. Jack was a delicious temptation that had fallen into her lap right when she needed him.

Maya leaned in and brushed Jack's lips with her own. He went rigid and tried to read her expression, but Maya felt she had already made herself clear. Slowly and carefully, Jack leaned in until they were breathing and exhaling the same air. His cracked lips joined hers. It was a gentle kiss, but when he started to pull away, Maya clasped her fingers behind his neck. No more walking away. Jack was hers until she let go.

Maya took his hand and led him below deck, straight to her stateroom. Stealing suddenly shy glances at one another, they unzipped their anti-exposure suits and unlaced their boots. Jack lay down in her rumpled sheets and reached for her from the bottom rack. The mattress was so narrow that they had to face each other on their sides to fit. Maya kissed him deeply and snaked a hand past his winter layers to feel the muscles of his flat stomach. Soon their hands were all over each other and their clothes came off piece by piece until they were two animal bodies, warm, odorous, and pressed together.

"Should I . . . ?" Jack whispered.

She pulled back to look at him, lips shiny with saliva.

"Get a condom from my room?" he asked with a thick voice, inching forward to close the gap between their faces.

She snorted a laugh just as he moved to kiss her. She couldn't help it.

"I'm flattered," she said. "Hope I'm worth your emergency condom."

"I have more."

She looked at him with such intensity that he admitted to having a whole box. Now it was Maya's turn to giggle uncontrollably.

"Sorry, sorry," she kept repeating. "Sorry, but you'll have to excuse me."

When she turned to get up, Jack tensed and held her tight until his senses overcame his lust. Maya felt around for her rumpled jeans and sweatshirt. There was a pair of flip-flop sandals by the door. By the time she stepped into the corridor and headed to the bathroom, she wasn't giggling anymore.

A whole goddamn box, she thought. Maya could understand one condom maybe, zipped into the change pouch of his wallet (because what man ever bothered with loose change), but a whole box? Did he sleep around that much?

Maya dropped her jeans down to her ankles and hit the head. *So what?* she thought. What did it matter when he was *here*, *with her*, looking so beautiful and bright against *Healy*'s drab interior. Maya told herself to be happy for that whole box of condoms. After all, getting pregnant in this mess would be the sorriest of states. Almost as a reminder, Maya saw a dried streak of reddish fluid smeared on her inner thigh, sticky to the touch. Her period was early. If Jack had noticed, he hadn't said anything.

When Maya returned to her room, he was gone. *So what?* she thought again, ignoring the sharp sting of being left. *You laughed at him, and now he's gone. Guess I'll be one less notch in his bedpost.* The door opened and closed quickly as Jack ducked inside. He didn't look her in the eyes or say anything as he kicked off his unlaced boots and sat back on her bed with an expression that was patient but eager. Looking at him and imagining what they would do made her body warm again. Before she could enjoy it fully, there was one more embarrassment to suffer through . . .

"I might get the white sheets a little messy—"

"S'fine," he said quickly. "We'll wash them in the sink later."

Maya walked into his embrace.

~∿∿∿~

WILL HE STAY? she wondered. (How many women had asked that question over the millennia? How many more until time ran out?) In Maya's limited experience, it was better to be the one doing the leaving. She sat up and swung her bare feet onto the cold floor.

"I gotta work," she said with a shiver.

They both knew she didn't *have* to work, she only *wanted* to work—and not as much as she wanted to be held in his warmth.

"Come back to bed," Jack said.

He yawned. Even with his face contorted, he was utterly handsome. *Just a little bit longer*, Maya told herself.

Crawling back beside his body was divine. She reveled in their stinkiness—musky sweat and thick applications of deodorant—like a French cheese. The bristles of his beard and his smooth lips stretched into a smile against the back of her neck. No doubt he knew his effect on women (and 7 percent of the male population as well, Maya figured).

"John and Yoko spent all day in bed together," he said, his voice muffled. "How's that for romance?"

His words tickled her skin.

"Love isn't romance," Maya said slowly. "It's something stronger."

She thought of her parents and how much they needed one another. What started as romance had become a necessity for survival. Maya was prepared for an awkward moment, but Jack wrapped his wiry forearms around her. She loved the threat of his genitals glancing her buttocks.

"That was just the first time," he finally whispered. "It gets better."

Maya believed him.

They listened to the vibrations of *Healy*'s engines until they suddenly stopped. An announcement from Captain Weber came over the pipes: the Navy had ordered *Healy* to stay at sea and await further instruction.

EIGHTEEN

INTOXICATION

◀ACK AND MAYA dressed for warmth and donned anti-exposure suits before heading outside into the night. Floodlights lit *Healy*'s deck in sharp relief. Jack saw other people gathered, but not as many as he hoped. Those who were holed up in their staterooms continued to fall into an unresponsive state, especially when they were alone. It reminded Jack of the eagles that drowned slowly in Seward Harbor, with no sign of struggle, only automatic blinking and breathing.

Jack and Maya stood by *Healy*'s outer railing and looked up. The polar night sky was like nothing Jack had ever seen; the multitude of constellations never looked so bright nor the darkness between them so devoid. Of all the remote places in Jack's many journeys, none were as remote. The green, glowing wisps of Aurora Borealis, looming dreamily above them, was one more testament to that fact.

Maya was practically pacing in place with excitement. She said the Northern Lights phenomenon was caused by solar wind interacting with atmospheric gases, but the scientific cause didn't seem to match the fantastical thing itself. Jack's imagination raced to find earthly comparisons for such a vivid green. It reminded him of the chartreuse absinthe that he drank in the French Quarter of New

Orleans. He could almost taste wormwood and green anise mixed with dissolving sugar on his tongue.

"You know that saying?" Maya asked, *"I wouldn't marry you if you were the last man on Earth!"*

Jack laughed until the cold air stung his throat.

"So, would you?" he asked.

But she wasn't smiling.

"I know I'm convenient," Maya admitted. "But I decided that I can't care why you're with me. I need you too much."

Jack took a breath and sighed. He promised Maya that he would say the words, but she had to promise not to say them back. He didn't know why, but that was when his relationships always went to shit. Maya frowned and said she didn't know which of them to feel sorrier for. Jack nodded, but he still put an index finger on her shivering lips. He needed to do this one thing right.

"I love you."

Closer to the flat horizon, clear of the Northern Lights, the Man in the Moon returned their gaze. His right eye socket was an impact crater, one of the largest in the solar system, Maya remarked. Getting hit with a cosmic impact was all a matter of probability.

"We could probably see UD3 with a regular telescope by now," she said, pressed against him.

It was such an awful fact that she whispered it.

"At least, that's what the news said while we were up by the North Pole. It's hard to find any coverage that's current."

Maya turned to Jack and asked, "Have you heard from your parents?"

"I told you, they emailed me while we were close to the pole, but I'd rather not talk about it."

"But since then?"

Jack said nothing, and she let the matter drop. The truth was that Jack stopped visiting the science lounge ever since the subject line "goodbye" appeared in his inbox with his mother's name beside it. Of course he would read her email eventually, and any others that may have followed, just not now. He couldn't. Could. Not. And so, when Maya talked about the world viewed through the internet, and all its terrible changes, he listened but said nothing.

They heard chanting close by. Jack turned to his right and saw one of the Coasties with her head bent over folded hands, lips moving quickly in prayer. There were many religious Christians making themselves more known. Several had instituted group prayer in the helicopter hangar and daily Bible readings broadcast over the pipes.

"Do you believe in God?" Jack asked Maya.

They had talked about so much over the days and nights spent together—but not that. Jack had been inside her body many times, and yet this question seemed to be almost too personal.

"I was raised Catholic," Maya said, after a long pause.

It wasn't an answer, only the start of an answer, at best. Jack wondered if Maya fell into the sizable population that couldn't defend the existence of God, but couldn't give up on it, either. After all, a world without a supreme being made more sense but was the bleaker alternative.

Jack was brought up Episcopalian and went to Sunday school in a stone church with stained-glass windows. As he grew older, Jack's faith slipped in unnoticeable degrees all the way down to a turning point. It came while Jack was stationed in Darfur, documenting a refugee camp with four other photographers and a shared interpreter. Stories from survivors were horrific: genocide, child soldiers, gang rape, mutilation, slavery . . . Jack saw a toddler no more than a few years old with a bloated stomach due to malnutrition and a parasitic Guinea worm sprouting from his bald head like a dangling string of spaghetti.

Surrounded by the carnage that humans inflict on one another, added to the random and senseless suffering that was life, Jack reached a state of overload. Another photographer, a more seasoned professional with a cockney accent and jaded sense of humor, saw Jack standing and staring. "Whatever God created us sure didn't stick around, mate," the man said with a clap on the back. And that was when the God in Jack's mind finally flatlined. He knew the saying *There are no atheists in foxholes*, but here he was, an old hat to war zones, shelling, and shooting.

"Pretend, for a sec, that you don't believe," Jack said to Maya.

He didn't want to debate something about which he had already reached a conclusion. He wanted to debate the things that God was invented to solve: chaos, meaninglessness, suffering, and death without heaven...

"Where does that leave us?" Jack asked. "Are you and I just walking, talking stardust?"

Maya squinted for an extended period of rumination. Then she spoke of her time as a graduate student under Dr. Charles Brodie, *Healy*'s chief scientist. In his office at Berkeley, there was a coffee table book of glossy color photos taken by the Hubble Telescope. Maya picked it up one day as he excused himself to take a phone call.

"I saw these giant columns of glowing gas and newborn stars," she said. "The biggest...*thing* in existence that I'd ever seen, that any human has ever seen. And it was so, so beautiful. Neon yellow, aqua, pink...I found out later that it was digitally colored," she said with a smirk. "I felt cheated. At first."

Maya said she got to thinking about what she was actually seeing: the birth and death of stars seven thousand light-years away digitally captured by an unparalleled feat of imaging technology, then assigned the colors of tropical sea life by a retoucher, printed on an assembly line, exchanged for monetary currency at a Barnes & Noble, and finally given on a wedding anniversary. Was that book and its pictures just reconfigured stardust, or was Maya seeing a wonder nearly beyond imagination?

She stopped talking abruptly. Her jaw hung slack.

"I just saw the streak of a satellite," she said. "It maybe..."

She tried to look at the sky in her peripheral vision.

"Maybe it was them?"

"Who?" Jack asked, craning his head back.

"The International Space Station," Maya said sadly. "I read online that there was no way to evacuate the astronauts."

Jack asked how that could be the case when something got them up in space in the first place. Maya shook her head.

"They're still up there. I guess they'll always be up there."

Jack didn't like the idea of a haunted space station where the bodies floated like their ghosts. When the cold was too much to bear, he took Maya by the hand and led her back indoors. Sexual relationships were forbidden on *Healy*, but rules were no longer anyone's biggest concern. In the red-lit corridors, they saw Ned exiting a bathroom with a stumble. Jack asked if he had gone on deck yet to see the Northern Lights.

"I've seen 'em before," Ned said. "More important that I take a big leak."

Maya slowed to a stop and tugged on Jack's hand. Her head cocked sideways as she looked at Ned more closely.

"Are you drunk?" she asked, with the corner of her mouth tilted up.

Ned snorted a laugh and shrugged.

"Whoa," Jack said. "And I thought *I* was the troublemaker."

"You are," Ned agreed, looking at the couple's clasped hands. "But who gives a fuck anymore. Since we are stuck out at sea, might as well hit up the stashes we keep for going on leave. A *smoke 'em if ya got 'em* kinda thing."

Jack remembered the flask hidden in his duffel bag.

"I got 'em!" he said.

"Me too!" Maya piped up.

She smiled wide and flashed those exciting incisors. Ned smiled back and nodded.

"Why don't you join us in the Coastie lounge?" he offered, before turning and ambling down the corridor. "And bring your trouble-maker friends."

Jack and Maya looked at each other, surprised. The two lounges were territorial, each forbidden to the other.

"I'll try and get some of the scientists outta their rooms," Maya said.

It was a great excuse to knock on doors and tell others to stop crying, stop drowning slowly in this existential nightmare, and come out and get blind drunk with the Coasties.

"Meet me back at my door," Jack said, and hightailed to his stateroom.

∿∿∿

GUSTAVO WATCHED JACK rummage around in his duffel bag as the young man extended an invitation.

"You should come," Jack said, head bent down. "It'll be fun. And it'd be good for you to get out of this cramped room."

Jack found what he was looking for and held it up: a silver flask.

"I'll come," Gustavo said.

"Wait, what? You will?"

Jack blinked and asked if he was sure. Gustavo nodded and extended his hand for the flask. As far as his bunkmate knew, he took a polite sip. But in truth, Gustavo didn't part his lips. Hard alcohol made him vomit and blackout. Still, he would play along. Drunken sprees were an important part of communal life. At least they always were for his people, the Wayãpi of the Amapari River in the Amazon forest.

Caxiri beer was brewed in his village from cassava, sweet potato, and saliva from the sweet mouths of women. Exclusions were reserved for the ill, for those practicing shamanistic ritual, and for women either menstruating or heavy with child, but all others were expected to partake. The sprees began with body painting using red *urucu* and black *genipa* dyes. Then one drank until they vomited, making room for more beer. At twilight and again at dawn, there would be dancing and singing by flickering lumps of burning resin. It was a time of joy and freedom from restraint.

Of course there were costs that came with the drunken sprees: fights often broke out; a man might beat his wife; a youth might be found hanging from a tree by his neck. But pain was expected and absorbed. Pain was a certainty in life, but joy... joy was the beautiful, elusive thing one clawed toward.

Jack gave his bunkmate a warm smile as Gustavo handed back the flask.

"My friend," Jack said, "you are full of surprises."

There was a soft knock on their door. Jack went to answer it but waved for Gustavo to follow along. Two people waited in the corridor illuminated with that strange, red light that flipped on at night. One was a young, tall, and bearded white man. The other was Maya, the small pretty woman he had met briefly the first time she stood in the doorframe while Jack rummaged around his closet. Gustavo could tell from the way Maya's body drew close and brushed against Jack's, the way she had to drag her gaze away from him to look Gustavo in the eyes, that they had become lovers.

Jack no longer slept in their shared room, but he didn't disappear altogether. He left his luggage and returned to get fresh clothes and give Gustavo food stolen from the galley. Sometimes Jack even visited their room for no other reason that Gustavo could gather, other than to make sure he was all right.

"Sir?" said the bearded stranger standing behind Maya. "If I may?"

Ceremoniously, he handed Gustavo a book and a ballpoint pen. Gustavo tilted up the cover and saw his own name in print. It was his most famous poetry collection, *The Majesty*. Its cover had a crude drawing of a Brazil nut tree with its roots and branches reaching, reaching. Gustavo refused to publish the collection without that drawing included.

"What is your name?" Gustavo asked as he opened to the title page.

"Carl," said the young man.

"Did you know, Carl, that my friend drew the picture on the cover years ago? His name was Zé Cláudio."

Gustavo didn't say that it was a dead friend from the Brazilian state of Pará, a murdered friend who died next to his wife as they sat astride their motorcycle; their two bodies pressed comfortably together made for an easier target.

〜〜〜

THERE WERE MORE than twenty-five Coasties gathered in their lounge. Maya spotted Ned seated at a circular table in the corner, playing cards. Soon as Ned saw the small party—two scientists and two guest passengers standing in the doorway—he smiled and called out, "They're with me!"

On his left was *Healy*'s man-overboard dummy Ralph, propped up in a chair by the table for comic effect. Ned had his arm around the dummy and held up his fan of cards for the both of them. On Ned's right was Malcolm, the crane operator, who smiled at Maya from behind his own closely held cards. Malcolm looked a good deal more sober and had a good deal more poker chips.

The other Coasties milling about were friendly and bleary-eyed as they passed around bottles and flasks. Maya held her bottle of Bordeaux tightly. She had a corkscrew in the pouch of her sweatshirt, but it didn't feel right to open the bottle without Charlie. She had tried to tempt him out of his stateroom, but he hadn't answered her pleading from the corridor. When she bent down and looked through the hole in his door, she only saw an empty desk and dark interior.

Two women approached to say how happy they were to see Gustavo out and about. The first was Ensign Camila Ortiz and the second was Ensign Leigh Ann Gates from the Morale Committee, who loudly hiccupped and slapped her hand over her offending mouth. Maya took the opportunity to ask them to check in on the chief scientist. Dutifully, they went, hiccupping down the corridor.

Jack offered to help Maya as she fumbled with the corkscrew.

"I'm okay," she assured him. "Go play."

So he did. Jack went to the poker table and sat on Ralph the dummy's lap. He offered his flask around and made a joke about mouth herpes. The players at the table all barked and sniggered with laughter. Jack was so hard not to like. Maya herself had tried and failed spectacularly. As if he could feel her eyes on him, Jack turned to her and smiled. Every hour they had spent together had the intensity of seven. They lived in dog years now with the fear of UD3.

There were Styrofoam cups on the long table in the center of the room, probably swiped from the Java Hut. Carl the postdoc brought over a stack for Maya to pour out small portions of wine to pass out. Everyone was grateful and lifted their cups to her.

"To the Arctic," Maya said, and lifted her cup as well.

The wine was delicious. For a brief instant, Maya closed her eyes and thought of home. When she opened them, a Coastie offered her a swig from his own flask. Maya accepted and winced at the fiery liquor. More flasks and bottles were passed around. The more they shared liquor and saliva, the more they clapped each other on the back and felt like old friends.

It didn't take much alcohol to make Maya tipsy, with her small body mass and low tolerance. She usually wasn't good at parties, but she tried to talk to everyone in the room and memorize all their names and ranks. Even the poet Gustavo grew more talkative, although his Styrofoam cup of wine never seemed to diminish. No one could bring up their families back home, so they talked about their big adopted family on *Healy*. For a time, they had good drink and stories of high adventure at the top of the world. In each other, they had solace and the hope of things returning to normal.

Conversation died as the two ensigns returned to the lounge looking bereft. Ensign Ortiz now spoke to Maya in Spanish, as if they were alone. Camila's face drew tight as she said that Dr. Charles Brodie was gone. Maya shook her head.

"We opened his door when he didn't respond," Ensign Gates whispered, looking between the two Spanish speakers. "He wasn't there. We searched several floors of the ship. If he doesn't turn up, it's likely he jumped overboard."

Camila handed Maya a folded piece of paper that the scientist had left on his desk. Maya recognized Charlie's scrawl:

Maya,
   I am so sorry. I fear I am losing my mind.

NINETEEN

THROUGH A TELESCOPE

KOUROU, FRENCH GUIANA
NOVEMBER 19
T-MINUS 74 DAYS TO LAUNCH

BEN GOT A CRICK in his neck as he stood in the largest cleanroom in the payload prep facilities, looking up at two massive solar arrays. Each consisted of five segmented panels that were supported on rigs running in parallel. Ben, Chuck, and Jin-soo stood between them, turning in circles for a panoramic view. The arrays spanned more than a hundred feet from tip to tip with glossy black solar cells filling in like scales on a dragon's wing.

"The arrays are nearly operational," Jin-soo said, his voice muffled by a mask.

All engineers were required to wear white cleanroom suits, nick-named "bunny suits," with masks, hoods, gloves, and boots.

"They will be complete and tested within a month. Ahead of schedule."

"Impressive," Ben admitted.

The light that brightened Jin-soo's eyes quickly dimmed as he remembered the reality: impressive, but not enough. Propulsion by solar power would be slow and wouldn't buy them any time to complete the hypervelocity comet intercept vehicle. It was this factor that dictated timing of the February 1 launch now counting down. On reflex, Ben checked his watch. And checked it again as Jin-soo and Chuck headed to the adjoining cleaning room.

"Love!" Ben called out.

She had been floating around the groups of engineers, translating between language groups. There were just under a hundred of them, the maximum number of persons allowed while still keeping a controlled level of contamination. After Ben waved her over, Love strode to his side.

"Engineers say the arrays will be ready ahead of schedule," she said. "That's good, right?"

Ben made a noncommittal noise, something like *Hmm*. As if to answer Love's question, a partially built HYCIV spacecraft was mounted on a wheeled gurney in the adjoining room. Its skeletal frame was a seven-foot cube shape with interior mechanisms exposed. Two engineers peeled off from a larger group surrounding the spacecraft. It took Ben a few seconds to recognize Ed and Stan (aka Ponytail Guy) from the core team. They walked over to Jin-soo's side and waited in silence with their shoulders slumped.

"Love, why don't you go offer your talents?" Ben said quietly. "Please."

Love gave him a wary stare before she joined the engineers circling the HYCIV and making adjustments. Once she was out of earshot, Jin-soo gave a status update. His team had to create and model the spacecraft while they were physically building it because there wasn't time to do the steps in sequence. The skin of Jin-soo's brow looked ashen and pinched as he quickly noted a miscalculation that cost his team precious time to reconfigure.

"My fear," Jin-soo said softly, "is that either we will not complete the HYCIV by launch or we will rush production to the extent that it will malfunction after deployment."

"That's everyone's fear," Ben sighed.

Jin-soo nodded. No one objected when he quickly transitioned into the latest modifications. It was a better topic of discussion for all of them.

Under any other circumstances, Ben would have zero tolerance for denial, hypocrisy, or bullshit of any kind. But in the case of the Effort, everyone had to ignore the elephant in the cleanroom, even as that elephant continued to smoke cigars, blare a horn, and tell inappropriate limericks while popping a giant erection. *What elephant? I don't see an elephant. Nope, no elephant here.* Because they needed to keep hope. Without hope they were possibly dead, possibly extinct.

The last thing Ben remembered clearly was his pondering a theory of comets and asteroids in the back of his mind. It was supposed that one of these foreign bodies could have struck primordial Earth and deposited the very organic molecules that became the building blocks of early life. Now a foreign body was threatening to wipe out all the brilliant creation of the last 3.8 billion years. Whoever said *The Lord giveth and the Lord taketh away* wasn't kidding.

There was darkness afterward, the same nothingness of unconsciousness. Ben was jolted out of this state with the feeling of falling and losing all balance and orientation. When Ben opened his eyes, Chuck was supporting a good portion of his weight.

"You were about to black out again," he explained.

"No I wasn't." Ben stood up straight on his own. "Jin-soo was talking about the lead impactor—"

"He was ten minutes ago," Chuck said.

Ben could swear that no time had passed, but the digital numbers on his watch said otherwise. Jin-soo looked at the floor.

"Maybe you should get some sleep—" Stan started to say.

"Maybe you should cut off that scraggly-ass ponytail, for God's sake!"

Several engineers stopped their work and looked over at the shouting.

"You did cut it off!" Ponytail cried, pointing to the hood of his cleanroom suit. "With scissors! You insisted!"

Did I really do that? Ben wondered. Hazy images of either memories or dreams suddenly replayed in his head. *Oh shit. Maybe I did do that . . .*

"Go to camp," Chuck insisted.

"I can take a quick nap outside with the others—"

"I'm calling a jeep."

Ben started to protest, but Chuck cut him off and asked the other scientists for a word alone. Jin-soo closed his eyes for the briefest moment of relief before walking off to resume his duty and bear their burden.

"Take care of yourself," Chuck said to Ben, "'cause I don't want your job. Don't make me take it."

Chuck turned, but Ben grabbed two fistfuls of his cleanroom suit. They weren't through, not with a threat like that. Chuck shoved him so hard that he lost his grip and fell backward onto the floor. They had never really compared themselves physically; theirs was a playing field for mental abilities only. As Chuck stood glowering, they both suddenly realized that he could kill Ben with his bare hands. Ben looked up at his friend in tears, like a child betrayed. Chuck's expression quickly softened. He moved to lift Ben up and hold him by the shoulders.

"I'm sorry," Chuck said.

"Me too," Ben agreed, with a tear slipping off the long slope of his nose. "I'm just so tired . . ."

He started giggling.

"Do you remember the night after I proposed the duck-and-cover maneuver? Back in 2014?"

Ben was the first to respond to comet Siding Spring's initial trajectory with a fully detailed proposal for NASA leadership. Ben delivered the coordinates to gather NASA's three orbiting satellites on the other side of Mars and use the planet as a shield from comet dust that could cost millions in damage.

The proposal had been just the beginning. When NASA

immediately approved it, Ben and his JPL team were in for the longer haul. He could remember spreading a sleeping bag in front of the desk in his office. He had looked out into the hallway and saw Chuck walking past, flossing his teeth while wearing pajama pants with the Budweiser logo slapped all over them. Before bedding down for a few hours, Ben called his condo's landline, and Amy answered it for the first time. She, and all of her clutter, had just moved in permanently. *When are you coming home?* she asked. Ben remembered her using that welcome word.

"And we thought *that* comet was going to be the test of our lives!" Ben snickered.

Chuck looked like he wanted to embrace Ben but didn't know how. He squeezed Ben's shoulders until they hurt.

"If anyone can save us, it's you," Chuck whispered.

Ben dipped his head in mute humility. That he could have a real friend who believed in him, and entrusted the planet to his care, was not to be taken for granted. For a brief moment, all the voices of doubt and hysteria in his mind went blissfully silent.

"Can you call Amy and tell her I'll be at the Penthouse?" Ben finally whispered.

"Penthouse" was the nickname Ben gave to Love's private utility closet on the second floor of the Space Museum. After the three of them became fast friends who supported and clung to one another in equal measure, Amy asked if the couple could join Love for a nap. Ben wasn't too surprised when Love agreed; Amy usually got what she wanted. Now the three of them sometimes nestled together in sleeping bags like pack animals in a warm, safe den.

Ben shuffled out of the large composite cleanroom in dejected defeat. Love joined him in the gowning room moments later.

"Why do I always have to escort you out?" she grumbled, as they tossed out their masks and gloves and hung up their bunny suits. "I'm an interpreter, not an enforcer."

"'Cause you're cooler and scarier than the rest of us nerds," Ben answered. "And you're my friend. So I listen to you."

They headed through a series of fireproof doors to the front exit of the payload prep facilities, made of more than fifteen buildings that looked like connected shoeboxes. Love started to say something and then stopped when two engineers walked past in the opposite direction. Obviously, she wanted to talk to Ben alone, which couldn't be good.

"How bad do you think things are out there?" she said, once they were waiting outside. "Now that they know?"

"Out where?"

"The world."

"Love, we can't think about that. There's too many other awful things we *do* need to think about."

"Easy for you to say. You've got Amy—"

"My parents are out there," Ben said. "My sister and her children are out there. I've got aunts, uncles, cousins, the whole tribe."

"I've only got one person out there," Love whispered. "But she's everything."

Her lips trembled silently as her eyes looked up to the night sky. Ben refused to follow her gaze; he refused to look up to that fucking comet. UD3 was now visible with an amateur telescope, barely. It appeared as a muted star. This smudge of light no larger than a pinhead was an eight-kilometer apocalypse if he failed.

Everyone stared up into space now: the soldiers standing guard on the center's security gates, the engineers waiting in line for the showers on the Space Museum parking lot—everyone but Ben. He didn't need to look up to feel what everyone felt. Death was usually such a lonely, individual suffering, but extinction had a shared quality. Ben knew he was selfish to be comforted by this, but misery loves any company it can get.

When a jeep pulled up, Love remained transfixed, but Ben

wouldn't ride three miles back to the Space Museum alone. The head of the logistics team was sitting in the back seat for an impromptu meeting in transit. In his previous life before the comet, the formal Mr. Kandegedara served as undersecretary-general for operational support at the UN. Ben had only met the Sri Lankan national once before the man joined his team holed up at the administration complex. Logistics worked best unseen, except for the marvel that was the Effort's infrastructure, staff, processes, planning, and so on.

Ben climbed into the back seat of the jeep and waited. The man looked grim but calm in flowing white linen clothes. Both hands were folded over his buckled seat belt; the top hand wore a gold watch and wedding band.

"Resources will become a major concern," Kandegedara said, with a thick accent and direct stare. "We are handling the situation to the best of our abilities."

He was prepared to stop there. Logistics and security were the only teams with access to external communications and transport beyond the Effort's perimeter. Everyone else was on a need-to-know-only basis.

"Might as well tell me what's wrong," Ben said, "or I'll start guessing at hypotheticals. I can't help it. It's what I do."

Kandegedara nodded. "Medical supplies won't be an issue," he offered. "We have access to stockpiles from the CDC."

That was where the good news ended. Kandegedara reported that hoarding and looting had wiped out most of the food already in distribution. Desperate people were migrating from cities by the millions to scavenge farmland and livestock. Kandegedara had tried and failed, along with government leaders, to set up defenses for several farming belts. But the acreage was too large and scattered to protect against armed militias, especially at night. Defenses in low numbers suffered massive casualties. Adding more and more soldiers required too large a portion of the farmland's bounty to feed and maintain, canceling out the purpose of the mission.

"That's not a major concern," Ben muttered. "That's a crisis."

Kandegedara agreed and continued.

"The Effort is prioritized, of course. We will receive all initial response resources of the UN, the Red Cross, and FEMA. As for the world...the American Midwest had record-setting rainfall that ruined crops. We estimated that grain stocks, being what they are, would last ninety-one days without another harvest, but those stocks are not evenly distributed. Half are in China—"

"Will the Effort make it to a February 1 launch?" Ben cut in.

"Possibly. If we limit our growth—"

"Freeze it, then," Ben said. "Body count stays fixed as of this moment. Not a single person joins our ranks unless another one leaves."

Kandegedara's jaw hinged slightly open, but no words came. Ben saw him worriedly turning his gold wedding band with the thumb of the same hand.

"It's what needs to be done," Ben said more gently.

But the man's eyes looked far away as he thought of someone close to his heart.

〜〜〜〜

AMY WAS SUDDENLY shaking him in his sleeping bag.

"What?" Ben croaked, blinking with difficulty.

His eyes were so dry.

"You weren't answering me," Amy insisted.

Ben said he was only sleeping, but Amy yelled that his eyes had been open and vacant. She was shaking. Ben pulled his arms out of his sleeping bag so he could wrap them around her.

"Maybe it's all these pills they force on us," Ben said. "Pills for anxiety, pills for insomnia, pills for side effects from other pills...They've got me zonked."

"I thought you were dead," Amy whispered, "but then I saw you breathing."

She was probably hallucinating with exhaustion; it happened to all of them. Ben unzipped her sleeping bag and coaxed her inside. He promised that he was as fine as he could be given the circumstances. Now it was Amy's turn to offer comfort.

"The nuclear team has made lots of progress," she said quietly. "And the Ariane rocket team is ahead of schedule."

Amy didn't mention the HYCIV team. Their status was confidential, and she was shrewd enough to know there was still a problem. Amy might not see the elephant in the cleanroom clearly, but she could see the shadow it cast. She avoided the topic because she didn't want Ben to break confidentiality, which they both knew he would.

"You showered," she said, drawing closer to cuddle. "Thank God."

Ben said he had to shower for the cleanroom environment; there wasn't time otherwise. One of his muscles spasmed so violently that he startled and tried to get up, saying there wasn't even time for sleep. Amy wrestled him like a mermaid by flipping her legs up and over to pin him down with the tail end of her sleeping bag.

"I may have found a diamond in the rough today," she said, trying to be more upbeat. "We processed twenty-three Chinese engineers at security. Only one of them was a woman. She's got these faded scars on her face. From a cleft palate, I think. Her boss man doesn't like her. She's only here because she's fucking phenomenal. It's gotta be why. Maybe she could join the HYCIV team—"

"You can't count on them."

"What?"

"The Chinese. They may go rogue like Russia and the others."

"Why?"

Ben sighed. Of course he would tell her.

"We think UD3 will hit mainland China," he whispered, even

though they were alone in the Penthouse. Amy absorbed the shock of his statement in silence.

"The odds are high," he added. "But we don't want anyone to know; there are too many dangers. After threat scenario fifty-three—"

"Where the asteroid split in two, right? Didn't you role-play Germany in that one?"

Threat scenario 53 was one of the very rare scenarios where reaction time was greatly reduced. Given that a typical time frame for any successful space mission was five years, countermeasures were rushed and unsuccessful. Instead of deflecting the simulated asteroid, interceptors split the rock, half of which exploded over Dhaka with a loss of twenty million virtual people. The other half hit the Philippine Sea and caused tsunamis that devastated the coasts of Japan, Taiwan, mainland China, the Philippines, Indonesia, and Papua New Guinea

Threat scenario 53 led to 54, 55, and 56, where countries outside of a trajectory might not want to hedge their bets with a failed deflection that resulted in several dangerous pieces of an asteroid or comet. In scenario 55, North Korea attacked a Japanese spaceport with short-range missiles.

"You're a good listener," Ben said, sniffing back a runny nose.

He was too bone-tired. That had to explain his fresh tears, that and his fear of losing either Amy or his sanity—or both—before his watch ran out of time. Doctors tried to put him on antianxiety meds, but they gave him such lucid dreams, where all his fears played out, reshuffled, and played out again. Amy died in more than a few, so he stopped taking those pills and tried some different ones.

"We don't want *anyone* to know, Amy," Ben said with a yawn. "Not our own people. Not our own government."

"You don't think . . ." Amy started.

The United States didn't have a policy for cosmic impacts outside their own borders. Ben wasn't positive that the president would have given up the country's entire nuclear arsenal if he had known that

North America wasn't in the direct line of fire. He might have kept his 6,185 warheads, knowing that Russia had kept their own 6,500 warheads. This was a risk Ben couldn't take, but he was falling back asleep and didn't have the energy to explain another danger that was far from new: apathy.

TWENTY

THE KNOWN WORLD
IN PAST TENSE

SOUTH BRONX, NEW YORK
NOVEMBER 19
T-MINUS 74 DAYS TO LAUNCH

R IVKA COULD HEAR the raids outside her windows—and they were getting closer. She risked a peek through the seam of her curtains. A group of men, ten or fifteen of them, stood between an old pickup truck and an apartment complex across the street. Rivka watched as they looped chains from their trailer hitch to the iron bars on a first-floor window. The truck driver gunned his engine and burned rubber until the bars ripped off the windowpane.

She saw the axe before she heard shattering glass. One by one, the men crawled through the window of the building. When the screaming started, Rivka sank to the floor and covered her ears. Hours later there was only silence, which wasn't better when you considered the implication.

Crazy with fear and loneliness, Rivka started hearing voices. Most were shrill as they told her to run for her life. Only one, a baritone with an echo, just wanted to say hello. The voice came from a heating vent beside her bedframe. Rivka got on her hands and knees to listen.

"It's Lamar," said the baritone. "From downstairs."

A smile found its way to Rivka's lips. She hadn't spoken to anyone since her cellphone died.

"You still a Yankees fan?" she asked, projecting down the vent.

"You still a fuckin' Mets fan?"

"Hey, this vent is in my bedroom," she said. "How much can you hear down there?"

"You lesbians're better than cable."

"Pervert!"

They laughed together, but it didn't last long. Rivka and Love were past tense. So much of the known world was past tense. Rivka pulled her folded legs to her chest and rested her chin on her kneecaps. She asked how Lamar was doing.

"Hungry and thirsty," he said immediately. "Lonely," he added after a bit of silence. "Keisha... Keisha's gone."

Keisha was Lamar's girlfriend. She had a killer figure and a sharp tongue. After things got bad, Keisha moved into their building for her own safety. Lamar was huge; six-foot-five with a wide, solid frame that could crush a person like a tipped vending machine.

"I told her to stay here with the door locked," Lamar said. "But I couldn't find much to eat or drink on my own. We were starving. One day I came home and she wasn't here. No one broke in, so she must have gone looking for water and food. You got any upstairs? I filled up my tub, but it's almost dry."

Rivka lied and said no. After a pause, she asked how many days Keisha had been missing.

"Since we lost power. Eleven days."

Rivka closed her eyes and took a breath.

"They're not coming back, Lamar. Not Keisha. Not Love."

"Yeah, I know," he said, barely audible.

"Then you know we need to get out of here."

It wasn't a question. If they stayed in the Bronx, they were dead. There was no fresh water and no food. The toilets were backed up with sewage, and the streets were full of armed gangs in daylight.

"You know my cousin showed up a couple weeks ago?" Lamar said. "Last anyone knew, he was doing time up in Sing Sing for armed robbery."

Lamar said that most of the guards at the maximum-security prison deserted their posts. The remaining guards were left with the dilemma of either releasing all the men or allowing them to starve to death in their cells.

"My cousin said bad men left that prison with just their jump-suits. Real bad. And he was no angel his self," Lamar admitted. "It's not just a comet we gotta worry about, Rivka. It's us."

"People have good in them," Rivka whispered.

Her voice grew stronger as she told Lamar that she was coming downstairs with food.

"You let me in," she insisted.

All that was left in her apartment was a half bag of rice cakes, a freeze-dried meal from a camping store that promised to be beef stroganoff, and plastic liters of bottled water. Rivka dropped the food and a water bottle into her leather bag and tiptoed down the stairwell. She scratched quietly on the door of 1B. Lamar opened it several inches along the length of a security chain. Rivka waited while he scanned the hallway to be sure they were alone.

Lamar had lost weight, although there was a lot of him to begin with. He stood shivering, leaner in his Yankees jacket and skull cap. Rivka was also down two notches on her belt. Her hourglass figure had a lot less curve. The breakdown-of-civil-society diet had done them both wonders. Rivka pulled the food and water out of her bag. His look of gratitude in the moment before Lamar snatched the packages and tore them open was like nothing Rivka had ever seen. Lamar swallowed without much chewing then downed the water in gulps. His eyes snapped back to her bag.

"That was the last of the food," she told him.

Lamar asked if she was lying again, so she showed him the empty bottom of her bag.

"Bet that's a real Prada bag," Lamar said sadly. "And here we are in the same boat."

"Yeah, well, time for that boat to set sail."

Manhattan was occupied by the army, or at least it was before the blackout. To reach Harlem, Rivka and Lamar would literally have to walk through fire, or—

"We'll swim it," she told him.

Lamar shook his big head sadly.

"Can't swim."

Rivka's shoulders slumped. Her eyes gave a look like, *You're fucking kidding me?*

"Was I s'posed to learn in my tub?" he asked.

Rivka had swim lessons in the chlorinated water at the JCC on the Upper West Side and later honed her skills summering in the Hamptons. She grit her teeth and pounded a nearby wall, then whimpered. Lamar muttered an apology, but Rivka wanted none of it.

"We'll figure it out," she said.

We...such a beautiful thing, as in, acting together rather than alone. Rivka put out her other hand, the one not throbbing with pain. Lamar took it and squeezed.

"We...We'll leave after dark," she said, wiping her eyes.

Rivka went back up to her room. Not to pack—they couldn't take much with them into the water—but to plan. How the hell was she going to keep Lamar from sinking? Rivka paced her apartment as sunlight faded to twilight. What would a Boy Scout do? What would Love do, besides leave?

Water bottles! Rivka opened one and dumped pristine, mountain spring water down her kitchen sink. They needed to float more than they needed to drink. Rivka emptied all but two of the liter bottles then recapped and packed them into two plastic trash bags. Rivka tucked her hand-crank flashlight and switchblade into the zipped pockets of her winter coat. It was November, and the air grew frigid and crisp once the sun went down.

As Rivka walked out her front door carrying the trash bags

by their drawstrings, she glanced back but kept moving. Without Lamar, she might never have found the courage to leave.

"You takin' out the trash?" Lamar asked, as he locked his front door behind her.

"More like saving your life."

She placed the crinkling trash bags on the floor and handed him one of the two unopened bottles of water.

"Drink up for the road," she said, and unscrewed the cap of her own bottle.

They clunked plastic in a toast, then pounded water. Rivka handed Lamar a trash bag of bottled air. She told him about the flashlight but didn't think they should use it until they were close to the water.

"It's dark out there," Lamar warned. "Darker than you ever knew."

He wasn't kidding. If not for the fat moon, they'd be blind. Rivka faltered at the front door of their building. She gave herself only a moment to feel the physical manifestations of terror: spiked heart rate, blood pressure and respiration; a flood of stress hormones preparing her to mobilize. Lamar took her hand and pulled her forward.

Gone were all the lights, traffic, and loud pedestrians gabbing to each other and their phones. In their place was a shadowed, concrete wasteland. Rivka could hear movements and see silhouettes dodging the moonlight. Raiders only came out when they could see.

"Look," Lamar whispered. "The Mitchel Houses are over there."

He lifted their clasped, gloved hands and used them to point at the tall developments like a compass needle. Having scavenged for food in the darkest hours of the night, Lamar was used to the new reality.

Rivka found her bearings and guided the both of them west toward the Harlem River. It was slowgoing. They couldn't see their feet and kept tripping on uneven sidewalks, trash, and noisy broken glass. Despite her disorientation, Rivka knew exactly where they needed to go. Most of the Manhattan eastern shoreline rose in a steep retaining wall up to Harlem River Drive. However, there was a section that had easier access to the water, the rehabbed Harlem River Park.

Rivka used to ride her bike over the Third Avenue Bridge and cruise along the path. Before returning, she would prop her bike against the wall of concrete at the water's edge. The barrier couldn't have been more than five feet above the river, and there was a small ledge leading out to marsh grass. Rivka had seen it as she looked out to the water, thinking of her parents on the Upper West Side where she grew up and the home she made for herself in Harlem as a young adult, telling herself she could return one day.

Rivka and Lamar followed Lincoln Avenue. It was eerily empty except for abandoned cars parked along the curb, their four doors spread open. They were being watched. Rivka saw the whites of a boy's eyes before he scurried around a building. She wished she had food to give him. She also wished their trash bags weren't so glaringly white and noisy. They came across a body lying in the wide road in a patch of moonlight. Rivka could smell it better than she could see it.

"Keep moving," she whispered, when Lamar started to slow.

"What if I know him?" he asked, swiveling his head back and forth on the lookout for Keisha.

"Keep. Moving."

Her whispers were hisses. Their hands clenched so hard they hurt. Lamar helped her through the absolute darkness of the Deegan Expressway overpass. Closer to the river, they saw an ugly glow illuminate plumes of smoke in the sky. Rivka smelled burning things that were never meant to be burned: plastic, polyester, rubber, and tar. Underlying the toxic fumes was the smell of human waste. Untreated sewage from the water treatment plants must have leaked into the river.

Lamar helped Rivka climb a chain-link fence and step over train tracks to reach shoreline two hundred yards south of the burning Third Avenue Bridge. Rivka flipped on her flashlight and pointed its beam across the river. It was still too dark to see their salvation in the form of park benches and tall lampposts, but they could see flashlight beams probing the dark of their destination on the other side.

"If those people catch us trying to sneak in, they could kill us," Lamar whispered.

Rivka shrugged.

"They can't blame us any more than we can blame them," she sighed. "We all want to live."

They both stripped down to their underwear and breathed through their mouths to avoid the stench. Rivka tucked her flashlight in her jacket pocket before stuffing her clothes down the sides of her bottle-filled trash bag. She was a good swimmer, but her muscles might seize up, and then she would need a makeshift lifesaver as well.

Rivka told Lamar to hold on to each deep breath; lungs were like balloons. Lamar stood shivering, looking up at the brilliant Milky Way stretching across the sky. He had never seen it, given the city's light pollution. They both studied it for a moment, seeing only a glimpse of the infinity that was the universe. Rivka took Lamar's hand and led him to the embankment. They might both drown in the next hour, but there wasn't much choice. Rivka thought of the orchestra on the *Titanic* who played as their ship lowered into the icy water. Sometimes you need to keep doing until the very end.

The water was rancid: a mix of ash, algae, rot, shit, and who knows what else. The temperature was a shock. Rivka told Lamar to kick, kick as hard as he could. Then she forced herself forward until she was up to her neck and gasping hard. Rivka pulled on the drawstrings of her trash bag as her body stiffened.

Kick! Kick!

The current wasn't strong, but it was difficult to make her muscles unclench. Rivka's nose kept dipping into the foul water.

She fought to keep her head up and risked a look back. Lamar was flailing, his trash bag strained like an anchored buoy in a wake, but there was nothing they could do for each other now. She kept heading for shore.

Kick! Kick!

There was room in her mind for this one word only. Even as she bumped into something half submerged in the water, a something that was most likely dead, there was only that one word for that one action. Even when a flashlight beam shone into her face, she kept kicking toward it. Lamar overtook Rivka; he was a fast learner with strong legs. Once he lifted his body out of the water and onto the barrier ledge, he caught his breath and then screamed her name.

Rivka kicked until she felt Lamar grab her shoulder and haul her up. She started to weep, but he was already pulling her by the arm toward a metal railing atop the barrier. Flashlight beams blinded them. Rivka saw a semicircle of shadowy figures that did nothing as Lamar struggled to pull Rivka and their two trash bags over the railing and onto solid ground, just as they did nothing to help the couple reach the ledge. Killing strangers was one thing, but doing nothing as they drowned...that was easier. Doing nothing was always easier.

Lamar and Rivka stood by each other on wobbly legs. They held hands and shivered violently in the harsh light. For a time, no one made the first move. It was a good sign. Lamar finally set his trash bag on the ground.

"Step away from the bags," a man barked. "Or you're going back in that river."

Lamar and Rivka did as they were told. They could hear their teeth clicking together. The man stepped forward. Light outlined his body in a stark halo. His rifle was pointed at the newcomers.

"You two alone?"

Rivka could only nod.

Please be human, she prayed, repeating both the verb and noun in her head. *Be human. Be human...*

Please.

In the halo of light, Rivka saw a camouflage pattern. She stepped forward and held out her shaking hands to grab the man's sleeve. He tried to hold her back at arm's length, but Rivka's numb fingers clumsily brushed the embroidered lettering on the chest of his jacket.

"Mm-McDevitt," she managed to read aloud.

The rest of the lettering spelled out US ARMY. The soldier's elbows buckled when he heard his name, and he let Rivka cling to his torso.

"I'm sorry," he said, patting her slick bare back.

"We should've helped you two, but we're nearly out of supplies and we're getting overrun..."

The soldier McDevitt sighed but seemed to remember his humanity as he removed his jacket and wrapped it around Rivka's shivering shoulders.

TWENTY-ONE

IMPACT SCENARIO 123

AMY HAD CAUGHT a second wind. Her actions now had a vitality that was lean and feral with all its fat starved off. In the Effort, Amy had found her home, and, improbably, it was right back on a military base.

The irony wasn't lost on her; for the first half of her life, Amy wanted to be anywhere *but* a military base. Much of her teenage years was spent holed up in a tiny bedroom, living in fantasy through books, graphic novels, comics, Magic: The Gathering cards, and used D&D game sets. Soon as Amy hit eighteen, she fled like a bat out of hell, leaving military life and avoiding all the negative associations she had foresworn: blind obedience, religious dogma, monoculture, and strict cleanliness.

Amy ventured west to bustling cities and reveled in the freedom and diversity that they attracted. She went to live music festivals, visited museums, attended a campaign rally, ate at ethnic restaurants, and loitered in public libraries. The only cause to look back on her former life was the aching loneliness and depression that soon set in. Amy was a social creature used to the human bonds of a tight-knit community. As a transplant living with other transplants in cramped apartments, relationships were all new and mostly transitory. She left the friends she made as she moved away, or they left her for new jobs, new locations, or the challenge of newborn babies.

And here, in the last place she might look, a spaceport turned international military base while facing planetary annihilation, Amy had finally found that familiar feeling of caring cooperation and shared purpose—but with the right tribe this time, her *chosen* tribe. These were the men and women saving Earth, just like her beloved science fiction stories, only now it was real.

This was the realization running through Amy's mind as her body suddenly vaulted forward against a seat belt. The jeep skidded to the shoulder of the road.

"Get down!"

Both UN peacekeepers in the front seat yelled for Amy to duck down. Her eyes caught the glare of headlights reflecting off white fabric; there was a human figure in the middle of the road wearing a lab coat. The driver kept one hand on the wheel while the other unstrapped his walkie-talkie to radio headquarters. The peacekeeper in the passenger seat unholstered his gun and called back to Amy without taking his eyes off the figure.

"Ma'am—"

"For the millionth time, call me Amy."

"We don't mean to overreact, but we have to be cautious."

Because of Ben, Amy thought. She was the glue holding him together, barely.

"Unidentified person is unarmed," said the driver, relaying information back to headquarters. "Looks to be alone. Wearing a security badge. Asian—"

"Chinese," Amy stated.

The engineers from mainland China all wore white lab coats as a formality.

"The Chinese engineers are testing the solar arrays back at payload prep," she added.

The jeep was less than two miles from the building, but what an engineer was doing out in the dark, standing in the middle of road, Amy couldn't say. Static crackled from the walkie-talkie.

"There's a security detail nearby," said a voice from headquarters. "Wait for backup."

"This could all be a fuss over nothing," Amy muttered.

"He's approaching!"

The peacekeeper on the right jumped out of the jeep, shouting and aiming his gun. Amy heard the Chinese engineer shout back—but in English. She opened her window and stuck out her head for a better look. The figure in the lab coat was closer now, squinting in bright headlights.

"I know her!" Amy screamed out the window.

Her gravelly voice rose above the others.

"She's an engineer with valid clearance. Put your gun down!"

Amy continued to scream until the peacekeeper lowered his gun, but he kept a hand raised with palm out.

"We have a positive identification," the driver whispered into his radio. "Female—"

"Zhen," Amy said. "The engineer's name is Zhen."

Dr. Zhen Liu, Amy remembered as she reached for the door handle.

"Just wait," the driver pleaded.

Amy grunted but did as he advised. Another jeep sped up to a quick stop alongside them. Three peacekeepers exited with flashlights mounted on their helmets. The one in the lead was a handler with a German Shepherd on a leash. Poor Zhen looked terrified, but the large animal was all business as he dutifully sniffed her clothes and shoes for explosives. The second peacekeeper waited with his semiautomatic rifle lowered as the third patted down Zhen's lab coat for weapons and scanned her badge with a handheld device. He lifted a thumbs-up.

"Clear," said the driver. "And her badge checks out."

"I could have told you that," Amy insisted. "I'm the one who processed her at security."

The driver listened to his radio and the shouts of the peacekeepers outside simultaneously.

"The engineer asked for you by name," he told Amy. "She wants to talk to you in private, but it isn't safe."

Amy didn't blame the peacekeepers for their apprehension. They didn't know that there was little to risk when the Effort was doomed to fail. The mission had been fucked from the beginning. Even as every simulated and imaginable scenario all led to failure (as Ben divulged in frantic whispers), the Effort continued with hope of the unimaginable, the irregular. And if anyone was irregular, it was the engineer standing in the middle of the road: the only woman out of twenty-three engineers sent to represent China, also the only one fluent in multiple languages.

Amy had a burning itch to google the engineer's name. Ben said that China had majorly upped its game as a spacefaring nation. Last year, it even led the world in orbital launches. What if this engineer was a part of that? Unforgivably, the logistics team flat-out refused to grant Amy special access to the internet. She had to fly blind, aside from her own observations—and others'.

When Amy approached Jin-soo weeks ago in the payload prep facilities, he was already aware of Zhen's potential, having received multiple reports of her methods to accelerate completion and then testing of the HYCIV's solar arrays. *Her methods were completely unique,* Jin-soo said in a hoarse whisper. *And I've seen a lot in my day.* It was only after admitting Zhen's singularity that Jin-soo finally agreed to show Zhen the planned construction of the HYCIV spacecraft.

Amy dashed out of her jeep. The driver lunged out and tried to block her path, but Amy continued until their bodies collided. She put her flat hand on his chest and leaned in. The intimate gesture startled the man, as she knew it would. Amy stepped past him and waved back the security detail until they gave her a wide berth.

Zhen finally stood alone, shielding her eyes against the headlights with both hands. The black hair framing Zhen's round face lifted in the tropical night breezes and grazed her full cheeks. She motioned for Amy to come closer. Noise levels from the layers and layers of barracks surrounding the space center security gates inhibited quiet conversation. Amy walked slowly until she was close enough to see the two linear scars on Zhen's upper lip, like shiny lines of candle wax stretching to her nose. The surgeries that had repaired her bilateral cleft palate were many decades in the past but still present.

Zhen's English was accented but surprisingly rapid and precise, just as Amy remembered.

"You asked Dr. Lee to show me the plans for the HYCIV," she whispered.

Amy nodded. She had a theory about Zhen's abilities and very little time to test it. So Amy had gone straight to Jin-soo with the hope he would consult Zhen on his HYCIV build.

"It would take two years to build that HYCIV model," Zhen ventured to say to Amy, "using all the donated subassemblies on the list."

But Earth didn't have two years.

"Do you have any *suggestions*?" Amy asked, putting an edge in her voice.

That was the whole goddamn point, after all.

"Only one," Zhen said, nervously checking her watch to gauge the passing time. "There may be a way to save us. But I need your help. I must know if there is a Chinese cargo plane still parked at the airport."

Amy looked back to her jeep and said that they could all drive to the Kourou Airport in less than ten minutes. It was easily accessible and secure within the outer Effort perimeter. Any unauthorized aircraft trying to enter the no-fly zone were radioed warnings and then shot out of the sky if they continued on course. (The noise was awful. Last time it happened, Amy covered her ears with her hands and kept moving. You had to keep moving...)

"Not Kourou," Zhen said, shaking her head. "I mean the airport where the Chinese all landed. The airport in Cayenne."

The difficulty of her request increased by an order of magnitude with that destination. The international airport in Cayenne was an hour's drive from the Effort perimeter, heading southeast along the coast. Zhen would need special clearance and a large security detail.

"*If* the plane is still at the airport in Cayenne, you must arrange a meeting," Zhen insisted. "I will need to speak to Dr. Schwartz and Professor Ochsenferrrd about the plane's cargo. We must be alone. No one can know."

Zhen finally stopped to let her words sink in. When Amy tried to ask about the solution to a timely spacecraft build, Zhen interrupted.

"*If* the plane is still at Cayenne, I will explain it to Dr. Schwartz and Professor Och—Ochsenferrr—"

"Just call him Professor. I can't say his name either."

Amy waited for more, but Zhen only looked at the glowing face of her watch and said that she had to return to her team at the payload prep facilities.

"And," Amy prodded, "*if* your plane *isn't* at the Cayenne airport?"

Zhen couldn't put the horror of that alternate fate into words. And she didn't need to; Amy could read them on her faltering expression: *Then the Effort will fail. Then humanity is living on borrowed time.*

~~~~

AMY HAD TO ask Ben to slow down and enunciate into his phone. Whenever he got manic, Ben spoke too quickly for the majority of brains to comprehend. Only the Professor could follow in real time.

"Slower," Amy insisted.

They argued more and more as time ran out, but really it was Ben shouting at her like he shouted at everyone else.

"Min-i-mal. In-terr-up-tion!" Ben said with exaggerated pause and menace.

Amy hung up and swallowed the lump in her throat.

No crying, she told herself.

This went against the advisement of Effort doctors, whose recommended procedure for extreme emotional turmoil was to (1) alert your supervisor to a necessary absence; (2) pick up a small pillow from dispensaries located at all major exits and corridors; (3) seek out privacy, because emotions are contagious; (4) cry, weep, and scream into your pillow for up to five minutes; (5) discard your pillow by the side of the dispensary; (6) alert your supervisor upon your return; and (7) continue your work.

No crying, Amy insisted, and skipped to the last part—continue your work. Amy had Troy Andrews from UN leadership reserve a small conference room in the Janus building right after one of the space flight team's sessions. Amy and Troy took the same jeep to Janus and waited for the allotted time.

"You brought the drone footage?" she asked.

Troy nodded and lifted his leather briefcase. Amy could remember when she first met him, soon after he flew down from Manhattan. He had looked like a successful stockbroker with gelled hair and a sterling silver clip holding his designer tie in place. But that was the beginning of August. In the following weeks, Troy stopped shaving and started wearing cotton T-shirts, but he still looked alert, as if he still belonged to New York's cultural and financial elite and was only playing safari. No longer. Troy was now haggard, sleep-deprived, and sweat-stained, like everyone else.

"Remember that silver tie clip you used to wear?" Amy asked, while they waited in the hallway for their allotted time.

Troy nodded. "The things I used to care about..."

Amy nodded. She still bleached her hair so that Ben didn't worry over the creeping growth of her roots and the passing time that they implied, but she was otherwise unadorned: no makeup, no jewelry, no perfume. She smoothed her greasy hair back into a half-ponytail with elastics she kept on her wrists. Amy had also done away with regular clothes, like many of the engineers, and wore an unmarked camo jumpsuit. With her unblemished pale skin, wide eyes, and platinum hair, she looked like a Victorian doll, only inked with a tattoo and dressed in military fatigues. Instead of looking like a joke, it somehow fit Amy.

After checking her watch, Amy knocked hard on their conference room door. Sounds of scuffling and murmurs came from inside. After a brief pause, Amy opened the door and walked right in. The space flight team was bringing their meeting to a close while griping about getting the shaft with resources because they were last in the line of defense. It was probably true. Without the success of all the other teams—HYCIV, nuclear, Ariane integration, security, logistics, and launch—nothing these astrodynamics experts said or did would make any difference.

Take a back seat, fuckers, Amy thought.

She was in no mood and would drag everyone out by the hair if it came to that. The space flight team got the message and scrambled with their laptops and papers. Amy dialed Ben. He was directly above them in the Janus meeting room, only a short elevator ride away. *Minimal. Interruption.*

"We're here," she stated, and hung up.

Troy connected his laptop to the flat panel mounted on the far wall. He opened a video file of footage captured by a security drone. Amy had seen them up in the skies. At first glance, without registering distance and scale, the military drones looked like small planes, nothing like the noisy commercial models that hovered like insects. The Effort's Predator models circled silently in wide arcs like graceful California condors, recording with optical and infrared cameras.

Video footage appeared on the flat panel with a paused time code in the lower corner. Amy saw an aerial view of tree cover like clumps of broccoli surrounding a long road leading to the airport on the edge of Cayenne. Troy advanced the footage, following the security drone as it flew south until an airfield came into view. Parked in the far corner was a very large, very wide plane—Zhen's Xi'an Y-20 with the red flag of the People's Republic of China painted on its dull metal tail. More than a hundred armed soldiers surrounded the plane in a staggered perimeter.

Amy heard Ben's voice in the hallway. He soon appeared dressed in his own military fatigues, pushing the Professor in a wheelchair. They were still discussing nuclear team business.

"Thank you for your time," Amy said the moment they crossed the threshold.

The Professor sat up and regarded her with a small smile. She knew that his doctors were very liberal with his codeine and gave him several days' worth of pills at a time, which the Professor could pop casually along with the mandatory Effort cocktail of antimalarial, antidepression, antianxiety, Ritalin, and (for those without heart conditions) amphetamines. He was now the most chipper scientist in any given room despite having the pallor of Death himself. Amy worried what his inevitable passing would do to morale.

As for Ben, leaning on the wheelchair's handles for support, he wasn't looking much better. He had fallen asleep while talking to a room full of engineers a few days before. His words had slurred midsentence, and his expression went slack. Before anyone knew what was happening, Ben crashed to the floor. He kept trying to stand back up but only fell down again and again. It ripped Amy up inside, but she could do nothing but make him sleep, eat, and swallow those damn pills. Everyone had to help Ben sacrifice himself for the cause. It made her ill.

She went to close the door and said that their discussion had to be confidential.

As she passed, Ben stated at full volume, "We don't have time for this shit, Amy."

He would never cut her off at the knees like this, never but for now. Amy cleared her throat and pointed up to the paused footage on the wall display. Troy addressed the Professor, avoiding looking at Ben as he eyed the growth of Troy's beard.

"It was one of our last arrivals from East Asia," Troy said. "China was the Effort's last signatory, if you recall. The plane landed in mid-November but remained parked to the side of the runways."

Amy saw the surprise on Ben's face as he finally recognized Troy Andrews, one of the UN overlords who had been holed up in administrative headquarters since the start of September. Even in this protected bubble, many had become unrecognizable to each other and themselves. But not Amy. She had never been more tired and strung out, and yet she was her best self.

"Why don't we just talk to him?" the Professor interrupted. "Why all the secrecy and cloaks and daggers?"

Light from fluorescent overheads bounced off his bald, liver-spotted pate. Amy could see beads of sweat despite the air-conditioning.

"I don't know why this has to be confidential," Amy replied, shaking her head, "but Zhen said she has the solution."

"Deus ex machina," the Professor scoffed.

Amy startled as a bolt of excitement ran through her body and tingled her extremities. How many times had Amy asked herself, *Is this comet real? How can this all be real when it feels so much like my sci-fi books and TV series?* There was something uncanny about it all—not déjà vu, but more like walking the familiar path of destiny.

"It's a term," Ben snapped into the silence.

Of course Amy knew it was a term. She and Ben had discussed the plot device countless times.

"Meaning..." said the Professor, who paused to look at Troy but still continued, "that unless your engineer can deliver a god, the likelihood of him having a solution for a successful HYCIV build within our ridiculous launch window is near impossible—"

"But not *im*possible," Amy said, finally regaining her senses.

She knew how loath scientists were to make that claim. The universe had proven them wrong too many times. The Professor sighed and nodded, conceding that all was supposedly possible if it wasn't impossible.

"But it's more likely that he is either wrong or lying," said the Professor sadly.

"She," Amy finally corrected him. "If Zhen is wrong or lying, then what are those soldiers guarding on that plane?"

The Professor's underbite quickly snapped shut.

Amy turned to Troy, but he was losing control of his faculties. The Professor had just admitted that the Effort's success was near impossible, a lost cause.

"Troy?"

His mouth gaped with the realization of doom. *Everyone and everything will die...*

"Troy!" Amy yelled at the top of her lungs.

He didn't even blink. The Effort doctors had labeled the condition UD3 catatonia. Amy rushed to Troy's laptop and scanned the crowded desktop. She opened another video file Troy had pulled from the drone security logs. The time code had advanced by just under two months.

"This footage was recorded days ago," Amy said to Ben and the Professor.

There were less than half as many Chinese soldiers standing attention in a sparse perimeter around the plane.

"Look at the wing," she urged Ben.

A series of plastic tarps spanned the edge of the plane's left wing and funneled down to containers on the ground.

"They're collecting rain because they're probably out of drinking water. Troy spoke to the security team still out there. They said the Chinese soldiers have been leaving one by one because they're starving as they run out of rations. They limp out of the security zone with just their guns, and they don't come back. The rest stay to guard that plane. Why?"

Neither man ventured a guess, but they weren't dismissing the question, either. The Professor tapped the length of the cane resting in his lap. With all ten arthritic fingers, he absently played a piano concerto while his eyes and thoughts remained fixed on the plane. Suddenly, his index finger lifted to point at Ben's head.

"Fortune-teller?" he mused. "In all those one hundred twenty-two impact scenarios, did any account for a deus ex machina?"

Ben shook his head. The Planetary Defense Conference scenarios all attempted to simulate plausible situations and outcomes. But here, in reality, they were approached with the implausible—and it was exactly what they needed. Truth could be stranger than the fiction Amy lived and breathed.

Ben nodded and said, "Let's hear what this Zhen has to say."

~~~

DEUS EX MACHINA translated from the Latin is "God from the machine."

Merriam-Webster's Collegiate Dictionary offers two definitions:

1. A god introduced by means of a crane ... in ancient Greek and Roman drama to decide the final outcome.
2. A person or thing (as in fiction or drama) that appears or is introduced suddenly and unexpectedly and provides a contrived solution to an apparently insoluble difficulty.

TWENTY-TWO

ZHEN

ZHEN STARTLED WHEN she saw a large cricket with waving antennae on the bottom of a solar array panel. She jumped back and looked up at all the black silicon cells that stretched to the ceiling—infested with crickets!

It couldn't be real. Zhen closed her eyes but had to open them before she lost her balance. The floor of the cleanroom felt tilted suddenly, but at least the crickets had vanished. She reached out to the engineer next to her and held on to his shoulder until her spatial orientation leveled. When Zhen turned to her neighbor, she saw light brown eyes above his mask with no epicanthic folds, a few freckles, and a mole above the right eyebrow. It was Albert, a member of the Guiana Space Centre staff. Zhen could have thanked him in French as she let go, but there was no need. They all steadied one another.

Albert continued to direct the engineers and technicians folding and packing up the completed solar arrays. Over the next couple of days, the arrays would be transported by rail to the Final Assembly Building, where they would fold on hinges like origami and stow within the Ariane rocket.

Zhen pressed a button on her watch and switched the digital display from the launch countdown to twenty-four-hour military time. It had been thirty-nine hours and thirty-eight minutes since Zhen had last slept. A quiet alarm would sound in twenty-two minutes as a warning that her faculties would begin to fail with increasing consistency; she would have more hallucinations, more disorientation, more fits of temper, more paranoia, and more impaired concentration. That is what Zhen had learned in the span of her mature lifetime, although she had never rationed sleep for this long a duration.

Her hallucinations at the payload prep facilities had been meaningless so far: bulging walls, human faces popping out of inanimate objects, or blobs moving in the corners of her vision. But crickets were lucky. Maybe it was a sign, beyond sleep deprivation, that the luck of the Effort was about to change for the better. Zhen lifted her hand to signal to Albert and three of her fellow engineers. They nodded quickly when she pointed to her watch. Zhen's forty-hour rest schedule was well known; only her supervisor, Quon, ever judged her for it. He had ordered the rest of the Chinese engineers to work until they dropped and had to be carried outside.

Zhen maneuvered to the wall of the large cleanroom, away from the mass of engineers and interpreters clustered below the remaining solar array panels. As she hurried along the wall, Zhen thought about the adjoining cleanroom on the other side where Dr. Jin-soo Lee and the rest of the HYCIV team would be toiling away on their impossible mission. Even with all the subassemblies procured at the Effort's conception, there were still too many complex parts that had to be built from scratch and tested within their launch window. The Effort was doomed—unless Zhen acted alone.

She checked her watch and quickened her pace, but it wasn't fast enough. Quon intercepted her and blocked her path to the exit. His eyes looked to her mouth, like they always did. He grimaced as he spoke because he knew about her scars under the mask's papery fabric, and he didn't like the deception of Zhen looking like a perfectly formed woman—pretty, even.

"We had another collapse," he reported. "Wang this time."

Zhen said nothing. She had already argued for scheduled intervals of rest for her team, but personal sacrifice was honored among the Chinese, even in the extreme, despite its sad waste. Quon's eyes darted furtively. They spoke in Mandarin, but there were several interpreters standing around or playing the wallflower until needed.

"I've heard rumors that you've met with their leadership," Quon said in a low voice, "in secret."

Zhen could feel her accelerating pulse in her ears and neck. She held her breath and waited for him to mention Amy and their meeting on the road.

"*I* am your superior. Not them. Not Dr. Lee," Quon said, nodding to the wall that separated them from the HYCIV team.

"You are not to speak with him alone."

Zhen felt immediate relief that he didn't know the extent of her actions—but she also felt anger. In working for the China National Space Administration, Zhen had always fallen in line. That was then; this was the time of extinction-event-class comet UD3. Zhen had to find strength and break out of the hard, form-fitting mold of obedience, like a weak chick breaking out of an eggshell.

"We are out of time," she said. "*All* of us," she added, daring to wave her hand around to circle every nationality represented in the cleanroom, the whole human family.

"Our orders were to *wait*," Quon hissed.

It was November when the Chinese engineers boarded a Xi'an Y-20 cargo plane and took off for South America. Leadership in Beijing had agreed to participate in the international effort . . . officially. Unofficially, the decision was split. There was a minority faction in talks with Moscow, agitating for China to join the Russian effort.

When Zhen's plane landed at the Cayenne airport, its human cargo of engineers disembarked and headed to the space center, but the soldiers and pilots remained to guard the plane and *wait*. Leadership in Beijing would either decide to join the Russian effort and recall all its engineers and resources, or it would fully back the international effort—and disclose the state secret that was the other cargo, a secret that could tip the balance between survival and extinction.

"The UN must be blocking communication from Beijing," Quon whispered, looking around him.

It was possible. Zhen had befriended many of the engineers on other teams using her fluency in English and French. Some whispered rumors that NASA calculated the comet's impact site in China. Zhen's government may have decided to join the neighboring Russians once they made their own calculations. The Effort would have blocked this information and ignored their demands. But there were other possibilities as well. An engineer named Cheung was the last of the Chinese to reach the Effort. He was a substitute for another engineer who died from a heart attack. With him came horrific news.

"Cheung said—"

"I know what he said," Quon interrupted her.

Zhen's jaw shut, but her glaring eyes spoke for her: *Now! Now is the time for you to lead us.*

Zhen was a forty-six-year-old woman with no hard power. Quon was her elder and a senior-ranked Communist Party member. He didn't have half of Zhen's intellectual capabilities or experience, but he shared the classified knowledge of what was packed and stored on their Y-20 plane. It was knowledge that could either save the Effort or continue to burn holes in their sanity while time ran out. But Quon made no move to act as they stood in silence. He was chosen to be a leader because he was a follower. Zhen stepped around him and didn't look back when he called her name.

After disrobing from her cleanroom suit, Zhen exited to the back parking lot of the payload prep facilities. Crushed cigarette filters squished under the soles of her shoes. A ring of guilty smokers stood by the door, sharing puffs from the last of the Effort's cigarettes.

Two of the smokers were Chinese. They immediately averted their eyes in shame as she passed, but Zhen could appreciate the normalcy of their habit. Even more touching was the way they closed their eyes to savor a nicotine-laced inhale and then wordlessly passed the precious smoke to their neighbor.

On the outer edge of the parking lot was a makeshift food bank and clinic. Zhen stood in a short line to receive a paper bag meal that she tucked into her lab coat pocket. To continue on, she had to step over sleeping engineers lying on the ground and others being spoon-fed like children. Most of the fat had been starved off their bodies through neglect. Zhen probably looked just as gaunt. Her clothes hung loose, and she missed her monthly bleeding.

Medics had hooked IV drips into some of the sicker engineers. If they couldn't be repaired on the spot, they were taken to an infirmary. Some returned, but most didn't. Zhen saw Cheung among them in his white lab coat. His hands shook violently, but his haunted eyes stared off into a distance no one else could see. Zhen stopped to whisper his name and shake his shoulder. Exhibiting symptoms of UD3 catatonia was dangerous, as it was rumored to be contagious.

"Cheung," she whispered. "Come back."

Zhen shook him harder, remembering what he reported when he first arrived: that Red China was once again a silent bloodbath. Cheung's parents and elderly aunt said the mass starvation that came with news of the comet was just like the midcentury Great Leap Forward. People ate grass and bark in the daylight, while babies and children disappeared in the night.

Cheung suddenly startled and blinked.

"It will get worse," he said, soon as his eyes could focus on Zhen.

"Home?"

"Everything," he replied, and looked away.

The world was falling into chaos and ruin. There was a strong possibility that no decisions came from the People's Republic of China because it no longer existed.

-ᴧᴧᴧ-

A DENSE, WOODED area surrounded the fenced perimeter of the payload prep facilities. To reach it, one had to first cross the parking lot at the back of the complex and hop a chain-link fence. When Zhen first ventured out into these woods, seeking a close and quiet place to sleep, she tied the end of a spool of coated wire to the chain-link fence. Quickly turning her wrists to let out more wire, Zhen walked backward into the trees. At seventy steps, she could no longer see the floodlights of the parking lot or hear humans above the ruckus of insects. At 132 steps, she found a cluster of strange trees: the first landmark she could recognize and remember.

The trees had dark globules, like grapes, growing directly on their bark. Zhen looped her wire around one of the trees, securing a sure path back to the complex, and plucked one of the strange fruits. Was it edible? She described it to an interpreter on her return and asked if locals ate the fruit, but he shook his head. No one had any exchange with the local Guianese, he said, except the armed soldiers outside the Effort perimeter. He looked so sad as he said it.

Every forty hours, Zhen followed her line of wire out into the woods. She was born and raised in Chongqing, one of China's megacities, and was used to concrete, signage, crowds of people, and the maps on her cellphone. She wasn't used to navigating her way through nature where every direction looked the same. But even at night with the moon tucked behind clouds, Zhen could find her way by keeping one hand on the wire and the other stretched out in front until it felt the bark of those trees with its bulbous fruit.

"To meet with me in private," she had told Amy, after hailing down her jeep on a road in the middle of the night, "you only have to follow my wire on a forty-hour schedule."

Zhen had pinned her hopes on so many risky unknowns because she had no other choice. This Amy, with the cyberpunk hair and tattoo on her arm, had to convince the leaders of the Effort to meet with Zhen in secret. Amy wasn't an engineer, military, or a government operative. Zhen wasn't sure of her official purpose, only that she didn't seem to answer to any authority. Others answered to hers.

There were other unknowns, ones that made Zhen's throat tighten, blocking speech and oxygen. Was the Chinese Y-20 plane still parked at the airport in Cayenne? Was the secret cargo still guarded by their soldiers? Zhen had checked the airtight containers after they landed in French Guiana. Her fingers were ever so gentle as she handled her own newborn, one that had taken three years of her life to gestate. All the containers were intact then, but what if they had been compromised since?

Zhen had to stop thinking. Terror kills the appetite. On top of that, Zhen found her bag lunch—two slices of bread with jelly and a paste of something that smelled like peanuts and looked like excrement—nearly inedible. Her stomach often shrank during the long work sessions, and filling it was uncomfortable. She would have to eat the rest when she woke.

Zhen took off her lab coat and folded it into a square. Not that she minded the formality of it. Zhen appreciated anything that camouflaged her physical form into something no one would question or even notice. But alone, outside of the air-conditioning, the coat was too hot and served better as a pillow. She placed it in the shade of a thick shrub and lay down.

Such a brilliant blue sky! Zhen was used to the low-hanging, gray mass of smog that plagued urban China, but here there was clean air with no taste, no smell, and no grit. She breathed deeply with her diaphragm and watched the pure white clouds drift and form strange shapes with both crisp and wispy outlines. Zhen closed her eyes and tried to sleep. She tried not to think about her family. They were probably dead, but...

Zhen came from a long line of mathematicians who had learned to survive against the odds—and this fact was her only reassurance. Zhen herself was a lucky product of her time as the second child born before the one-child policy was introduced. She was a pigtailed five-year-old with red scars on her upper lip when Deng Xiaoping came to power in 1978 and brought reform that opened China's borders and economy.

Zhen's family pooled their money to send Zhen's older brother, Kuo, to Cambridge, England. Zhen never expected to be a "sea turtle" who left China to study abroad, even if her family could have afforded such an extravagance twice. Her mother wanted her to apply to Peking University, and her father wanted her to apply to Tsinghua University, but Zhen couldn't imagine not coming home to her parents. She was more than happy to enroll in Chongqing University as the youngest pupil on record.

In 1989, Zhen turned sixteen and prepared to graduate with honors when student protesters gathered at Tiananmen Square and refused to leave. The Liu family read about the occupation in the *People's Daily* while other state newspapers turned a blind eye. The protestors drew sympathy and hope in readers and triggered buried memories in others. When an announcement came over the radio in May that the Chinese government would impose martial law in Beijing, Zhen's mother became frantic.

"It is happening again," she whispered to the walls. "They will disappear. They are too young to know."

The horrors under Chairman Mao and his Workers and Peasants' Red Army surfaced in her mind.

"Leeches," she told Zhen one night, pacing in her bedroom. "There were leeches in the rice fields."

She slapped at her shins as explanation. Zhen's newly orphaned mother had joined the millions of youth sent to farming communes in rural China.

"I can still see them," she confided to her daughter.

The memory of looking down in freezing water crusted with ice and seeing her bare legs standing covered in the dark parasites and dripping red blood from their bites was so vivid, it bordered on hallucination.

"I can't go back," Zhen's mother promised herself. "They will have to drag me out of this apartment in a wooden box."

Zhen's father was more lucid and direct.

"If you fall on the wrong side of a revolution, Zhen, you will be crushed. And all our hopes for the future will die with you. Our family will be shunned. I will lose my job, and we will be beggars."

He could see that Zhen's ears and mind were open to the promise of democracy, but she did not understand the dangers. He had to appeal to her reason and duty. Whether people were ruled by the greed of the few or the idiocy of the masses, Zhen's father explained, it wasn't worth the destruction of their family. He spoke calmly, but Zhen could still hear fear in his voice along with her mother's footfalls as she turned in tight circles.

Zhen owed her family everything. Instead of joining the democracy movement of 1989, she stayed home while soldiers of the People's Liberation Army sprayed bullets into their people. Purges soon followed. Zhen was allowed to graduate from university at the head of her class while several other students and professors disappeared from the public eye. Life was allowed to move on for those who stayed silent and afraid. And so it moved on for Zhen.

Many of her friends got married in the years after university, but Zhen had no suitors. If one looked past the scars, she was within the normal range of plain to pretty. But no one looked past the scars. Zhen's parents could afford to be kind about it. After all, their son would continue the family line. Zhen was their lucky number two. They encouraged her to continue her education. Female PhDs were called *di san xing*, or the third sex. But Zhen was already unmarriageable and had little to risk.

By twenty-eight, she was considered one of the *sheng nu*, or "leftover women," like the pieces of gristle and soggy vegetables that get pushed aside and left on a dinner plate. Everyone assumed Zhen would remain in academia, but the government recruited her, like her cryptographer grandfather, shortly after she earned her doctorate. Party leadership wanted a stronger space program, one befitting a major world power and one that would be a source of national pride.

In order to enter the program, Zhen had to pledge her loyalty to the legacy of Mao Zedong and join the Communist Party. She did this while handing over her passport and dreams of traveling around the world. There was no other way but to keep her head down, watch after her family, and meet the expectations of others. Zhen survived but made a promise that when the time came, when there was more to gain and less to lose, she would rise and stand honorably with the righteous. It was her destiny.

TWENTY-THREE

THE MEETING

KOUROU, FRENCH GUIANA
JANUARY 14
T-MINUS 18 DAYS TO LAUNCH

I HIGHLY RECOMMEND a good enema," the Professor announced.

"So noted," Ben said, pushing the old man's wheelchair toward the Janus lobby.

He let the Professor prattle on, loopy with painkillers. Amy offered to take over, but he ignored her. Ben was leaning down on the handles of the wheelchair as much as he was pushing forward.

"I don't mean to sound ungrateful," the Professor was quick to add. "Codeine was a comfort. And now morphine is an absolute godsend—but they clog the pipes something awful."

Now that the Professor had graduated to morphine, he needed to receive his doses in person at the infirmary. Suicide was becoming a particular threat among many at the Effort, such as psychological trauma, disease outbreak, air attack, internal sabotage, and raiding from local French Guianese who had managed to cooperate in storming the outer perimeter and overwhelm enough guards to seize their weapons and break through. With each new threat came a new set of rules strictly enforced.

When Ben, the Professor, and Amy reached the lobby doors, a jeep was waiting outside. Walking into the heat and humidity of French Guiana was like walking into a soft wall. Ben crouched down beside the Professor until he could see his own likeness reflected in the thick glass of the old man's spectacles.

"You sure you won't come?" Ben asked the Professor.

Sweat gathered on the old man's clammy skin.

"I'll head back to the nuclear team," the Professor said. "Physics, I can handle. Jungle humidity is another matter. Not kind to electronics or old men."

Two peacekeepers got out of the jeep and approached. One lifted the Professor up as if he weighed no more than a child while the other folded his wheelchair to stow in the back. Ben and Amy watched the jeep drive away.

"He looks awful," Ben said.

"So do you," said a voice behind them.

Ben and Amy startled and turned to see Love, standing in front of the lobby door in her military jumpsuit with her arms crossed.

"What are you doing?" Ben stuttered. "You need to stay with the nuclear team."

"Fuck you, Ben. I may not be the genius you are, but I'm not stupid. I know something's up."

Love would have said more, but another jeep pulled up to the Janus building.

"Oh shit!" Ben cursed. "It's the Disasters."

Two women stepped out of the back seat wearing red vests with Red Cross emblems. One was a psychiatrist from a Presbyterian family in Vermont. She had a tall, wiry body and prominent chin and nose, like a Halloween witch. The ER surgeon, on the other hand, was from Houston. She was small and round in stature but demanded the respect one was owed for doing the Lord's work. Both were veteran volunteers with Red Cross Disaster Response. When they appeared like gray-haired banshees, it meant you were ready to be pulled back from the brink of self-destruction and spirited away for medical treatment. The women immediately walked up and introduced themselves.

"Hang on, did the Russians put you up to this?" Ben interrupted. "Oleg thinks shrinks are hilarious."

"That may explain their high suicide rate," the tall psychiatrist countered. "But no. A concerned colleague asked that we reach out to you—"

"No time," Ben said, "and I'm stealing your taxi."

He darted between them and got into the back seat of their jeep. Amy got in beside him, but before she could shut the door, Love stepped inside.

"Move your skinny asses over," she barked. "I'm coming, too."

Amy nudged Ben in the ribs with her elbow until he scooted left. Ben told the driver to head for the payload prep facilities.

"Why payload prep?" Love asked, as she buckled up.

"That's what we hope to find out," Amy admitted.

〜〜〜

BEN LOST TIME in the jeep. He must have fallen asleep, because he opened his eyes and saw everyone staring at him. They were idling in the back parking lot of the payload prep facilities. Ben fumbled with his seat belt and tried not to fall as he stepped out. Old cigarette butts littered the asphalt. Reps from the logistics team had already doled out the last of the cigarettes. Food, medication, and supplies were being rationed, which likely meant the rest of the world was starving. The Effort had become a greedy organ that sucked up the remaining blood of civilization as it dissolved.

Ben stepped over and around sleeping engineers dressed in fatigues and curled up on their sides.

"Like downtown Tokyo without the suits and ties," he muttered.

And just like businessmen working to exhaustion in downtown Tokyo, the Effort engineers had their share of collapses, breakdowns, and heart attacks from fatigue and chronic stress.

Ben, Amy, and Love scaled the chain-link fence surrounding the parking lot. Ben was slower and clumsier in his weakened state.

"Could this be a trap?" Love whispered, as the forest closed in around them.

Ben gave a humorless laugh and shrugged.

"But, then why risk it?" Love insisted.

"Because there's nothing to risk," he blurted. "We're all dead. Dead as doornails. Unless this...She"—he motioned ahead—"knows something the rest of us don't."

Love halted. Her legs buckled, and she crumpled to the ground. There was some type of fetal position she was supposed to assume; the Disasters demonstrated it during a mandatory seminar on psychological trauma, but Ben wasn't paying attention at the time.

Amy moved to hold Love as Ben walked away. Love would have to get up and keep going, just like he did. And if she didn't...One had to let go eventually, he surmised. Much as he deeply loved it all—the planet, his life in the new millennium, Amy, his parents, sister, nephew and niece, memories of Southern California, Love, and the rest of the Effort—he had to let them all go. Ben's internal caring mechanism was beyond its breaking point, and his synapses were flooded with antidepressants. Every time he tried to cry into those Effort pillows, it was like trying to squeeze tears from driftwood.

Ben walked ahead until he spotted a strange cluster of trees. At first sight, the branches looked as if they were covered in black, globular spots, like plump parasites.

"The plane is still there?"

Ben jumped and turned in a full circle. The voice was close. He spotted an Asian woman in the shade of a large bush, struggling to rise. She wore a tank top and shorts but quickly unfolded a white lab coat and pushed her arms through the sleeves.

His curious eyes scanned her face and latched on to her scars. Zhen caught his stare.

"Double cleft palate—"

"Yes," Ben interrupted, and still felt human enough to look away.

"Where is Amy?" Zhen asked.

As if on cue, there was keening noise from the distance behind Ben.

"She's helping a friend," Ben said quietly. "Look, you wanted me, you got me. So let's start with who the fuck are you, and why the fuck should I care?"

This gave her pause.

"Zhen," she replied.

"Zhen, I'm Ben Schwartz."

The engineer blinked and remembered to bow with respect.

"The plane is still there?" she asked again.

Ben nodded. The woman put a hand on her heart and took a deep breath. Ben didn't know what he was expecting, but it wasn't this. When Amy first told him about an engineer claiming to have a solution, he thought Zhen was either a liar or a shit mathematician with bad calculations. He could sniff out a bad actor from across a room. So, shitty at math, then.

"Let's get on with it," Ben prodded. "What's your solution?"

He had already exhausted all possibilities as far as his mind could stretch. He was prepared to shatter Zhen's hopes for a solution just as he had shattered Love's hopes for a future. They give you a job to do, you might as well do it.

Zhen started to tremble and breathe quickly. She had to will the words up from deep inside.

"The *Tianlong*!" she said in a rush.

If this woman was expecting lightning bolts, they didn't come.

"A spacecraft," she explained. "The next generation of *Hayabusa*."

"*Hayabusa*?" Ben asked, shaking his head. "You mean JAXA's *Hayabusa*?"

"Yes," Zhen said, expecting the question, but still angered by it. "The Japanese space agency built the *Hayabusa* and *Hayabusa 2*—"

Of course Ben knew this, just as he knew that the *Hayabusa 2* was currently navigating deep space toward a C-type asteroid thought to contain organic and hydrated minerals from the primordial universe.

"But the *Tianlong* is Chinese," Zhen insisted. "The word is Mandarin for Heavenly Dragon. We built it in secret. *I* built it. With many improvements."

Ben tried to form a question. The garbled word he managed was a mix of *what* and *how*.

"Our network hackers are . . . most impressive"—Zhen's admission was not without shame—"and unconcerned with the intellectual property rights of foreigners."

"You stole the technology."

"It's here," she said.

"You . . . you have a duplicated *Hayabusa 2* spacecraft—"

"Not just duplicated," Zhen said, gritting her teeth, "duplicated and *improved*. The next generation—"

"Where?" he shouted.

"Here," Zhen repeated. "Packaged up in pieces on that plane in Cayenne."

Ben's mouth opened and closed, gasping for air. He sank to the ground but felt suddenly weightless. If this was all true, Zhen really was a god lowered onto the stage in the second act to deliver her grace. Ben was light. He was a helium balloon floating in that beautiful blue sky above.

He must have lost time again. When he opened his eyes, Amy was kneeling over him with red-rimmed eyes. Ben turned his head to see Zhen and Love standing next to each other.

"You thieves," he said to Zhen. "You *beautiful thieves*!"

Zhen shook her head, frowning. After starts and stops in English, she released a diatribe in Mandarin.

"She's saying the ends would justify the means," Love translated. "Because scientific understanding benefits all."

Zhen nodded quickly and said that both the Americans and Japanese had been in the early stages of missions to sample liquid water found on Enceladus and Europa in the hopes of discovering proteins, the building blocks of extraterrestrial life. Zhen knew her leadership wanted to beat them to it. They wanted to show the soaring, fire-breathing might of China and win the space race, where Zhen just wanted a chance to compete.

Ben was listening, but he was also making a mental inventory of all possible subassemblies in a *Hayabusa 3* that could be repurposed in Jin-soo's HYCIV spacecraft. *Oh, fuckety fuck!* he thought. *The Hayabusa 2 had an ion engine!* If the Effort's HYCIV was powered by an ion engine instead of solar energy, it would be much faster. And if the spacecraft could get to the comet faster, the Effort could push out its launch window and gain more time.

Ben held up his watch and switched the display over to their launch countdown.

He would have to recalculate a reduced launch window and reprogram the Effort's two redundant rubidium master clocks, counting down with perfection. As he imagined the weeks— *months!*—that could be saved, Ben released a fluttery, nervous laugh. All of their watches would need to be reprogrammed, but Ben was far from complaining. Since the first sighting of UD3 in July, Ben could finally gain ground in the fight against time.

"My God," he sighed. "I'd be crying tears of joy if it weren't for the meds."

Amy opened her mouth, but before she could ask what the hell was going on, Zhen said, "There's a problem."

Of course, Ben figured. There was always a problem, but with the parts of a *Hayabusa 3* available, at least the Effort had a fighting chance. Amy helped him sit up as Zhen explained that the *Tianlong* and its borrowed *Hayabusa 2* technology were a national secret. Her orders were to wait until leadership gave disclosure. Zhen took the chance to ask if Ben knew of any communications with China, but he was just as in the dark.

"What I am doing..." Zhen continued.

She looked to Love and spoke again in Mandarin.

"Treasonous," Love translated.

Zhen thought the word sounded suitably ugly and nodded. Ben bit into his upper lip and counted to five before he asked if she was joking.

"Seriously though," he insisted, blood in the crevices of his front teeth. "What part of 'big fucking comet go boom' do y'all not understand? What part of annihilation leaves any room for this nationalist bullshit?"

Zhen didn't disagree, nor did she feel understood.

"You are not Chinese," she said simply. "You can imagine, but you can't know us."

Ben opened his mouth, but there was no argument against the truth of the statement. Not that it would stop him from taking the *Hayabusa 3*—if it really was at the airport—by any means necessary. Zhen could see the quick decision in his eyes.

"The Effort will get our *Tianlong*," Zhen promised. "But you will do it *my* way. With as few deaths as possible. These are my soldiers. My people."

She stepped forward and awkwardly extended her palm.

"This is how you do deals?" she asked. "Like in the movies?"

Ben looked to her open hand but said, "I need that ion engine."

It was something between a warning and a threat, but Zhen was determined; her hand never pulled away.

"I know UD3 will hit China," she said.

NASA had tried to keep the comet's trajectory secret, but there was nothing to stop others from doing their own calculations.

"I want this as much as you," she assured Ben.

He finally shook her hand, letting slip the words, "Deus ex machina."

Zhen shook her head and stated that she didn't speak Latin, only Sichuanese Mandarin, Cantonese, English, French, and minimal Russian.

"It's...a term," Ben explained.

"Meaning?"

His mouth hung open. Ben snapped it shut and shook his head, still acting as if he had been hit over the head with an iron skillet. He leaned his chin on Amy's shoulder and dared to say that success was possible.

"And it is our only option," Zhen said.

Her smile seemed to say that she knew these stakes like a fish knew water.

-᠕᠕᠕᠕-

IT DIDN'T TAKE long to gather all the Chinese engineers into a conference room by the offices of the payload prep facilities. Zhen insisted on talking to her countrymen first. Many of them were friends who had worked beside her on the Chang'e 4 rover that landed on the far side of the moon the previous January. The door to the hallway was propped open so that two peacekeepers could straddle the entryway and keep an eye on things. Love Mwangi sat just outside, leaning her back against the wall. Amy sat beside her, and Ben paced the hallway, hissing expletives.

"There's no telling what they might do to one another," he shot out.

Ben already regretted his promise not to intervene until necessary. Twenty-five peacekeepers stood on each end of the hallway ready to quell a revolt by force. Zhen began to speak but was quickly cut off. The peacekeepers in the doorway lunged inside and exited seconds later, dragging one of the Chinese engineers out into the hallway. Zhen appeared in the doorway, holding her neck with both hands. When her hands dropped back to her sides, Ben saw red scratches and welts on her throat.

"Comrade Quon should be barred from this room," Zhen said with difficulty.

She didn't linger to watch the man disappear down the hallway, screaming, his legs dragging behind. Nothing would deter her from telling the truth. Ben waved several peacekeepers into the room to stand beside Zhen as she announced the existence of the *Tianlong* spacecraft. Questions from the other engineers were tentative at first. Then they grew heated and even toxic. Mandarin came fast, loud, and layered as they interrupted one another. Love closed her eyes so she could concentrate and interpret.

"Some are angry—"

"No shit," Ben muttered nervously.

"—that Zhen didn't tell them sooner. Others are angry . . . that she made this decision on her own. The spacecraft wasn't hers to give away. They are saying . . ."

Love waved Ben over so she could whisper in his ear and repeat all the angry questions and conspiracy theories hurled at Zhen:

What if this defense effort was meant to fail?

What if the rest of the world was willing to take its chances on a future with no China? America had tried to wipe out communism with war, but here was UD3 to finish the job. Meanwhile, their government might be trying to recall them all for a defense effort back home. What if Zhen was blocking communication?

Zhen finally spoke up, and the room fell silent. Love paused before interpreting her words into English: *The Effort is real. It is the only defense effort that can destroy UD3. Either help us save the planet, or get out of our way.*

Ben smiled at the word *us*. It didn't refer to the Chinese, or the communists, or the cultures of the East. *Us* was the Effort; Zhen had joined them and raised the flag high.

She came and stood in the doorway and waited for the other engineers to file out into the hallway. She didn't look any of them in the eyes, not even when one briefly laid a hand on her shoulder.

"Some of these men should come with me to Cayenne," Zhen said to Ben. "It may encourage the soldiers to lay down their arms."

Ben had to object. The airport on the edge of Cayenne was less than an hour's drive beyond the Effort perimeter. Only minimal security guarded the forty miles of highway leading southeast along the coast to the city. Ben admired Zhen's bravery, but it was too dangerous, and she and her team had proven themselves too valuable.

"Zhen, I've heard it's bad out there. Really bad."

"I have to go," she said.

Zhen got to call the shots; that was their deal. Ben sighed.

"You'll need air cover. And an armed convoy—"

"And me," Amy said, stepping forward. "I'm going, too."

Ben opened his mouth, but Amy was a faster draw and louder.

"*I* knew how this story was supposed to end. *I'm* the one who found our deus ex machina. Let's not forget that."

Amy glared at everyone around her; no one would be allowed to forget that, least of all Ben.

"I can't lose you," he pleaded.

"You won't. Success is our only option."

She smiled. Amy was the love of Ben's life, but it was her choice and she had already made it. He looked between the two women and ceded command of the Cayenne mission.

TWENTY-FOUR

CAYENNE

KOUROU, FRENCH GUIANA
JANUARY 15
T-MINUS 17 DAYS TO LAUNCH

BEN WAS ANXIOUS to move quickly, but Zhen insisted on waiting for daylight. Approaching the Cayenne airfield in darkness might look like an attack, and Zhen wanted to avoid bloodshed, if it could be helped. The SWAT team was suspiciously large already, but Ben had flat-out refused to reduce headcount any further.

At the first light of dawn, fifteen Humvees parked in a long line at the administration complex. The commander of the SWAT team led Zhen and Amy to their assigned vehicle and the pile of body armor left for them on the back seat. His own body was covered with segmented pieces that looked like a carapace. Zhen picked up a green-gray helmet and ran her fingers over the pockmarks on its surface.

"I want to go!" Love called out, jogging along the line of Humvees until she reached the two women.

The convoy already had a Mandarin interpreter to negotiate with the Chinese soldiers if Zhen got injured or killed. Amy told Love she had to stay and help Ben.

"Where *is* he anyway?" Love muttered, scanning their surroundings.

Ben was nowhere to be found. After the Cayenne mission logistics were arranged throughout the night, he had quietly disappeared.

"He said he couldn't watch me leave," Amy replied. "It's better this way."

She strapped on a bulletproof vest and eyed the gun strapped to the SWAT commander's thigh.

"Gimme one of those," Amy said, pointing.

"What?"

"I have a license to carry. I've been at target practice since I was eight—"

"I'm not arming a civilian," he said. "I have ten snipers in the lead Humvees. They'll get in tactical position and cover you."

"They better," Amy snapped.

One by one, drivers flipped their ignitions. The SWAT commander got into the passenger seat and adjusted his headset. Amy pulled Love into a crushing embrace that ended with a gentle push away. On the sidewalks of Chongqing, before UD3, such tall and exotically beautiful women as these would gather a crowd of gawkers—Zhen included. But this was no time for distractions. Zhen strapped on her helmet and crawled into the back seat.

She closed her eyes and tried to envision the Cayenne airport. Ben had shown Zhen video stills in time progression to prepare her. At the beginning of the footage, there were over a hundred Chinese soldiers left to guard the plane, but their numbers reduced rapidly as time wore on and resources ran out. Zhen saw still images of soldiers dragging their own dead off the airfield.

"Do they have the Discovery Channel in China?" Amy asked, settling into the back seat.

Zhen opened her eyes and saw that Love was still standing by the curb, watching them. Amy didn't look anywhere but forward as she described a documentary series on nature.

"My favorite was the one on penguins," Amy continued.

The birds were safest on the ice, she said. Predators like leopard seals, orcas, and sharks swam the waters, but so did the fish and krill that penguins needed to eat to survive.

"They would all line up on the edge of the ice and look down into the water, waiting."

Amy bowed her head to demonstrate. The side part in her hair was just starting to darken at the root, so Amy was human after all, not a colorful and exaggerated character in a *manhua* comic book.

"But the penguins were scared..."

Amy said that it was always one of the bravest penguins that dove in first. The rest followed almost instantly in a big splash.

"It just takes one to lead," Amy finished.

Zhen nodded.

"The loadmaster," she said, to show she understood.

Zhen had bonded with the loadmaster as they worked together to carefully load all of *Tianlong*'s subassemblies into the fuselage of the plane and secure them for the long flight from China to South America.

"He could be our bravest penguin."

"I was talking about *you*," Amy said, looking at the dark bruising and lines of ruby scabs across Zhen's throat.

The SWAT commander gave the order to move. As their Humvee slowly accelerated, Love jogged alongside. She slapped her palm flat against the glass of the passenger window. Amy immediately placed her palm against it. Their fan of fingers and lifeline creases matched up for a moment, until Love's hand slipped off as she fell behind.

The Humvees drove smoothly in sync with ten-meter gaps between them. Soldiers at the security gate of the space center grounds waved them through to the military barracks beyond. Everywhere one looked, there was a grid layout filled with tents, Humvees, tanks, kennels, storage containers, and so on.

"So massive," Amy gasped.

After five miles, the convoy reached the Effort's outer perimeter of tangled barbed wire and soldiers wearing the light blue helmets of UN peacekeepers, the olive green of various armies from around the globe, or the black of the French gendarmerie from the Guiana

Space Centre. Zhen saw a checkpoint straight ahead. The line of vehicles came to a stop.

"It's the Disasters," Amy barely whispered.

"The what?"

Amy had to clear her throat to explain: "Disaster Relief with the Red Cross." She pointed to several unarmed people walking from the checkpoint down along the line of jeeps. Bright red vests peeked out from under their body armor. The SWAT commander lowered his passenger window and signaled to a tall white woman in the lead. She approached their jeep and opened Amy's passenger door. Long, stringy gray hair hung from her helmet and swayed as she clambered into the back seat and stepped over Amy's knees with long limbs.

"Is—is it Ben?" Amy asked.

Zhen's seemingly fearless ally suddenly looked stricken.

"No, no," the gray-haired woman said quickly.

Zhen stared at her faded-blue eyes and pointy nose in profile as she buckled the middle seat belt.

"We thought it best to accompany you and the other engineers. It's been five months since you arrived?" she asked.

Amy was still shaken and could only nod.

"So five months of seclusion within the Effort," the gray-haired woman continued, making the point out loud.

She paused to turn to Zhen and introduce herself as Dr. Clayton with the Red Cross—a medical doctor, a psychiatrist—she clarified, assuming Zhen may be used to PhDs.

"And you, Dr. Liu, left China in the middle of November?"

Zhen nodded.

"I was in quarantine before I left China, but I heard what happened on the outside," she said, thinking of Cheung's stories and shaking hands.

"You may have *heard*," the psychiatrist conceded, "but you haven't *seen* with your own eyes. Not until now."

The Effort had to fight for the survival of the species, Dr. Clayton said carefully. This fight had to be won at any cost. That meant any individual, any family, any populated city, country, or continent.

"We've had to make very cold, calculated decisions that we could never have imagined ourselves making. And we will keep doing whatever is necessary. And so will you, Ms. Kowalski and Dr. Liu, because there is no other way."

One would think this foreboding statement would keep Zhen on the edge of her seat, but the body needs what it needs. Shortly after the convoy exited the Effort's perimeter, Zhen nodded off.

Bullhorns woke her. Zhen bolted and winced at the pain in her bent neck. Amy was rubbing her tired eyes and looking disoriented. Bullhorns blared again, making them both jump. Voices echoed in French and English. Zhen was slow to translate the regional French into something like: *Stay back!*

The flat land allowed a clear line of sight for miles. Armed soldiers lined both sides of the highway at ten-meter intervals, facing out to hundreds, no...thousands of gathered people. Here were the French Guiana locals that Zhen had wondered and worried about. And they were starving; stick legs and arms poking out of filthy clothes.

"Stay behind the line!" a voice blared in English.

Another Humvee overtook theirs in the left lane. It had its roof open at an angle that provided cover for the standing gunner. Speakers protruded from the vehicle's rear, broadcasting warnings.

"Just the patrols," the SWAT commander said to the women in the back seat.

He had to project above the clamor of loudspeakers and low-flying helicopters. Ben had said that the Cayenne airport and connecting highway were still loosely protected by the Effort's multinational armies, though no planes had landed in more than a month. Zhen saw that most of the Humvees in the convoy had also opened their roofs to allow standing gunners.

"Why..." Amy asked as her blond head swiveled back and forth, "Why aren't we helping these people?"

Dr. Clayton took a full breath.

"French Guiana has a very small population density. Luckily for us. Easier to defend against," she added under her breath. "Not all of its people are starving like this. Some were employed by the space center and kept on for the Effort. But the region's economy was heavily dependent on the French mainland for subsidies and goods. No longer..."

The doctor said that most local supply chains had broken, let alone a global one that has to cross the Atlantic Ocean. French Guiana had strong gold mining and timber industries that steadily cut away at the Amazon forest, but currency had no value now, and no one needed a new mahogany dining set these days.

"That leaves the population with subsistence fishing, hunting, and farming. Small scale. Nothing worth us stealing—"

"You would steal from these starving people?" Amy growled.

"The Effort would steal from anyone," the doctor admitted. "We have the world's brain trust on an ultimate mission, and the armies needed to protect them. That requires a lot of calories."

Dr. Clayton counted off the ravaging of local food sources by the French Guianese: cattle, pigs, and chickens had been slaughtered; capa, tapir, and monkeys in the bordering forest had all been shot and eaten; vegetable fields had been ripped up; savanna trees had been stripped of fruit.

"Traditional fishermen are surviving," she offered. "Well, as long as they can avoid getting killed for their catch. Our surveillance drones have spotted them hauling in crabs, prawns, and fish. Humanity hasn't managed to plunder the bounty of the sea—just yet."

"How do you know all this?" Amy interrupted. "You're just a psychiatrist. The logistics and administration teams don't tell the rest of us anything."

Dr. Clayton maintained her calm and soft demeanor.

"We inform members on other teams about the state of the world very minimally," she agreed. "Lately, I've been the one who does the telling. In the past, when it wasn't done by a professional, not enough was done to monitor the situation."

The doctor didn't elaborate.

"We don't have food to spare," Dr. Clayton said quickly, just as Amy pointed to the people outside the vehicle and opened her mouth, ready to yell. "But we do have enough fresh water. We used to set up dispensaries along the highway, but it attracted too many desperate people. There were organized attacks on our soldiers. After that, we stopped letting them get close. We drew the line—literally. Even so, we offer them protection," Dr. Clayton added. "That's why they gather at the line."

Amy looked to the psychiatrist and then at the SWAT commander. "Protection *from what?*" she asked.

"From one another," Zhen whispered. "That smell..."

When she breathed through her nose, Zhen smelled fire-roasted pork. Amy must have been too upset to notice.

"Yes," the doctor said sadly. "We're not the only ones doing the unthinkable. Our soldiers tried to bury the dead, but there were too many, and the bodies weren't doing any good stuck in the ground."

So there was cannibalism among the starving masses. Cheung had said that it was happening back home in China, but here it was right beside them. The Effort was like a snow globe: an environment in a bubble that kept them all focused inward and oblivious to the horror on the other side.

The locals grew more desperate as the convoy passed by. With hollowed eye sockets and dry mouths, people begged for help. But no help was coming. The Effort was hope for all humanity—but not for them. Zhen felt the first signs of fear as a sinking in her stomach. There were so many; they could overturn the Humvees and drag them all out through the windows if they acted together.

A group of frightened children held hands as men pushed them from behind toward the road. Just as Zhen realized the ugly shock of children used as a human shield, the SWAT commander leaned back and assured the three women that they were safe. Ben had arranged for more air cover to protect the convoy. Amy stuttered in disbelief.

"You're not actually going to shoot—"

The sound of a helicopter drowned out her words. Warning shots pelted the earth in staccato rhythm. The crowds scattered, screaming.

"Jesus fuck!" Amy shouted. "Those are unarmed people! Children!"

The doctor only spoke when the noise died down. She didn't have a voice like Amy's.

"Our soldiers have been stoned to death. They've been beaten and ripped apart by mobs."

Amy opened her mouth, but Dr. Clayton kept talking.

"Our orders are to protect this defense effort at all costs. Right now, that's the two of you—and that airport."

She pointed to the road ahead, but Amy didn't turn to face forward. Instead, she leaned over her lap and put her hands over her ears. Luckily, she didn't see a young teenager break free from the line and run toward the convoy. The girl held her arms outstretched from a T-shirt whose silkscreen had faded to white. Zhen couldn't hear what she was saying above all the voices yelling for her to stay back. Twenty feet from the highway, bullets burst into her chest cavity from a gunner just ahead. Just twenty feet, so close that Zhen could have thrown her a bottle of water, so close that Zhen could have done something to keep her alive and not a heap of skin and bones receding in the distance.

Zhen heard Amy weeping into her lap. Zhen's own ragged breaths came quick and shallow. Dr. Clayton fixed her steady, pale eyes on Zhen and spoke slowly.

"We have the most important mission in the history of the planet."

Zhen understood.

"Breathe."

Of course she understood, but what if it was all for nothing? What if the plane took off in the night, or what if the cargo was damaged? What if people were devolving back into wild animals and cold killers for nothing? Zhen lurched and vomited a stream of bile onto the doctor's shoes.

Soon as she stopped gagging, Zhen apologized.

"I usually get it in my hair," Dr. Clayton said, trying to smile.

Their stone-faced driver leaned back briefly.

"Go ahead and cry," he told Zhen. "I do. When I'm not at the wheel."

Zhen wiped bile from her lips. French Guiana was not a densely populated region. What of the cities? What of the megacities of China where her parents and brother lived? What happened to the only people who ever loved her? Were they cut up into pieces and roasted on a spit, like a child's nightmare?

A helicopter made another low pass and shot up the ground ahead of them. Crowds of people ran from the road, trampling others who tripped or were pushed underfoot. One body didn't move from the gunfire. It was an Asian man in a white lab coat smeared with dirt. Half his face was slack, like it was melting, and the other half was dazed and frightened.

Zhen recognized Ts'ao Wu, the Chinese engineer who suffered a heart attack and was rushed to the Effort infirmary. Interpreters from the UN told the rest of the Chinese engineers that Wu had died in surgery. The Effort's logistics team had already contacted the Chinese government and arranged for Cheung to replace him. Was Zhen seeing Wu's ghost? Or was it that these crowds of people weren't just the locals because the Effort was discharging its infirm—at the least. Instead of Wu, it could very well be Zhen abandoned out there. It might be yet, for who could not notice that the Effort stockpiles were depleting? Ground meat and fresh produce were used sparingly, barely enough for flavor. Engineers were no longer allowed to fill their plates. Rations were doled out carefully in single portions only.

"Breathe," Dr. Clayton prodded.

Zhen lifted her gaze to the brightening expanse of sky and focused on the traffic control towers of the Cayenne airport. Her breathing eventually slowed into an even rhythm, but she didn't take her eyes off those towers. She tried not to blink.

⁓⁓⁓

"WE'VE ARRIVED," the SWAT commander said.

Amy sniffed hard and sat up. Her face was red and slick with tears. When her eyes locked with Zhen's, she nodded. It was time to actively forget the highway wasteland behind them. As Dr. Clayton said, they had their mission, and it was the only mission.

The convoy passed through the Cayenne airport's guarded gates and proceeded along the airfield perimeter. Gunners stood down and resealed their roof panels. Zhen saw that all the parallel runways were empty—except for the Chinese Xi'an Y-20 plane parked in the far corner, right where Zhen left it. She slapped one hand over her mouth to stop noises issuing from her lips. There it was in front of them; all was not lost.

The Humvees parked in three rows starting at a fifty-meter distance from the plane. The SWAT commander handed Zhen an extra pair of binoculars and told her to stay put as he exited the vehicle. Zhen had to shift to the middle, nearly in the tall doctor's lap, in order to see the plane from their vehicle's position in the middle of the third row. She counted sixteen Chinese soldiers in baggy uniforms trying to stand at attention with their rifles. As she was counting, two collapsed, and only one of those was able to struggle back up to his feet.

More soldiers limped out of the plane's hatch. There could still be a lot of them inside. The plane's forty-seven-meter-long body with its extra-wide fuselage had a maximum cargo capacity of sixty-six tons. Its name translated to *Chubby Girl* in English. Zhen re-counted a total of twenty-three soldiers blocking her from the *Tianlong* inside. She would have them all shot if it came to that. But she hoped with all her heart that it wouldn't. These soldiers were dying as they continued to hold their ground with complete selflessness for duty. How could she not be fiercely proud of her people?

The SWAT commander returned to report that his snipers were all in position. Behind him stood eight of the Chinese engineers who had come to help. Zhen saw Cheung in the lead. Of all the UD3 catatonia cases that Zhen had seen, all had worsened rapidly. Yet, here was Cheung, suddenly clear-headed with purpose. Perhaps the afflicted had a path of return after all.

When Zhen stepped out of her vehicle, the smell of roasting meat was twice as strong. It drew unbidden memories of her mother's sizzling, spitting wok. Zhen felt her mouth fill with saliva. She heard a stomach gurgle and growl in anticipation but didn't know if it was hers. Bodies want what they want.

Zhen took off her sweaty helmet and politely ignored the SWAT commander's protests. She wanted her face clearly visible as she approached the plane. Cheung took off his helmet as well. The soldiers wouldn't recognize him. Cheung came to the Effort on a later flight, but he was still Han Chinese, the same blood and history. When Zhen took a few steps forward, Cheung was the only engineer who walked by her side. The rest fell behind.

Amy tried to join the engineers, but Zhen shook her head.

"But, if you need me—"

Amy didn't need to finish. The two women had already come so far by relying on each other's help. And Zhen didn't need to look up to see all the drones and helicopters that Ben had sent to protect them. She passed their moving shadows along the concrete of the runway.

The helmets of the Chinese soldiers swiveled as they tried to keep track of all the SWAT soldiers, squatting behind the open doors of their Humvees, while keeping an eye on the small group advancing toward them. They were completely outgunned but stood their ground with their fingers on their triggers. Zhen whispered for Cheung to walk slowly and carefully.

"Stop!"

Zhen and her group halted. She followed her ears and recognized the Chinese major with embroidered stars on his shoulder insignias. He stood behind his men, closer to the plane's hatch, yelling in English for all to hear. Zhen scanned the soldiers' faces but didn't see the loadmaster or the pilots. Hopefully, they were still inside the plane.

A young, emaciated soldier dragged himself over to the group of engineers with his gun lowered but ready. He smelled like sweat and rot. Zhen greeted him, but he didn't smile. The soldiers had all been quiet on the long journey to South America. They didn't know about the *Tianlong*; they only knew the cargo was a state secret that could alter the fate of China.

"We've received no word from Beijing," the soldier reported to Cheung in Mandarin.

The pilots had orders to turn on Chubby Girl's systems once a day for communication back to command.

"Fetch the loadmaster," Zhen said to the soldier.

No one moved. From the corner of Zhen's vision, an engineer with the family name Bao walked up from behind to stand on her other side. Bao was a short man, and so he had to tilt his chin up to look the soldier square in the eyes and repeat Zhen's command to fetch the loadmaster. The solider gave a look of wary relief before retreating; he must have known that all their waiting and suffering would be over, one way or another.

The young solider conferred with his major. Together, they disappeared into the fat belly of the plane. When they reemerged, the loadmaster was with them. Zhen's hands and feet started to twitch with nerves. The three men stopped about six meters from the group. The loadmaster looked between Zhen and the major, who had unholstered his gun.

"Was that *you* who made the rainwater catchment?" Zhen called out to the loadmaster.

She slowly pointed to the wing on the far side of the plane draped in tarps. The loadmaster had training as a mechanical engineer. On the voyage, he had good-naturedly teased Zhen about her pristine lab coat by showing off all the gear oil streaking his military uniform. He said that they needed to make a different kind of camouflage for the likes of him.

The loadmaster nodded and stepped closer, closing half the distance between them. The major and his soldier crept closer as well.

"You look strong," Zhen said, noting the loadmaster's strength in comparison.

"We're out of food." He then admitted, "The last of it went to the major, the pilots, and me. You should have brought pork buns with you. It would've been polite."

When he smiled, his ashen lower lip cracked and bled. Zhen said that she had brought food, fresh water, two doctors, and four medics. She meant for her words to travel even as their temptation caused pain and trembling in the soldiers. The major's stare turned colder.

"I've thought about you," the loadmaster said to Zhen, taking two steps closer, "while we were alone out here. Waiting."

His name was Dewei. Zhen wasn't surprised that she stayed on his mind, just as he had stayed on hers. Theirs had been a quick kinship that didn't come easily to Zhen. Dewei didn't need to be kind to her—most didn't and most weren't. And yet, he showed her pictures of his young wife and infant daughter back in China and then asked about Zhen's own family. They talked for the majority of the flight, stopping only to catnap and then start up again.

Dewei didn't mention the large containers he had to maneuver onto the plane, but he was brave and curious enough to ask about Zhen's thoughts on the comet. The topic of UD3 had become taboo in much of China. Speaking its name invited unimaginable death and destruction into a conversation, but he still did it. And what's more, he admitted he was scared for the future.

"You must think of all children now," Zhen told Dewei quietly. "Just as you think of your own daughter."

The suspicious major moved closer.

"That cargo is a spacecraft," Zhen said, raising her voice. "We need it to stop the comet. Unload it now."

Dewei nodded. This was the order he had waited for. As he turned, the major shouted again in English.

"Stop!"

The loadmaster held up his hands but spoke defiantly.

"Whatever is in that plane, we need to give it to them. We need to end this."

The major yelled without taking his eyes off Zhen and the SWAT team.

"We don't have orders."

"And we never will," Dewei insisted. "Give it to them."

More Chinese engineers flanked Zhen until they were all standing shoulder to shoulder. The major lifted his gun and pointed it at Dewei's head, taking aim at the first detractor. A sniper bullet knocked the major off his feet before he could discharge his weapon. There was a moment of silence and indecision. Then one Chinese soldier set down his rifle. Then another. And another.

TWENTY-FIVE

WEBER'S WARNING

Jack's parents inhabited his dreams. He was usually lucid enough to know they were both probably dead—and Jack told them so. In some dreams, his mother and father nodded in sad agreement, but in others, they held out hope for their real selves. Jack woke one afternoon alone in Maya's lower bunk. The memories of his dreams were already fading, but he could still recall his mother pointing to the scar on his neck and asking, *Remember Germany?*

Jack didn't remember the military hospital in Landstuhl very well, but he did remember the stray piece of hot shrapnel in the Syrian city of Homs. Jack also remembered waking up on the flight to Bethesda Naval Hospital. His parents were beside him. They had immediately flown to Germany and then flown right back to the States forty-eight hours after their only child survived surgery for a nicked artery.

When it was time to be released to a caregiver, Jack had no one but his mother; he had broken off his last relationship right before leaving on a dangerous assignment. Mrs. Campbell readied his old bedroom in their house back in northern Virginia. It was easy at first. Jack was foggy from pain medication, and his mother was gentle. When she spoon-fed him soup and antibiotic pills, Jack teared up with each painful swallow. He was still so close to death that she forgave him then.

But the days passed and, by small degrees, their patience ran out. Mrs. Campbell filled the silence with talk of her familiars. Some of it was harmless enough: milestones like birth, marriage, and death. But that usually transitioned to gossip, judgment, and competition. Jack knew his mother hid pettiness behind good looks, charm, and polished manners. Others were easily fooled, while Jack saw the underlying comparisons over money, real estate, dress size, popularity, successful children, cruises, tennis—in fewer words, everything that Jack found superficial. Laid up inside the same four walls he thought he had escaped, Jack was his mother's captive audience, just as in childhood before puberty stoked his fire and told him to get the hell gone.

When it was time to peel away the surgical tape and remove Jack's bandages, her fury percolated to the surface. *Your father and I won't always be around to take care of you, you know*, his mother said, losing the smile she always wore like a favorite lipstick. *You need to settle down with the right girl and a steady job that won't keep trying to kill you.* Jack balled his fists, but the fight left him soon as his mother broke down in tears at her first look at the jagged stitches, running from his collarbone to the corner of his jaw.

Jack reached for her, but she batted his hand away and cried out, *You did this to yourself!* Jack answered slowly, *No, Mom. This was a piece of metal. What I did was expose the truth about attacks on civilians.* He knew that his parents assumed his injury, one that nearly cost his young life, would be a call for major change. They assumed wrong. Jack realized that he thought he had been running away from his parents, while he was really running from a sheltered life like theirs, spent at a desk or a country club. He was better built for the great wide open, fighting and dying for what mattered.

When Maya returned to her room, Jack was rubbing the scars on his neck. He pulled his hand away and reached for her, but Maya brushed by and squatted by the sink cabinet.

"I woke up and you weren't there," Jack said to her bent back.

It sounded needy and desperate to his own ears.

"Do you have any Dramamine?" Maya asked with her head still in the recess of the cabinet. "I'm out."

He told her to look in the pouch of his *Healy* hoodie that was cast off somewhere on the floor. Maya and Jack were sick as dogs, but they weren't the only ones. All passengers and inactive crew were advised to medicate and take to their beds. Even as Jack sat, seemingly stationary, his body orientation told him the truth: *Healy* was rolling along the Bering Sea with sixty-two-knot wind speeds and twenty-foot waves slamming into her red chest. The ship's engines were running at full power just to maintain position.

Maya found the pill bottle in his hoodie. She took in water from the sink with cupped palms and swallowed, then smoothed down the crown of her tousled hair with wet palms.

"There's gonna be a vote tonight," she said to her reflection in the vanity.

Maya said she ran into a Coastie on her way back from the head. He informed her that there would be an announcement over the pipes for all to gather in the helicopter hangar at 2000 hours. Captain Weber wanted to put to vote whether to stay in the safety of the ship until supplies ran out, or to return to Seattle or even Joint Base Lewis-McChord if the city was too dangerous.

Jack reached out for Maya a second time. Not since he was a child holding the fabric of his mother's clothes in tight fists did he feel such a hysterical need for another person. There were moments when they couldn't bear to be on opposite sides of the same room. In bed, they held each other's bodies so tightly their forearms trembled with fatigue, but no matter how close their embrace, it never felt close or comforting enough.

"I guess the others won't get a vote," Maya said. "You know, the ones who've...stopped talking."

No one bothered with the *Healy* accountability form anymore, so it was hard to tell who had succumbed to the comatose state. Suicides were also harder to find ahead of the smell. By the time the crew disposed of the body overboard, the rest of the ship knew about it anyway.

When Maya ignored his hand the second time, Jack jolted with something of a laugh. He was too self-aware to miss the irony.

"What's so funny?"

Maya sounded angry. Jack smiled at her, but it wasn't the usual flashing of perfectly straight, perfectly white teeth. This was a lopsided smile that made him look young and exposed.

"I've always run away from the people who loved me. Who *needed* me," he admitted. "I've put whole time zones and continents between me and mine. Now here I am, *needing* because I can't handle UD3 alone."

Jack lay back and wondered if every solitary consciousness eventually suspects that reality was created for them only. *Healy*'s cramped quarters, with nothing to do but fear loneliness and stew in guilt, were a personal hell that felt to Jack like proof of this far-fetched speculation.

Remember Germany?

"Oh God," Jack whimpered. "My parents..."

His mother's last email from back in late September couldn't be tucked away and compartmentalized any longer. He had to face it, to face her.

I don't know where you are, Jack. Just that you are not with us.

How carefully his mother worded that statement of fact, not wanting her last communication to serve as incrimination. Her care did nothing to erase his crime of absence.

We are running out of food. Your father wants to take the car and drive further from the city. We have a canister of gas that he hid in our bedroom closet so we could keep an eye on it at night. I left a key to the house under a rock by the birdbath. There are too many things to say. I don't know where you are, Jack. Just that you are not with us. We love you and will pray for you. We will pray for us all.

Jack turned to the wall and started sobbing. Moments before, Maya didn't want Jack to touch her, crowd her, further invade her personal space, but she immediately got back into bed and pressed against his long, curled shape until it stopped shuddering.

~~~

CAPTAIN WEBER SPENT too many sleepless nights combing the internet. Most familiar sites and search engines were down with a *503 service unavailable* error. He tried to remember or even guess URLs to try. Satellites on the ship detected no new inbound email communications either. *Healy*'s ISP in Seattle was no longer functioning. The last communication from the Navy on November 26 reported that the overwhelmed Army and National Guard had pulled out of several West Coast cities and retreated to islands and peninsulas with natural barriers.

Weber had last heard from his brother with an email in late October, stating that Seattle was "a living nightmare." Even the suburbs were "bad, very bad." People carried weapons with them: guns, crowbars, lead pipes, and baseball bats. They didn't say hello to one another, but they nodded to convey a message: *I understand that we are both human beings doing what we can to survive, and I wish you all the luck, but if you threaten me or my family, I'll bash your skull in.* Bodies lay mangled in the streets.

Weber's brother promised to take care of his wife, Karen, and their two children while he was still away at sea. Both families planned to pack up their campers and drive into Washington's national parks, where they might find safety in the deep forest, for a short time at least. Karen left a warning in her heart-wrenching goodbye.

I love you, Martin, more than my life. The children love you just as much but don't come home. It's no one's home anymore.

Weber was just over fifty but had two young children. It had been difficult for Karen to conceive with him gone for so many long voyages to the Arctic. They had given up hope by the time she got pregnant during a Christmas leave. A beautiful daughter and son were brought into the world three years apart on the same sunny day in September, never to be taken for granted. He swore to find the three of them in the chaos or most likely die trying.

Until Weber could reach dry land, he prayed. Hard. In between rote recitations, Weber questioned the purpose of the comet. Was UD3 God's way of culling the unworthy, like the floods in Genesis? Did God wish to set back the clock of civilization to biblical times, when life was more righteous? But what if there were no survivors? UD3 was big. Too big. Why would God kill all His children? Were they only a failed experiment?

At 1945 hours, Weber made an announcement over the pipes that it was time to gather in the helicopter hangar. *Healy's* second-in-command joined him on the walk over. They didn't say much, but it was nice to have someone by his side as he entered the hangar and faced the crew and passengers. Weber walked to the center of the large space and cleared his throat.

"Thank you for gathering here tonight..." he began.

It sounded like the hollow introduction of a funeral. Weber was never ready with the right words while in the moment. They only came after draft upon draft of feeble attempts. He pulled a folded piece of notepaper out of his uniform pocket. One side was covered with the perfect, slanted script that nuns had beaten into him before computers made the craft obsolete.

"We have no communication with leadership. It is time to make our own decision," he read aloud. "It may not be standard military practice to put decisions to vote. But rules were not written for days like these."

The captain looked at everyone, even the people standing in the back. Weber was a tall man (thank the Lord) and still wanted to be the sort of leader who looked into the eyes of others.

"If we remain at sea, as long as we can, we'll continue to have the safety of this ship. We won't suffer along with the rest of our families, friends, and neighbors. But that is a form of suffering unto itself. You will have to live with the choice of letting them go."

An image of Karen came to mind unbidden. She wore her favorite sundress with the floral print at the hem. He could never remember the name of the flowers. She always laughed and rolled her eyes when he asked.

"If we return to mainland instead," Weber said, swallowing emotion, "we will have to face what they have faced..."

Did he have to put such horrors into words? Did he have to say murder, rape, gang rule, death cults, and even rumored cannibalism out loud?

"You've all seen the last reports. You've heard the same stories. Seattle is a disaster zone. We could take the Puget Sound past Tacoma and anchor at Steilacoom. It's a three-hour hike to Joint Base Lewis-McChord, if it's still operating. That's your safest bet but, honestly, I don't know your chances..."

He had to stop there. The decision went to vote.

"All in favor of returning to mainland?"

Captain Weber immediately raised his hand and counted all the voters who followed suit.

"All opposed?"

The decision would be close, and a few voters were abstaining by looking at the floor, racked with indecision. Weber noted that most of the remaining scientists now raised their hands to stay at sea. They were either young and unmarried or lived outside of Washington State. Weber also noted, with a sinking stomach, that some crewmembers had hands raised—and all of them were women, who would be easier targets for violence.

His eyes caught two clasped hands raised in the air for a double vote. One belonged to a scientist and the other to a guest passenger, a photographer who always walked the deck with a camera. This couple was inexplicably, undoubtedly in love. Of course they would want to stay safe on the ship, Weber thought, as long as they had each other.

"Majority votes to return," he announced.

And now they had only to wait and wonder what they would return to. *Healy* was sailing from the Arctic with its time frozen in the past; the ship was a capsule of a civilization that had taken millennia to build. Like a house of cards, it had all come fluttering down into the bloody anarchy of their new present.

~~~~

EVERYONE ON *HEALY* did their best to provide privacy and protect Maya's and Jack's strange good fortune in finding love. In this spirit, Captain Weber approached them two days after the vote.

"There may be a way," he whispered, "to keep what you have. While you can."

They listened.

Healy was nearing the Aleutian Islands. Weber told the couple they could take a month's worth of supplies onto one of the ship's survey boats and disembark in the morning. If they followed the captain's coordinates at a steady pace, they would reach a small island recently abandoned by its native Iñupiat population. Thawing permafrost had caused its buildings to tilt, buckle, and sometimes collapse. Rebuilding was pointless when rising sea levels were returning the island to the Bering Sea at the rate of three to nine feet a year. The captain told Jack and Maya that any homes still standing could make for a temporary shelter out of the wind and weather. Then, at daybreak the next morning, they could continue southeast and reach the chain of Aleutian Islands.

"Follow the islands east until you can find a settlement that will take you in," Weber said. "You'll need their help, because you'll die out there on your own."

Weber told himself this was the right move, despite the couple's ashen faces. Even if they failed to find an accommodating settlement, at least they would have more time together in relative safety. It was all anyone could hope for this side of heaven. It was more than the captain could hope for.

~∿∿∿~

WHEN JACK OPENED the door to his stateroom, Gustavo was seated at his desk studying an unfolded map. The smaller man's chin and neck had stayed smooth throughout the entire voyage with no need of a razor. By comparison, Jack looked like a Viking with his full ginger-blond beard and shaggy hair that covered his ears and nape.

"Sloppy Joes tonight," Jack said, pulling food wrapped in damp napkins out of the pouch of his sweatshirt and placing it on Gustavo's desk. "Emphasis on sloppy."

Instead of grabbing a change of clothes from his closet, Jack pulled out his two empty duffel bags.

"Can you keep a secret?" he asked, without looking back.

Gustavo's silence was answer enough.

"Maya and I are leaving in the morning," Jack confided.

He grabbed an armful of clothes from the closet and stuffed them into one of the bags.

"We're gonna try to find a village on one of the Aleutian Islands and wait this out with them. There's no reason for the two of us to risk...what might happen to Maya on the mainland. She thinks her family is dead, and I don't know where mine is 'cause I'm the world's shittiest son."

Jack grimaced and finished packing all his shoes and clothes in silence. When he saw a thick stack of printouts on the floor of the closet, he grabbed them and finally turned to his bunkmate.

"Ah! Every poem you've ever written," Jack said, holding them up. "I printed them out in the science lounge."

He tucked the stack of paper into a duffel bag carefully.

"Taking *them* with us is kinda like taking *you* with us, right?"

Gustavo returned Jack's smile. Jack thought it such a beautiful expression that he reflexively snapped a picture with the camera around his neck.

"You still have film and batteries?" Gustavo asked.

"Three more batteries. And it's all digital. Nothing's analog anymore," Jack admitted. "When the memory fills up, I'll probably delete everything and start over. I can't *not* take pictures."

Somewhere in early adulthood, Jack had molded into his occupation. There was no way for him to purge photojournalism because it was at his core, despite being useless in current circumstances. Jack put the cap back on his lens and let the camera hang from its strap. It was a familiar weight. Without it, he felt a nagging worry of forgetting something.

"I'll miss you," Gustavo said honestly. "There is family and tribe. And there are those we chose."

He won't survive Seattle, Jack couldn't help thinking. The whole trip, Gustavo had acted like death was right around the corner waiting for him. And now it was. But what about Gustavo's people?

"How remote are your Wayãpi villages in the Amazon?" Jack asked. "Could they still be safe?"

Gustavo took a deep breath.

"Could," he said softly.

The Wayãpi in the northern state of Amapá lived in the deepest part of Brazil's remaining forest, Gustavo told Jack. Half of their designated lands fell in a large reserve and the other half fell in a national park. Much of the forest was impassable on foot. Aside from rivers and skies, the only way to access Brazilian Wayãpi lands was one long dirt road that connected to a small mining town.

"My people will fight for their lives," Gustavo said. "They always have. And when they can't fight, they will hide. Some say there are still places no white man has seen."

"Do you know what all this means for them?" Jack asked. He tried to explain one of the many streams of thought that had run through his head when there was nothing for him to do on the ship but think. Gustavo's poems spoke of the Great Hungry Machine that was modern civilization and the billions of humans who worked its cogs. Everything living was fed to the Machine: forests, animals, rivers, and fish. It consumed and poisoned, seemingly unstoppable until a dark comet rounded the sun.

"For the first time in hundreds of years, the Wayãpi will be left alone in the forest," Jack told Gustavo. "At least until the comet hits or doesn't. Promise me you'll let that sink in. This is the very thing you've always wanted, right?"

Gustavo's jaw hung speechless. The words were already sinking in.

Jack pulled the straps of his duffel bags over each shoulder.

"Bye," he said.

This moved Gustavo to place a hand on Jack's shoulder.

"There is no word for goodbye in my language," he explained. "There is no translation, because my people don't leave each other. Except for me."

He held on to Jack's shoulder, squeezed, and then let go.

In the morning, Jack was gone.

TWENTY-SIX

GULP ISLAND

AT A PUNCTUAL 0700 HOURS, Weber met Maya and Jack by the Arctic gear locker. Suitcases and duffel bags lined the corridor by their feet. Both were dressed in sensible civilian clothes: jeans over long underwear, ski parkas, and wool caps. They stood close to each other. Weber felt a glimmer of envy that he squashed immediately.

"I have a gift," he announced, too upbeat to be believed.

He propped his new fishing rod against the wall and set down his heirloom tackle box.

"This was my grandfather's," the captain explained, with a hand lingering on its scarred leather.

Weber had planned to give the box to his son on his sixteenth birthday, but as they say, the best laid plans...Maya opened her mouth and started to protest, then stopped. These were times to swallow guilt and take what you were given.

"Thank you," she said.

Weber turned and got down to business. The Arctic gear locker stored all equipment and supplies for *Healy*'s short-range missions and surveys. Drinking water wouldn't be a problem with all the snow and rain. Everything else...would be a problem. Weber grabbed a duffel bag and started packing.

"Storms have gotten worse these last few years," he said, reaching for two folded Gumby suits in small and large sizes. "And with a warmer ocean, there's a lot less ice as a barrier. I'm hoping you'll find a good structure on the island. One with a strong foundation."

He crossed to the other side of the locker and announced each item before placing it in the bag: flashlight, utility knife, first aid kit, fire lighter with a refill can of butane, and weatherproof tarp. Jack laughed. Weber had heard that the photojournalist was quick with a joke or a story of high adventure. He was popular with the Coasties, despite being an outsider.

"Reminds me of those logic puzzles," Jack explained. "You know, 'You are crossing to the dark side of the moon.'"

You are crossing the dark side of the moon. Choose only fifteen items to take on the journey and list them in order of importance to your survival...

"One kid always listed the oxygen tank at number five," Jack said. "Tops."

"Not on my watch," Weber muttered.

He showed them how to use the flare gun before packing it.

"I can't supply you with a real gun," the captain insisted, more to himself.

There weren't enough weapons to spare; arming these two would leave someone else empty-handed when they reached mainland.

"Sir?"

The three of them jumped at the sound of a man's shout. The ship had grown so quiet.

"Lieutenant Colson reporting, sir."

The lieutenant was under the supply officer's command. He had keys to the locked pantry and orders to pack enough proteins and carbohydrates to last two people one month.

"I ordered takeout," the captain said, wanting to show his own sense of humor.

He led the way back into the corridor and found Lieutenant Colson standing by a duffel bag. Colson's mouth was tight at the corners. Food hoarding was becoming problematic. The more it continued, the less food they would have to divvy up before they anchored.

"Thank you, Lieutenant. That will be all."

Weber stepped forward and lifted the duffel bag of food in his spare hand. Something ugly manifested in the lieutenant's face as he stared at the supplies being gifted to a pair of civilians, but Weber turned his back and nodded to Maya and Jack, who scrambled to gather up his fishing gear with their own bags and suitcases.

Balancing a duffel in each hand, Weber led the couple down a series of narrow corridors connected by watertight doors with levers designed to stop the spread of flooding water, smoke, and fire—but not the threat of a cosmic impact, apparently.

They stepped lightly and tried to ignore noises coming from behind closed stateroom doors. Weber preferred the noises (weeping, praying, shouting, and so on) to silence. Silence was a bad indicator. There wasn't much *Healy*'s overwhelmed medical staff could do for the comatose, aside from arranging an IV drip of fluids.

Midway along *Healy*'s length, they stopped for Maya to catch her breath.

"What's this island called?" she asked. "Our way station before we reach the Aleutians?"

"Depends who you ask, like most things," Weber replied. "On the ship, we call it by its coordinates. On a map, it's labeled Taylor Island, if it's labeled at all. The Iñupiat who lived there must have had a good name for it, back in the day, but I can't remember. No one remembers the good names. Just the bad."

He gave a small smile of apology.

"Then what's the bad name?" Maya asked.

Her eyes were so dark that the pupils and irises merged into solid spheres. She reloaded her tiny frame with bags, grabbed the handle of a rolling suitcase, and held the captain's tackle box close to her chest.

"I can't pronounce it in their language, but it means swallowed whole," Weber said. "Gulp. Like a fish."

The three proceeded to *Healy*'s stern and emerged from a hatch. Temperatures on deck hovered at the freshwater freezing point. Flurries partially melted in the air and fell as a white drizzle. A twenty-three-foot rigid hull inflatable boat was already secured at the top of the ship's stern ramp. Weber strode quickly and climbed in first. Maya struggled to step over the hull with her short legs, but Jack was quick to help her after unloading his bags. They sat quietly behind the steering console as Weber pointed and explained each of the controls.

"You'll follow these coordinates and reach the island by afternoon," Weber said, plugging numbers into the console's digital interface. "Tomorrow morning, you'll need to refuel."

He lifted his chin to three canisters already secured in the front of the boat.

"Then head southeast and keep an eye on the compass needle."

He pointed to the horizon. In the wet glare, the Bering Sea was a dull-metal gray. The couple looked to one another with doubt mirrored in their eyes. Fear of rape and vicious deaths had driven this decision. Now fear of freezing in winter slowed their step. They might escape the mainland, but not fear.

Weber asked if Jack or Maya had any questions. When they both shook their heads, he pulled a key from his cargo pocket. Maya hesitated. *Wait!* her black eyes said. Weber knew he would have to move quickly before they lost their nerve. He flipped the boat's ignition himself.

"Godspeed," he blessed them, and shook each of their hands.

Maya and Jack looked equally terrified and grateful.

Hurry . . .

Weber removed the boat's safety straps. After *Healy*'s stern door lifted, the speedboat jolted and lowered backward to a white, frothy wake. Sounds of roaring water swelled as the retrieval line hooks released. The boat launched at speed with Jack at the wheel. The man turned for a final glance back at *Healy*'s bright red flank. Captain Weber stood at a railing, his tall stature dwarfed by the colossal ship, his hand lifted against the shadows of fog.

~~~~

ALL THROUGH THE day's voyage, Maya kept looking back to the distance where they had left their mother ship. They had runny eyes and noses in the wet cold, but Maya's sniffing could have been more than that. Jack only looked ahead to their destination. He had also formed strong bonds while in the mental trenches of possible extinction, world calamity, suicide, and news reportage that literally made him vomit. Yet when the time came, it was easier for him to detach from both *Healy* and his former life. Jack was always good at running away.

"I see the island!" he called above the wind.

Jack maneuvered with the boat's pump-jets and angled south toward Gulp Island's soot-colored beaches. Fog thinned in time to reveal a seawall of rocks capping the island's northern shore, a measure by former inhabitants to buy time against storms. The wall ended midway along the island's two-mile expanse. Jack steered farther south and turned inland.

"How do I stop this thing?"

Maya reached over and shut off the engine to reduce their speed. The boat coasted and rode in the waves along with bobbing pieces of trash. Jack hopped out when the hull bumped up onto the beach. He grabbed a nylon towline and worked with the surf to pull the boat's nose clear from the water. Maya took his hand and stepped onto the beach. Both were wet and shivering. Jack's jeans were soaked.

"We need to stay dry," he said.

Maya nodded in a daze. Jack unpacked the neoprene Gumby suits for them to pull on. Even with the hoods down and collars unzipped, Jack and Maya looked ridiculous.

"We're going to freeze to death looking like Muppets," Jack joked.

And they laughed about it. Laughing was essential; to be taken on the journey to the dark side of the moon.

Jack took Maya's hand and led her across a narrow beach to the base of a ten-foot cliff. They dug the floppy feet of their suits into eroding silt and clambered up. Jack's camera swung on its strap and bounced against his chest. With three-fingered mitts, they made fists around the long, wild grasses poking out of melting slush and pulled at the earth by its hair.

At the top, Jack and Maya could see the full, treeless expanse of the island. Many objects were hidden under lumps of snow. Whatever they were, they weren't worth the effort of relocation. Neither were the leaning, single-story houses made from wood planks and corrugated metal. Some tilted by only a few degrees, while others' whole foundations were buckled and warped. If Maya and Jack were afraid of this odd-angled ghost town, they didn't speak of it. Wind folded around them in the silence, feeling their shapes.

Finally, Maya slid back down the cliff, leaving deep skids with her heels. They returned to their boat on the trash-strewn southern shore. Jack kicked at a crushed water bottle, then toed a tampon applicator.

"Shame we can't eat plastic," he sighed.

Maya found the captain's tackle box and clumsily popped the clasp with mitted fingers. Lifting its lid, she saw wooden trays filled with fishing hooks and lures in shiny candy colors.

"There are large concentrations of schooling fish in these waters," she assured the both of them. "Walleye pollock, Pacific cod, herring, sablefish. If we can feed ourselves, and maybe a few others through winter, we won't be too much trouble to take in, right?"

"What if one of us dies before the other?" Jack blurted out.

Maya set the box back down and nuzzled her lover's ginger-gold beard.

"One of us *will* die before the other," she reminded him. "That's the way of it. Before UD3 and after."

"After?" he asked with eyebrows lifted. "You mean the international defense effort that was in the news? You think they have a shot?"

Maya waved the question aside. She asked if Jack had ever seen a horseshoe crab. The species was nearly half a million years old. Its ancient self had survived all previous mass extinctions, even the great Permian extinction that had killed up to 96 percent of all marine species.

"So there's hope?" Jack asked. "Either way?"

Maya looked to the ocean. Primitive life once slithered out and evolved, for better or worse. It could happen again.

"There's always hope," she said.

Maya was wiser and stronger than all of Jack's other lovers, with a rare mix of sweetness and grit. She and Jack were an unlikely match. Only a polar ice cutter and a comet could deliver them into each other's arms. Jack loved her so much it rendered him speechless.

So he snapped a picture with his camera.

"Pictures?" Maya laughed. "Still?"

"Yes. Still."

The stories Jack captured with his Nikon made his own life's story as well. They mattered, still. There was meaning in the making.

"You've probably had a lot of survival training, right?" Maya asked.

Jack nodded, frowning. Maya was smart and sensible, but only he could keep them alive. He felt the sweaty fear of being in grave danger beside someone precious; it was a new feeling.

"Have you ever been starving?" Jack asked.

"I've been hungry."

He shook his head: not the same. Something inside Jack cracked.

It wasn't real, but psychosomatic; his scarred body telling him this woman had finally made him fragile.

"We need to find shelter and set up camp," Jack said. "I know what to do. There's hope for the two of us as well."

He stepped back and took a wide-angle shot of Gulp Island, their lodgings for the night. He would continue to capture the human experience for as long as they, and their batteries, could last.

TWENTY-SEVEN

TRUE SOLDIER OF THE WAYÃPI

BRASÍLIA
MAY 24, 2011
NATIONAL CONGRESS OF BRAZIL

> *The true soldier fights not because he hates what*
> *is in front of him, but because he loves what is*
> *behind him.*
>
> —*G. K. Chesterton*

Have you ever been surrounded by such a brilliant blue?" Father St. John mused.

The floors and leather upholstery in the Senate chamber were ultramarine, the same blue on the Brazilian flag hanging limp on the stage. The priest looked up from his seat in the upper gallery's front row to the domed ceiling, which shimmered like fish scales. Father St. John blinked away tears from either too much sunlight or too much beauty in a man-made structure that housed such corrupt men and women. Two out of every three members of Congress faced criminal accusations, ranging from bribery to murder.

"Niemeyer architecture," the priest whispered in Gustavo's ear. "One of our own."

"Our own?"

"Sorry, Brazilian. Niemeyer was born in Rio de Janeiro."

Gustavo ignored this. The priest was Canadian and Gustavo

was a Wayãpi Indian—or an Indigenous person, or whatever name Brazilians were using these days. Both men had lived in the forest and on its dangerous frontier for the majority of their lives. At sixty-eight, Father St. John's hair and beard were still full but completely gray. He was no longer thin, but that common fat-thin of elderly men with a paunch on which he rested his folded arms. His long, skinny legs were knock-kneed like a curassow bird. Gustavo was in his late forties and had long hair that was still black but without luster.

"Is the list ready?" Gustavo prodded.

Reflections in the priest's pale irises vanished as he looked back down at Gustavo with something close to pity.

"If I didn't know you better," he said, reaching for the leather satchel propped against his sandaled feet, "I'd tell you to enjoy beauty wherever you can find it. But I *do* know you better."

Gustavo had met Father St. John, and all the books the priest kept locked away from the forest's cockroaches, when he was eight years old. An evangelical missionary had sent the boy to find a priest living in a cabin beside a settlement of miners. The missionary wanted Gustavo to be baptized, but Father St. John had no interest in converting a child who didn't understand the meaning of it. He was not a missionary, but he did have a mission. *I heard the cry of my people*, he always repeated. The statement was both complicated, for all its many references, and simple. "I Have Heard the Cry of My People" was a letter signed and released by northeastern Brazil's bishops in 1973, denouncing systemic violations of human rights. It was also a statement attributed to God in the Book of Exodus as he spoke of the oppressed Israelites. Once more, it was Father St. John's own sentiment since he had left the land of his birth to answer this cry.

"Body count is nine hundred thirteen." The priest sighed, pulling a stack of papers out of his satchel. "We can't count missing persons, unfortunately. Only corpses."

The Walking Dead List supposedly tallied up all the names of activists who pressed for labor rights, Indigenous rights, sustainable farming, and environmental justice—until they were murdered for it. The number was a gross underestimation; the forest had a bad habit of drowning out screams and swallowing up evidence. But the names of those who undoubtedly lost their lives to greed and violence were something that couldn't be denied.

Gustavo dropped the papers on his lap without a glance. Large numbers still confused him, and he already knew the names of all the brave people reduced to ink on paper. The Walking Dead List existed for those who didn't know. Gustavo swiveled his head to survey the busy gallery with full seats and bodies packed into the standing room behind them. He had wanted to approach a reporter about publishing the list and wasn't expecting so many.

"I've never seen so many reporters turn out for the forest," Gustavo remarked.

"They're here for *you*," the priest insisted.

Father St. John had tried and failed to instill the significance of a Nobel Prize in Literature. Gustavo wasn't going to attend the award ceremony in Stockholm and chided his friend for being so characteristically optimistic about the stated prize. *No one has that much money, Sinjin,* he would reply, calling his friend by his family name.

"If the reporters are here for me, then they're not here for the forest code vote?" Gustavo said.

"Perhaps a few?"

The priest was an optimist, not a liar. Weakening the laws that had governed the forest since 1965 was historic. But the media served the public, and the same public that generally supported the environment in opinion polls also elected the corrupt politicians who fought to exploit and destroy it.

There was a double flash of a camera at the back of the gallery. When Gustavo turned around, another flash blinded him. Father St. John laughed at his puzzled expression.

"Get used to it," he added.

Teasing Gustavo while teaching him and nudging him toward love, in every Christian sense of the word, were Father St. John's favorite pastimes.

A senator made his way to the podium at the front of the chamber. Father St. John sat up straight and frowned.

"I know I must love all God's children," he said, "but this one's a real bastard."

The federal senator was a rich cattle baron turned politician, a powerful member of the rural bloc. At the podium, he wore an expensive suit with a Brazilian flag pin on his lapel. Before the man became a senator, he was local governor of the frontier state of Rondônia, where he wore simple clothes and a brimmed straw hat. He wanted to appear as a man of the people—more specifically, rich cattle ranchers like himself.

"*Meus amigos,*" he said, with arms outstretched, and continued to address his fellow senators in Portuguese.

When his eyes scanned the gallery and caught sight of Gustavo, he smirked. Gustavo wasn't used to being seen, especially not by men like that. He felt his pulse quicken as they regarded each other with calculated hate.

"I see more white faces judging from above," the senator said, growling the syllables.

He pointed an accusatory finger up at Father St. John, a pale Canadian Jesuit working with the social justice wing of the Church.

"Those hypocrites from the north tell us not to develop our lands because we are hurting the Indians and the animals. Who the hell are they to say this during a recession?"

He laughed and threw up his hands.

"I'll tell you who . . . they are the ones who sold their forests, skinned all their animals, and slaughtered their natives. That's who. The North American colonies were built on blood-drenched lands."

Father St. John looked at his feet but didn't budge from his seat.

He had told Gustavo that the massacres of his ancestors were more reason to fight against massacres of the present—not less.

"The rest of the West has grown rich from their lands," the senator argued. "Now it's our turn."

The chamber resounded with applause from the floor, making him even more bold.

"If the Amazon is the lungs of the world," the senator shouted, "then the world must pay us to breathe!"

One by one, senators stood to cheer and bruise their palms with clapping.

"We've lost," Father St. John whispered.

He wasn't wrong—the code amendments passed with a majority in both legislative houses—but before the ballots were cast, a congressman stepped up to the lectern microphone unexpectedly. The former environment minister looked out at the gallery in a shocked daze.

"Something terrible has happened," he said into the microphone.

Only a respectful stranger, like this man, would refer to them as José Cláudio Ribeiro da Silva and Maria do Espírito Santo. To everyone who knew and loved them, they were Zé and Maria. That was how the couple had introduced themselves to church members in the state of Pará after they started receiving death threats in 2008. The land that they rented from the government for sustainable harvesting was under attack from illegal loggers and charcoal burners. Members of the church hired a lawyer to file official complaints to government agencies on their behalf, but police protection was refused.

Zé wouldn't run from his home, and he wouldn't back down. He talked to anyone who would listen about the value of the rainforest and what was being done to it. He took pictures of all the trucks carrying off felled logs from burning forest and emailed them to police and reporters alike. Just last year, he was invited to speak at a TEDx conference and had his speech posted to YouTube. But as media attention spread across Brazil and beyond to the international community, Zé and Maria became bigger targets.

And so it was Zé and Maria who were sprayed with fifteen bullets. It was Zé and Maria who would be laid out in matching coffins with white polyester silk framing their faces to hide the ragged holes where assassins had cut off their ears as proof for payment.

"I'd like to call for an investigation into the double homicide—" the senator started to say, but a roar of booing from the floor drowned out the rest of his words.

Father St. John's jaw hung open as the rest of the upper gallery audience looked at one another in shock. Gustavo saw a familiar face, the Greenpeace director sitting six seats to the right, shake his head in sadness but not surprise. Amid all the commotion, the Senate called a recess. Several people in the upper gallery filed out and took to the stairs. One journalist making his way to the aisle whispered congratulations for Gustavo's Nobel award.

Read one of your poems at my funeral, Zé had said to Gustavo. *The one about my beautiful Majesty.*

Father St. John swallowed something of a moan and said humanity should thank God for all the dirt of the earth. Without that dirt, the faces of the dead would be unbearable.

"There will be more," he warned. "And the Belo Monte dam proposal will get approved next week."

And as collateral damage, a vast amount of rainforest would be submerged underwater, including the traditional homeland of the Kayapo people. Gustavo leaned over the gallery's metal railing, staring daggers at the eighty-one senators directly below.

"Fifteen bullets," he said. "Fifteen. All the fingers on three hands."

Of course the number of bullets wasn't for the newly dead but for the still living. They were for him, Father St. John, and all the others who resisted exploitation by the rich and powerful.

"Our enemies hire assassins to do their devil's work," Father St. John said.

Gustavo continued to study the men below, stripping himself down to his single, dogged mission of destroying the destroyers.

"And they will never see the inside of a jail. But you would, Gustavo."

Gustavo finally turned to look at the priest. His friend must have seen past his sickened soul, straight to the murderous intent lodged at its core like a pit.

A plump white man approached Gustavo in the aisle. All of him looked white—his hair, his beard, his linen shirt, and the undersides of his arms and stout legs. Only the red burn on his face and the tops of his arms had color.

"I'm with the Intergovernmental Panel on Climate Change," the man said, extending his hand. "And I've read all your poetry collections."

Gustavo ignored the other man's open palm.

"Today was...one tragedy after another," the man conceded, putting his hand back at his side. "But isn't that why we need poets? Tragedy is your trade."

Light from the domed silver ceiling flashed in his wireframe glasses.

"And the Amazon isn't the only tragedy, the only battleground of climate change," he said. "There is another for you to write about..."

Only the environments that were most hostile to human civilization, the Amazon and the Arctic, had been spared from its massive destruction—until now. The white man offered to take Gustavo on an ocean voyage to show him melting icebergs, drowned polar bears, beaches littered with trash and starved murres, abandoned Inuit villages, and rising sea levels. He handed over a business card, which Father St. John accepted as Gustavo remained motionless.

"Dr. Charles Brodie," the priest read aloud. "University of California, Berkeley. The Turner Foundation Endowed Chair Professor of—"

"Just call me Charlie," the man offered.

After he left, Father St. John pocketed his card.

"That kind of voyage would grant you an American visa with no questions asked," he whispered. "An escape from all this—"

They were interrupted by a young man walking toward them from the gallery. He stopped in the aisle and bowed in deference as he introduced himself in Portuguese as the Brazilian bureau chief for the *New York Times*.

"I'm mainly covering a different vote," he admitted, "but the forest code interests me personally. I'm trying to build a story that will gain enough readership to publish."

Gustavo waited silently. He didn't have any advice on how to make Brazilians care.

"A statement from you would mean a great deal," the man explained. "Perhaps enough to make a difference."

Gustavo only wished to be left alone to grieve for Zé and Maria and stew in hatred, but he knew these selfish activities achieved nothing. He rose and nodded to the bureau chief. As they headed for the stairs together, another journalist followed them, armed with a pencil and notepad. Yet another pulled out his cellphone and started recording video as they reached the Senate chamber floor.

A few of the senators had left for the break, but many remained to chat or answer emails on their laptops. Gustavo spotted the rural bloc senator in a large group of cohorts. His face was a caricature of competence and fraternity as they showered him with congratulations on his speech. When the senator locked eyes with Gustavo, his mask fell away in his surprise. Gustavo stepped up to the microphone with a look that said, *Now it is my turn.* More and more journalists gathered below him.

Gustavo described the aftertaste of a poisoned river: the bitter metal of mercury and the sour burn of pesticides. The taste, and the floating fish, only came after your children had already drunk their fill. Gustavo described acres of smoking ash that had once been verdant forests noisy with animals. The death of the forest was also the death of life for hunter-gatherers like the Wayãpi and harvesters like Zé and Maria.

He lifted the Walking Dead List in one hand and described a pile of bones. If he were to reach in, he might pull out the jawbone of Sister Dorothy Stang, an American nun who taught sustainable farming to the rural poor renting federal land. She was shot with all six bullets of a revolver from a gunman hired by a rancher. The jawbone was still and silent, no longer giving voice to their cause.

Reaching in again, Gustavo might pull out a femur from one of the "root collectors" who illegally cut down and burned the forest. These men were rarely the ones who profited. Some were easier to kill and bury in shallow graves. In death, they joined the dead zones of forest they had burned.

Before reading off the names of his list, Gustavo thought of the senator from the rural bloc.

"Meus amigos," he said, slapping the list over his heart.

TWENTY-EIGHT

ESCAPE

AMAPÁ, BRAZIL
APRIL 3, 2019

THE FIRST THING Gustavo remembered in that small stretch of wretched time was anger—his usual kind, which is to say nothing of the blinding rage that came later. It was the road sign that caused it, the one along the drive from Wayãpi lands to the frontier town of Pedra Branca do Amapari. The sign stated that the lands were protected, but what was stated was not the reality.

The southern half of the Wayãpi's designated territory lay within the RENCA reserve, which housed the world's largest remaining forest as well as deposits of gold, manganese, iron, and copper. In 2017, Brazil's president tried to abolish the reserve's protection but was luckily, blessedly, blocked by a federal judge. That same year, an illegal mine was shut down a mile from a Wayãpi village. Several years later, the fight was still the same.

"Our warriors have guns like the Brazilians," Gustavo's twin brother, Tuír, called out.

He sat in the back seat of Father St. John's jeep, blinking with the wind and pulling long strands of hair from his eyes.

"We have bows and poison-tipped arrows. We are brave and will fight to the death!"

Gustavo sighed. Yes, the Wayãpi men were brave, but the rifles the government had given them were decades old and their bows weren't real, not like the Grandfather People made them. Father St. John said that the government had many methods to keep Indigenous villages under control. This particular method started with gifts from the modern world: matches that saved a family from the tedious chore of starting a fire with a spark; manufactured cloth that saved them from having to grow cotton, spin it into yarn, dye it with *urucu*, and weave it into fabric; rifles with bullets—but only in exchange for their bows and arrows.

Villages grew dependent on these gifts as their traditional ways of survival were forgotten. And then the matches ran out, the fabrics tore, and the rifles needed more bullets. Indians had to obey the government and watch helpless as the boundaries of their lands shrank.

Gustavo leaned over from the front passenger seat to hand his brother a bundle of clothes. They were almost at the edge of town. Tuír grumbled as he struggled to find the armholes of the shirt. He wasn't used to white-man clothes, but then he wasn't used to Father St. John, automobiles, or the town of Pedra Branca do Amapari. He definitely wasn't used to running for election to the town's city council.

"There is more than one way to do battle," Gustavo told him. "We have no say about what happens to us until we can get an Indian in government."

He turned back around as Tuír pulled on khaki shorts and removed his loincloth. Father St. John kept his bespectacled eyes on the rough terrain ahead and let the brothers yell at one another in Wayãpi.

"Why don't *you* do it?"

Tuír asked this just as Gustavo was checking his cellphone for a regained signal.

"It needs to be a Wayãpi who lives with our people in the forest," Gustavo replied.

What he meant was, it should be a *real* Wayãpi and not one who had to leave the traditional ways to try to save them. Gustavo barely remembered his true name. Too often, he thought of himself by his Portuguese name, the one a missionary gave him with a shrug, as if to say, *Why not?*

"I am the voice of our tribe with poetry," Gustavo called out. "You need to be the face."

Tuír laughed and said they had the same face. He wasn't one for metaphors.

"I do my share," Gustavo insisted. "That's why *I* get the death threats. Not *you*."

"You do for the *other* Indians," Tuír countered. "You even do for Brazilians more than you have ever done for Wayãpi."

There was truth in this. Gustavo had fought for the land rights of Indigenous peoples and peasant farmers alike. Father St. John insisted that allies needed to unite, or it would be hopeless. It had to be all of Brazil's powerless united against mass destruction and exploitation by loggers, miners, agribusiness, cattle barons, and oil refiners. This battle took Gustavo away from Wayãpi lands. It took him to the trade union leader of the rubber tappers, Chico Mendes, before he was murdered. It took him to Zé and Maria when they were still alive. It had taken him to Paris and to Washington, DC. In the meantime, Gustavo didn't recognize Tuír's two sons as they grew unseen.

Father St. John pointed to a gas station coming up on the side. He needed to refill before they headed into town to his modest parish, where he and Gustavo now lived when they weren't traveling. All three men got out of the jeep after he parked. The priest disappeared into a small store to pay for gas at the register.

"Make a real bow," Gustavo said to his brother.

Tuír gritted his teeth and shook his head. He said he didn't want a bow. He could hunt so much more easily with a rifle. He needed to use bullets now that the animals had grown scarce.

"Make another bow," Gustavo insisted. "Try."

"You don't remember how hard it is," Tuír said. "You have to find the perfect wood near the Capoeira headwaters. It needs to be shaved down with the jawbone of a white-lipped peccary. When we lived by the Nipukú River, there were herds of them in the forest. My sons have never seen a single peccary in their lives—"

"Or a real bow," Gustavo added.

You can't teach your children what you forget.

"The Wayãpi must remember the ways of the Grandfather People—" Gustavo started, but Tuír barked a laugh, as if to say, *These words from you? You who wear khaki shorts with a cellphone in one pocket and a wallet in the other.*

Again, Gustavo felt his anger rising. When they were children, no one in their village could tell the twins apart at first sight. Not until Tuír showed his quick temper, or Gustavo laughed. They said that Gustavo loved to laugh so hard that he fell over backward, but he couldn't remember a time when he wasn't sad, resigned, or angry.

"Stay here," Gustavo said, before he turned and walked away.

It was one of the little ways the twins hurt one another; their instinct was to remain at each other's side.

Gustavo was in the store when it happened. He was trying to read the small print on the packaging of a new phone card. In one second, he realized that his eyes were failing with old age. In the next, bullets shattered the shop's windows. Gustavo dropped to a crouch and covered his ears until the deafening gunfire stopped. When he lifted his head, Gustavo saw Father St. John slumped against the counter, bloody and dazed. Gustavo scrambled over to him, trying not to skid and fall on shards of glass. He held the old man's face in one hand while the other patted his body, searching for mortal wounds. The priest groaned in pain, but he wasn't shot, just cut and bruised all over. Gustavo looked through the shot-out frames of windows.

My brother!

As he jumped up, the priest grabbed his leg. Gustavo yanked hard. Twice—three times before he could pull free from the old man's tight grip. Tires squealed on the road outside. By the time Gustavo raced out the door, a red truck was already peeling off down the road into town. Tuír was lying by the parked jeep with his face up, eyes and mouth open. Blood darkened his orange polo shirt to a wet crimson. The flap of one ear was cut off.

Gustavo stared down and saw a lifeless body identical to his own. He thought he saw himself with empty eyes looking up at the sky. Those last words thrown at his brother would haunt Gustavo forever. *Stay here*, he had said to Tuír. And so his twin had died in his place.

~~~

HEALY IN THE GULF OF ALASKA
DECEMBER 28
T-MINUS 35 DAYS TO LAUNCH

STAY HERE...

Gustavo had stayed outside that gas station. Time had frozen, trapping him in a small piece of the past with no urge to break through. Numb shock gave way to waves of acute pain as he relived the murder and felt Tuír's absence. Gustavo had read so many poems about the aftermath of war in which soldiers felt severe burning, itching, and clenching motions in their missing limbs. Gustavo felt these pains for his missing twin, now a phantom self.

His more lucid moments of grief were tinged with a bitter and hopeless despair over the inevitable extinction of the Wayãpi. For how could he save an entire tribe when he couldn't even save his own brother? And so Gustavo stayed there, in that time of horror and death. Until now.

He stuffed a piece of cornbread into his mouth, chewed, and

swallowed. Then he ate a spoonful of beans as he considered his bunkmate's parting words: *For the first time in hundreds of years, the Wayãpi will be left alone in the forest. Until the comet hits or doesn't.* Jack was right. Suddenly the Wayãpi were no more doomed than the rest of humanity. In fact, they were better off in the safety of the forest with their knowledge of how to subsist and survive.

Gustavo ate more beans as he felt the burden of saving the Wayãpi and their lands lift from his shoulders—thanks to a comet. When his awareness fully returned to the here and now, Gustavo looked down and saw that his plate was scraped clean; he had eaten a full meal. Everyone on *Healy* had encouraged Gustavo to eat more on the journey: Jack, Ensign Ortiz, the members of something called the Morale Committee, but things had drastically changed. Two Coasties had to search the pockets of his poncho and jeans for smuggled food before Gustavo was allowed to leave the mess hall.

On the way back to his room, Gustavo peered out of a porthole and shielded his eyes from a setting sun like a glowing ember. He thought of Frost...

> *Some say the world will end in fire,*
> *Some say in ice.*

There was a Wayãpi myth of the Great Fire that Ends the World, but Gustavo couldn't remember where the fire came from. Did it come from the starry skies? Or did it come from people? The Wayãpi themselves stole fire from the jaguar, when they were still animals and birds and the jaguar roamed in human form. With the power of fire, the Wayãpi learned to speak; they became human while the jaguar became an animal that could only roar in anger. Was being human about power? What about the power of destruction?

A woman passed behind him in the corridor, ripping on the nail beds of four fingers with bloody teeth. Gustavo couldn't catch what she was muttering.

It wouldn't be long before the ship anchored. There were announcements over the speakers, what Jack had called the pipes, that alternated prayers from the New Testament with instructions for gearing up and reporting to a lifeboat. Gustavo reached the entrance to the crew lounge and heard loud male voices.

"Government called for good helicopter pilots," one stated. "They were flying them to South America, where they need to be able to take off and land vertically in the jungle."

Gustavo peeked in and saw a few men seated at a table in the corner of the lounge. The voice belonged to a big young man called Ned, who was slouched over a fan of playing cards.

"Who says there's still a need?" another man said. "Who says there's still a government? We've been at sea for almost five months."

"All that matters," Ned replied, "is the defense effort at the equator. Captain Weber said so himself. So *if* there's still an Effort, then I'm the helicopter pilot to find it."

Ned cursed his "shit cards" and said he was going to "hit the head." Gustavo backpedaled just as Ned exited the lounge.

"You are traveling to the South American equator?" Gustavo asked, nearly breathless.

The big Coastie startled and looked down. Ned had met Gustavo during a night of drinking under the Northern Lights. He had been quiet and watchful in Gustavo's presence. *I've never met a Nobel Prize winner*, he finally said sheepishly.

"Well, I'm flying to Fort Hood in Texas," Ned said after a pause. "If it's still there. Our military was transporting personnel and supplies to the European spaceport in French Guiana. I'm hoping to catch a ride south."

"Show me where you will go," Gustavo commanded, pulling out the folded map he kept in his pocket.

Ned bent down and located the mouth of the Amazon River

where it chipped and fissured the southern continent like the rim of a ceramic bowl. His index finger traced north along the coast, past the Oyapock River, to French Guiana.

"Here," he said. "I think."

Gustavo's insides felt the heat of a terrifying hope. If the young man was to be believed—and Gustavo had grown accustomed to suspending all belief a long time ago—Gustavo wouldn't have to die in this frigid and barren place. He had traveled to the snowy edge of the earth, and now he could go home.

~~~

CAPTAIN WEBER PAUSED by a porthole on his way to the weapons locker. Fog blocked first light; it was difficult to see where the Puget Sound of Washington ended and where fog and rain clouds began. Weber was grateful for the low visibility. No one on the coast would be able to see *Healy* until she drew close to anchor by the docks. There was no need to attract trouble when they would find it soon enough.

The fog wouldn't help *Healy*'s pilot, however. Weber couldn't help a smile when he thought of Ned Brandt, a strapping, clear-eyed young man with an unpredictable depth of character. When he wasn't losing his shirt at poker in the crew lounge, Ned was reading Steinbeck novels while eating twigs of jerky. On deck, he was the first to lend a hand to the other crewmembers or scientists. Backbreaking labor and long hours never stopped him from smiling or remarking on the beauty of cerulean water. He even used the word *cerulean* before farting into the wind as he paused to admire. Weber wasn't supposed to have favorites, but he did.

The captain walked to the ship's weapons locker and found Ned waiting in a flight suit. As soon as *Healy* passed the mouth of Commencement Bay, he would lift off.

"Well, this is one way to get out of gambling debt," Weber joked as he reached into his pocket for a key.

Ned's eyes crinkled when he smiled. His face was young but also freckled with exposure.

"The defense effort could use me," Ned reminded him.

It could use a Hail Mary more than anything, but Weber only nodded. Ned tried to thank him again for the extra fuel, but it wasn't necessary. Ned was the ship's sole pilot, so the fuel in the Dolphin helicopter's tank would only go to waste. Weber had ordered his men to drain the Dolphin and pack up the Jayhawk with as many canisters as she could hold.

"What's your plan B, son? Just in case you can't hitch a ride south from Fort Hood," he asked Ned, but they both knew he meant, *Just in case there is no Fort Hood.*

Ned said that he was still working on a plan B. The captain pursed his lips and nodded.

"Sir, something I want you to know," Ned said. "When I picked *Healy* for assignment, I was picking you."

Ned offered his hand, but the captain embraced him briefly and patted his meaty shoulder.

"Godspeed," he blessed. "Now, let's get you armed."

Weber unlocked the weapons locker and lifted a semiautomatic rifle from the rack.

"We're not talking polar bears or hostile smugglers anymore," Weber conceded, "but the same rule applies: When you need to shoot, you shoot. Period."

"Yes, Captain."

Ned took the rifle, but his eyes lifted back up to the gun rack.

"Have you decided who's gonna get the rest?"

Weber frowned and averted his eyes.

"I'm advising them to travel in groups and protect each other."

It wasn't an answer because Weber didn't have an answer. There was no right way to divvy up a small number of firearms among a large crew about to make a run for their lives. He had looked at the problem six ways to Sunday and still couldn't determine a just decision.

"You said 'them,'" Ned said. "You're not headed to Lewis-McChord with the others?"

Weber shook his head and said he was headed for the Cascade Mountains and would take his chances on his own, like Ned. The younger man gave a quizzical smile.

"The funny thing of it is," Ned said, "I'm not going alone."

TWENTY-NINE

WE ARE BORN OF LOVE

CHONGQING, CHINA
1986

ZHEN'S MOTHER HAD no tolerance for her daughter's dried tears and the shame prescribed by others. She understood that Zhen was a girl with a very slight facial deformity, and for that she was bullied and made to feel less than worthless, a bad element that needed to be stamped out of a community. But Zhen was beloved by a family that had fought too long and hard to give in now.

"Words don't draw blood," her mother insisted. "You don't know real suffering."

She paused from chopping garlic for their dinner and wiped her hands on her apron. This was usually when her mother began telling horrific stories that Zhen knew by heart and still feared, but Zhen was twelve years old. While she tried to be invisible outside the safety of home, she was testing her voice inside it—especially with her mother.

"You don't know what I know," Zhen said quietly. "Because you're not me."

The logic was faultless, but her mother still looked stricken. Zhen used the silence to continue.

"No older boys called you a shit-eating sewer rat because of this," she said, pointing to her upper lip.

Zhen's scars had paled, but her upper lip was still slightly lifted and skewed from reconstructive surgery.

"They have a point," Zhen admitted. "I do look like a rodent or rabbit, without the whiskers."

What she didn't say was, *No one will want to kiss this mouth.*

The girls at school talked about boys incessantly, but Zhen could only listen at a distance. She might wear the same uniform, but she was not one of them. She was different in too many ways. Zhen knew it. They knew it. And knowing made it all the worse.

Zhen walked past her mother into the family room. The Lius still didn't have a TV like most of their neighbors in the apartment building, much to Zhen's disappointment; she found the science and near magic of broadcast images fascinating. Zhen's father said that the Liu family didn't spend carelessly on appliances; they invested in their children. Zhen had had two facial surgeries before she was old enough to remember. Kuo, her older brother by four years, had been privately tutored in several foreign languages during secondary school and now studied in Cambridge, England. Despite these large investments, the Liu family wasn't struggling. Comrade Liu was the manager at the Chongqing power station and was held in high esteem. The family owned a nice dining table set carved from rosewood. A sofa sat against the wall, framed photographs covered the walls, and a bookshelf was full of hardbacks with titles such as *Power System Engineering*, *Electric Fields and Circuits*, *Thermodynamics*, *Differential Calculus*, and the latest cookbooks gifted to Zhen's mother to inspire her utilitarian meals.

Zhen folded her coat over the arm of the sofa before she continued down a small hallway. Their apartment in Chongqing had two bedrooms: Zhen's parents slept in the larger master bedroom, and her grandfather now slept in the smaller one. He had come to live with the family over a year ago after his wife passed. Zhen didn't mind sleeping on the sofa and moving her clothes into neat piles against the family room wall. Her paternal grandfather was a national hero, a mathematician who had survived the Cultural Revolution by working for the military's intelligence unit as a cryptographer. On the other side of her family, Zhen's maternal grandparents were university professors before they were labeled class enemies and sent to *laogai* camps, never to be seen again—no bodies, no graves.

Zhen saw cigarette smoke hanging in a haze by the smaller bedroom door. One would think that Zhen's grandfather loved cigarettes more than anything in life, but he had to love her more, because he stubbed them out in a ceramic ashtray whenever she visited. Zhen never complained, but he knew the smoke made her cough. She knocked on the bedroom door and waited, and then knocked again. Her grandfather slept a lot; living so many decades was exhausting.

When Zhen entered the musty bedroom, her grandfather was sitting up in one of the twin beds. He lay against pillows propped against the wall. A quilted blanket covered the lower half of his thin body. His brown face creased with a sunken, toothless smile, like the fissures of a walnut. Zhen took heart. How could she be all the ugly things her bullies claimed while in the loving arms of such an important family?

Her grandfather plucked his dentures from the bedside table while Zhen unzipped her backpack and pulled out a thin stack of papers. She didn't want to show schoolwork, only her personal investigations: Zhen work. Her grandfather nodded as he inspected her technical drawings.

"Part of our wall clock," he said, pointing to plastic cogs rendered in the silvery graphite of Zhen's pencils.

She had flipped their clock over on its face to get to the black plastic cartridge that attached to the hour, minute, and second hands. Using her father's tiny screwdriver, Zhen had opened the cartridge and disassembled the inner workings piece by piece. After close inspection, Zhen drew several pieces on a page at three times the scale in near perfect proportion. Finally, Zhen rubbed her pencil eraser through thick applications of graphite, creating white smudges that mimicked light reflecting off copper wiring or the glossy dark surface of a battery cylinder.

When her grandfather handed back the stack of drawings, Zhen flipped on the bedside lamp beside them. She tapped her stack on the nightstand to square up the edges, then held it up to the light. Her papers looked as translucent as the skins of a pan-seared onion. Clock pieces on every page overlapped in their original configuration. Zhen's grandfather even saw the plastic teeth of several cogs interlock. He smiled and embraced his granddaughter with pride. The stench of stale cigarettes and sweat made Zhen breathe through her mouth, but she still held him tight.

"And it worked when you put the pieces back together?" her grandfather asked.

He often told Zhen that his full approval had to be short lived because she was young, and it was the job of the young to learn and improve. Zhen released his narrow shoulders and nodded quickly.

"And you hung it back on the wall before your mother noticed your tinkering?" he added.

Zhen giggled and instinctually covered her smile with her hand. When she was younger, she couldn't remember how many years ago exactly, Zhen had tried every facial expression she could think of in front of a mirror. Both smiling and frowning tugged on the scars below her nose and exaggerated them. After this discovery, Zhen covered her mouth when she felt it stretch with expression. The habit made her grandfather very sad.

"Please don't hide your smile," he reminded her.

Zhen slowly moved her hand; she couldn't deny her grandfather anything.

"When I was young and strong, I protected my family from the entire Red Army," he muttered, "and now I can't even protect them from ordinary assholes."

He sighed and pointed to her drawings to change the subject. The tip of his finger rested on the sketch of a tiny cylinder of metal that Zhen couldn't open without fear of breaking it.

"And what do you think is inside this?" he asked.

"The thing that keeps the time?"

It was the only part of the equation that was missing. Zhen's eyes could trace the transition of electric power that began with the battery and ended in the mechanical power of a stepping motor that moved the cogs that turned the hands—but where was the precision and control? Zhen's grandfather didn't seem too surprised or disappointed when she had no further guesses.

"What was the one word printed on the clockface?" he prodded.

"Quartz?"

He lifted his eyebrows. And here Zhen always thought it was the name of a company, not a mineral inside! She tried to ask questions, but a fit of coughing and wheezing gasps interrupted her grandfather's answers.

"Ask your father about quartz crystal oscillators when he gets home from work," he finally managed to say. "I shouldn't have all the fun."

Zhen's grandfather lay back on his pillows, spent, exposing the bony knob of his throat. He had only one more question for her, the same question he always asked before gently patting her on the shoulder to dismiss her.

"And your mathematics?"

He had pushed his children and grandchildren toward the useful profession of engineering for their own safety and sanity; pure mathematics was once considered a pastime for bourgeois intellectuals, and cryptography led to obsession and madness. Whatever the application, however, math was the universal language at its foundation. This language was innate to the Liu family, such that they could not only speak it from a young age but sing with full lungs. Zhen assured her grandfather that her test scores were very good. Only after he pressed her did Zhen admit that they were perfect.

When she stepped into the hallway, her mother was silently standing close to the bedroom door. She turned and walked back to the family room. Zhen followed, quietly repeating her grandfather's request for his afternoon tea and his comment that the afternoon noodle broth didn't have enough Sichuan pepper.

Zhen's mother turned and planted her feet.

"I get angry at you sometimes," she admitted.

Zhen hung her head as she sat on the sofa and pulled books and worksheets out of her backpack. She hoped her mother would leave her to concentrate on schoolwork—not that she needed concentration. Zhen often got in trouble with her math teacher because she never wrote out equations, just the answers. Doing calculations in her head was much faster and allowed more time for Zhen to sit at her desk and think of more interesting equations. Her teacher knew better than to accuse Zhen of cheating, but he often lectured the class on the dangers of arrogance as he paced up and down rows of desks, pausing at Zhen's. He was very wrong. Zhen didn't enjoy watching her classmates struggle with solutions that came to her instantly. It didn't make her feel superior that she had a better handle on mathematics than her teacher; it just made her feel more alone.

"It's not that I don't care," her mother insisted. "It's that I care too much. When you let those bullies hurt you, you let them hurt me."

Zhen nodded and swallowed hard. Her eyes stung.

"You must be brave," her mother pleaded. "Wear your skin armor."

In the Zhou dynasty, warriors had stretched dried rhino skin into coats of armor. The grandmother who had told these stories to Zhen's mother was taken away and never returned. Zhen's mother didn't have her own mother. She only had Zhen.

"I will be brave," Zhen promised out loud.

Light reflections swam in her mother's dark eyes, a purer white than Zhen could achieve with the strenuous rubbing of her pencil eraser.

"A quartz oscillator is a tiny crystal cut from quartz in the shape of a tuning fork," her mother said, sniffing a runny nose.

Zhen listened as her mother explained the properties of quartz: after applying a voltage, the mineral could vibrate back and forth an exact number of times per second, creating an electrical signal with a precise frequency. This was the precision and control that was missing.

"Quartz clocks are better than pendulum clocks that depend on gravity, which changes from valleys to mountaintops," her mother added.

She smiled and pointed to Zhen's school backpack.

"May I see your drawings?"

-∿∿∿-

THAT NIGHT, ZHEN woke with a painfully full bladder. She tried to fall back asleep, but it was inevitable that she would need to use the washroom. Zhen wiggled her feet into slippers and stood in the moonlight. Tiptoeing soundlessly, Zhen heard noises from her parents' bedroom. She pressed her ear against the door and heard the creaking and metallic plings of shifting weight on a wooden bed frame and coiled box springs. Her mother's voice was muffled but understandable as she spoke to her husband.

"I want Zhen to be tutored in languages like Kuo."

Zhen held her breath. The world outside of China was still an exotic mystery that she had only begun to experience secondhand. Foreign students had returned to China's universities in the last several years. Zhen's father had invited several to his home to teach his son languages like Russian, German, and Italian. His wife served tea at the rosewood dining table, where lessons were conducted. Zhen helped her mother so she could hover and listen. She felt like her cryptographer grandfather, on a mission to decode the hidden order of what sounded like a babble of noise.

Zhen had even seen a few American movies. They were dubbed in Mandarin, but still—they were *American*! China's president Li Xiannian had been the first to set foot on American soil just last year. In this new era of history, who could guess what the future would bring as it opened wider?

"Tutors are a large expense," her father said, taken aback and wary that his wife might insist.

He knew her too well. She said that the tutoring would only be necessary for two years, until Zhen would be full grown and ready to apply to university. Zhen's jaw dropped with such an equally exciting and terrifying prospect. She would be fourteen in two years, which was two years younger than her brother when he left for England, and four years younger than the average student. Would a four-year age gap make her peers kinder or crueler?

"And I'll go back to work one day," Zhen's mother added wistfully.

She didn't need to elaborate. Zhen's mother, the other Comrade Liu, had been an engineer before she became a wife, daughter-in-law, and mother of two children. It was an unspoken understanding that she would return to her calling when her father-in-law was dead and her children grown.

"Why?" Zhen's father finally asked. "Why does Zhen need to learn languages when we can't afford to send her abroad like Kuo? And why does she need to apply to university so young?"

Zhen felt heat radiate from her cheeks. Her father worked so hard for the family that Zhen rarely saw him. When he was home, he tried to spend time with his dying father and visit the grave of his mother. Troubling him with Zhen's own desires and well-being seemed shameful; it would make her the most selfish child in

Chongqing. Zhen squinted her eyes shut as she waited and worried over her mother's answer.

"Because Zhen is my daughter, and I want this for her."

She spoke as if the matter was already settled. Zhen's mother was dutiful and quiet, but strong willed—a confusing mix. The mattress squeaked; she must have shifted and turned over on her shoulder to face the wall, ending their conversation.

THIRTY

SKIN ARMOR

ZHEN WAS LATE reaching the Final Assembly Building. She insisted on remaining at the infirmary to check on the remaining Chinese soldiers from Cayenne. Only days ago, two had died within hours of each other, their bodies too weak to fight kidney failure. Zhen held their hands and listened to their last words. They were not alone, as much as anyone cannot be alone at death.

Zhen visited the infirmary as much as she could and let the staff know her soldiers were important. As for her own importance, it was beyond question. Zhen's reputation as the possible savior to humanity had spread throughout the Effort. All eyes now looked to her with wonder and gratitude. There was little doubt that she was the reason the Cayenne soldiers were still treated well, while other patients disappeared mysteriously, leaving empty cots stripped of their sheets.

"Zhen! Over here!"

Zhen was several meters from the exit when she heard her name. She turned to see a very old man lying in one of the beds with an IV drip. He became more familiar as she walked over and began to resemble the photographs of a younger, healthier, clothed Professor Tobias Ochsenfeld.

"We finally meet in the flesh," he said. His grin was first earnest and then wry as he added, "As disappointing as that may be."

The Professor's bleary, bespectacled eyes still managed an intense, observant stare that he now trained on Zhen's facial scars. The left was slightly shorter than the scar on her right, skewing her upper lip by only a few degrees. Here was a renowned astrophysicist and mathematician that Zhen held in the highest regard, and yet his eyes went where all eyes went.

"Does my face offend you?" Zhen asked. "With our insistence on symmetry as a selection effect?"

The Professor's face suddenly animated.

"You've read my essays!" he exclaimed. "Ah, that... that is a treat. So few of my peers even bother."

It took him longer than a pause to scoff, like it was a waste of breath to add such an obvious statement. "But of course you're beautiful. All young and healthy people are beautiful. They're just too stupid to know it."

He said peer, Zhen thought. *He said I was a peer who was beautiful.* Zhen had to cut their conversation short, but she rolled this thought around in her mind, like the tongue rolls a savory morsel. Outside of the infirmary, Zhen breathed in the night air and stopped to look up. Until she had arrived in French Guiana, Zhen had never seen stars with her own eyes. With all the pollution and light in Chongqing, space equated only to mathematics and images on computer screens or Xeroxed scientific papers.

Staring up at the infinite cosmos left Zhen awestruck. Here was the magnificent and mysterious universe whose reality reached even further than the expanding view of humanity, from elusive particles of matter to swirling galaxies in deep space. Even as Zhen tried to study the stars above, they remained sharp in peripheral vision but faded in direct line of sight, deliciously unknowable.

Dewei, the loadmaster, caught up with Zhen just as she was about to step into a jeep. He and the two Xi'an Y-20 pilots were lucky enough to make a full recovery. Standing before her in a clean military jumpsuit, Dewei had regained a healthy amount of weight.

"I'm a good engineer," he said in Mandarin. "I can work. Please, I need to leave this place."

Zhen smiled and said that the work of the HYCIV team was already finished. The rest would be up to others.

"Come see for yourself," she added, and motioned to the jeep.

Dewei eagerly hopped into the back seat beside Zhen. On the drive, she explained that the Ariane rocket had already traveled by rail from the Integration Building to the Final Assembly Building. *So close!* There was only one step left in their launch campaign: placing the HYCIV into the rocket's upper stage and capping the nose cone.

The peacekeeper in the front passenger seat of the jeep radioed ahead of their arrival. As they pulled into the front parking lot of Final Assembly, Zhen spotted Jin-soo in a military jumpsuit, impatiently pacing back and forth. She hadn't seen him without his cleanroom mask, cap, and bunny suit for some time. Jin-soo's hair had gone from steel gray to white, as if the mission had sucked the color and life out of every fiber. They were all husks—but today, they were *happy* husks.

"It's nearly topped out," he said, breathless. "Hurry!"

Jin-soo grabbed Zhen's hand and pulled her toward a building comprised of two joined rectangular structures—one narrow and stretching almost ninety meters tall, and the other long and squat. Dewei jogged to follow them into the long half, where there was a gowning room to suit up. When they all entered the other half, Zhen craned her neck to marvel at the fifty-meter-tall Ariane rocket. Jin-soo wouldn't let Zhen stop moving.

"This is your last chance to see the HYCIV," he said, frantic.

Dewei remained gaping on the ground floor, dodging scurrying engineers as Jin-soo led Zhen to a lift elevator built into the lattice of scaffolding that zigzagged floor to ceiling. There was a mass of metal everywhere in beams, cranes, steps, and four platforms with guardrails that bridged the distance from two opposing walls out to the rocket at the center of the room. Engineers in white suits swarmed around the infrastructure like mites that grew smaller as Zhen ascended to the highest platform. She tried not to look down as Jin-soo pulled her out to the center, which curved to encircle one side of the rocket.

Two people standing in the bend both turned to greet Zhen with utmost respect. Zhen had yet to meet any of the Europeans on the Ariane integration team. The man introduced himself as Marcel, the director of the spaceport, or what was the spaceport before it was transformed into the Effort. He was a substantial man with distinguished wrinkles around freakishly blue eyes. The woman introduced herself as Anneke, the assistant director. She was the tallest woman Zhen had ever seen.

"We've taken good care of it," Anneke said, lifting her strong chin toward the HYCIV already nestled within the main stage of the rocket.

Zhen walked over for one last look. She could see the top of the HYCIV's box shape with its two high-gain antennas like foil-wrapped dinner platters. On its side, there was the ion engine of her *Tianlong* ready to power through space to save precious, precious time. Zhen knew every circuit, every centimeter of its structure. Its image blurred as her eyes watered.

"I dreamed it would find alien life on an asteroid," Zhen said wistfully. "But its destiny is the destruction of a comet."

"It will destroy a destroyer, yes?" Anneke said.

Zhen had to smile. *Yes.*

The sound of weeping made her turn around. Jin-soo was a mess of tears.

"I am *amazed . . .*" he gasped.

Marcel patted his shoulder and nodded in agreement.

"I turned out to be a better scientist than even my most arrogant imaginations. And I'm a Frenchman!" he laughed. "I suppose we all have UD3 to thank."

But no one wanted to agree out loud. Anneke took his hand in her own and smiled to show she understood. Marcel took her hand gratefully and brought it to his mask, forgetting the fabric in front of his lips. *Of course*, thought Zhen. Under these extremes, acquaintances became intense lovers or enemies, or both. And how could they not, even if the woman was a full foot taller, which Zhen couldn't help finding awkward.

Marcel gave the order to lower the rocket's six-meter conical nose from a ceiling crane. They watched in silence that was broken with a loud "Zhen!"

Only one person would shout with such a rough and raspy voice in such a large echo chamber: Amy. Zhen steeled herself and leaned over the guardrail to look all the way down. Most of the suited figures on the floor were indistinguishable except for the two waving up at her. Amy was one, of course. Love the interpreter was probably the other. Zhen waved back as Amy made her way to the lift elevator.

"Zhen!" she heard Dewei call out from the opposite end of the floor.

Everyone wanted her attention. Zhen's raw emotions were sparkling-hot colors, like fireworks.

"Zhen!"

She saw him standing by the mobile launch table, pointing to the side of the rocket and bouncing on his feet with excitement. Technicians had just peeled a sheet of adhesive off its glossy white surface, leaving three black stencils. The first was a black rectangle, but the other two were Chinese characters.

"Usually we require a six-month lead time for artwork," Anneke said, "but we made an allowance."

Zhen assumed she was joking but couldn't be sure.

"Now, will you tell us what everything means?" Anneke prodded.

Zhen was honored with naming rights for the rocket. Ben Schwartz insisted until she agreed and submitted two Hanzi characters. The first represented a stretched animal hide, starting with a head of horns and ending with the tail:

革

The second represented a turtle shell and could signify armor, a protective shell, or fingernails.

甲

Paired together they were *gé jiǎ*, or skin armor, in the literal English translation. Zhen explained to the Europeans that their HYCIV spacecraft was the armor that would save the planet from UD3, if all went according to plan.

What Zhen didn't explain was the name's personal significance. *Be brave*, her mother said of the insults raining down on her daughter. *Remember this and wear your skin armor . . .*

And here was that same shameful girl now a woman and the Effort's hero, the Professor's deus ex machina—scars and all. Her mother would stand tall and burn bright with vindication if she knew, in the small chance that she was still alive.

Amy exited the lift at the top platform and strode over, speaking to Anneke and Marcel like she was already in the middle of their conversation.

"Zhen gave the rocket a name and I gave it a flag—but not for any one nation. The Effort is international, and honestly, there are no nations anymore," Amy added. "This is bigger. This is everything."

Everyone on the platform looked to the black rectangle, the new flag of their defense effort, and saw a cut-out circle exposing the white surface of the rocket. Here was planet Earth centered in a dark universe, everything surrounded by nothing.

Amy joined Zhen at the guardrail and leaned against her shoulder. Zhen was always surprised at how easily and confidently

Amy touched people—surprised and also pleased with the comfort it gave. They hadn't spoken about the world outside the bubble of the Effort and probably never would. Dr. Clayton had checked in on Zhen a few times to pull her into a quiet corner of a room and ask how she was coping. The doctor's blue eyes pierced Zhen like a needle: to extract in as painless a way as possible. But Zhen didn't say much, wanting to focus all her energy on the Effort to reach moments like this.

A narrow section of the wall slowly slid upward, eventually leaving a rocket-sized opening speckled with stars. The fully integrated Ariane rocket was ready to travel by rail to the launch pad, marking twelve hours to scheduled launch.

It was such a grand spectacle, such a hopeful step toward survival as an Earth-bound species, that no one noticed the Disasters step from the lift elevator onto the platform. Amy only turned around when Dr. Clayton touched her lightly on the arm. Amy blinked at the doctor's Red Cross vest as the realization sank in. She asked what she always asked: "Is it Ben?"

This time the answer was yes.

ZHEN NUDGED HER way through tightly packed, camo-clad bodies in the Jupiter building's VIP room. The air-conditioning blasted to combat the rising heat. Maximum capacity had to be capped at a squished 275 occupants; only the Effort's team leadership could gain entry and witness the mission control room on the other side of the glass partition. Others had to watch the monitors mounted in all the space center buildings or listen to the countdown by radio.

"Move aside!"

Zhen looked toward the direction of the voice and saw Stan from the HYCIV team. Ben always referred to him as "Ponytail Guy," but here he was with a fresh buzz cut close to the scalp. Stan continued to shout at people to move out of Zhen's path. No one complained once they turned, saw her thin scars, and realized who she was. Bodies parted to make a narrow path toward the glass partition. As Zhen squeezed through, she saw more familiar faces. Ziggy from the nuclear team lit up with a smile to see her.

"So close," he whispered with shaking fists.

Jin-soo said nothing as she passed, but he reached out to graze her cheek lovingly. Zhen had never been touched this way. She had to turn and look ahead to stay in control of her emotions. Chuck waved her over to his side, where he was speaking with Marcel in front of the glass partition. His paunch tightly stretched against the middle fabric of his jumpsuit. Both men paused their conversation to offer nervous smiles. Marcel looked ill.

"I've launched more than five hundred Ariane rockets from that room, but I've never felt like this. Wish I had a cigarette."

Zhen looked through the glass to the mission control room. Anneke stood, but all the other Europeans on the launch team sat in rows in front of touchscreen tablets, telephone docks, microphones, metric screens, and dials. Spanning the far wall above them was a ten-meter mounted screen with split views of live feeds. Larger views captured the launch pad at different angles. A smaller view on the bottom left captured a room with more than thirty seated individuals: the space flight team. A smaller view on the bottom right was all black except for back-to-back universal and count-down times.

The room suddenly vibrated with the sound of a soft tearing from above. Chuck told Zhen that the security team had fighter jets and helicopters patrolling the no-fly zone in case there was a country still capable and dumb enough to launch a missile attack.

"Excusez-moi," Marcel said. "I need to go vomit."

As soon as the Frenchman was out of earshot, Chuck moved to reassure Zhen.

"Don't worry," he whispered. "The launch will be recorded for Ben. And the history books, of course. Ben won't have to miss it completely."

As soon as the HYCIV and Ariane rocket were both on tracks bound for the Final Assembly Building to be mated, Ben Schwartz had collapsed. Breathing and blinking but otherwise nonresponsive, doctors diagnosed him with UD3 catatonia. There wasn't much they could do but hook up an IV drip and hope for the best.

Chuck told Zhen that Amy had broken the historic rule of conduct: *Don't punch the messenger in the face.* Not only had she punched Dr. Clayton after she had delivered the news, but she knocked out a front tooth as a result. Chuck didn't hide his admiration then or now as they heard her rusty-nail voice in the VIP room. Zhen saw the crowd part down the middle with griping on both sides about jutting elbows and stepping on toes. The Professor emerged in his wheelchair with Amy pushing from behind. They must have come straight from the infirmary.

"You are all interrupting my dying process!" the Professor wanted everyone to know.

But he was chuckling at his own gallows humor. The morphine drip attached to his wheelchair might have had something to do with it.

"It's good to see you again," Chuck said with relief.

"Then we must really be in trouble," the Professor guffawed.

He looked through the glass, over the heads in mission control, and up to the monitor views.

"Look at them," he said, using his cane to point. "My space flight team! Like Thoroughbreds stomping at the gates waiting for the starter pistol. They can't believe it's finally going to be their turn!"

If the launch succeeded, and if the rocket's nose cone successfully separated to deploy the HYCIV spacecraft, then the space flight team had to steer the craft on a collision course with comet UD3 and detonate its nuclear payload on target.

Amy stepped around the Professor's wheelchair to touch Chuck on the arm and lean in.

"It's okay," she said. "Yuri and Julie are watching Ben for me. They'll be there if he wakes up."

Amy looked to Zhen and managed a smile.

"Skin armor," Zhen told her.

"That's right," Amy agreed. "Time to be tough. We've got a fucking rocket to launch."

A voice from the room's loudspeakers echoed, "T minus five minutes."

They looked at one another and listened to nervous chatter that vibrated the glass partition.

"I wish Ben was here," Chuck sighed.

The Professor agreed and said that in all the simulated impact scenarios that Ben had played out in the past, he still couldn't have predicted the remarkable chain of events leading them through to the uncharted future.

"He'll come back to us," Amy insisted.

She took Zhen by the hand and led her away from the partition, toward the rows of chairs in the back of the room. The crowd parted and two people jumped up to offer their seats. It was a nail-biting relief to be a seated bystander now that the work of the HYCIV team was finished. The Effort was in the hands of the launch team, then the space flight team, and then fate itself.

"T minus one minute."

The VIP room fell silent. Amy, usually fearless, grabbed Zhen's hand and held it tight. They looked to the countdown on the monitor.

T-minus 41 seconds.

Zhen whispered that Amy's grip hurt. Amy looked down and forced her clenched fingers to loosen.

T-minus 8 seconds.

In the next few moments, operations would execute automatically, and there was nothing the human species could do. The only choice left was to either shut their eyes or leave them open. Zhen left hers open, even as flare from the rocket boosters left negative imprints on her vision.

"Liftoff!"

The Ariane 5 rocket launched up into the blue sky and over the open sea. Zhen watched, quaking with fear as her mind made a running list of all possible malfunctions. The Ariane shed its rocket boosters and payload fairing and continued to soar with the power of its cryogenic main stage. The upper stage ignited next and burned hydrogen in order to reach speeds of 21,000 miles per hour.

It started as a murmuring as heads turned to look at one another and ended as a deafening blare of screams and cheers. Bystanders lifted their arms in victory. Zhen stood on the seat of her chair to see over all the raised fists. Her eyes caught the Professor, banging his cane against his metal wheelchair and hollering to get Chuck's attention. The rocket would deploy the HYCIV twenty-seven minutes after liftoff. He had to get to his space flight team.

The Professor probably knew his body wouldn't last to the time of intercept with the comet, but he would cling to life as long as he could, as all do. As soon as Chuck got behind the wheelchair and pushed it through the crowd like a steamroller, the Professor smiled. He smiled so wide that his ancient face looked ready to shatter into a million pieces.

THIRTY-ONE

¡REZA!

AFTER THE DISCOVERY of UD3, Enrico and his parents drove every night from their high-rise condo in Mexico City to the basilica to pray. Hail Marys went to the Virgin of Guadalupe, patron saint to the Americas, and now Saint Medard, patron saint of protection against bad weather—which was the closest they could get to a cosmic impact. Priests handed out prayer leaflets with an eagle hovering above the young Saint Medard, sheltering him from rain.

"But the eagles have drowned," Enrico whispered.

He read science blogs that described beaches blanketed with drowned birds washing up with the tides. Enrico's mother hissed for him to be quiet. Her pleading eyes never left the fabric shrine of the Virgin hanging behind bulletproof glass. Enrico crumpled his prayer leaflet and tossed it to the floor of their pew; he had no patience for false promises.

When the basilica became overcrowded, Enrico's family prayed at home. The city already had over 20 million people in a country of a quarter billion. As a first comet trajectory and then a second hit the news, Catholic pilgrims flooded in to reach the shrine. Enrico stopped going to school. His father stopped going to work. The armored car that waited for them in the mornings stopped coming.

For a time, Enrico basked in the beautiful novelty of spending time with his father, who was a virtual stranger to him. Enrico was ten years old and well above his peers in math, sciences, and reading comprehension. Eager to show off, he located UD3 through his telescope from the balcony of their fifty-fifth-level penthouse. It was a faint pinprick of light between Mars and big, banded Jupiter.

"Looks far away," Enrico said, which seemed to please his father.

Together, they went online and researched the growing momentum for an international defense effort. The world's best engineers were sent to South America to design and build an intercept vehicle that could knock UD3 from its trajectory. Military aircraft passed overhead on their way south, like a long migration of metal birds.

"What if the Effort's a lie?" Enrico's mother asked, as they watched from their balcony.

She didn't bother to whisper. His parents no longer tried to hide the truth that everyone could already see.

"Just for show," she added, "to keep us from killing one another?"

Enrico's father shrugged. He found the Effort comforting, even if a deflection proved impossible.

"Then it's a nice lie."

"Lies are lies," Enrico piped up.

But he believed in the engineers on those planes and their mission. He believed in the power of science ever since he saw one of his own cells under a microscope, stained blue and giggling in saliva. Now *that* was a miracle that had nothing to do with the saints.

When the power went out, the family lost their air-conditioning, hot water, oven and microwave, internet access, phone chargers, and television. Enrico's mother wept on the sofa, clutching her remote control. A few weeks before, celebrities from her favorite *telenovelas* had joined in a televised prayer vigil for the global crisis. Each of the celebrities read from prayer cards as favorite character clips spliced into the visuals. Enrico's mother kept the channel on 24/7 until the screen went dark.

"They were like my friends," she told Enrico. "Now I'm cut off and alone."

"You still have us," Enrico said. "And we're real."

She locked her arms around him and sighed into his hair. Enrico inherited her dimples, but not much else. She was a beauty queen with gold skin and hair. Marriage proposals came the day of her *quinceañera*, but she waited. Sure enough, Enrico's father spotted her while traveling on business. He was the president of a national bank, slight in stature but immaculately dressed in a pressed linen suit and wire-rimmed glasses.

Marriage, Enrico's mother proclaimed happily, was just like her *quinceañera todos los días*—but better. Who needed costume jewelry when you had a three-carat engagement ring and credit terms at designer shops? Who needed a tacky party at a hotel in the suburbs when you dined with the mayor and his wife in Polanco? Enrico's mother maintained that it was all a fairy tale.

Except that life never is, Enrico's father always replied. His job was very stressful and gave him insomnia. He encouraged Enrico's love of science because he had imagined life as a field biologist until familial duty pulled him toward finance. *Dream while you're young*, he whispered to his boy.

But it was difficult to dream as the comet grew closer. Its slow increase in size was both terrifying and too predictable for a ten-year-old. Enrico pulled his drone out of his bedroom closet and carried it to the balcony. When he strapped on the goggles, he saw his unrecognizable city through the darting and hovering eyes of a hummingbird. More and more pilgrims arrived at the basilica every day. Parked cars and RVs clogged streets and highways. Thieves crept along the line of vehicles at night, siphoning off any fuel they could find with hoses and canisters. Such stealth was unnecessary. All eyes, except Enrico's, were trained ahead and looking for salvation.

When the drone's batteries died, Enrico switched the lens on his telescope and trained it down instead of up.

"Looks like we're back to spying the old-fashioned way," his father called out.

He always hated the drone.

Enrico named the city Tent Town after pilgrims spread fat-caterpillar sleeping bags onto the ground and hung a colorful patchwork of bedsheets for curtains. They lit prayer candles after dusk. Looking down from his balcony, Enrico thought of the firefly sanctuary east of the city in Tlaxcala. Only the prayer lights didn't blink in syncopated rhythm; they burned steady, illuminating the hands and faces of God's faithful.

Enrico's mother stood by him at night. She either waited for a turn at the telescope or leaned over the rail and into the updraft, shaking gold strands of hair out of her eyes and the crease of her full lips.

"So pretty," she whispered.

It was such an awe-filled, confused statement that it almost sounded like a question. The lights were lovely, but there was a putrid smell on rising gusts. There was hysteria in the echoes of collective prayers from below.

The pilgrims' candles burned out by the end of September, leaving only darkness. About that time the water and sewer systems both failed. New arrivals to the city increased, but not all were convinced that God was watching. Cartel gangs, always the scourge of Mexico, came armed with machine guns and machetes. They pillaged the last of the pilgrims' food and water.

Enrico's mother stopped joining him on the balcony. She retreated to the master bedroom and prayed with her grandmother's rosary beads for her family first and the pilgrims second. Enrico's father said nothing as he emptied the mixing bowl she used for a chamber pot out the window.

Residents in Enrico's building were still better off than most. They were rich and connected and had longer access to scarce food and supplies. But being better off could be dangerous, which was nothing new. Enrico always had armed chaperones when he ventured beyond the building gates and small security details at each of his birthday parties. Being the only child of a wealthy power couple made him a bigger target.

Enrico helped his father pile all their furniture and belongings into the condo's fire exit stairwell. Everything but their beds and mattresses was used to create an impassable obstacle. Anyone intrepid enough to scale the twelve-foot walls surrounding their building, break through steel doors to the lobby, and climb fifty-five flights of stairs would still have their work cut out for them.

"But what about the neighbors?" Enrico asked. "What if they need our help?"

He thought about the widow Padilla Hernandez and her Chihuahua, Sancho, who lived two flights down. The frail woman kept doggie treats in one pocket of her purse and Pica Fresa candies for Enrico in another.

"We don't have neighbors anymore," his father muttered.

"Then what about us?" Enrico asked.

He dragged a light aluminum-tube chair from the balcony to the interlocking mesh of objects.

"How will we get out?"

"We'll take the elevator like we used to do," his father replied.

"But what if we don't get power back?"

Enrico's father said nothing, just as he said nothing about his bedbound wife or the gunshots from the streets below. Instead, he went for his Bible. Enrico joined his father as he sat cross-legged like a child in their empty living room. His glasses had smudged lenses, but their metal frames still shone in the window light. As a bank executive, he had never looked so unkempt, with his growing beard, running shorts, and sweat-stained undershirt. Both parents, once larger than life, were now looking desperate and mortal.

It was all prophecy, he explained to Enrico: hunger, swords, blood, and death as the stars of heaven fell unto the earth, even as a fig tree casteth her untimely figs, when she is shaken of a mighty wind...Enrico fidgeted as his father read Revelation aloud. He fingered impressions in their wall-to-wall white carpet, where there used to be custom furniture.

"What happens when our food runs out?" Enrico interrupted.

"Then we pray," his father snapped. "Can't you see what I'm showing you? If you're so smart, why do I have to spell it all out?"

His father stood up too quickly and almost fainted. He staggered into the master bedroom. When he emerged hours later, his arms were full of empty containers. Back when the family still had running water, they had filled up their Jacuzzi and every type of makeshift vessel: mugs, glasses, bowls, vases, detergent bottles, both halves of a Chanel sunglasses case, and so on. All but the Jacuzzi were now empty.

Father and son transported the empty vessels to their balcony. Enrico placed his lucky Cruz Azul football club cup in a good spot but didn't bother to hope. The city would get a centimeter, maybe two, of rain in a month, if they were lucky. The whole exercise was, as his mother said about the defense effort, probably just for show to keep from killing one another.

Enrico whined about his cramping belly because he couldn't help it. His father added Saint Monica to the receiving end of his prayers, patron saint of disappointing children. When the crying began, Enrico's father couldn't take it. He always said it was a woman's weapon.

"*No llores,*" he screamed at his son's tearful begging. "*¡Reza!*"
Don't cry, pray!

He tried to hide his own tears and pointed up to the ceiling. *Pray!* But God wasn't floating up in the clouds. Enrico knew because he looked with his telescope. His father retreated to the master bedroom and locked the door for good. Enrico tried praying, but it was just a repetition of words. His mind was too free and obsessed over memories of food. Every time he knocked on his parents' bedroom door, there was either silence or shouting.

In his loneliness and need for distraction, Enrico gravitated to his telescope. He didn't need its powers of magnification at night. UD3 was now visible to the naked eye. Instead, Enrico lowered his sights from the heavens down to the hell on earth. There he witnessed a man use a machete on another, swinging it like a baseball bat. Enrico ran into the living room in a fit of screaming.

His father opened the bedroom door but didn't step out. He waited at its threshold for his son's nonsensical noises to calm into something intelligible.

"We have to help them!" Enrico finally managed.

Tears ran down his cheeks. His hand shook as it pointed to his father's desk against the bedroom wall. There was a loaded magnum revolver in a locked drawer that he wasn't supposed to know about. It was too late for one poor, blood-covered pilgrim, but that revolver could save the next.

"We don't have bullets to spare," his father said.

"But we *have* to help them."

Enrico's father gripped his son's arm, tight enough to bruise, and dragged him to the adjoining bathroom. The Jacuzzi tub was nearly empty.

"Save your tears," his father said, and went back to his prayers.

Enrico crawled under their bed, shivering. He couldn't shut out the images locked in his head. He said prayers in rapid, jittery bursts. Nothing happened. He listened to his parents pray on the mattress above him. His mother whispered Hail Marys. His father confessed his sins aloud to Saint Jude, patron saint of lost causes. He said the things no one wanted to know, least of all his family.

By morning, Enrico crawled out from under the bed. The walls of his mind were still blood spattered, but he was restless. Enrico returned to the balcony. He looked into his telescope. In the age of the internet, most preadolescents knew more than they should. Enrico had peeked at images of death and pornography. What Mexican boy with a computer hadn't looked at cartel videos of chainsaw beheadings? But those horrors were recordings. By their very nature, they happened in the past and could be stopped with the click of a button. Enrico never watched to the end—but he did now. After dry heaving over the railing, Enrico's empty stomach settled. The hours passed. Then days.

It's amazing what one can get used to. Not only could Enrico watch the carnage over time, he couldn't tear his sick-curious eyes from it. Enrico watched gangs plunder Tent Town. Some pilgrims fell to their knees to pray and ask for mercy, but it just made the process easier with a sweeping slash to the throat or face. The things they did to the young women were the worst of it. What would happen to Enrico's beautiful, golden mother if their barricade failed?

Gangs cut away muscle and severed thick limbs to pile onto bedsheets and sleeping bags from Tent Town. They hauled away the meat and left bowels, bones, heads, and shit in the streets. Enrico realized that what his parents always told him as a child was true: there were people like monsters, lurking out in the world, ready to gobble him up if he wasn't careful.

A new smell mixed with the stench. It reminded Enrico of Saturday mornings when he woke to his mother cooking breakfast. She fixed up bacon and eggs with black beans and salsa, all the while chatting on her cellphone. *Do you ever put that damn thing down?* his father asked from the breakfast table. But his eyes lifted above a spread of *El Universal*. He loved to watch her, and she loved to be watched by him.

Enrico knew he shouldn't lie to himself. Nice lies were still lies. He knew what that breakfast-bacon smell had to be, but it didn't stop his mouth filling with saliva. At a time when there were no neighbors, no more talk of a defense effort, and no planes in the sky, could he eat people? Was it better to die like the pilgrims and go to heaven, or eat them and live, even if it would damn him for eternity?

There was a blur on the horizon. Enrico ground the heels of his hands into his watery eyes, but the blur remained. Heat distortion? Only when he switched his telescope lens did he see the hordes more clearly: endless streams of people trekking into Mexico City from the south and east. Here were the desperate from all of Central and South America. Enrico couldn't have comprehended their sheer volume, or just how much the masses of modern *Homo sapiens* had grown to dominate the planet. There was no room, and yet they kept coming. Gangs couldn't kill fast enough and were swept under the sea of crazed people and crushed. Bodies piled up, releasing a choking stench. Enrico stopped breathing through his nose, but he could still smell and taste it.

Pilgrims kept climbing on top of one another, pleading for deliverance. *Too much*, Enrico thought, trying to shake everything out of his head. *Too many. Too much*... He fainted. When he opened his eyes, with his scraped cheek resting painfully on concrete, Enrico saw a small flash. Four foil-wrapped pieces of chocolate were expertly hidden within the thick latticework of the balcony railing.

Enrico's mother hid chocolate for him every year on the Feast of the Virgin. He must have missed these pieces. Enrico ripped off the foil and gulped down the chocolate pieces without chewing. He inspected the railing twice over before a realization struck him: he didn't share. He hadn't even had the inkling to do so until it was too late. Selfishness was no way to thank the Virgin, whose painted skin was milk chocolate born from both Indigenous peoples and their European conquerors. It was no way to thank his own mother, the woman who couldn't help spoiling her precocious son with sweets, comic books, kisses, and the latest model of drone.

Enrico knocked on his parents' bedroom door and waited. It was unlocked. His father was sitting on the edge of his bed with the loaded revolver in one hand. A cloud passed over the setting sun.

"*Lo siento*," Enrico whispered to his mother and father.

There was chocolate in the creases of his frown. *I am sorry.*

His father hid the revolver under sweat-stained sheets. He put a skeleton arm around his son's skeleton shoulders and leaned in until their foreheads rested on one another. Forgiveness was unnecessary. Enrico was his child. Children were the receivers of unconditional love. Even in a world staring down the nose of a bullet, they were still the means to a future.

Box springs sounded as Enrico's mother got up and staggered to the windows on wobbly legs. Her fingers touched glass and traced a drop of rain.

"Do you see?" she whispered.

Was it a hallucination? Or was it rainfall? Drinking water might only grant borrowed time, but it would be spent with family—no fairy tale or *telenovela*, but real. Her most simple prayer had been answered with a miracle.

THIRTY-TWO

OFF SCRIPT

OCATE MESA, NEW MEXICO
JANUARY 8
T-MINUS 24 DAYS TO LAUNCH

NED NEEDED TO sleep after clearing the southern end of the Colorado Rockies on their fourth refueling stop. They flew over a mountainous forest and landed on a high grassy hill with a clear view in all directions. They had to land in remote positions that could be easily defendable if pursuers ever caught up to them.

"I wish the Jayhawk wasn't so damned loud," Ned said to Gustavo, once the helicopter's black blades wound down.

The sound attracted attention. Roving gangs of armed militias shot at them from the ground. Survivors crept from their hiding places and ran screaming and waving for help. Ned said he couldn't wash the thought of all those desperate people from his brain. And what's more, they made landing very dangerous; a quick-moving horde could be the end.

Ned ducked into the strap of his semiautomatic rifle and let it hang from his neck as he high-stepped around the Jayhawk and pinwheeled his arms, stretching cramped muscles. Gustavo had spent enough hours in the body of the helicopter, lying next to the extra fuel and supplies, that he was rested and not nearly so stiff.

He took out his laminated map of the Americas and located French Guiana. Ned had said that the Kourou airport, their final destination, was midway on its northern coast. Gustavo would have to trek south to reach the Oyapock River on the border of French Guiana and the Brazilian state of Amapá. Ned had a compass in his duffel bag. He wouldn't need it once they landed in Kourou and he joined up with this Effort he kept talking about. A compass could guide Gustavo when the sky was clouded or hidden by thick canopy.

Once Gustavo reached the Oyapock River, he would follow it southwest to where it met the Camopi River. There were settlements of Other Wayãpi where the two rivers joined. Gustavo had visited these settlements many years ago. The language of these northern tribes, split from his own Wayãpi back in the age of the Grandfather People, sounded different from his own but not enough that he couldn't understand it. Gustavo could talk to the Other Wayãpi of the Oyapock River. They might offer him shelter and even help him return to his own Wayãpi villages in Brazil by the Amapari River.

Gustavo stepped into the belly of the helicopter to check his rations. Water wouldn't be much of a problem in a rainforest, but food would. He hoped there would be more rations to spare at the Fort Hood military base in Texas. When Gustavo hopped out onto the ground, Ned said they must be somewhere in northern New Mexico, but that didn't mean anything to him. Outside of New York City, the North American landscape was all unknown to Gustavo. He turned in a circle and shivered in his poncho. He was used to hot, wet, green forests at the equator, but this forest was cold, dry, and golden. Long, pale grasses didn't bend but crunched underfoot.

"How much longer until Fort Hood?" Gustavo asked again.

"Jesus, you're like a kid on a car trip," Ned griped. "Like I told you, little more than five hours of flight time with two more refuels."

"What if it isn't there—"

"I dunno," Ned said quickly. "Pray? Probably die. We'll deal with it when we get there. Now make yourself useful and set up the sleeping bags. I need to go take an elephant dump."

Ned was usually cranky from hours of flying, but it didn't take long for his better nature to resume on the ground. Gustavo carried their sleeping bags from the helicopter to a bare patch of earth and unrolled them just as he heard Ned wail. Gustavo sprinted to the other side of the hill and found Ned standing by the fly-covered remains of two people. Their clothes and meat had been stripped, leaving desiccated, sinewy skeletons with stained underwear. Gustavo tried to measure how long the dry decay had been left in the sun. He could still see lots of telltale footprints and broken turf from a struggle.

"We can't bed down here," Ned said. "Jesus. They look like a man and woman. Were they married?"

Gustavo turned away from the gore and told Ned he needed to sleep.

"I hate this place now," Ned announced.

"Don't waste your hate on places. Save it for people."

"Is that from one of your poems?" Ned asked, sarcastic.

Gustavo ignored him and kept walking.

"What're your famous poems about, anyway?" Ned asked as they headed back to the Jayhawk. "Dreams? Beauty?"

"War."

Ned snorted.

"Well, that figures. Which war?"

"Mine," Gustavo said.

He climbed into his sleeping bag for warmth and sat up alert. Ned stretched another minute before lying down. The rifle swung from his thick neck. Gustavo asked to hold the gun so he could keep watch while the other man slept. They were never safe unless they were in the air. Gustavo didn't see any dangers within several miles of where they landed, but then he hadn't seen those bodies, either.

Ned said nothing as he pulled the brim of his cap down over his eyes and shut them, twitching restlessly. An awkward silence passed, broken only by Ned's muffled farts.

"I saw you had a Bible in your bag," Ned finally said.

"You looked through my bags?"

"Once," he replied, shameless. "When you set off to empty the piss jars at the last refuel. You know, I was raised on those parables. Back in Oregon."

Gustavo had also been raised on those stories, as well as those of the Grandfather People. All peoples seemed to have their own myths of how they came to be and how they could continue.

"What about the end?" Ned asked. "I don't remember what the Bible said about the end, but I know it's in there. Was it like this? 'Cause—and I'm just thinkin' out loud here, but I think we've gone off script. I think we're taking a page from the Donner Party."

"The what?"

"I'm saying that if we end up as nothing but Godless cannibals . . . I don't think I wanna be part of that future. No, sir, I'm not going down like that."

In some ways, Gustavo felt sorry for his companion. In others ways, he found him spoiled. The end was not a new threat for Gustavo's people or any of the peoples subsisting on what was left of the natural world. The end was not new to all the animal species on the brink of extinction.

"Ever wonder if it's your turn?" Gustavo asked, unable to contain his envy.

"What?"

"Your civilization," Gustavo clarified. "What if it's your turn to die out and fade from history? What if that comet is your Christopher Columbus? Your Portuguese and Spanish conquistadores?"

"What'd you mean, *your*? We're in this together, Gustavo. Just because you're not white—"

But it wasn't race that formed a boundary. Ned didn't understand, and Gustavo didn't have the words to explain it.

"I'll need your compass," Gustavo blurted.

Ned snorted again. He gave a litany of grievances that Gustavo did his best to tune out. He hated relying on strangers. He hated

THIRTY-THREE

BARE BONES

KOUROU, FRENCH GUIANA
MAY 8
T-MINUS 47 DAYS TO NUCLEAR DETONATION

THREE DAYS AFTER the successful Ariane launch, Love saw a tall, shaggy man waiting by the door of the Penthouse, her utility closet in the Space Museum. He wore the same military jumpsuit as Love. His long beard was unkempt, and one of the lenses of his eyeglasses had a crack running through it.

"This is against the rules," the man told Love immediately. "We still have the mission."

Whether to prove a point or acting on paranoid reflex, the man checked his watch for countdown to interception and nuclear detonation.

"Then why are you here?" Love shot back.

"Amy Kowalski can be convincing."

It was true. Amy would also lie down in traffic for a friend, no matter that she was desperately waiting for the mind of her lover to return to his body. When Love came to her at Ben's bedside in the infirmary and begged for a favor—now that humanity had a fighting chance—Amy agreed.

"I need you to find someone," Love said to the man, pulling her shoulders back and lifting her chin.

Love understood the Effort rules: there was the mission and nothing else. No room was left for family, country, religion, ideology, or even self. All had to be sacrificed for the greatest purpose in the history of the species. Love had followed the rules faithfully, but now she was breaking them. Letting on to her heavy guilt wouldn't get what she wanted, however.

"Her name is Rivka Shulman. Caucasian, brown curly hair, brown eyes. She lives in the Bronx but was subletting an apartment in Harlem. Her parents live on the Upper West Side. She might have reconciled with them—shouldn't you be writing this down, or something?"

Love stepped forward until she was less than three feet away. She looked at the man closely, under the beard and disheveled hair, under the dead-eyed stare cracked in half.

"Troy Andrews," she said finally. "You've changed."

He was no longer the handsome, smiling man from UN headquarters in Manhattan.

"It's best to remember your home and family as it all was," he said softly. "Trust me."

Troy stepped past her and made for the stairs.

"Will you look for her?" Love called out.

Troy didn't look back as he answered with a voice that was tired and sad, but resolute.

"Your girlfriend is dead, Love."

But these were just words spoken by one man. Love shook her head. *No, not Rivka.* She sprinted ahead of Troy and turned to block in his path.

"You want to know?" Troy sighed. "Everyone wants to know— until they know."

But Love was ready to beat the truth out of Troy if she had to. He saw it in her eyes. Troy readied his hands for a fight as he breathed deeply to fill his lungs and say what he knew.

"New York City was a disaster zone, like the other major cities..."

Those who could get out, did. The rest, Troy said, were stranded as services shut down. Once the markets and restaurants were picked clean, there was nothing to feed more than 8 million New Yorkers surrounded by concrete. Hoarding and looting were rampant. Local law enforcement failed as officers stopped reporting for duty to stay home and protect their own families. Municipal systems and supply chains broke as more and more people stopped going to work out of fear as the murder rate spiked. And that was only the beginning.

"We were in touch with UN headquarters while they still had power," Troy said. "Manhattan had walled itself off from most of the violence in the outer boroughs. Paratroopers dropped down in October and gave them a shot in the arm in terms of food and restored order, but it was temporary."

Love's jaw was moving without sound. She finally managed a small voice.

"I didn't know—"

"You didn't have to. You were lucky that way."

Troy hung his head and said he was sorry. He looked like he meant it, reluctantly; there didn't seem much sorrow left in him to give.

"We lost contact with headquarters after their power grid failed in the hurricane. That must have been around when the accident happened."

"What hurricane? What accident?"

Troy blinked several times in a row.

"There was a nuclear accident during a hurricane on the East Coast," he said slowly. "Our drones detected massive levels of radiation near a reactor in Connecticut. We found the explosion."

Once the power is out, Troy said, a nuclear facility running on backup generators has a limited window to shut down the reactor. It wasn't too surprising that something went wrong in one of many nuclear reactors clustered by the coast, given the circumstances: a good portion of the personnel had abandoned their posts after more and more police guarding the facilities abandoned *their* posts; the minds of the rest were clouded with existential dread; they must have figured the world was about to be smashed by an extinction-class comet anyway; and the lives of operators and their families were in danger from lawlessness and natural catastrophe with severe flooding and high winds.

"It was the winds that caused the most trouble—"

Troy started and stopped himself.

"Anyway, blame the hurricane," he said. "That's always easiest."

Troy sidestepped around Love and reached the top of the stairs. Love suddenly switched from standing slack-jacked and dumbstruck to sprinting and lunging at Troy. She grabbed the fabric of his jumpsuit. He looked prepared for her reaction, just not her speed and strength.

"I want to know," Love croaked, "all of it."

"But you don't. My own wife and two children—"

"I don't care about you!" Love barked.

And at that moment, she didn't. All Love cared about was her Rivka. Troy narrowed his eyes and wrested free of her grip.

"The hurricane caused high winds to travel south along the coast," he said. "It would have carried radioactive clouds toward North Carolina's Fort Bragg. That's the nation's biggest military base. They couldn't let that happen."

Troy shook his head and said the government ordered pilots to seed the clouds over southern Connecticut, southeastern New York, and northern New Jersey with silver iodide to sow rain that wrung out all the deadly radiation. Love squeezed her eyes shut and shook her head violently. *No, not Rivka. No!* Troy mistook her refusal for disbelief.

"What do you think Russia did after the Chernobyl accident?" he asked. "To save Moscow and the larger cities to the northeast, they sacrificed everyone to the southwest. The smaller cities of Gomel and Novozybkov had black, radioactive rain as all the fallout was dumped on them—"

"Stop!" Love screamed.

Troy looked away, pained, and told Love to save her pity. Hurricane season was long over. It was spring, and most of the people in New York City had died of starvation by now. If they had stayed alive this long, it was by any means necessary.

"There was no food for months and months," Troy whispered. "Nothing but the meat on their bones, if you want to count that. Some did. They figured morality wasn't doing them any good. You can't eat it."

Love didn't move or speak as Troy rushed past her and took several stairs in each stride. She heard him call out on the way down.

"Finish the mission. It is our only hope."

JUNE 2

T-MINUS 22 DAYS TO NUCLEAR DETONATION

SEVERAL TIMES, LOVE had to stop rooting around in her gutted luggage to double over in ragged breaths. When weeping was inevitable, she curled up on the floor of her utility closet and howled. Goodbyes were always final in Love's experience. Since her days in the orphanage in Nairobi, everyone in her life had an expiration that they knew like they knew their names.

When Love turned seventeen—an approximate age based on a designated birthday—she prepared for a mandatory discharge from her only home. Love packed up her hand-me-down clothes and the foreign novels that the nuns had given her. All the holy mothers were gathered by the door of the orphanage whispering prayers in many native tongues: Swahili, English, French, Spanish, and German. Sister Ellen's voice rose above the rest. She had held Love as a bawling infant soon after her birth mother died. She even gave Love her name and willed fate to be kinder to a destitute orphan.

Before Love headed out to the nearest bus station, Sister Ellen placed a hand on her shoulder. She knew that Love had suffered under their roof, despite their vigilance. Sending a teenage girl off into the world on her own was like feeding her into the lion's mouth, but they had little choice. *Open your heart when it is safe*, Sister Ellen whispered. *Let the light in . . .*

Sister Ellen may have meant Jesus. She may have meant a husband in Kenya and children who would follow. It was doubtful she meant a sassy, smart, and sexy Upper West Side Jew with big brown eyes, big hair, and a big heart. But that was exactly who Love let in, and they basked in each other's light for a time.

Love wiped her eyes and nose on the sleeve of her jumpsuit before taking it off. She suddenly wanted to feel and look like a person, like herself. After pawing to the bottom of her suitcase for her tangled clump of jewelry, Love saw the Mets baseball hat she stole from Rivka's closet on the night she left New York City. It was the only part of her lover that she could keep.

Love felt the cap's orange embroidered letters and thought of her Rivka: her wry sense of humor, her smile and laugh, the ripe fullness of her body, the way she always tried to coax a smile. On the night Love abandoned Rivka for the Effort, there was no talk of love. Left unspoken, it was there as she placed her switch-blade on Rivka's pillow and walked out of their Bronx apartment unarmed. Love had found *love*, her calling since she was given a name.

Love hopped down two flights of stairs wearing one beaded earring with a dangling feather, the same earring she wore on the day of her arrival in French Guiana. Love ran through the lobby of the Space Museum out to the front entrance, where Zhen and Amy were saying their goodbyes. And here, like before, she realized she loved people at the verge of losing them.

"Sorry, I wasn't sure I could do this," Love muttered, then cleared her throat.

Zhen stood patiently. She had finally swapped her white lab coat for a military jumpsuit and steel-toe boots that looked too big.

"I want to give you something," Love said, placing the baseball hat on Zhen's head. "Even though you don't look like much of a Mets fan."

Zhen asked for a translation.

"Means you don't look like a jackass," Love clarified. "But it'll keep the sun off your face."

She adjusted the plastic snaps in the back.

"Looks better on you anyway," Love whispered in Mandarin.

Zhen asked why Love never wore the cap herself. Love replied that she wasn't much of a Mets fan, either, but more of a fan of a fan.

"It belonged to someone very important who will look over you now," Love added. "Someone I loved."

Her fingers drifted up one last time to touch the hat's embroidery. Love was ambivalent on religion in adulthood, but she always believed in ghosts—the bad and the good. Zhen smiled and turned to look at an Asian man waiting for her in the back seat of a jeep. He nodded when she pointed to the hat, but he didn't smile back. When Zhen turned back to the two women, her own smile had thinned into a tight line of fear.

Love felt an emptying in her gut: a familiar survivor's guilt. The Effort had purged nearly half of its staff. Love was still shocked— and she was a distrustful person to begin with. But it was hard to argue with the reality that there wasn't enough food. Half of their heroes were left to hang in the wind in order to save the remaining half who had to complete the mission. Love was one of very few interpreters chosen to remain on what was officially termed Bare Essentials. Chuck, Jin-soo, the Professor, and the rest of the Space Flight team would also stay to keep the HYCIV on course to intercept UD3, eject and detonate its lead impactor on the comet's surface, and steer the nuclear charge into the crater. All other staff would join the unofficially nicknamed Bare Bones discharges.

Love opened her mouth, but she struggled to speak of the emotional thunderstorms that raged inside her. Instead of forcing out words, she reached for Zhen and held her instead. At least she could do that. Zhen wrapped her arms around Love's torso and squeezed.

"I'm allowed to cry now, right?" Amy asked Zhen.

She burst into tears without waiting for an answer. Amy always did what Amy wanted. Zhen embraced her next, and Amy dropped her head onto her shoulder. Love watched her crown—unremarkable, greasy brown hair that grew to platinum—bob with hitching cries.

"Bring Ben back," Zhen said into Amy's ear.

Amy nodded and winced, but the words pushed her to stand up straight and wipe at her runny eyes and nose. To Love, Amy had only grown more beautiful as each desperate day passed.

"I will," Amy agreed. "I saw him look at me the other day. His eyes focused, I swear it. Ben will come back, just like your friend Cheung did. And I'll be there when he does."

Amy's scratchy voice was the only sound that made Ben stir and blink, like a dreamer who wanted to wake.

"But what about *you*, Zhen?" Amy cried. "You may have saved the goddamn world, and yet here you are."

Zhen took Amy's and Love's hands in each of her own.

"Not me," she said, and smiled bravely. *"We."*

〜〜〜

GIVEN HER STATUS and contribution to the Effort, Zhen and her friend Dewei were the last nonessential staff to be discharged. They were each given backpacks with a generous amount of supplies: packaged food, water, a field first aid kit with penicillin, antimalarial pills, water purification tablets, mosquito netting, sleeping bags, and so on. Zhen was grateful. Most discharges got nothing but a canteen of water. However, carrying anything worth killing for was a danger in itself.

Zhen saw the southern checkpoint on the Effort perimeter approaching ahead. It felt like only days since she had last seen it on the way to the Cayenne airport, not the months she barely remembered from working to exhaustion. Zhen's heart raced and her palms sweated. Time was such a relative thing, especially when you had none. *Will I die today?*

Her jeep parked in front of the checkpoint gate, where fifty French soldiers clustered in a black mass with barking dogs.

"Keep the dogs away from us!" Zhen shouted.

She could see Dewei was just as terrified. They deserved some dignity. Almost immediately, the handlers pulled back on their leashes until the animals disappeared in the crowd. Zhen looked to Dewei and nodded. He stepped out of the jeep and hefted his backpack onto his shoulders, and then helped Zhen with her own. The French soldiers were humble and sad, but firm as they explained their role. Turning to Dewei, Zhen explained in Mandarin: *They're saying we can't come back.*

Grim-faced, he nodded.

"Miss Zhen!"

The shout came from the perimeter. A soldier in a green camo uniform ran along barbed wire toward her with his rifle pointed down.

"Miss Zhen, wait!"

He stopped in front of her, panting. There was an American flag stitched on his uniform. His rifle was larger than the others with a long, thin muzzle and mounted scope on top.

"Miss Zhen, we never got to meet," he said between breaths, "but I was in the security detail at Cayenne. I was the sniper who..."

His eyes were hidden behind sunglasses, but his face angled slightly toward Dewei.

Zhen translated for Dewei: *This is the man who saved your life.*

Dewei opened his mouth and took a step back. He bowed to the soldier with his heavy pack. The sniper nodded back briskly. It must be difficult to be thanked for killing another man.

"It's been a good morning," the sniper offered. "No one's fired a shot and the road's been mostly clear. Mostly."

He said it in earnest, but with a good deal of pity. When Zhen asked what made for a bad morning, he started to say one thing then changed his mind and said another.

"How's Amy?" he asked.

Zhen forced a smile.

"Strong."

This was hurting her. She would lose control soon. Zhen nodded to the French soldiers manning the gate. She was as ready as she could be.

"Discharge!"

Their shouts rang out in French and English first. Interpreters along the perimeter repeated their shouts in a range of languages. The French soldiers opened the gate manually and stepped aside. Zhen didn't move. Dewei took her trembling hand and pulled her gently one step forward. Neither of them expected to get very far or live very long.

"And don't worry about those two," the sniper said, nodding toward the highway. "They were discharged an hour ago. One of 'em is still in shock."

Zhen looked down the road and saw two figures wavy with heat distortion. One large figure sat on the asphalt, while a smaller figure tried to pull the other up to a standing position.

"I thought we were the only nonessentials left?" Zhen asked.

"You probably were," the sniper replied, "but we had the last plane from Fort Hood land today. Brought a few brain doctors and surgeons. They had a devil of a time tracking down those kinda specialists in this mess, but they'd do anything to help Dr. Schwartz and the others with the catatonia."

He pointed to the figures.

"Stragglers from the plane. As long as discharges keep a distance, we don't have to shoot 'em," he said matter-of-factly, and then squinted into the scope of his rifle for a better look within its crosshairs.

Zhen shuddered a breath. She squeezed Dewei's hand and led him past the gates, which were pushed back into place immediately.

"I've got your back again," the sniper called out, but Zhen didn't turn around.

Bullhorns blared and made them startle. An interpreter shouted warnings in poor Mandarin. They had to keep moving forward. Zhen walked as fast as she could with her heavy pack. Eventually the two wavy figures on the highway solidified into two men with duffel bags. The smaller, older man had darker skin and long hair. He looked somewhat Asian but definitely not Han Chinese. The young white man on the ground had a beard and a half-stricken, half-delirious expression that stretched into a smile when he saw her.

"The Mets suck!" he shouted.

Zhen dropped Dewei's hand and reached up to touch the baseball cap Love had fitted on her head.

"Did the guards say anything about me?" the young man asked, his smile gone.

"That you have to keep moving," Zhen replied. "We all have to keep moving or they'll shoot."

With that, the smaller man grabbed the larger one by the arm and tried again to bring him to a stand. He seemed aware of imminent danger, but his friend was like a resting ox. Dewei stepped around to help. He grabbed the young man by his leather belt, then angled his feet together and leaned back to leverage the combined weight of his body and backpack; he was always a good loadmaster. The young man on the ground tilted and finally stood up. His eyes never looked away from the checkpoint.

"If I could just talk to them again—" he muttered, looking to the perimeter of barbed wire, soldiers, and live ammunition.

He started walking toward the checkpoint. Dewei hollered and grabbed the duffel bag slung over his shoulder. He planted his legs like a wedge but only dragged forward several meters. The older man screamed and boxed his friend on the ear to stun him. Zhen dropped her pack and sprinted around them.

"Don't shoot!" she shouted back at the soldiers.

Hundreds of eyes were watching. Hundreds of mouths shouted *Hold fire!* at one another. Zhen still mattered, even outside the Effort's perimeter. She stepped up to the bearded young man until her face was right below his.

"You. Must. Stop!" she shouted.

There would be no talking, she assured him, only shooting. The young man's face suddenly sagged with realization and fatigue.

"But I've come so far..."

Zhen said that she and Dewei had come much farther, from the other side of the globe, but it didn't matter. The Effort no longer needed them.

"We must leave," she said.

The young man allowed Zhen to pull him in the other direction with his friend and Dewei right behind. They walked in silence along the highway until they could no longer see the Effort's perimeter, only the occasional soldier standing fifty yards apart on the asphalt.

"This road leads southeast to Cayenne," Zhen said, pointing to the sparse line of soldiers and a patrol jeep blaring warnings far in the distance. "We don't want to stay on this road. I know. I've seen what comes next."

The smaller man looked up at the sun and then pointed off to the right, due south. He took off his leather shoes and socks and left them behind on the highway before stepping onto dry grass. The younger man followed. He looked back over his shoulder at Zhen and Dewei and nodded for them to come along.

Dewei looked to Zhen and frowned.

"We can't trust these men," he whispered.

Dewei was right. But the one man was very big and strong. And the other had purpose and place; he looked like he belonged as he melted into shade from the bordering forest. Zhen was a small urban dweller who had given herself up for dead as soon as she was discharged from the Effort. At least the two men in front of her were a new development, a step away from that prediction.

Zhen took Dewei by the hand and led him away from the highway leading to Cayenne. Dewei followed, shaking his head. He would follow her anywhere, he said, but didn't have to like it. The group trekked through forest until they reached a river, probably a tributary of the Kourou River. The river was too wide to cross on foot, so they followed its bends until they reached a narrow bridge.

On the opposite bank, Zhen saw several wood-slat houses on stilts. One house stood less than fifteen meters from the bridge. The pile of bodies was visible only from halfway across the water. Zhen froze. Dewei turned back to her, his raised eyebrows forming a question. He had been too busy watching the other men in front of them and had missed the danger surrounding them. Zhen had to point because she couldn't speak. The other men crossed the bridge, but only the large one stopped to gape. Zhen saw his whole body sigh and his wide shoulders slump at the horrific sight. Some of the bodies were small children.

Zhen forced herself to cross the bridge, but she refused to move for a closer look. Dewei stood beside her and shielded her view until the big man walked back over to join them.

"I'm guessing these houses are already picked clean," he said. "That would explain the family rotting in a pile over there."

He put his hands on his hips and took a few breaths.

"Do you two have any weapons?" he asked, suddenly looking

Zhen in the eyes. "Those Effort bastards took my rifle before they spit me out on the road."

Zhen shook her head.

"Well, I still have my hunting knife," the man said. "And a compass. Maybe we could help one another. Because if we stay out in the open, we're going to die. And if we hide in the forest, we're going to need *him* to stay alive."

He pointed to his friend, who had finally stopped far ahead to look back at them, agitated.

"My name's Ned, by the way."

"What is he saying?" Dewei whispered in Mandarin.

Zhen's eyes flitted to the pile of bodies lying next to the stilts of what was their home. Those bodies had names once, too.

"What do you need from us, Ned?" Zhen asked in English.

He sighed but nodded and got to the point: Ned and his friend were almost out of food.

"So we give you food," Zhen said, "and your friend will guide us through the forest...to where? To do what?"

"He'll find us fresh water," Ned said, perking up. "He's looking for a certain river that will lead him to a big village. There'll be food there. They clear land for gardens, and they fish and hunt. And there are lots of villagers. We'd be safe."

"And then what?"

"And then we *don't die*," Ned said, lifting up his hands. "At least not today and not tomorrow. What more can you ask for?"

Zhen nodded; she had no better plan and was living on borrowed time anyway. She put out her hand, like they did in Western movies, which made Ned snort a laugh. They shook in agreement and started off toward the smaller man.

"Okay then, Gustavo!" Ned called out to his friend. "We're all coming with you. These guys are going to share their rations, and I'm the guy that got you here. Your turn."

The man named Gustavo looked back at Zhen and Dewei and

shook his head. Ned pulled him off to the side for an argument in hissing whispers. Ned finally shouted, "Well, do you want to get there alive?"

Gustavo cursed to himself. The words started in English but morphed into a strange language Zhen had never heard.

"South," he commanded. "And don't slow me down!"

He turned and refused to look them in the eyes for days.

THIRTY-FOUR

INTO THE FOREST

FRENCH GUIANA
JUNE 9
T-MINUS 15 DAYS TO NUCLEAR DETONATION

GUSTAVO WALKED AHEAD of the others, turning to slip between tree trunks, high-stepping through the brush, and keeping an eye out for danger. Wayãpi were sure-footed in the undergrowth with their dexterous feet and strong big toes. Their soles were flat and hard with calluses but still graceful while balancing on a tree trunk or bridging a wide stream. The soles of Gustavo's feet had grown too soft, but they would harden again.

He set a brisk pace the others couldn't keep. The more they slowed him down, the more he thought bad things, like how two people could survive longer on the rations they split in four every night. Gustavo yearned to reach the Oyapock and find his people, but as himself and not as someone who would murder his own friends in their sleep. He had to keep reminding himself who he really was, like a prayer or shamanistic chant.

I remember Father St. John. I remember our church in Pedra Branca. I remember writing poetry about our losing battle...

Before meeting the priest, Gustavo thought, *before I took the Portuguese name Gustavo, I was Wanato of the Wayãpi by the Amapari. I remember knowing what the Grandfather People knew: how to start a fire, how to beat a vine whose pulp can stun fish in the rivers. I remember all the trees, plants, and animals. I remember all the stars that hang in the sky...*

Wanato smelled burning. He swiveled his head to look back at the bare soles of his moving feet. They were darkened with ash. It wasn't long before the group reached a large clearing where the underbrush was scorched down to sharp, broken roots for as far as the eye could see. Where there was once every shade of green and the full music of creatures, there were now blackened tree stumps and silence. The lingering smell of char hung thick in the air.

Wanato stepped more carefully across the wasteland and told Ned to check the compass. They needed to stay as close to due south as the terrain allowed. When Ned didn't answer, Wanato turned back to see the three of them struck dumb and motionless at the scale of destruction.

"This is nothing," Wanato yelled at them. "Keep moving."

Other than boats, the first motorized vehicles that Wanato had seen as a child were construction vehicles—and he had screamed in terror.

I remember that my name is Wanato and I am Wayãpi, he chanted in his head. *I remember why my people don't kill butterflies . . .*

Wanato's father once asked his son a long time ago, *Why don't Wayãpi kill butterflies?* This was an easy answer for the boy. *Because butterflies look after the vines that tie the sky to the ground and keep it up.* Wanato's father had nodded in the dying firelight and asked what happened when the Old People killed all the butterflies. This was back in an age when the world was new and Wayãpi were like children. *The sky fell to darkness*, Wanato whispered. *The Old People couldn't hunt . . .* The words came so quickly that Wanato had to gasp for breath toward the end of the story as Yaneyar the hero brewed *caxiri* beer and enticed his Wayãpi people to drink, sing, and dance until the sun rose again.

~∿∿∿~

THEY WEREN'T COVERING enough ground by the time the sun set. Wanato let his imagination sprint ahead as he tried to will his future into existence. His brother's beautiful wife would be the first to lay eyes on him, Wanato decided. She would go into shock as he emerged from the forest after the most challenging quest of his life. He might need to whisper his name to assure her that he wasn't his twin brother and that the world hadn't completely turned inside out. The dead hadn't risen, but the lost had returned. Wanato would reach for her as tears slid down their cheeks. Senses regained, she would grab hold of him and wail with joy.

With that, the rest of his family would come running. His old aunt would place her shaking palms on his shoulders. She would need to feel him to believe in the miracle of his return to the Earth's hot and fat middle from the ocean of ice at its northern pole. And his brother's sons—who could have been his own sons, by the looks of them—would sit beside Wanato by the fire and listen to stories of snow and ice, a metal ship that was as big as a village, a picture taker named Jack, and a flying helicopter that lifted him into the air and brought him home. Over the days and nights, he could fill the hole his brother left and gain the family he never had ...

Wanato spotted a familiar vine and darted to examine its choking hold around a dead trunk. By the time the others caught up to him, Wanato was smiling.

"Japu bird's snot," he said in English, and pointed.

He told them it was the vine's Wayãpi name. During the days of the Old People, the japu bird started sobbing and didn't stop until the whole forest was covered in his snot.

"Gross," Ned said.

But Wanato's face was melting from something hard into something soft as each familiar thing caught his eye.

"How many days have we been at this, Gustavo?" Ned asked, and clenched his jaw.

Wanato never understood the white man's obsession with counting things. What did it matter how many days they had been in the forest? Did it change anything to know?

"Twenty-one days," Zhen said immediately.

She didn't say it with an accusing tone, even though they were starving and miserable. Their skin was slick with dripping sweat, and welts from blood-sucking insects had made their joints swollen. One of Zhen's eyelids was so puffy it wouldn't open. The men were shirtless, exposing pronounced rib cages, knobby spines, and sharp shoulder blades.

The others had followed Wanato for days and days (twenty-one, according to Zhen), silently grateful for his drive and knowledge of the forest. Wanato saw the movements of a poisonous snake where the others saw only leaf litter. He saw the broad, waxy leaves that could carry the embers of a fire or be bent to funnel rainwater straight into their canteens. At night, Zhen and Dewei selflessly divided their food into small, equal rations until it was all gone. Now their stomachs were long empty and their strength and spirits were failing.

Ned limped up to Wanato. He stumbled so often that Zhen and Dewei stayed close and grabbed hold of his arms when he tilted. They went down hard with the big American every time.

"I know you're happy to be home," Ned said carefully, "but we're gonna die if we don't eat."

Wanato had been angry as they left the highway and headed into the forest. He didn't want the worry of trying to keep three other people alive. But he owed his life to Zhen and Dewei for the food that had sustained them this long. And to Ned, he owed his return home. Wanato's gratitude was boundless, and truth be told, he found the young man endearing on the days he had patience. Wanato didn't want to leave these three unless there was no other choice. He owed them that. And he owed himself the peace of mind that he had done all he could for them.

"We need a new plan," Ned told Wanato.

"No, same plan. We find the Oyapock," Wanato said. "We are close. If you want to give me the compass to hold—"

"Not a chance. You're not done with me until I say so."

"Then keep us headed south," Wanato said, and led the way forward.

~~~~

THE NEXT DAY, just before dusk, Ned fell and wouldn't get up. Zhen and Dewei tried to pull him to his feet, but he wouldn't budge. Wanato doubled back and crouched beside him.

"Just go," Ned said softly.

He gave the compass to Wanato without looking him in the eyes. It might have been shame, or maybe he always expected to be left to die. Zhen couldn't get him to say much while the four of them sat in the underbrush, too exhausted to slap away mosquitoes. The sun crawled across the canopy.

"The daylight's almost gone," Ned finally said to Zhen.

It must have been easier to talk to her. There was a kindness about Zhen that drew you in.

"You should go while you can," Ned almost pleaded.

Zhen spoke Chinese to Dewei, who nodded in agreement.

"We will wait with Ned until morning," she said to Wanato. "You can go."

They were all releasing him from blame. Wanato held the compass, looked down at his feet, and gave them a silent command. If he waited any longer, if he tried to say goodbye, he wouldn't be able to do what he must. Wanato stood and trudged ahead with all his remaining strength. He didn't turn around, but he felt their eyes watching his back.

I couldn't save them. How many times had he thought this, and would he ever believe it?

Wanato kept moving and focused solely on the hunger that tried to claw its way out of his belly. Starvation didn't recognize friends, family, or lovers, only its own pain. Wanato focused so hard that he nearly tripped and twisted an ankle on something round and partially hidden by underbrush. It was another familiar part of the forest: a large seedpod. Wanato picked it up and turned in circles, scanning the forest. Then he saw a grove of the largest trees in the whole Amazon.

Wanato hurled himself back the way he came, clutching the seedpod to his chest. As soon as he could take in enough breath, he screamed Ned's name. Zhen hollered back in the distance, leading Wanato back with her voice. When he found them, Ned bowed low to hide his tears. Wanato had to crouch.

"I can save you," he whispered to Ned.

The American grabbed him in a shaky embrace.

"Just a little farther," Wanato said quickly. "I swear it."

He pried off Ned's hand and placed the hard pod onto his palm.

"What the hell is this?"

Ned looked up into Wanato's eyes and saw a new excitement and urgency that brought him to stand on failing legs and wipe his tears. Wanato led the way, with Zhen and Dewei in the middle and Ned at the back, stumbling and holding on to tree trunks when he fell. They reached the grove of trees whose trunks rose above the canopy. The dullish seedpods littered the ground by their roots. Wanato used Ned's hunting knife to saw off the top of one and pull out a large, rough seed with a seam along the pinched edge of its shell.

Ned crumpled to the ground. "Brazil nuts!" he gasped.

Ned looked like he didn't know whether to smile or cry with relief. He did both as Wanato cut into the seed's seam with his knife, shelled it, and tossed it to Ned. Wanato stood just out of reach as he continued to toss the Brazil nuts one by one. He had to avoid getting locked in Ned's grateful grip before he could dispense the foods his friend so desperately needed. Dewei bowed in gratitude when Wanato threw him a shelled seed and then returned the favor with a seed he had just shelled with his small utility knife. The young man was good with tools.

"Brazil nuts aren't nuts at all," Ned blubbered, sniffing a runny nose. "They're seeds. Go figure."

Wanato had come to learn many things about Ned: his stubbornness, humor, and indigestion, but the things that he most admired were Ned's capacity for empathy and wonder in all situations.

"You should read poetry," Wanato told him, although he had no idea how that could be possible now.

The Brazil nuts (which were really seeds) were oily to the touch and delicious. Zhen said she lost count of how many Wanato and Dewei both doled out, they were that good. Wanato furrowed his brows as his hands kept moving.

"Wayãpi can count up to four," he told her. "After that, we say there is 'a lot.'"

Zhen laughed and hid her smile behind one hand.

"Then there is much we can teach one another," she said.

Wanato looked over at her and went still. There had always been so much to teach and learn, but too few would listen. Wanato spent his adult life hitting up against the wall of ignorance on all sides and almost gave up.

"Lesson one from us Wayãpi," he said, and pointed to the grove. "Save these trees!"

In the days before the comet, it was illegal to destroy Brazil nut trees because they created such a valuable export. But laws alone weren't enough to protect them and their delicate ecosystem. Brazil nut trees only bore fruit in virgin forests where the right pollinating bees could thrive. The trees only bore children where the agouti could eat its seeds with its sharp rodent teeth and bury the others for later.

Saving the Brazil nut tree was a lesson his dead friends Zé and Maria knew well. There was one of these trees on the federal land that the couple harvested. Zé named it the Majesty for its immense splendor and once fended off illegal loggers with a shotgun when they tried to invade. It was a war with the Great Hungry Machine on one side and the Majesty, the tree of life, a giver instead of a taker, on the other.

Wanato could remember Zé—everything wide: his face, his eyes, his nose, his smile, those hats he always wore with tufts of gray hair spilling out—as he handed Gustavo a pencil drawing of the Majesty for the cover of his poetry collection. Wanato could picture him at the end of his TEDx Talk, before he thanked the live audience and exited the stage. He said, "It's in our hands, and we have the future before us—and we have to decide."

"Meus amigos," Wanato muttered sadly, and brought another Brazil nut to his lips. *My friends...*

~~~~

THEIR BELLIES SWELLED and got to work digesting rich proteins, fats, and fiber. Ned ripped farts and groaned about his stretching stomach. They couldn't have set off hiking even if they wanted to. Moving a safe distance from the grove and its falling pods, they lay down and huddled in pairs under two nets that kept the mosquitoes and cockroaches off their faces.

"We got lucky," Zhen whispered. "So many will starve. Millions. *Billions.*"

"All the people left in the cities," Wanato agreed.

He could remember the first time he walked through a city as a young man. There were more people in Macapá than he imagined even existed. He asked Father St. John, *What is feeding all these people?*

He had only known the forests, rural farms, and even frontier towns with gardens and chickens running underfoot, but the city had no way of producing food, not that he could see.

"Both you Debbie Downers better shut up and go to sleep," Ned growled.

~~~~

WANATO DIDN'T KNOW how much time had passed before he woke and pulled back the mosquito netting. Zhen was already standing alert and looking up. Windows in the canopy revealed a clear sky.

"I've counted the days and hours," Zhen stated, still looking up, "down to T-minus zero to detonation of our spacecraft's nuclear payload."

"Is this it?" Ned whispered, desperately trying to read Zhen's shadowed expression. "Is the comet coming to hit us? Is this the end?"

The forest was eerily silent. The insects and frogs all watched and waited. There was a flash of light that burned an afterimage they tried to blink away. Dewei sat up and opened his mouth, but Zhen shushed him.

"Do you feel that?" she whispered.

Wanato felt vibrations in his chest and ears. Fiery streaks suddenly zipped across pockets of sky in the canopy. Leaves, branches, and insects rained down from high above.

"Meteors!" Zhen gasped. "Those are shattered pieces of the comet. We hit it!"

More meteors burned trails toward the horizon. Ned tilted his head all the way back.

"Hope it hurt, fucker!" he shouted up, laughing and crying.

Wanato watched the sky blur through his tears. How could he not be grateful to the comet, now that it was deflected? UD3 had succeeded where he had failed; it brought the destruction that could save Indigenous peoples and their forests from extinction, if only they could remember their traditional ways. It had also brought a civilization that was poisoning itself to a halt; it saved humans from themselves. Nothing by any stretch of his imagination could have been so effective.

After the meteor shower ended, the sky glowed with a strange light that was strong enough to cast shadows.

"Do you see that aurora?" Zhen asked in the silence. "It's charged particles from the nuclear blast reacting with the Earth's magnetic field. The comet would have impacted Earth by now. It's been deflected."

The aurora looked like an alien sunset on another planet—or a sunrise.

"This is not the end," Zhen said to Ned, with a lump in her throat. "This is our second chance."

She shot her fists up high. Afterward, she said she could feel all the people of the Effort and all the remaining survivors under the same glowing sky lifting their squeezed fists and screaming, the many becoming one victorious.

〜〜〜〜

THE GLOW HAD faded into familiar stars by the time they set off with as many of the Brazil nuts as they could carry. Without pain from starvation, without the fear of death and ultimate destruction, they could ignore difficult questions for the time being and just enjoy life itself. They joked and smiled. Zhen told the group stories about the Effort and the spacecraft they all built together. When Ned pulled back a curtain of flowering vine, hundreds of small butterflies scattered into the air. Zhen gasped and clapped in delight. Dewei also found a colony of flared, golden mushrooms growing on a decomposed log.

"Gustavo! Food! Food!"

The young man could now pronounce their names and string several English words together. Dewei pointed to the mushroom colony, eager to please their leader, but Wanato shook his head. Ned asked if the mushrooms were poisonous. Wanato shrugged and said he only knew that the Grandfather People didn't eat them.

"For hunter-gatherers, your Grandfather People were pretty spoiled," Ned grumbled.

Wanato shrugged again and smiled. His ancestors could afford to be picky when they knew how to make bows and poison-tipped arrows, how to grow cassava in bad soil, and how to scrape off the poisonous peel of the root and soak it to make *caxiri* beer, flat bread, porridge...there were so many things the Grandfather People knew.

By the middle of the dry day, they hadn't passed any streams and their canteens were empty. With one misery abated, they felt another creep in, trading hunger for thirst. Wanato knew they had to reach water soon as they descended a slow incline.

"Will you take off that ridiculous Mets hat?" Ned snapped at Zhen.

They all had racking headaches from dehydration. Zhen stopped to cock her head and think, then said simply, "No."

But she didn't budge. They all stopped moving.

"Now what?" Zhen finally asked Wanato. "What will happen to the three of us? Do we stay with you and your people until it is safe to leave the forest and return?"

Wanato nodded, but he was doubtful. He didn't know if the world would ever be safe for Zhen again; it had never been safe for Wayãpi to begin with.

According to the Grandfather People, they were forever fleeing. To escape epidemics, mass slaughter, slavers, and missionaries, Wayãpi migrated north along great rivers and split off like its headwaters. Some families, like the one headed by Wanato's father's father's father, followed the Jari River's tributaries deep into forests that became the Brazilian state of Amapá. Other Wayãpi continued north as far as the Oyapock River on the border of what became French Guiana. Most of these Other Wayãpi settled where the Camopi River joined the larger current, but there were also rumors of other tribes, secret tribes that hid themselves away from danger.

As Wanato continued south with Ned, Zhen, and Dewei following in his well-placed footsteps, he began to worry. Would the Other Wayãpi of French Guiana remember him? Would they accept the three foreigners in his care, or would they resort to violence? Wanato wouldn't blame the villagers for defending themselves against a perceived threat. Contact with foreign invaders usually ended in death and loss—but not always.

Wanato's great-grandmothers were young girls when a scientific expedition reached their village. Those were days before contact with gold prospectors and the government. The event was a landmark because it was guided by a curiosity that kept greed and massacre at bay. The foreigners didn't spread disease and stole nothing from the village. Instead, the strange men—exhausted and probably ill with malaria—presented colorful glass beads with tired smiles. In return, the Wayãpi gave two headdresses with bright macaw and toucan feathers and several arrows. The bond they made that day was brief but unbroken.

The foreigners wished to continue down the Jari River in their canoes. Many Wayãpi archers watched them embark with their arrows notched. The foreigners waved in parting but kept their rifles in reach. No one was a fool, but neither did they want to fire the first shot and kill something that sparked wonder. They chose to watch and wait. And so, behind the fear and distrust of every new encounter with non-Wayãpi, there could also be a small hope that wonder would stay the arrows of warriors and win out.

When Wanato heard a rush of water, he jogged ahead to find a river, but it was not the Oyapock. Ned caught up to him and hollered with joy. The four of them filled their canteens and dropped in water purification tablets. Wanato left the others to rest on the bank as he scouted the area. Maybe they still had another day of hard hiking to reach the Oyapock, but maybe not? Was this the Eureupousine River? Wanato had never seen it, but he knew the river was close.

Vegetation grew thick and scratched at Wanato's skin. He stepped into a small clearing and saw a tree with a thick thatch of woven palm leaves obscuring its branches. Wanato realized he was staring at a hunter's hideout at the same instant a Wayãpi man leaned into view with a bow stretched taut and an arrow aimed at his heart. Wanato stopped in shock and marveled at the real Wayãpi bow and an arrow tipped with bloodred macaw feathers. The man's loincloth was made from rough cotton twine and dyed with *urucu*.

The tribes that kept themselves secret, he thought. *They hid deep in the forest and remembered how to carve and string a bow like the Grandfather People.*

Wanato knew the warrior recognized him as both Wayãpi and an invader. The warrior would spend only a few seconds on a decision. He could release his arrow and kill the invader, defending his people and their lives in the forest. Or he could choose wonder and try to create a human bond that crossed their divide.

Wanato smiled and laughed with joy, nearly falling over backward as he reveled in the few seconds of time when both of those perfect possibilities could exist together.

THIRTY-FIVE

DREAMS

THE SECOND DARK AGES
NORTH CASCADES NATIONAL PARK, WASHINGTON

FOR THE THIRD time that day, Captain Weber fell and lost his sight. The Cascade Mountains went black with fuzzy, unresolved points of lights.

This is it, he thought. *This is where I fall and don't get up.*

Weber was dying of starvation. The lands surrounding Tacoma's suburbs had been stripped of all vegetation, as if consumed by plagues of locusts rather than starving humans trying to digest grass and leaves. Weber lived on rations from *Healy* until he escaped the city and found freshwater lakes. He had kept several lures and line from his heirloom tackle box before giving it away, and Weber was a skilled fisherman, but he hadn't made a catch in days. He knew that many of the survivors were cannibals by necessity, but he couldn't bring himself to cut flesh from human bodies. One could lose a sense of meaning, religion, ideology, love, and hope but still cling to a sense of self, even if it was formed on those lost things.

This is how the stranger found Weber: collapsed next to his duffel bag with a dazed expression. Delirium was common to those living and dying in what came to be known as the Second Dark Ages.

"Coast Guard, right?"

The stranger's voice came from twenty yards away. Weber turned and readied his wasted body for a fight he would lose. The stranger held a semiautomatic rifle and wore a kind of woodland camo that wasn't military-issued.

"My father was in the Coast Guard," the stranger said, pointing at Weber's filthy working uniform.

Lightweight binoculars hung from the man's neck. He must have read the white stitching on Weber's chest that spelled out "COAST GUARD" as he tracked him through the forest.

"Junior lieutenant. He was always grateful to the Coast Guard for keeping him out of Vietnam. Ah, sorry. Probably pisses you off to hear things like that. Meant no disrespect."

Weber waited—to be shot, to be surrounded by an ambush, to have his duffel bag stolen...The stranger made several cautious steps on soft mud. He was stocky and wore a belt but didn't need to. How could he have so much meat and fat on his bones? How?

"Par—"

Weber cleared his throat and tried to speak again. It had been weeks since he heard his own voice whisper a hymn.

"Pardon me, sir. But do you know where I can get food? I'm too weak to walk."

The stranger nodded, like he could see as much. A gloved hand rested on his gun.

"Where you headed?"

"To find my family," Weber said. "They left the Seattle suburbs for the parks. I was at sea when all of this..." He was too exhausted to elaborate. "Happened."

"Being on that ship probably saved your bacon. At least in the beginning," the stranger said. "Few could have made it this long on their own."

His hooded eyes squinted.

"I can see that that uniform was made for a man of your height, but if you're coming with me, I still gotta check. Wait here."

The stranger left Weber shivering in the mud. It was pointless for him to crawl into hiding. To find his family, Weber had to live. To live, he needed food. And if he needed food, he needed this stranger with the ample waist. A cold rain fell as he waited and prayed. He had lost track of the days, but it had to be early autumn judging from the new snowpack on the mountains.

Weber heard an engine above the patter of rain and saw a truck emerge with large off-road tires. It moved slowly up the incline, slaloming pine trees. The stranger parked and hopped out of the driver's side. His right hand still steadied his gun, but his left held a coil of nylon rope that he threw in a sloppy underhand.

"Tie me a bowline knot."

Weber looked to the rope and then up at the stranger.

"If that's really your Coast Guard uniform, you'll know how," the man explained. "If not, then you probably stole those clothes and gear, and I'll have to waste a bullet."

Weber picked up the rope and tied a bowline knot with shaking hands.

"Good. And no hard feelings. Can't have people killing and impersonating an officer. Against the rules of war, right?"

Weber tied a reef knot and then a sheepshank for good measure.

"Now you're just showing off," the stranger muttered. "Get in."

Weber stood and fainted. When he regained consciousness, the stranger had him by the crook of his arm. No doubt Weber weighed less than a scarecrow.

"I gotcha," the other man said. "Just a few more steps."

He helped Weber into the passenger seat and went back for his duffel bag. It was much lighter than the day he disembarked *Healy*. All that was left was a canteen half-full of lake water, a compass, a first aid kit, a spare set of wool socks, a sparker fire starter, a rain poncho, and a knife. Weber started out with a flashlight that allowed him to travel at night and hide in daylight hours. The small device was undoubtedly a lifesaver before it ran out of batteries.

The stranger sat in the driver's seat and leaned over with his eyes trained on Weber. His left hand squeezed into a tight fist.

Weber held his breath. The other man's nose had large pores and hairy nostrils that flared with Weber's stench. The truck's glove compartment popped open. When the stranger leaned back, Weber felt something land in his lap. It was a granola bar.

Weber fumbled quickly but couldn't open the flashy foil packaging. The stranger had to snatch it out of Weber's hands and rip into the foil with his teeth before tossing it back. Weber ate the bar in two bites, barely chewing. He licked his fingers as he shed silent tears, because of the nourishment, and because there wasn't enough of it.

The truck's engine revved. Its windshield wipers made slow arcs to clear the drizzle. Weber likewise swiped at his damp, bearded cheeks with the back of his hand.

"Thanks for the food. Name's Weber," he added, because it was all he had to offer in return.

The stranger's hawkish eyes darted between the forest in front and the passenger to his right. They caught the silver eagles on Weber's collar tips.

"Nobody cares about names anymore, Captain."

He looked over at Weber's chiseled face. Beneath the dirt and desperation, he must have seen the ghost of a dignified figure.

"My father would've liked you. You are what he wanted to be. Or, does that mean he would have hated you? Who knows?"

The stranger had a northern, rural accent and stressed *o* vowels like a Canadian. *Whooo knoooows.*

"What I do know, Captain, is that you should've stayed on your ship."

Weber's lips moved without sound to form *Healy*. The name of his ship was US Coast Guard Cutter *Healy*. His days on polar expeditions seemed like quiet, ice-filled dreams. All days before the comet and its deflection seemed like dreams in the new reality.

It was the dead of winter when Weber's ship anchored. The crewmembers and scientists all banded together in small groups that headed for Joint Base Lewis-McChord while Weber struck out on his own. He couldn't see far in such thick fog, but he heard a woman screaming in the distance. Instead of running toward her, he ran in the opposite direction. In a time of war, Weber wouldn't think to abandon his own crew. But this wasn't war. This was survival in the face of an apocalypse, a face that wasn't human.

The truck descended slowly by zigzagging around trees and crushing saplings under its monster tires. Lake Chelan came into view through the treetops, pearlescent with morning fog. Growing up, Weber used to camp in the valley and swim in the lake. In good weather, its surface was a clear reflection of the sky. "God's Country" is what his father called the North Cascades National Park—but it wasn't now.

Weber spoke up when they reached the smooth road running parallel to Lake Chelan's southwestern shore. Roads meant people, and people meant danger. He had tripped over too many bodies hidden under the snow. Weber figured there had to be a reason this well-fed man ventured out into danger alone. Even armed to the teeth, he was taking grave risk.

"Where were you headed?" Weber asked.

"Such a nice day, I was on the winery tour."

Weber hiccupped a small laugh, surprising them both. The stranger returned a sideways grin. They passed an abandoned Buick along the side of the road with its gas cap left open.

"Are you looking for loved ones?" Weber pressed. "Like I am?"

The other man didn't answer right away. His mouth twitched as he started and abruptly stopped after two words. Maybe he was trying to think up another joke, or a lie.

"I was looking for a woman," he finally admitted, with a shrug. "Until I saw your uniform in the trees and got curious. Survivors come to the lake when they run out of water. I got plenty of supplies so... figured I'd have more luck in the love department than I have in the past. I'm the new Brad Pitt, don't yah know."

Weber couldn't help thinking of his wife, Karen. She was in her late forties, but still attractive. At summer picnics, she turned the heads of much younger men with her long, tanned legs. He tried to empty those thoughts from his mind.

"May I try the radio," Weber asked, changing the subject.

"You won't get a signal. Hasn't been jack shit in nearly a year. No radio, no TV, no internet. All dark."

"But that's how it could happen, right? How survivors, the decent ones, could communicate and find one another?"

"I dunno. You tell me."

"Okay, then, I'm telling you. Radio waves could be the way."

That had been Weber's hope since he saw the dazzling meteor shower in the summer sky—fiery streaks of ice, dust, and rock blown from the body of a giant comet—which meant that there could be hope for all of God's creatures once more. Weber asked if the man believed that things could still go back to the way they were before UD3 had come and gone. The stranger shrugged.

"I'm not sure things are much different. We've stopped *pretending* to be civilized, that's all. We've lost our polite manners and our electronic gadgets and showed the animals we always were under it all. We were still competing with one another to survive—just with a more complex and subtle set of rules. I mean, I didn't kill anyone before UD3, but that doesn't mean I didn't want to."

Weber said nothing. He wondered if things shouldn't go back to the way they were after all. Perhaps things should be altogether different? Better? Or wiser, at least? He stared at the road ahead and saw what looked like an eviscerated human torso, a rib cage and trailing spinal column. It still saddened Weber that none of the victims would receive a proper burial.

"We're going south," Weber said. "But I was headed to North Cascades."

"You were headed nowhere fast, is more like it. I'm bringing you back home with me. You could use a hot meal. And a good wash. You reek."

His face went suddenly serious.

"Buckle your seat belt," he ordered.

A group of haggard men was walking beside the road. They carried heavy plastic bottles of water that they dropped in surprise. One stepped to the middle of the road and waved his hands above his head. His shouts, the red fabric of his down jacket, his frantic movements all said *Stop!* But the truck leapt forward, accelerating above ninety miles per hour. The stranger's jaw was set, his mind made up.

Weber braced his weight. He wasn't one for moral inaction, but he had no way of knowing if the man in the red jacket meant to harm them. These were different times; many horrible actions were justified. Weber closed his eyes, but there was no sickening thud to interrupt his silent prayers. When he looked back, the man in the red jacket was tumbling down the embankment. He must have jumped to safety at the last second.

"Good that we didn't hit him," Weber said in a long exhale.

The stranger grunted and mentioned all the damage a deer had already done to his fender. They were silent for the rest of the trip.

⌇⌇⌇⌇

THE CLOSING OF the driver's-side door woke him. Weber bolted upright, but he was strapped in by a seat belt. It was already twilight and the drizzle had stopped. Weber watched the stranger's shadowed figure through the windshield as he approached a ten-foot-tall chain-link fence topped with three rows of curled razor wire that looked like widow's lace against the sky.

A section of the fence slid back when the stranger pushed with his meaty arms and shoulders. He got back behind the wheel and eased the truck through the gate with its headlights off.

"Was this a prison?" Weber asked.

"No. It's home. That wire is to keep people out, not in."

Weber didn't blame the man for turning off the truck's engine and taking the keys with him when he stepped out to close the gate.

They drove down a long and narrow dirt road. When the underbrush cleared, Weber heard the crunch of tires on gravel. There was a building forty yards ahead, like a modern-day fortress with high concrete walls. Weber saw a large satellite dish on its roof, outlined against rose- and lavender-colored clouds. A metal garage door was the only interruption in the wall facing them.

"Here's where I get lazy," the stranger admitted.

He reached up and pressed something behind his rearview mirror. The garage door lifted and folded along segments as it retreated into the wall.

"How . . ." Weber started. "How were you so ready?"

"It's funny," the man said, looking more sober.

He stepped lightly on the gas.

"I was ready for every other reason under the sun. Terrorist attack, currency collapse, Ebola outbreak . . . but a fucking comet? I mean, ya gotta be kidding me."

Weber nodded and gave a tired laugh. Depending on how you looked at it, UD3 was either the least funny situation in an infinite amount of other possibilities—or it was hilarious.

The truck came to a stop as the garage door extended back into place. Weber unfastened his seat belt in the absolute darkness.

"Just wait," the stranger whispered.

Overhead lights flicked on.

"Jesus," Weber breathed.

"No, not Jesus. More like energy from solar panels," the man said, sounding pleased.

With the granola bar and a few hours' sleep, Weber was able to walk without help. He shuffled along slowly after his host.

The other man reached the door and flicked on a small flashlight mounted on the end of his rifle.

"I don't use lights where there are windows," he muttered. "It could attract them."

He shut off the overhead lights and opened the door. Weber tried to follow the flashlight's thin beam pointing down the gun barrel. It was a surreal view, like one of those first-person-shooter videogames he had seen in the crew lounge on his ship. The stranger crossed the first room and stood to the side of its only window. He picked up his lightweight binoculars and scanned the darkness outside. Weber stole a moment to look around. The room had no furniture but was cluttered with piles of objects: collections of electronics, clothes, and weapons. The soles of Weber's boots skidded on grime.

The men crossed two more rooms before reaching a windowless kitchen with a wooden table and chairs. The stranger helped Weber into a chair and flicked on the overhead lights. They both blinked rapidly in the dazzling light. Electricity. How could Weber have been so ignorant to its everyday miracles?

The stranger pulled out his jingling keychain and unlocked the door to his basement larder. Gun and flashlight in hand, he disappeared down a flight of stairs. Weber looked around the kitchen. He saw a cast iron stove on legs with its thick exhaust pipe reaching to the ceiling. The walls above and below the cabinets were bare.

When the man returned, he had two cans clutched to his chest with one hand. The other held his gun with his trigger finger ready. Weber made no sudden moves. His stomach groaned like a kettledrum.

"I know," the other man promised. "It's coming."

He let go of his gun and let it sway from its strap. There was a can opener lying on the kitchen counter beside an old dog collar. Weber would have used his teeth on the metal like the starving animal he was. The thought of food was almost unbearable. He needed a distraction.

"Do you have a dog?" Weber asked, making fists with trembling hands.

Soon as he asked, he wished he didn't. People ate their pets, and they trapped and ate all the wild animals they could find.

"I *had* a dog. Now I don't."

Weber's silence must have betrayed his thoughts.

"I didn't eat him," the other man snapped as he took off his gloves. "He died two years ago. He's buried in the back. In one of his holes."

"I'm sorry."

The other man shook his head, like he was shaking free of the thought, and emptied baked beans into a bowl.

"Got a feeling you won't mind it cold," he said, carrying the bowl and a spoon to the table.

Weber took the bowl from the stranger's hands and tipped it up to his open mouth.

"Easy," the man said gently. "Eat slow as you can. Easy! You're gonna—"

Choke. Weber hacked until tears ran down his reddened face. As soon as he could breathe, he spooned up the remaining beans and sauce. Metal scraped against ceramic. Weber's host was already opening the second can. He took a seat at the table as he poured out the contents. Weber's eyes watered again as he finished his second helping but this time because of overwhelming gratitude. How could he ever repay the man beside him? He wiped up the streaks of sauce with his finger and licked it.

"You're the first person I've talked to," the stranger admitted. "You know, after I lost contact."

Weber cleared his throat. If talking was what this man needed, then Weber would happily sing for his supper. He asked questions and listened to answers. The other man used to be some sort of cybersecurity expert, where a constant state of paranoia might be a competitive advantage. Back on *Healy*, Weber and the rest of the crew used "Before the comet" to describe familiar life before that August, but this man used "Before I lost contact." He must have been a recluse who only spoke to other humans through satellite via emails, blog posts, money transfers, and live chats.

"Didn't you get lonely?" Weber asked.

"I connected with people all the time."

"But never face-to-face."

The man shrugged. "I never fit in with people. I preferred Jax."

"Who?"

"My dog. Jax was his name."

The corner of Weber's lips turned up. "I thought no one cares about names anymore."

The other man considered the words given back to him.

"Andrew," he said, holding out his hand.

Weber's hand was filthy, but Andrew took hold of it. He wasn't the type who liked to be touched, so he forced his grip and held on.

"Are you a Christian, Andrew?"

He pulled away from Weber's hand. "Nah, just doing my bit for the Coast Guard. My old man woulda wanted it that way."

The stranger's eyes suddenly stopped on Weber with a fixed stare.

"You won't find your family," he said sadly. "I know that's not what you wanna hear. And it's not something I'm supposed to say. But it's the truth."

Weber lowered his blue-denim eyes.

"Well, I said it," the other man continued. "But, come morning, when you take leave, you can forget I said it. If need be."

He got up and fed split logs and tinder into the stove. There was enough water in the large kettle for Weber to soak a washcloth and rub away the dirt and sweat from a fruitless search. As soon as the water turned gray, the other man refilled the kettle from a well pump and set it to warm again.

That night, Weber slept with a full belly under a stranger's roof.

He dreamed of his wife and children. He dreamed of eagles coasting in the breeze. He dreamed of children in the future, born into an unknown age that would be whatever they made of it.

In the morning, Weber remembered his dreams and forgot the truth.

THIRTY-SIX

TWO KNOCKS IN YEAR 4 AC

THE SECOND DARK AGES
PEDRA BRANCA DO AMAPARI, BRAZIL

THERE WAS A knock on Zhen's bedroom door after Sunday prayer. As expected, Gustavo was standing in the second-floor hallway with a canvas bag slung around one shoulder. Many voices echoed below from the townsfolk of Pedra Branca do Amapari as they either chatted by the wooden pews or took their conversations outside the church to stretch their legs.

Gustavo usually attended both the prayer and the townhall that followed shortly after. However, the next rainy season was nearly upon them. Each was announced with a sudden blast of wind, followed by steady downpours that could last as long as a quarter of the solar calendar. Travel was difficult in all the flooding for friends and enemies alike. Gustavo had to return to Wayãpi lands while the dirt road connecting the town was still passable on foot.

"Ned will be ready soon," Gustavo muttered.

He shared a little smile with Zhen. Ned was a favorite with the townsfolk. The grannies waved for him to bend down so they could kiss his cheeks. The men clapped him on the shoulder. Women blushed and their children reached up to be lifted high in the air. Ned didn't understand most of what they all said in Portuguese, but he would smile and nod. When it came time to hold hands in group prayer, his large hands were warm and strong.

Gustavo's gaze wandered over Zhen's shoulder to the interior of the bedroom, so she stepped aside and invited him in to wait for their local celebrity. Gustavo hesitated at the threshold. Five months ago, he had done the same before deciding to cram into his old bedroom across the hall with Ned so that Zhen could have this larger bedroom with several windows. It once belonged to a Canadian priest, a man who raised Gustavo like a son. Father St. John was traveling abroad when the imminent impact of comet UD3 caused so much panic that major airlines suspended flights. No one knew what became of him, along with so many others stranded far from home.

Zhen opened the top drawer of a wooden dresser, where she had carefully placed the priest's personal effects for safekeeping, but Gustavo didn't want to take his things with him, and looking at framed photos "hurt too much." Instead, Gustavo walked up to the stacked shelves of books against the far wall. His fingertips glanced rows of leather spines and tapped three gaps where books were missing. Gustavo must have memorized the priest's library, because he named the missing poets.

Zhen pointed to an armchair and a table by the window. Two books rested on the small round table. They were the same collection of poetry, but one was in the poet's native English and the other was translated to Portuguese. Zhen had been comparing them line by line as the chants of "Ave Maria" floated up from the church below.

"You'll help Ned with Portuguese?" Gustavo asked.

"We're helping each other."

It was true in every sense of the word. Despite a difference in age, gender, race, nationality, personality, and all the rest of it, Ned was Zhen's closest companion; all the family she had left.

"You'll give our love to Dewei?" Zhen asked of Gustavo. "And tell him we said goodbye?"

Gustavo nodded with his head hung low. For a time, the four of them were family, living in the Wayãpi village of Aramirã.

They borrowed axes from the other villagers and built a house on stilts with wooden plank walls and a thatch roof. Gustavo had immediately swapped his clothes for a loincloth, called a *tanga*. Dewei and Ned did the same after a week of hauling planks and sweating through their clothes. *The humidity is killing me,* Ned said to Zhen. *And I feel completely overdressed. Like a grizzly bear walking around in a full tuxedo.* It took months for Zhen to walk around with only a square of cotton fabric tied around her waist like a sarong, and she regretted all that time spent hot and uncomfortable.

Nearly as soon as their house was fully built, Gustavo married his brother's widow and moved into his own house. That left the three of them to hang their hammocks in one of four corners and then try to earn their place in the village. Ned and Dewei didn't hunt with the Wayãpi men. They were too clumsy in the forest and scared away game; they couldn't shoot an arrow straight and couldn't keep up with the chase without tripping on the underbrush. Instead, they helped burn, clear, and till small plots for gardens.

As for Zhen, she joined the other women in their endless chores. They bathed before dawn, before the men, so as not to be "lazy women" according to the Wayãpi men. They tended gardens, prepared cassava, and ground it into a flour that was kneaded into flat bread that they dried on their thatched rooves. The women also tended fires, gutted animals and fish, and roasted the flesh. They even brewed *caxiri* beer with cassava and their saliva for village drinking sprees. Women worked all waking hours while holding and nursing babies or keeping the toddlers safe from scorpions, fire ants, large trees with shamanistic power, and the Amapari River, where the great anaconda, Owner-of-the-Water, lurked.

Dewei soon married a young Wayãpi girl and asked Ned to help him build a house of his own. Both he and Gustavo lived with their new families, but they managed to stay present for Zhen and Ned.

The four of them had saved each other from death and witnessed the narrow escape of their planet together; that wasn't something one should forget.

Zhen and Ned continued to live together. Instead of the linear timeline of the modern world they once knew, nature followed a cycle. There was birth and death, sunrise and sunset. There was the fireside under a night sky pregnant with stars and the glow of the Milky Way. There was the pain of rotting teeth, peeling sunburns on Ned's freckled back, and wounds on the hardened soles of their feet, but there was also the fullness from warm flat bread and the weightlessness of resting in a netted hammock. There was the dry season, and then the soggy, miserable rainy season, and then the dry again. Three years of this cycle passed in the Wayãpi village before the first raid.

Forty-one Wayãpi were killed, two girls went missing, and a quarter of the village's gardens were ripped up as a band of invading Brazilians quickly stole all the food they could carry and retreated back on the single road leading out of tribal lands to the frontier town of Pedra Branca do Amapari. One hundred and eight Wayãpi died from an illness that spread like wildfire within days. Wayãpi had no immunity to the diseases of large populations.

The second raid on the village of Aramirã occurred six months later and was even more deadly. Gustavo had stepped into the role of chief, like his father and twin brother before their deaths. He ordered all the dead bodies, Wayãpi and Brazilian, to be burned. Despite these measures, there was another outbreak.

Gustavo insisted that the raiders weren't the townsfolk from Pedra Branca. They had to be complete strangers migrating from the southeastern cities of Macapá and Santana by the mouth of the Amazon River. The townsfolk of Pedra Branca had lived separately but peacefully beside the Wayãpi for decades, Gustavo argued. They knew one another, and people couldn't take a machete to the face of someone they knew. (Zhen and Ned confided in each other that they had their doubts. People could and did do this.)

Gustavo had sworn to himself that he would never leave his people once he returned to them, but they were in grave danger from the outside world—again. After the third raid on the village, he decided to journey to the town where he had lived the majority of his life to see what had become of it and what could be done about the raiders who had to be coming through their roads.

Ned and Zhen couldn't let Gustavo head off into danger alone, but Dewei chose to remain behind in the village. His wife had given birth recently. Dewei had already left two children behind in China for a top-secret mission that took him on a one-way flight to South America. When life gives you a chance at redemption, you seize it and hold tight.

"There Zhen is!" Ned called out from the second-floor hallway. "Hiding in her room during prayer again."

He smiled with two rows of teeth bright against his bushy, dark beard. Ned enjoyed what he called "giving Zhen shit for skipping out on church." Zhen reminded Ned, yet again, that she wasn't hiding. She was from China; Communism was the only religion allowed. With that, Zhen tried to change the subject like she always did when guarding her atheism from her lovable, pushy friend.

"Thank you for letting us stay in your home," Zhen said to Gustavo as they descended the stairs of the parish together.

But Gustavo shook his head.

"My home was always with the Wayãpi. This town is the path where I was *called*. It was where Father St. John was called as well. A mission isn't the same as a home."

But they could be the same. The Effort was both Zhen's mission and her home. It was where her abilities reached such heights that they shocked her.

Gustavo had already said most of his goodbyes, but more than a hundred townsfolk still gathered in the street outside the parish to send him off. There wasn't an easy affection between them, for Gustavo wasn't like Ned, but there was respect and true appreciation for all he had done to give them back their community.

The parish was on the far side of the town, less than a mile from the dirt road leading to Wayãpi lands. Zhen, Gustavo, and Ned walked shoulder to shoulder down the empty paved street. Before the comet, the town had been evenly split between rural farmland on the perimeter and buildings clustered around the main road and inside a bend in the Amapari River. Four and a half years after the deflection, or in the middle of 4 AC, as Ned referred to his new calendar abbreviation for "after comet," the municipal buildings, shops, and houses were nearly all abandoned. Many inhabitants had been killed in raids, and many more had become farmers on the edges of town.

The only families who lived in the buildings along the road were headed by men like Ned, who served in the local militia. This was the only job the townsfolk were willing to support through taxes on their harvest of rice, corn, beans, cassava, pineapples, oranges, bananas, and melons. It was very dangerous, but it brought honor and paid a lot of produce.

Zhen could remember the first time the three of them walked inside some of the abandoned buildings five months ago. Luckily, they wore clothes for the journey to Pedra Branca and could breathe through their sleeves, although they still choked on the stench of death. The three of them hiked out to the closest farmland and saw much of the same: entire families slaughtered with their bodies lying where they fell. *They're not fighting together*, Gustavo had barely whispered. *So they die a few at a time. Before the rest know to flee.*

With that, Gustavo had run to his parish and found the hidden key to the building, right where the priest had always left it. Gustavo rang the church bells until the townsfolk left their farms and gathered outside. They had prayed for the return of the priest and their God. But here they got a poet, an engineer, and a pilot with no plane. Many of the townsfolk wept in disappointment.

Gustavo didn't despair. He called the first of the townhalls. There were so many people they filled the pews and the street outside. Gustavo raised his voice so that it carried and told the townsfolk that if they didn't make a stand and fight back, they would die. Raiders would go farm to farm and outnumber a single family. There needed to be a militia to patrol the town's perimeter and ring the church bells to signal an attack. All the men would have to come running to fight. If they didn't find safety in their numbers, they were doomed.

"Are you sure you wish to stay in Pedra Branca?" Gustavo asked Zhen and Ned suddenly.

The other two nodded vigorously as they walked. Ned looked to Zhen with shared understanding.

"I'm so grateful," Ned insisted. "Everyone I ever met in the first twenty-seven years of my life is probably dead...I'm only alive because of you and the others."

The Wayãpi were the most decent of peoples who had saved their lives at every turn. The warrior they encountered by the Eureupousine River had stayed his arrow. He was from an unknown tribe, but he understood enough of Gustavo's words to know that the Oyapock River was their destination. He even hiked with them for half of a day to get them headed in the right direction and then pointed ahead with a frown that needed no translation: *Leave these lands and don't come back.*

Once the band of four found the Oyapock River, they followed it upstream until they reached a village of "Other Wayãpi," as Gustavo called them, on the northern bank of French Guiana. This was the September after the deflection, and they were starving again. The Other Wayãpi remembered Gustavo and took in both him and his ragged friends with no complaint. It took Gustavo, Zhen, Ned, and Dewei a week to regain their strength and heal their blisters. The

Other Wayãpi wove carrying baskets from palm leaves and fastened shoulder straps made of soft bark. They packed food that lasted well: bananas and *kwaky*, a grainy porridge made from cassava flour. They even wrapped smoking embers tightly in a waxy palm leaf so the group could take fire on their journey across the Oyapock River to the southern bank of Amapá, Brazil. It took them another month to reach Aramirã.

"I'm so *very* grateful. But life in the village is a life for someone else," Ned said. "It's a life for you, Gustavo. And for Dewei, but not for me. Not for Zhen, either."

Ned was two meters tall—or "six-foot-four" as Ned insisted when they sparred over the metric system. His skin was pale and covered in dark hair. The Wayãpi stared and pointed up at his full beard and hairy chest, calves, and thighs. The names of Wayãpi adults were considered private and guarded carefully. Many had Brazilian names or nicknames that they answered to instead. Gustavo's name wasn't really Gustavo, but that was what everyone in the village called him. It wasn't long before Ned caught on to his nickname.

What're they calling me? he asked Gustavo, and pointed to a group of men sitting on a log by a fire. Gustavo translated immediately: *Big Ugly. That's your nickname.* Ned was taken aback. *Why would you call me that?* he asked the men directly. Gustavo translated English to Wayãpi. One of the men answered matter-of-factly and Gustavo translated back. *He said, "Brazilians are all ugly." I know you're not Brazilian, Ned, but invaders have carried so many different flags over the generations. It's just easier to lump you together sometimes.*

Ned let it be known that he was a mix of Scottish, German, and Norwegian descent. (Although, Zhen had to admit, he might as well have been full Neanderthal from the Ice Age when physically compared to these Amerindians.) What's more, Ned added in a raised voice, he had had to partake in diversity and inclusion training along with all other Coast Guard personnel—a course these Wayãpi had obviously skipped.

Ned disappeared for a few days after that. Gustavo and Dewei grew worried, but Zhen asked that they give him some time alone in the forest. She had realized, with a tug on her heart, that Ned—a strapping and well-proportioned American white male—had never been an ugly outsider until this moment. And inside the isolated Wayãpi gene pool so perfectly adapted to the literal polar opposite environment, that is all Ned would ever be.

They reached a gas station on the edge of town.

"I hate this place," Gustavo said.

He stared down the abandoned store and empty pumps like an enemy. Zhen knew that this was where Gustavo's twin brother was murdered. She and Ned said nothing as they kept walking. All of them had lost their real families, and only time could ease that pain.

The asphalt paving soon ended, and they continued onto a red-dirt path and wide clearing that cut through the forest toward Wayãpi lands like a trailing wound. The unpaved road stopped just short of the village, constructed and then abandoned in the 1970s when the Brazilian government ran out of funding. This had saved the mostly secluded Wayãpi, while other tribes were exposed to the modern world and wiped out.

Gustavo halted and pulled his T-shirt over his head. Zhen and Ned turned around to give him privacy as he took off all his clothes and tucked them into his canvas bag. When they turned back, Gustavo had tied cotton twine around his waist and draped two pieces of red fabric over his groin and buttocks.

"I don't think you'll have any more attacks in the rain and flooding," Gustavo said, "but stay alert."

Ned was already pretending to dust off one of his shoulders. Gustavo gave a half smile but looked to the pink and purple scars on the other man's forearms and biceps. The deeper gashes had dark dots at the edges where Zhen had tried to stitch the flesh together with sutures and a curved needle from her first aid kit.

The scars hidden under his shirt were even larger. At least they had healed without too much infection to leave Ned ready for the next raid.

"Try and stay on the other side of a knife," Gustavo said kindly, and he reached up to embrace the bravest of fighters.

Ned hugged back hard and closed his eyes for a brief moment. You never knew when you would see someone again, if at all. Gustavo hugged Zhen next and promised to return to town when the rains stopped. She and Ned watched the back of Gustavo set off under a high noon sun. His long hair was still fully black, while Zhen's was lightly streaked with strands of steel gray. He told them Wayãpi hair was always black: black at birth and black at death.

By nightfall, Gustavo would arrive at his village, made safer now that the small town of Pedra Branca was willing to stand together and fight off raiders from the southeast. Gustavo's village had his wife, formerly his brother's wife but a widow no longer. It had Gustavo's nephews, whom he had adopted as sons. This village had everything Gustavo had ever wanted.

～～～

AT DUSK, THERE was a visitor outside Zhen's bedroom on the second floor of the parish. Zhen had used her chamber pot minutes before hearing the knock. She tried to breathe through her nose to determine how bad the smell was. Without modern amenities, they were faced with their animal nature again, noses rubbed in it.

"Zhen?"

It was Ned come to return the missing collection of poetry to the priest's library now that the light had died. Ned had to report for a night shift with the militia, but still he lingered.

"I, ah, when I came to pick out a book, I peeked at your little nest over there," he said awkwardly, and pointed to a corner of the room where Zhen had collected cellphones, laptops, bedside radios with alarm clocks, car antennas, wires, and various other equipment, all under a plastic tarp.

"Nest?" Zhen repeated.

She smiled wide without covering her scars with her hand.

"Yes! My nest for a *xǐquè*!"

"What?"

"*Xǐquè*. It is the name of a bird. They are curious collectors. I think they line their nests with shiny objects."

"Magpie?" Ned guessed.

Zhen nodded and said that the English word sounded right, but she wasn't sure.

"I have a favor," Zhen said, suddenly remembering. "There's a large satellite dish high up on the roof of a building. I'd like you to get it for me without breaking your neck."

Ned clapped his hands together with excitement.

"Yes ma'am. Do you think any satellites are still working?"

"As you say, only one way to find out."

Ned laughed and said, yes, he did say that.

"You think four years is enough for the great human race to get their act together?"

"No," Zhen admitted. "But maybe someday? I wonder what that would even look like. Have we seen it in a past civilization, or would it be something new?"

Zhen sighed as she tried to skim her knowledge of the last several millennia. So much went wrong, she had to admit, but so much went right. How could they bring back the good without making the same mistakes all over again?

"Maybe that someday when we do get our act together," Ned said, "maybe that will be the day when I help Dr. Zhen Liu get to where she is needed most?"

But they were in the most remote forest left on the planet. It was a natural barrier that protected them from grave danger, but it was also a barrier blocking the way back to what was once modern civilization. They had crossed that barrier once, but they had Gustavo as a guide, the Wayãpi villages by the Oyapock River as safe havens, and a lot of luck to keep from starving along the way.

"They'll need someone like you. Whoever *they* is," Ned continued. "But the journey will be so dangerous. You'll need me, and I'll need a mission. You got to be the hero. I want my turn."

"You are already a hero," Zhen said simply.

Ned bowed his head. That he didn't protest with false modesty meant that he knew it was true. Zhen walked over and lifted the tarp covering her collection. Her fingers itched to get to them. Soon...

The lead engineer from the Effort in French Guiana always referred to scenarios of the future. As Zhen saw it, her magpie nest had several. Scenario 1, worst case, Zhen would enjoy moments of nostalgia as she touched and tinkered with these artifacts of great human endeavor. Scenario 2, Zhen could build two short-range radios so that the town could warn the Wayãpi village in Aramirã of attacks. Scenario 3, the best of the possibilities, Zhen could build a radio strong enough to bounce off the ionosphere so she could listen for others. She would listen for Ben Schwartz, Amy Kowalski, Love Mwangi, Jin-soo Lee, and all the others. The Defense Effort for Comet UD3 had completed its mission, but would there be any survivors who could join a new effort for a new world?

Ned squatted beside Zhen and picked up a cellphone with a dead battery.

"The professor on the show *Gilligan's Island* jiggered a battery out of coconut shells, seawater, pennies, and, like, hairpins."

"What?"

"It was a joke," Ned said quickly. "Sorry about the American pop culture. I mean to say, *Imagine what you could do with all this crap on your floor!* Dewei said you're a genius that can solve the impossible. You did it at the Effort."

"I didn't save the Earth with my brain," Zhen said. "I saved it with diplomacy."

She giggled at Ned's baffled expression.

"Deus ex machina," Zhen whispered with a sudden glow. "That's what they called me..."

IN THE END, modern civilization was not undone by a comet, but by its very threat. No one knew how much the human population dwindled by the Second Dark Ages. The only communications were from hunters and fishermen, who all described the same hardships. Complications from childbirth were killers, and infant mortality was high. These dangers were almost lucky, because they only applied to the fertile. I was lucky to be born so soon. My mother was even luckier. She told me her childbearing hips were finally good for something.

I was an only child. Both my parents claimed that this was for the best. My mother said that feeding another child would have been too difficult. My father said that he didn't want to risk losing his wife. Still, it wasn't a choice. My mother was once a scientist. She told me our rainwater wasn't clean. It only looked clear because I couldn't see the chemicals and pollutants with my eyes. My mother said she could taste them and often gave a saying from the Known World: *You reap what you sow.*

But I didn't know any different; water tasted like water. The Known World wasn't known to me or any of the other children born in the dark; it existed in the survivors only. On bad days, comet refugees on Atka suffered nightmares, post-traumatic stress disorder, and even the catatonia. On good days, some hummed the melodies of pop songs and spoke of professional sports teams and reality television. *Remember?* they asked, as they slid their index fingers across their flat palms, scrolling through news feeds on make-believe smartphones. Some even drove make-believe cars while make-believe texting and crashing into a make-believe pile-up. My mother had another saying from the Known World: *Old habits die hard.*

I loved to listen to talk about the Known World. During the long Alaskan nights of winter, our community usually gathered in the school gym, nestled together under sealskin blankets with stone oil lamps burning by our feet. The other children were noisy, but I was silent so I could hear. My mother said I was like my father, Jack, a keen observer who used to capture photographic images. She asked if I was taking pictures in my head as I stared. *Maybe?*

The adults talked about democracy, the internet, slavery, war and peace, the Constitution, books, plays, songs and solid gold albums, movies, poems, and museums with all our artifacts kept safe inside. My mother taught me about science and chemistry. My father taught me about photography, journalism, recorded history, and manufactured propaganda. Their stories became my stories.

I was eleven years old when the Message Bottle washed up on the shores of Atka Island. The message was written in Russian that no one could translate, but it was the first we had heard from survivors outside of the Aleutians. The Message Bottle was all we talked about for many moons. What would happen when pockets of survivors found each other? What did they want to be as they came out of the dark?

They say that each new age dreams up the next. My parents wondered out loud if our future wasn't so unknown; perhaps we all knew exactly what it should be if only we could embrace it and let go of the comforts of the past, selfish as they were. As new leaders would be elected, as new dictators and warlords cleared a bloody path to the top, as more and more children were born in an era not to be taken for granted—it would become time to decide what to do with that second chance. We would die by our decisions and mistakes, or live to tell our stories.

AUTHOR'S NOTE

I researched and wrote this story on weekends when my time was my own. The details won't be perfect, much as I want them to be.

I must give credit to the volunteers at Wikipedia who started me off with a basic understanding of just about everything. For deeper dives, I searched the best news outlets for English speakers: *The Economist, NPR, BBC News, The Guardian, The New Yorker, National Geographic, Rolling Stone, HuffPost, NBC News, International Business Times, Slate,* and *The New York Times*. If there is a heaven, journalists from these publications should have reserved parking at the gates because there is no democracy without a free press.

The Defense Effort for Comet UD3 pulled from existing theories and collaborations toward planetary defense. The original HAIV (Hypervelocity Asteroid Intercept Vehicle) model belongs to Dr. Bong Wie and his team at the Asteroid Deflection Research Center Department of Aerospace Engineering at Iowa State University. The Post–Cold War collaboration between American and Russian nuclear physicists was best described by one of its participants, Dr. Siegfried S. Hecker. I named the character Dr. "Ziggy" Divjak from the Effort's scientific core in his honor.

I have never boarded a polar icebreaker, but I learned from those who documented their experiences on *Healy*'s scientific expeditions, especially Dr. Katlin Bowman, Alan Guo, and Bill Schmoker. I have never been to the Amazon or witnessed firsthand its environmental devastation, genocide, and assimilation of Indigenous peoples like the Wayãpi. I was largely informed by two books written by two phenomenal individuals: *Getting to Know Waiwai: An Amazonian Ethnography* by Alan Tormaid Campbell and *Blood and Earth: Modern Slavery, Ecocide, and the Secret to Saving the World* by Kevin Bales.

José "Zé" Cláudio Ribeiro da Silva and his wife, Maria do Espírito Santo, were sustainable farmers that were murdered together in 2011. The killings were announced, as they were in the story, in the Brazilian Senate as it debated proposed changes to its Forest Code. An article in *The New Yorker* by Jon Lee Anderson titled "Murder in the Amazon" recounted how a block of "ruralistas" senators booed when a legislator called for an investigation into the murders. I quoted an unnamed senator: "If the Amazon is the lungs of the world, then the world must pay us to breathe." This statement was actually made by a senator from Rondônia in an interview with *NPR*'s Lourdes Garcia-Navarro.

ACKNOWLEDGMENTS

The Effort wouldn't exist without Karen Kosztolnyik of Grand Central Publishing. Karen believed in the manuscript and its full potential. Her insights nudged me to add more structure, more depth, and more heart. The second champion to make this all possible was my agent, Suzanne Gluck of WME. Not only do Suzanne and Karen command a great amount of respect in the publishing industry, they are also everyone's favorites. Lucky for me, I landed with the exceedingly capable *and* decent.

They keep good company. I am indebted to the rest of the Grand Central team, especially Ben Sevier, Rachael Kelly, Luria Rittenberg, Lori Paximadis, and Michael Morris. I continue to benefit from the support of my own team at WME: Caitlin Mahony, Andrea Blatt, Sanjana Seelam, Troi Henderson, Siobhan O'Neill, and Anna Dixon. Their efforts connected me to Oliver Gallmeister at Gallmeister and Susanne Stark at DTV, and I am grateful for the early enthusiasm of these individuals in France and Germany.

Drafts of *The Effort* received invaluable wisdom from readers Chris, Bernadette, and Matt. I love these three tremendously and take liberties to arm-twist them for feedback. Earlier drafts also received consultations from six literary agents at the 2017 Unicorn Conference: Zoe Sandler, Sarah Bedingfield, Andy Kifer, Rachel

Crawford, Julia Kardon, and William Callahan.

While I come from obscurity, I've been working on long-form fiction since the first grade. Allow me a quick shout-out to the editors at the transatlantic webzine *The Bees Are Dead* for publishing my first work of flash fiction. My gratitude also extends to family and friends in Philadelphia and Milwaukee who have read my previous work and encouraged me further. You don't know how important your praise was to a struggling amateur. Well, maybe you do if you've read this far.

One final acknowledgment for activists who risk their lives: the Walking Dead of South America and beyond. Many have died protecting the forest and its creatures. The rest of us have failed to pick up their torch in these dark times. As a backlash to our greed and complacency, I see rage from the next generation: children taking to the streets. These new inheritors are our hope—and that is where I left this story.

READING GROUP GUIDE FOR

THE EFFORT

DISCUSSION QUESTIONS

1. *The Effort* references both documented impacts, like the asteroid explosion near the Russian city of Chelyabinsk in 2013, as well as many "near-miss" events—one as recent as July 2019. Do real-life events like these shift the book—and a threat like dark comet UD3—from science fiction to speculative fiction?

2. The defense effort in the book is pulled from existing theories and collaborations toward planetary defense—and the unforeseen consequences of nationalist politics and noncooperation between nations. Ben, however, remains steadfast in his belief that "science has no borders." In the current political climate, do you believe nation-states are more or less likely to come together in the face of looming catastrophe? Why or why not?

3. The narrative revolves around an international cast of characters, whose mixed reactions to the comet propel the story line forward. Whose decisions did you identify with the most? Did you have a favorite character?

4. Jack wonders if Gustavo was invited on the *Healy*'s final expedition so that his poetry could immortalize the Arctic and its wildlife. How, in this instance, is Gustavo's art similar to Jack's photojournalism? In your opinion, what is the most effective method of capturing a feeling or moment in history? Do you lean more toward an artistic or an objective journalistic approach when it comes to chronicling?

5. In chapter 3, several characters arrive at the Guiana Space Centre complex and enter a building named Janus. A member of the staff informs them that Janus was the Roman god of gateways, beginnings and endings, and duality. Why do you think the author chose to highlight the features of this particular deity?

6. In chapter 4, Jack claims that "some things can't be explained by science," whereas Maya insists that "all phenomena have cause and effect...we just don't always understand what those causes and effects are." Do you agree with Jack or Maya? Why?

7. When family members of the novel's protagonists started slipping out of the narrative—characters like Love's girl-friend, Rivka; Jack's mother; and Captain Weber's wife, Karen—how did this make you feel? With families and friends increasingly living in different cities around the world, how would an event like UD3 affect you and your family?

8. News coverage—from trustworthy sources and perpetrators of "fake news"—heavily influence characters' behavior

in *The Effort*. Online comments from readers particularly illustrate how fear, paranoia, ignorance, and prejudice can warp people's ability to differentiate fact from fiction. With people reading increasingly polarized media content these days, how do you think bridges can be built between individuals who disagree on fundamental issues?

9. As the comet moves closer to Earth, some characters turn to religion, while others confront their atheism and the idea that there isn't a reason for chaos. Did the novel inspire you to reflect on some of our world's "big questions," including but not limited to life, death, meaning, morality, religion, and spirituality?

10. How would you react if you were told a comet was hurtling toward Earth and would likely make impact in the next few months? How do you think society would respond?

11. The author uses foreshadowing as a narrative tool throughout the novel: for example, the dying eagles in the Arctic hinted at a biblical passage that alludes to the downfall of mankind. Did other foreshadowing elements in the novel surprise you? Why or why not?

12. In chapter 11, Dr. Charles Brodie quotes musician Joan Baez when he says, "Action is the antidote to despair." Do you agree or disagree with this statement? How does this idea contrast with the catatonia that eventually takes hold of so many characters?

13. Zhen ends up being *The Effort*'s true hero—the deus ex machina who saves the world from UD3. Her engineering

solution, however, stemmed from a risky decision to disobey her superiors. Do you feel Zhen's bravery originated from her early conversations with her mother and interactions with bullies? Throughout your life, how have you, like Zhen, steadily developed your "skin armor"?

14. In the Second Dark Ages, Jack and Maya's child describes life in the new age. The child has never experienced things we take for granted, such as electricity, modern medicine, government, the internet, and so on. As someone who has lived before the Second Dark Ages, what would you miss the most? What would you miss the least?

15. It is not the comet, but the *threat* of the comet, that results in the devolution of civil society. Rioting, starvation, and dwindling resources catalyze the real violence that brings about the Second Dark Ages. But the novel ends with hope: humanity has a second chance to rebuild, to learn from past mistakes, and to live in an era never to be taken for granted. What do you think people could do *today* to actualize a similar "second chance"—to live better, be better, and create a better world?

VISIT **GCPClubCar.com** to sign up for the **GCP Club Car** newsletter, featuring exclusive promotions, info on other **Club Car** titles, and more.

 @grandcentralpub   @grandcentralpub   @grandcentralpub

ABOUT THE AUTHOR

Claire Holroyde is a writer and graphic designer living outside of Philadelphia. *The Effort* is her first novel. She invites you to visit claireholroyde.com to learn more.

YOUR
BOOK
CLUB
RESOURCE

VISIT
GCPClubCar.com

to sign up for the **GCP Club Car** newsletter, featuring exclusive promotions, info on other **Club Car** titles, and more.

 @grandcentralpub

 @grandcentralpub

 @grandcentralpub